I0661711

The Luna City Compendium #2

Containing: Luna City IV,
A Fifth of Luna City,
And
One Half Dozen of Luna City
In One Complete Volume

By
Celia Hayes
& Jeanne Hayden

Geron GA & Associates

San Antonio, 2019

ISBN-13 978-0-989782364
ISBN-10 0989782360

Cover design by Alex of 3iii Graphics

Printed in the United States of America by Lightening Source, Int'l. and distributed by Ingram.

Geron & Associates
A Division of Watercress Press.
2019

Dedications and Acknowledgments

Thank you to the readers who love the series, and demanded a further chronicle of events, lives, and loves in Luna City. To my family, friends and the memory of those who have gone before. *Semper Fidelis!*

Jeanne Hayden

The Luna City series is dedicated with affection to those residents of Texas small towns who have not only welcomed us over the past half-dozen years of doing book events and markets, but who have also served as an inspiration by telling stories which are woven into this continuing chronicle: Fredericksburg, Boerne, Bulverde, Beeville, Goliad, Gonzalez, Comfort, Richmond, Junction, San Saba and Harper, Giddings, Llano and Lockhart, Richmond, New Braunfels and Kerrville. Thank you all for your continuing inspiration. Special thanks are due again to Larry H. for expert advice on the cooking, classic French kitchen-management, and catering aspects of this and the previous Luna City chronicles, and gratitude to J. "Pouncer" Melcher, of Lancaster, Texas for attentive beta reading and extensive suggestions, and to the late Professor John Igo, of San Antonio, who read an early version of the first Luna City Chronicle and encouraged us to continue with the tale.

Celia Hayes,
San Antonio, 2019

Contents

Luna City & Environs

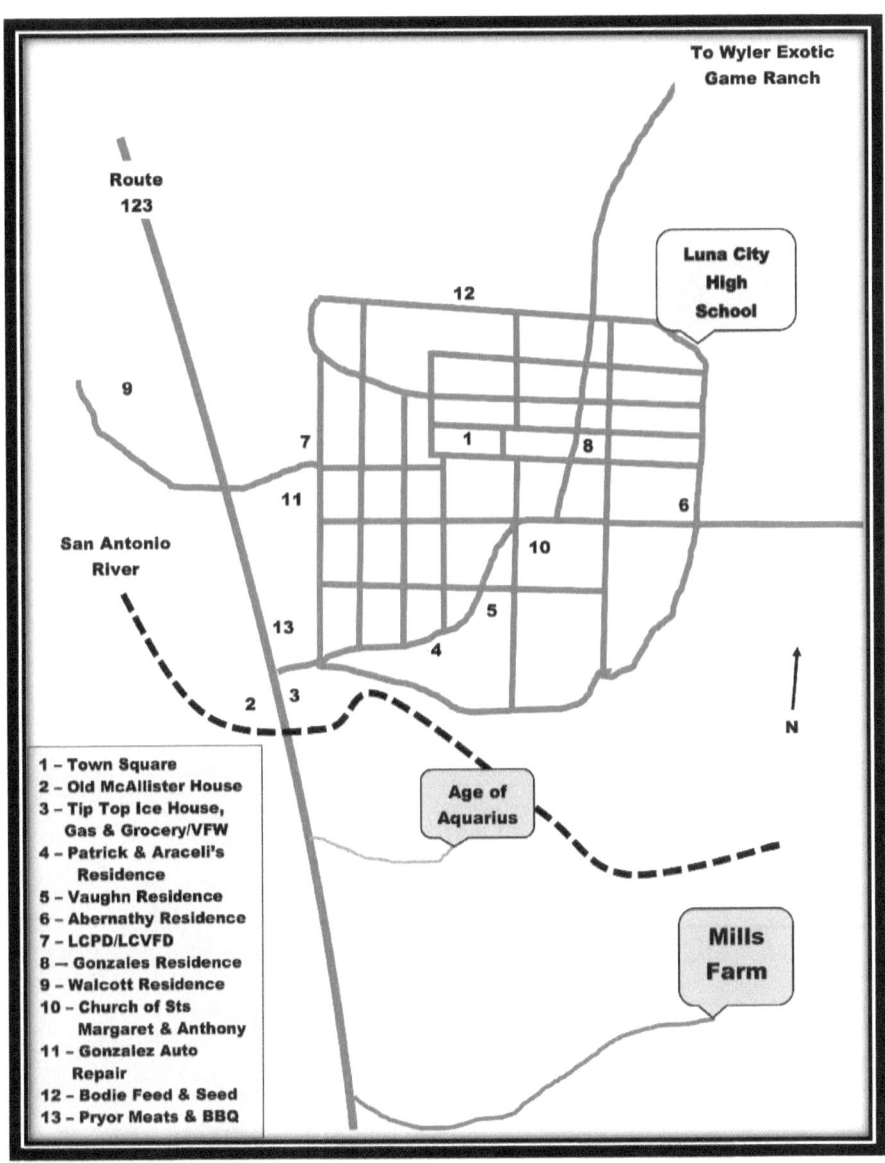

To Wyler Exotic Game Ranch

Route 123

Luna City High School

San Antonio River

N

1 – Town Square
2 – Old McAllister House
3 – Tip Top Ice House, Gas & Grocery/VFW
4 – Patrick & Araceli's Residence
5 – Vaughn Residence
6 – Abernathy Residence
7 – LCPD/LCVFD
8 – Gonzales Residence
9 – Walcott Residence
10 – Church of Sts Margaret & Anthony
11 – Gonzalez Auto Repair
12 – Bodie Feed & Seed
13 – Pryor Meats & BBQ

Age of Aquarius

Mills Farm

Luna City Town Square

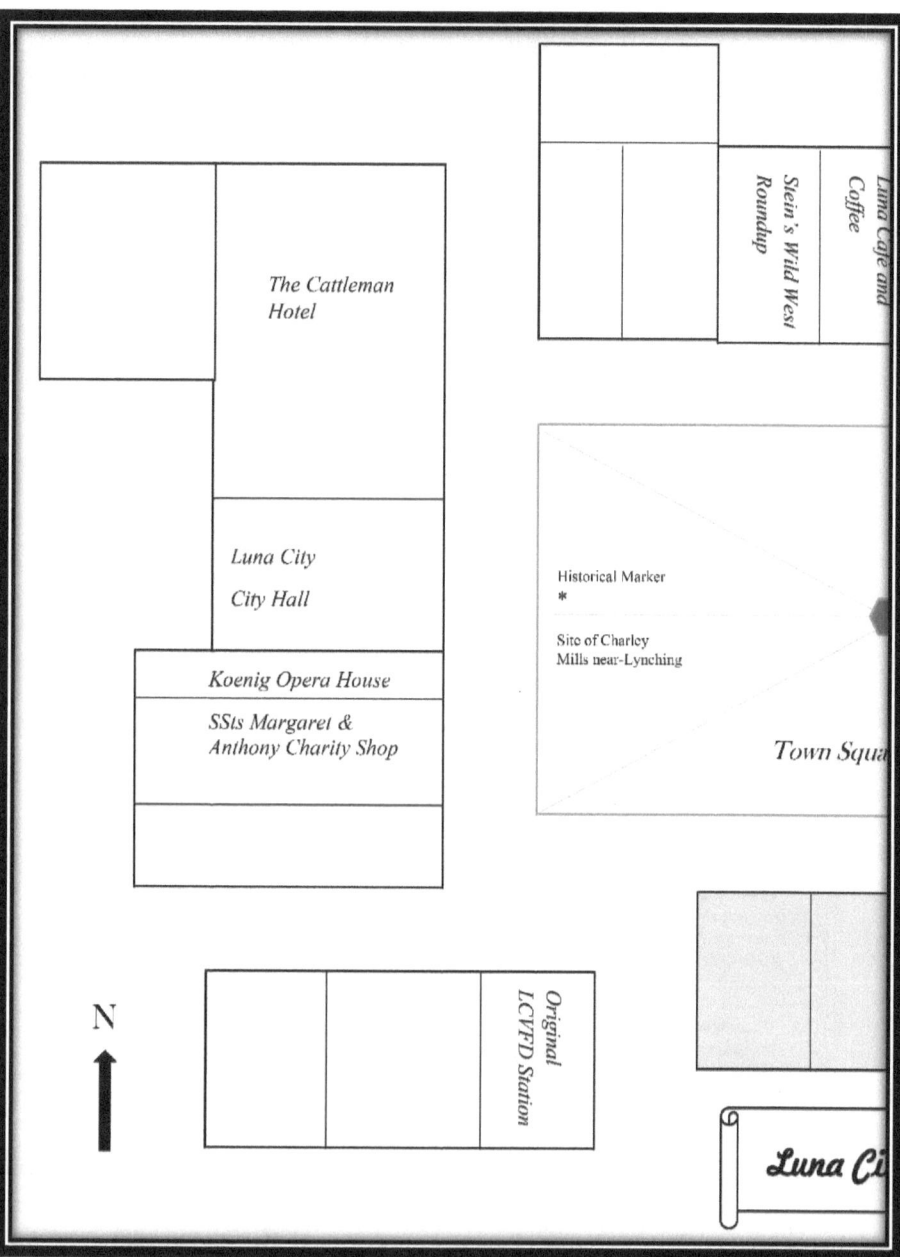

The Cattleman Hotel

Luna City City Hall

Koenig Opera House

SSts Margaret & Anthony Charity Shop

Stein's Wild West Roundup

Luna Cafe and Coffee

Historical Marker
*

Site of Charley Mills near-Lynching

Town Squa

Original LCVFD Station

N

Luna Ci

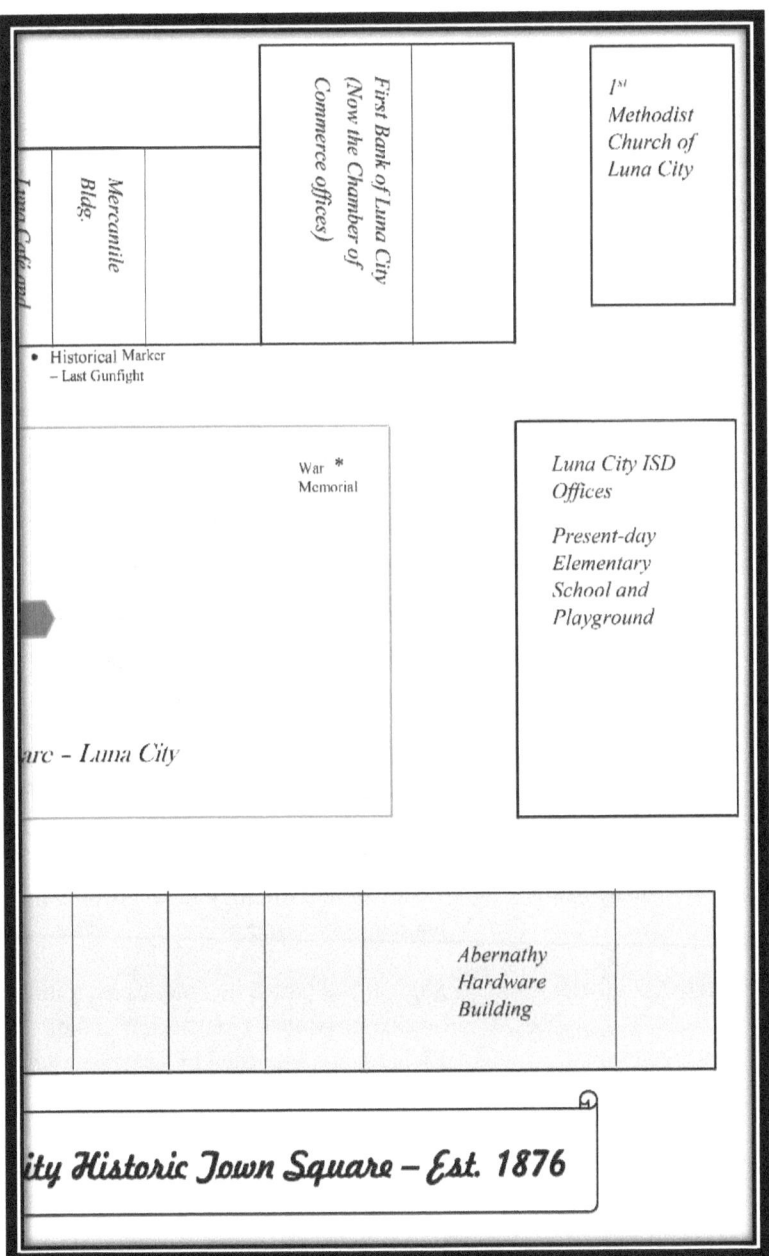

First Bank of Luna City
(Now the Chamber of
Commerce offices)

1st Methodist Church of Luna City

Luna Cafe and

Mercantile Bldg.

• Historical Marker
  – Last Gunfight

War * Memorial

Luna City ISD Offices

Present-day Elementary School and Playground

are – Luna City

Abernathy Hardware Building

ity Historic Town Square – Est. 1876

Cast of Characters

(An asterisk marks those who are deceased)

Richard Astor-Hall

(Ricardo to his friends in Luna City, Rich Hall in his previous life)

A former celebrity chef, who through a chain of circumstances, finished up in Luna City, managing the Luna City Café and doing the occasional catering event.

Martin Abernathy

Widower, father of Jess, mayor of Luna City, hereditary owner of Abernathy Hardware.

Jessica "Jess" Abernathy

Daughter of Martin, qualified CPA, Air Force Reservist, champion barrel-racer, significant other to Joe Vaughn.

Benny Cordova

The devious and ninja-skilled general manager of Mills Farm.

Samantha "Sammi" Colquhoun

Sometime actress, media personality, and ex-girlfriend of Richard.

James Wyler "J.W." Ellis*

Grandson of Doc Stephen Wyler, once boyfriend to Jess Abernathy, best friend of Chris Mayall.

Dwight David "Music Man" Garrett

Coach of the Mighty Fighting Moths and band music master.

Alberto "Berto" Gonzales

Student and part-time limo driver, younger brother of Araceli Gonzalez, friend of Richard, and grandson of *Abuelita* Adeliza Gonzalez.

Sylvester Gonzales

Gaming geek, computer nerd, USMC veteran.

Roman Gonzales	Construction contractor.
Roman "Romeo" Gonzales	Cousin of Berto and Araceli, former oilfield worker, currently top male model, married to Susannah Wyatt, no longer an unwitting focus for strange and unearthly energies.
Adeliza "Abuelita" Gonzalez	The revered and feared matriarch of the Gonzales/Gonzalez clan, dedicated Food Channel watcher, and Richard's biggest fan.
Araceli Gonzales-Gonzalez	Older sister of Berto, married to Patrico, mother of Angelika and Mateo, manager, assistant cook, head waitress at the Luna Café & Coffee.
Patrico "Pat" Gonzalez	Husband to Araceli, drives a tanker truck for an oil company in the Eagle Ford Shale Oil Field.
Hernando "Nando" Gonzalez*	Korean War fighter ace, local hero, for whom the high school gymnasium is named.
Judith "Judy" Stillwell Grant	With her husband Sefton, the owner of the Age of Aquarius Campground and Goat Farm, the last two holdouts of a 1960s commune.
Sefton Grant	Husband of Judy, landlord of Richard.
Katherine "Kate" Heisel	Gonzales cousin, reporter for the *Karnesville Weekly Beacon*, significant other to Richard.
Christopher "Chris" Mayall	Manager, Tip-Top Icehouse, Gas & Grocery, bartender at the VFW, Navy veteran, amputee participant in marathons, medic - Luna City VFD, best friend of J.W. Ellis, and friend of Richard.

Leticia "Miss Letty" McAllister Oldest person in Luna City, WWII Red Cross service, kindergarten teacher, friend to Chris Mayall.

Douglas McAllister, Phd * Miss Letty's older brother, professor of history, and author of *The History of Luna City*.

Phillip Noel-Barrett Actor, media personality, once romantic rival and frenemy of Richard.

Xavier Gunnison-Penn Unsuccessful international treasure-hunter.

Andrew Pryor Oilfield geologist, headquartered in Karnesville, owner of small BBQ restaurant

Patricia Wyler Pryor Granddaughter of Dr. Stephen Wyler and Miss Alice, wife of Andrew Pryor, HS girlfriend of Joe Vaughn.

Georg Stein Native of Germany, a retired corporate lawyer, passionate reenactor, owner of Stein's Wild West Round-up, married to Annise.

Annise Stein Co-owner of Stein's Wild West Round-up.

Joseph "Joe" Vaughn Army veteran, local football hero, chief of the Luna City Police Department, significant other to Jess Abernathy.

Clovis Walcott, (Colonel, USAR/Ret.) Retired US Army Reservist, currently consulting engineer, keen reenactor.

Sook "Isabel" Walcott	Korean-born wife of Clovis, socially ambitious, and the tiger-mother from Hell.
Jeremy "Jerry" Walcott	Oldest child of Clovis and Sook, a student nurse and family care-giver.
Robbie Walcott	Younger son of Clovis and Sook, bright and wildly curious, potential kitchen trainee.
Belle Walcott	Daughter of Clovis and Sook, lead trumpet in the Mighty Fighting Moths Marching Band
Susannah Wyatt-Gonzales	Regional manager, at VPI, sexual stalker of Richard
Collin Wyler	Son of Doc Wyler and Miz Alice, father of Patricia, international financier, serial husband, and treasure-hunting enthusiast.
Stephen "Doc" Wyler	Owner of the Wyler Exotic Game Ranch, a qualified veterinarian, part-owner of the Café and second-oldest resident. Father of Collin, grandfather of Patricia Pryor and J.W. Ellis.
Marigold Amy Yasbeck	A student, and semi-girlfriend of Berto, formerly known as the child actress Amy Butler.

Luna City IV

Luna City Volunteer Fire Department
Established 1878

Up in Smoke

"Come on! Move it!" Jess commanded, as she thrust her cellphone into the depths of her briefcase-handbag. Behind the counter, the switchboard was lighting up like an old-fashioned pinball machine and Sergeant Gonzales settled her headset and returned to her more urgent duties. "I'll drive you all back to your place – but hurry! And when we get there, don't do anything stupid, 'kay? We'll have it all covered – and I promise, we'll try and save what we can!"

"Be careful, Babe!" Joe Vaughn shot over his shoulder as he dove for the front door of the Luna City Police Department HQ. Chris had already beaten him, with his teenage medic-apprentice on his heels, leaving the ambulance stretcher marooned in the middle of the waiting area. Gunnison Penn lay supine and abandoned on it, his mountainous buttocks crowned like the Alps with a wad of white dressing instead of snow.

"Hey! What about me?" he shouted, his flushed countenance reflecting an expression of more than his usual irascibility. "That vicious beast bit me! It has rabies, I'm certain … I demand…"

"Take two Motrin and drink plenty of water," Chris replied. "Sorry, pal, we got us a for-real emergency. We'll get back to you as soon as …"

"Azúcar does not have rabies!" Judy Grant sobbed. "You hit him first! And if he catches anything horrible from biting your nasty ass …

you will never be welcomed back to the Age of Aquarius, and that's a promise!"

"Look, Mr. Penn, Azúcar had all his shots ... Now come on, Judikins!" Sefton Grant had his infuriated spouse by one elbow, but it did not prevent her from belting Gunnison Penn across the head with the woven Andean peasant bag which served Judy Grant as a purse.

"Did I do that?" Judy spat as Richard caught her other elbow. "I'm so sorry – and I hope that hurt!"

"Mrs. Grant," Richard begged, "Compose yourself, let us fly away home – your house is on fire ... hell, why does that call a nursery-rhyme to mind?"

"Can we move it?" Jess demanded through tight-clenched teeth, and they were all through the narrow front door of the Luna City PD's offices, moving at speed towards Jess' bare-bones little yellow Jeep Wrangler. With Richard's assistance, a curiously resolute Sefton stuffed his still-sobbing spouse into the back seat – which left the front passenger seat to Richard. Jess spun out of the joint Luna City PD/VFD parking lot in a screech of brakes and a spray of gravel, a short length in the wake of Luna City's two pumper-trucks, all ablaze with lights.

The winter sun had barely slipped below the horizon, the sky the bleached color of a sea shell – it was still light enough to see in the light twilight. Jess and her little yellow Wrangler joined the cavalcade of lights and motors, burning up the raddled, rut-ridden road which was the turn-off into the Age of Aquarius Campground and Goat Farm, raising a storm of dust barely detectable against the massive column of smoke rising from the glade of oak trees where the Grant's yurt burned.

Jess slid her Wrangler into a slap-dash halt some distance from the pumper-trucks, in the driveway which had formerly been the lane between the campground and the Grant's eccentric compound – the yurt, and other outbuildings.

"I'm sorry," she said, over her shoulder to the Grants. "It looks pretty well gone. It was nothing but framework and felt and all that, wasn't it?"

"Yup," Sefton replied, with remarkable stoicism, considering that it was his family home of four decades going up in roaring red and yellow flame. Now that Jess had turned off the engine, Richard could hear it plain – a sound to turn bowels and soul to jelly, the full-throated, blast-furnace roar of fire, fire well-along. "I … we built it – we can watch it go, Judikins."

"Stay here," Jess commanded. She had already gone around to the back of the Wrangler, yanking an assortment of heavy clothing out of a duffle-bag and pulling them on over her street clothes. Richard noted, out of the corner of his eye, that a half-dozen other new arrivals to the scene of catastrophe were doing the same. "We'll try and save the other shit and the trees … Richard – I'm counting on you, don't let Sefton and Judy do anything stupid."

"Only things," Judy Grant replied, remarkably stoic after her previous hysteria, although her cheeks still glittered with fresh tear-tracks. "Only things, Jess. Don't let anyone risk their life for materiel things."

"I know – don't fret," Jess said, as she pulled a massive helmet over her head, and pulled the face-mask down over her countenance. At a determine jog she went off towards the gathering of similarly-clad figures. Richard soon lost her among the bustle of volunteers, made anonymous in form-concealing gear and helmets, deploying hoses from off the back of the pumper-trucks in a manner which suggested much practice.

It had rather surprised him to see that bystanders among those camped at the Age had also turned too, with a couple of garden hoses and a number of buckets – a valiant but fruitless effort, which that straggle of old Aquarians gratefully yielded to the better-prepared and equipped members of the LCVFD. A handful of them – sweating and soot-stained joined Richard and the Grants, attended by the Grants three very excited dogs.

"Sorry, man," the first of them said, when he could be heard over the roaring fire and the vociferous dogs. He looked about the same age as Sefton, save being a little cleaner-cut than the latter, who looked like a younger and less run-to-seed Willie Nelson "We did what we could, but it went up like a torch."

"No sweat, Bigbee," Sefton Grant shrugged, still amazingly stoic. "Any idea how it started?"

"The sweat-lodge, I guess," Bigbee replied in a plaintive voice, as Judy embraced the dogs. "We thought the fire was out, when all the ruckus started … I swear to you, man – Rickover and Daisy, they grabbed some of your stuff from inside, though. You got insurance, so at least you can start again, make the ol' commune HQ even trippier than before."

Sefton cleared his throat. "We don't have any insurance, Biggs … well, not on the yurt and our personal shit. Only on the van, 'cause it's required. You remember, all this wasn't built to code, 'r anything like that. We winged it back in '68 and we been winging it ever since. Judikins, she wanted to live lightly on the land, ya remember."

"Well, damn, Sefton!" Bigbee shook his head. "How you gonna rebuild, then? You gotta live somewhere. Can you swing it out of pocket?"

"Prolly not," Sefton shook his head, his countenance more lugubrious than ever. "We make just enough from the place to scrape by, pay the sales taxes 'n permits an' all, keep the place running."

"Sorry, man," Bigbee digested this unfortunate intelligence. "Real bummer, having to start all over. Can your kids help?"

"They got their own lives, man," Sefton shook his head. "I can't ask that of them – they're stretched as tight as we are, with their kids going to college an' all. We'll figure out a way." He heaved up a deep sigh, which turned into a cough on a drifting wisp of smoke. Bigbee thumped his back.

"Look man, you can crash with Wanda an' me in the RV tonight, but we gotta get back to College Station by Christmas Eve. We're doing Christmas dinner with the Dean and his family, or we'd stay longer. Ya know, you could come and crash with us for longer, just to get your head straight…"

"No can do, man – not with the dogs, an' the goats an' hens an all. It would kill us, to walk away leaving the place unattended," Sefton answered. "The critters need us. But thanks for asking." He fetched up a deep sigh from the very depths of his soul, and added. "We'll get by … us country boys always do."

Judy was crying again, kneeling on the tumbled ground with her arms around the dogs – those three large mutts of undetermined lineage, all of whom had chosen the Grants as their personal and much-adored humans after being dumped in the countryside by previous owners. "Our paradise is ruined, Seftie," she sobbed. "That awful man – he was the harbinger of war and discord! He spoiled everything – it's all his fault!"

The dogs pressed close to her or Sefton, shivering and whining in distress. Richard viewed them with faint loathing. He was not particularly an animal person and Judy's display of emotion vaguely offended him, his upbringing being of the old-school stiff-upper-lip persuasion, no matter how far he had fallen from that ideal in employing strategic temper tantrums as a form of theater. Sefton's uncouth stoicism was rather more acceptable to Richard. He was loath to admit that he had become guardedly fond of them both, or at least progressively less annoyed with their eccentric conduct and overt social familiarity. Somehow, he could hear the voice of his aged Gran, chiding him for being a snot in thinking he was above them, somehow. The Grants had been very kind, over the last year and a half, renting him the Airstream made cozy by the efforts of the Gonzales/Gonzalez clan, presenting him regularly with fresh eggs in exchange for the bucket of vegetable scraps and peelings that he brought daily from the Café – scraps upon which the Grant's flock fell with avid greed. The way that the chickens could scarf down peelings – especially of fruit was a source of never-ending amusement to Richard. And Sefton's unparalleled homemade mustang-grape wine … for a continuing supply of that ambrosia, he would forgive much. He might even absent himself from the old Airstream and give it over to them for an indefinite period – it was theirs after all, and if they needed a place to stay … he could always go stay with Chris.

After ten or fifteen minutes, it appeared that the combined efforts of the fire department volunteers were bearing fruit – in such a brisk and efficient manner that he could hardly credit the evidence of his own eyes. But the roaring flames had been doused in a protest of sizzle and gouts of steam thrown up as a last protest. One stream of water from the hoses now turned on the nearest of the scorched trees, while the other turned on the black-cinder remains of the yurt as if to say, 'now, stay out, you bastard!'. There was a definite slacking of interest on the part of bystanders, now that it the initial excitement was over. It wasn't as if there was all that much substantial to burn, anyway. After a few minutes of concerted effort, volunteers methodically began rolling up hoses and stowing them on the first pumper truck, before scattering to their own vehicles.

"I say," Richard cleared his throat in a hesitant fashion, as Jess – still hooded and androgynous in her turn-out gear approached them all. "It appears as if the fire is well and truly quenched. I would offer …"

Jess shed the heavy helmet in one splendid gesture. "Hey, look – it's just about done, and we managed to keep it from going too deep in the trees. It's still too hot to start poking around for what you can salvage, so don't even think it. You both need to go someplace and … adjust. Now. My place is yours for as long as you want. I've moved in with Joe, all my personal stuff is gone, but … there's sheets and towels and things, and furniture and all. Take the dogs, there's a corral out back for Azúcar. Stay as long as you need – here's the house key, but I don't think the back door is locked."

"Thanks, Jess," Sefton answered, taking the key which Jess wrangled off her key ring, while Richard looked on, simultaneously relieved and yet still resentful. So much for his unborn generous gesture.

In the Offices of the Karnesville Weekly Beacon

"Kate! Get in here and tell me what in the name of Dog has been going on in Luna City!"

Kate Heisel, bright-eyed and ready to plunge into another week of work on the regional newspaper on the morning after the last of the holidays, was in the chief editor's office almost before Acey McClain finished bellowing, and as a sprinkling of superannuated dust from the ancient light fixtures in the offices of the Karnesville Weekly Beacon ceased sifting down like a gentle benison on the various desks below.

"Yes, Chief – right away, Chief!" she chirped. Acey McClain, grizzled, slightly hung-over and well over twice her age, scowled thunderously.

"Dammit, Kate – do you have to be so cheerful first thing in the morning? I'm not Lou Grant and you are not Mary Tylor Moore. And don't call me Chief!"

"Sure, Chief," Kate grinned at him and took out her notebook, perching on the narrow wooden guest chair opposite her boss. "It's a legitimate form of aggression, being offensively cheerful first thing in the AM. Think of it as a workout for your liver. Get the old blood flowing … the birds are singing in the trees, the sun is shining, God is in his heaven and all's right with the world…"

Acey McClain gave his pungently expressed opinion on that state of affairs and Kate's grin widened. She made a show of jotting down several of the more interesting terms of abuse, and when he had finished, remarked, "Wow, Chief – that last isn't even biologically possible … unless one is maybe triple-jointed and has a taste for … never mind. You were asking about Luna City over this last week."

"That's what I like about you, Kate," Acey McClain sat back in the monumental and heroically battered leather executive chair which had been the badge of office for editors at the *Karnesville Weekly Beacon* since it had been the *Daily Beacon*, sometime around 1962. "And why I put up with your flagrantly disrespectful attitude. You're the most purely un-shockable female that I have ever met. So – back to my original question: what in the name of Dog and all the Angles in heaven has been going on this last week in Luna City? I swear, if it weren't for them, we'd have nothing to print except the legal notices, the minutes of the last garden club meeting and the police blotter."

"About the usual, Chief." Kate licked her pencil-point – an affectation adopted from her close watching of old movies about the news business. Kate was a great believer in professional traditions. "Let's see … there was a fire at the old hippy hang-out by the river, just before Christmas. Burned the main establishment to the ground, but no one hurt and nothing much lost. The place wasn't insured, though … but neighbors are weighing in. The new marketing director at Mills Farm has offered them one of their residential trailers for the owners to live in, while they rebuild."

"What caused the fire?" Acey McClain was always curious about that. The answer to that question in his own hard-bitten crime-beat reporter past had earned him a more-than-average number of above-the-fold, huge-typeface-headline-stories during a very long career in the big-city print news business.

"They think that a fire in a sweat-lodge wasn't properly extinguished," Kate replied. "The investigator for the LCVFD is all but certain about that. No story, Chief. Now, the mass-brawl that happened immediately before the fire ..."

"Now you're getting to the nut, Kate," Acey McClain sat forward in the leather office chair, all eager attention. "What was that all about? I heard that some asshole got bitten in the ass by a rabid llama – true?"

"Not the rabid part. The llama in question did have all his required shots." Kate flipped over to another page. "I double-checked with the veterinarian ... Doc Wyler. Doc Wyler of the Wyler Lazy-W Ranch."

"Oh, Dog," Acey McClain shuddered, almost imperceptibly. "This asshole didn't pick a fight with him, too? The biggest ranch and the richest guy in Karnes County? And a man who lovingly cherishes his grudges like they were prize breeding stock?"

"Not so far," Kate replied, still chipper as a squirrel with a winters-worth of stored away acorns. "As a matter of fact and according to eye-witnesses – and I have a list of them," she flipped through another couple of pages. "All names available on the Talk of the Town blog. The asshole is one Gunnison Penn of no definite fixed address other than Canada. He struck the llama in question first; I have photographic proof of it. You know, Chief – it's great how everyone has a cellphone with camera capacity in their pocket, these days. There is a clear case of self-defense to be made: Gunnison Penn clearly hit the llama first."

"That Canuck treasure-hunter guy?" Acey McClain looked even more alert. "He's back again? Guess he must have beaten the last injunction – the one filed for harassing the family of that kid that found a pristine 1892 20$ gold piece at Mills Farm?"

"You don't have to remind me, Chief – I was there, and the kid's mom is my second-cousin. Yeah, that guy, and he's gone again, lucky for Luna City. He definitely got the message. He packed up and went, as soon as he got a stitch or two and a shot of antibiotics at the Med center," Kate snickered. "I cornered him in the parking lot there after he was released, asking him for his reaction. "

"Good girl, Kate!" Acey McClain radiated approval. "*Sixty Minutes* material, no fooling, kid – you'll be in the big-time, any time!"

"God no, Chief – I've got some standards! Back to the all-hands punch-up on the banks of the San Antonio River. Another party of individuals charged in the brawl – three guys trying to do a stand-up for a YouTube feature about the mysterious Luna Lights…"

"What was it about those lights," Acey folded his hands together and regarded his most energetic and enterprising young reporter with happy anticipation. "You find out anything about them? Optical illusion, secret Pentagon aircraft, mass hallucination – what?"

Kate fetched up a deep sigh from the depths of her news-hungry yet strangely ethical soul. "Fire lanterns, Chief. All that it was. I talked to Sefton Grant and his crew of superannuated hippies. They were celebrating the Solstice, or some such crap. They launched fire lanterns – you know – those paper hot-air balloons, with a candle burning under them, about twenty minutes before that guy with the cellphone recorded three of them drifting over the road. I even checked with the weather service – the prevailing wind at that time would have sent them in a westward direction. Fire lanterns – nothing more."

"For sure, Kate?" Acey scowled across his desk, and Kate sighed again. She brought out her cellphone. "I drove around, between Falls City and Kenedy. By pure luck and knowing the exact direction in which the wind was blowing at that particular hour, I found where one of them had landed. I gotta pal at KSAT-Weather in San Antonio. The evening turned damp and cold, and this one came down near Hobson. The owner was pretty p'oed. He had a barn full of hay which it landed next to and he let me take one picture. Sorry if it's blurry – he was yelling at me as if it were my fault. I'm not saying it was aliens, Chief … it was fire lanterns."

"All right, then, Kate." Acey McClain sat back in the executive editor's chair, mildly disappointed. Aliens, or supposed sightings of them were almost as good for producing huge-typeface headlines as criminal arson. "What next? Who else was party to the mass punch-up?"

"A bunch of ghost hunters," Kate consulted her notebook. "They were actually pretty casual about it all, except when it came to joining in the brawl. I guess tracking 19th century mayhem makes you pretty laid-back regarding the current version. They were looking for the Agua Dulce ghost riders, or the emanations thereof. Their video looks darned good; subtly creepy, like the *Blair Witch Project* on an even smaller budget. The thrill is in the suggestion, you see … or rather – what you don't quite see. But no actual hard data there. Actually, I've always believed that the legend of the Agua Dulce ghost riders is one of those folk-tales. You know, a story told to scare the ever-loving crap out of kids. The other Mills Treasure-hunters; they didn't have any more luck than Gunnison Penn, but they're still holding out, when last I checked."

Acey McClain steepled his hands, finger-tip-to-fingertip and looked over them, magisterially. "I've been hearing about the lost Mills Treasure for years, Kate. Last year was about the first time I heard enough to make me think it is any more substantial than the Agua Dulce ghost riders. So what do you really think about the Mills Treasure?"

"I base my opinions on the certainties, Chief," Kate replied. "No observable certainties – no opinion. But I did have a nice telephone chat last week with the man who is the established expert on the Mills Treasure – Collin Wyler."

"That Collin Wyler? Jeebus, Kate, he's more elusive than the Loch Ness monster! I have it on good authority that he doesn't talk to any media reps less exalted than the top reporters from the *Economist* or the *Wall Street Journal* … the *New York Times*, if he is in a mood to go slumming. How did you manage that scoop?"

"Well," Kate licked her pencil and assumed a becoming expression of modesty. "He was visiting the home-place for Christmas, being between wives, I guess. Mom's second-cousin Patricia is the housekeeper there. I've always had the private house number, so I took a chance. He's really a sweet guy, Chief, and he was so helpful."

"Be careful, Kate – he's a notorious pussy hound, and if he's between dates-o' the-moment…"

"Really, Chief, don't be disgusting. I would never mix personal with professional. Besides, he's older than my Dad!"

Acey did note that his sharpest reporter was blushing slightly, but decided not to make note of that. Discretion was the better part of valor. "So, what insights into the notorious missing Mills Treasure did he favor you with?" he asked with heavy sarcasm.

Kate licked her pencil again. "He's been looking for the Mills Treasure since … he was a kid," she replied, with all seriousness. "He even told me some things about Old Charley that I didn't even know. I could hardly take notes fast enough. His take on it is that, yes, there was a treasure hoard at one point. The old scoundrel kept it in the pit under the old farm latrine, until about 1911. It's his opinion based on extensive research that Old Charley dipped into it as he needed funds for this and that … and by the time he croaked, he had used it all up. Nothing left – all gone to support his various shady enterprises, through exchanges and transactions which can never be traced at this late date." Kate snapped her notebook closed with an air of finality. "It's his considered judgement that the Mills Treasure is a chimera, an illusion – a mirage. All these searchers looking for it are after the illusion. If that search gives them a purpose …

hey, everyone needs a purpose, or at least, a hobby. I consider him a subject-matter expert, Chief. I'd accept his conclusion as provisionally final, until evidence to the contrary is unearthed."

"So – no treasure," Acey McClain sighed. "Another local illusion shot to hell. Thanks for the low-down, Kate. No one does research as thoroughly as you do. Oh … speaking of Luna City," he added, as Kate stood up. "There was one more thing – I got a call from some cable TV show producer last week, just before we shut down for the holiday. You ever heard of *Ala Carte With Quartermayne*? I don't watch the Food Channel, so I have no idea of who he was talking about … but they're looking for shooting locations in Texas for next season."

"Oh, sure," Kate beamed. "You have too heard of him, Acey! That's Allen Lee Mayne, used to be quarterback for the Broncos back in the day. He's doing a restaurant show now; blows into town with a film crew, he and his sidekick hang out with the staff of a two small local places, watching them prepare their signature dishes – then they shoot the breeze with the customers and judge which of the two are the best. It's a blast to watch, he's a funny guy and he loves good food."

"No kidding … well, that will be a top story, when and if it happens. The producer said something about a big-time chef running a dinky little eatery in Luna City that they were interested in. He was asking about some guy they called Rich Hall, the Bad Boy Chef? You know him?"

It completely escaped Acey McClain's attention, the very slight hesitation before Kate replied, "No one by that name doing business in Luna City, Chief. That all?"

"For this morning, yes – thanks for the briefing."

Gone Home

Like all nine-day wonders, the burning of the Grant's long-time home eventually slid to the back of community consciousness – or so Richard thought, at first. Christmas passed, then New Years. The old Aquarians scattered, as did the ghost hunters and the UFOians, although a few brave hold-out treasure-hunters remained in a small tent on the far side of the now-deserted campground. Even they scampered, the morning after a hard freeze early in January painted the trees and grasses with white frost and killed every last bit of greenery. The ice-cold and the subsequent bitter wind stripped the last leaves from the oak trees. Richard, secure in the Airstream, with a heap of quilts on the bed and relishing the warmth emanated by the tiny yet efficient heater, watched them go without a pang. Now he had the campground entirely to himself, which – he admitted candidly to himself – he mostly liked.

But … be did miss eccentric and colorful bulk of the yurt, crowning the slight rise of hill above the campground meadow and the field where the goats lived and grazed. It didn't even make a romantic vision of a ruin – it was just a sad, pathetic pile of wet ashes and carbonized wood, a void where something familiar had been.

He should have had a clue, though – the weekend after New Years', when for a brief day, the site became a hive of activity, people combing through the carbonized wreckage; mostly strangers, although he recognized a few of them; the Grants themselves, Jess Abernathy, Joe Vaughn almost unrecognizable in grubby jeans and sweatshirt, armed with heavy work-gloves and masks against sharp edges and dust that rose from every movement. They were all working methodically through the site with rakes and sieves, turning up unidentifiable, soot-covered lumps of this or that from the remains. When he returned at mid-afternoon from Sunday brunch at the Café and spotted several familiar and unfamiliar vehicles parked at the edge of the grove, curiosity led him to wander up, the bucket of vegetable scraps and peelings for the chickens in one hand an excuse for indulging in it. About a third of the blackened footprint left by the yurt was swept clean, the picked-through ashes and cinders bagged and thrown onto the back of the Grant's makeshift vehicle.

"Hi, Rich … looking for salvageables, before Roman Gonzales brings his bulldozer over to clear the site, " Jess greeted him. "You know … that stuff that didn't burn."

"Find anything so far?" Richard asked. It wasn't a very inviting site, reminding him of a particularly unrewarding archeological dig – lots of unidentifiable, oddly-shaped charcoal-colored lumps, covered deep in soot, centered on the single old-fashioned cast-iron wood-stove which had once provided heat in winder to the yurt.

"Some of Judy's cast-iron skillets and Dutch ovens," Jess replied, turning over some debris with her rake. "Some plates and glasses, all melted together. Forks, knives, and spoons … I suppose they can be polished up and used again, but I don't know why anyone would bother..." she picked up a square, flattish object, and wiped it off on an indescribably filthy bandanna tucked into her waistband, revealing fire-mottled blue enamel underneath – a casserole lid.

"Judy – I found this lid," Jess called across the site. "Will the rest of it be around close?"

"Oh, yes!" Judy beamed, as she hurried across, followed by Sefton. "That's the Danish modern one that my great-aunt gave me for a wedding present – I always baked Lentil Surprise in it. It doesn't look damaged at all! It was on a shelf, all together with the pots and pans..."

"Here's the rest of it," Jess sounded pleased, as she fished up another, larger lump, and Judy clasped both objects to her somewhat sagging breasts. "They don't look much damaged at all ... I guess you could go on using them."

"I will!" Judy burbled happily. "Why, I'll make a batch of Lentil Surprise tonight – the kids always loved it so! You are welcome to join us for supper – you, too, Richard, and Jess and Joe ... the kids are driving back to San Antonio tomorrow morning, and I'll make plenty for everyone."

Beyond her, Sefton made a brief grimace of discomfort, which Richard heroically pretended not to see. Judy's Lentil Surprise ... the best one could say of it was that it resembled something disgusting left on the ground by a dog with bowel movement troubles.

"I'm sure it will be wonderful, baked in your lovely indestructible casserole," Jess replied with so little hesitation that Richard didn't doubt she was also making an excuse. "But Joe and I have a commitment to supper with Dad, and Gram and Grumpy tonight, so we can't make it..."

"And I have to get up early in the morning, so I'm making an early night of it," Richard interjected smoothly. Sefton looked even glummer, although Richard supposed the presence of their family must provide him some relief from Judy's notoriously awful cooking.

18

"You hadn't ever met our boys," Judy burbled, seemingly undismayed. "Sefton, Junior – when he was growing up we called him Spirit River. And Cassidy Sundance … he's the middle child. He went and joined the military; Casey Grant, can you imagine? How terribly militaristic, and bourgeois! Sunny – short for Sunflower … she was such a disappointment to me! She had such artistic talent, and gave it up to be a dental assistant. She wants to be called Serafina now, but I always think of her as Sunny…"

"It's a good living, and I always liked Sunny," Jess put in. "How's she doing, anyway?"

"Very well," Judy answered, with a determined air of good cheer. "Her husband just expanded his practice and she's campaigning for a position on the school board. Honestly, sometimes I just don't know where we went wrong with that child." She hugged her reclaimed casserole again, adding forlornly. "I'll take it to Spir – to Junior's house with me, Seftie. You won't mind, will you?"

"You do that, Judikins," Sefton said. "The boys always loved lent … what you cooked."

Richard looked from one to another. Sefton, always rather lugubrious of expression, somehow looked even more depressed. "You're leaving the … Age for a time, Mrs. Grant?" he ventured, and Judy nodded, suddenly appearing as depressed as her husband.

"It's just for a while," she explained. "It's all the bad energy, since the fighting, and the awful fire. It's … dragging my own chakras into bad alignments, depleting my own positive aura. I can hardly sleep at night. And with no place to live here, until Seftie rebuilds … I may as well not sleep at Junior's house than not sleep anywhere else. I'm not as young as I once was. I absolutely must measure out my vital energies, day by day."

"Quite understandable, Mrs. Grant, quite understandable," Richard nodded wholly sympathetic, although he was torn in deciding who he felt more of it for – Judy or her still-adoring and long-suffering spouse. "Let me know if there is anything that I can do, in the meantime."

"You can keep an eye on my Seftie for me," Judy replied, coquettishly. "See that he has a good meal for himself now and again – I know what these lonely single men get up to! Cheap greasy junk food, full of carcinogens and chemicals! Why, what you bring for the chickles every day would be better for my Seftie than that!"

"You may depend on me, Mrs. Grant," Richard switched the bucket to his other hand, while Jess stifled a giggle, and silently formed the words 'Lentil Surprise.' "I believe most strongly in excellent food, for every person, every day. Mr. Grant will never starve, when I am around." '*Or drive to Karnesville for a cheap hamburger,*' he added silently, and took his leave, thinking that Judy probably wouldn't be gone for very long. How long would it take to clear away the debris and re-erect a new yurt, after all?

The Bennington Patriot Riders

The Bennington Patriot Riders is a New England-based motorcycle club principally (but not exclusively) composed of military veterans and family members, loosely affiliated with the national Rolling Thunder, Inc. organization. The club was founded post-World War II, but saw an influx of new members in the early 1970s. It is registered as a non-profit organization, and supports several military-oriented charities such as the Blue Star Mothers, Soldiers' Angels, the Fisher House Foundation, the Red Cross and others. Their colors are blue and gold, and their club patch features a representation of the Bennington Battle Monument.

The Riders participate in national events such as the annual Rolling Thunder Ride for Freedom or Ride to the Wall, a massive motorcycle rally held annually in Washington DC, on the Sunday of the Memorial Day weekend. Members gather silently in the Pentagon parking lot, and at the stroke of noon, fire up their machines and slowly process to the Vietnam Memorial. The Riders participate in a yearly transcontinental road trip. In even-numbered years, they cross from Montpelier, Vermont, to Portland, Oregon via the upper mid-West states, and down the Pacific Coast to San Diego. From there, they cross to Houston, New Orleans and to Jacksonville, Florida, and then up the East Coast and back to Montpelier. In odd-numbered years, they reverse the itinerary; traveling south and then west across the southern states. The exact route varies every year, which generally takes two weeks. The Patriot Riders prefer to travel by secondary roads rather than the major interstate highways. This long-distance ride is usually scheduled for early spring, and usually draws forty to sixty participants.

A

Castle of Straw

As it turned out, a new yurt was not in the cards, for reasons never quite explained to Richard, but which he assumed probably had something to do with an officious council authority withholding planning permission – although on second consideration, that seemed most uncharacteristic for Luna City, where the height of officious council authority was Miss Letty McAllister sternly admonishing a pair of skate-boarding teenagers doing tricks off the stairs to the Town Square bandstand. Several days after the salvage party, a bare-bones house trailer appeared at the other end of the campground – a plain, utilitarian structure delivered by a massive truck with the logo of Mills Farm emblazoned on the side. The truck was being driven away, as Richard pedaled up the rutted road. He didn't recognize the driver, a burly middle-aged chap who waved genially at him as the truck ground slowly past.

He found Sefton Grant, hooking up the various power, water, and sewage lines to the new trailer. "I say, Sefton – another guest?" Richard ventured. The new trailer – which from the slightly battered condition it presented to a closer view – was quite definitely not a recreational vehicle, or anything like that used by the regular visitors.

"Of a sort," Sefton grinned and scratched his bristly cheek. "It's on loan, from Mills Farm, can you believe it? First generous thing those bastards have done in thirty years. New management, y'know. For our use, until the rebuilding is done. It's a man-camp trailer, they have a bunch they use for overflow staff in the summer. Guess they don't know that rebuilding will take a mite longer than calculated."

"Oh?" Richard calculated the tone of his voice to indicate mild sympathy, not invite further confidences, but Sefton shrugged.

"Well, it's like … the money to build again. The yurt was OK when we were younger, and we added a lot to it over the years. It's just that now I have to do in a few months what we were years working on, and the bread just isn't there, all at once in the here and now."

"I'm certain you'll think of something," Richard's attempt to be bracing was not entirely feigned; Sefton was immensely creative, a scrounger and a tinkerer of no small skills. "Look, I promised your good lady that I would see you had a good meal now and again … how about a vegetarian pasta bake, with cremini mushrooms, spinach and fresh buffalo mozzarella? I'm perfecting a recipe for the luncheon menu at the Café, and I'd appreciate your input. Say – around six o'clock?"

"Sure thing, Rich," Sefton grinned, revealing a set of amazingly healthy white teeth. "Say, what wine goes best with your pasta bake – red or white?"

"Whichever one you feel like drinking," Rich answered, his own heart lifting at the prospect of a jug of Sefton's mustang-grape wine. The man was as good a vintner as his wife was as rotten a cook.

"Six o'clock, then," Sefton pushed his battered boonie hat further back on his head, and squinted at the cloud of dust rising from the lane which led into the Age from the main road. "I got a visitor, man – old Jaimie Gonzalez, from across the way. You know, him with the horses that are always getting out. He's bringing me a load of straw bedding for the goats."

"See you at suppertime," Richard withdrew into his tidy aluminum cocoon, and busied himself with setting out and prepping the various ingredients for the pasta bake, chopping the meagre fresh herbs that he had on hand, loosing himself agreeably in the process. In this, he was interrupted by a tentative knock on the door, just as he slid the baking dish into the pre-heated, nearly toy-sized bake oven. "It's open!" he shouted; the next moment, Berto Gonzales let himself into the trailer.

"'Lo, Ricardo," he said, bashfully as was his usual habit. "Whatcha making? Something good?"

"Pasta bake for dinner," Richard replied. "What brings you out here?"

"Uncle Roman stopped by with some stuff he had left over from a reno-job," Berto explained. "A bunch of slate tile, some metal roofing, and a coupla glass windows 'n patio doors. He asked me to come along and help unload, if Sefton wanted it. That smells good, Ricardo." He looked so longingly in the direction of the oven, that Richard could only sigh and ask if he wanted to come over for supper, as soon as he and Uncle Roman had unloaded the bounty which they had brought.

"Sure!" Berto beamed happily at him. "Ya mind if Uncle Roman comes? Aunt Conchita has a church meeting, so we were gonna go to the Whattaburger in Karnesville but your cooking is better, any day."

"I should bloody well hope so," Richard replied. "To the best of my knowledge, worthy as the proprietors of that establishment may be, they were not trained at Cordon Bleu in Paris."

"Is there a cooking school in Paris? I didn't know that!"

"Of course, there is," Richard snapped. "France is the very home of haute cuisine."

"I thought you meant Paris in Texas," Berto looked like a hurt puppy. Richard couldn't decide if Berto was taking the piss ... or if he really believed that the Cordon Bleu school of the culinary arts was indeed in Paris, Texas. Richard reached deep inside of himself for the manners and consideration which he had always been told were essential for a gentleman.

"Well, there might very well be a school of cooking there," he ventured, after taking a very deep breath. "But the place where I trained was in the original Paris. In France. Go tell Roman that the two of you are welcome … and that Sefton is bringing a jug of his homemade wine to the party."

"Awesome!" Berto lit up like a newly-decorated Christmas tree. "Like last time! I hope Sefton can use the stuff we brought…"

Across the campground, an impatient car horn beeped, several times. Richard looked out the window over the cooktop, and saw that Roman Gonzales by his laden pickup truck. "I think your uncle is giving you a hint," he said, and Berto scrambled out the trailer door and went galumphing across the empty campground. Richard shook his head. If there was a God in this heaven which everyone around here spoke so much about, then He must spend a lot of time watching after naïfs like Berto.

It was mild enough to eat outside on the little patio – which, really, was the only space big enough to serve up a meal to three relatively normal-sized men. The dining area in the Airstream might accommodate a pair of anorexic teenage girls, three if they didn't have sharp elbows. Richard hastily constructed a first course of packaged fresh spinach, adorned with dried cranberries, crumbles of feta cheese and seasoned pecans, tossed with a dressing of reduced blood-orange juice and olive oil, and sacrificed a baguette of his own café-fresh French bread to the demands of hospitality. On reflection, this was a necessary sacrifice; he had his reputation to consider, his standing in the community. After more than a year in Luna City, the necessity for and the advantages of being considered a part of such a community had been thumped into him as if with heavy clubs. Following the comprehensive disaster in the launch of his top-of-the pops London restaurant, Carême, Richard suspected that if he hadn't finished in Luna City, likely he would have drunk himself to death. If not that, then drooling and talking to himself in some top-flight and secure rehab facility. His good fortune in arriving in Luna City had been by chance and a private charter-flight pilot miss-hearing the name of the city to which he should have been delivered. For that, he owed an enormous debt to the citizens of Luna City, as exasperatingly opaque as they often seemed to be.

Just as he brought the pasta bake out of the oven and Sefton poured another round of savory rich red mustang-grape wine for everyone, another dust-trail appeared in the lane.

"Hey, it's Mr. Walcott!" Berto exclaimed, transparently thrilled as a child at a yearly pantomime upon spotting a favorite star, as the shiny black and heavily chrome-adorned SUV crept slowly up the lane. "I wonder what he is doing here?"

The driver of it observing the gathering at Richard's trailer, the SUV felt a tentative way across the lumpy campground in a manner which suggested someone with uncertain vision in a strange room. At the edge by the Airstream, the black SUV pulled in, and Clovis Walcott emerged from the driver's side. No one emerged from the passenger side. Obviously, Clovis' uber-demanding spouse was not with him; a circumstance for which Richard sensed that everyone else present at his al-fresco dinner was breathing an invisible sigh of relief. Most everyone liked Clovis Walcott; Sook Walcott, the champion tiger-mother of Luna City – indeed of Karnes County and perhaps of South Texas in general – was respected and feared, but the prospect of her company not relished by the cognoscenti. Now, Berto greeted Clovis, with the artless charm that only Berto could bring to bear.

"Hi, Mr. Walcott; where is Mrs. Walcott? I thought you went everywhere together?" *(A nice way of saying that Sook Walcott accompanied her husband like she was his parole officer.)*

"Hi, Berto. It's Sefton I came to see, actually. My Little Bride is in New York with Belle over the holidays; checking out the residence hall, and giving the place the once-over," Clovis grinned. "Just making certain that Julliard is good enough for our daughter."

"So the Missus backed down," Roman drawled. His daughter Beatriz was the same age as Belle Walcott; the girls were – as much as Richard tried to escape knowing such small-town trivia – in the same graduating class at Luna City High School. "You must have done some fast talking, Clovis."

"I pick my marital battles," Clovis retorted, equably. "And fight them with My Little Bride only when absolutely necessary. <u>When</u> I do, I usually win. But I didn't come out here to discuss my domestic arrangements; I just got back from Hong Kong last night, and the first thing I heard this morning from Robbie when I got up for breakfast was that the Grant place had burned to the ground while I was away. I thought I'd come over as soon as I was done with business for the day and make certain that you were all right. You and Judy doin' OK, then?" To Richard's ear, Clovis sounded completely sincere. The Age of Aquarius was an institution; Judy, as a descendant of an original founders, counted as being from one of the old families, like Miss Letty, Doc Wyler, the Bodies and the Abernathys, whereas the Walcotts were parvenus of relatively recent arrival.

"Getting' by," Sefton answered, terse and stoic as the cowboy hero in an old movie. "Thank-ee for asking, Clovis. You wanna drink?"

"Of your homemade stuff? Twist my arm, podner!" Clovis accepted a glass offered by Berto, and Richard sighed. Wine as ambrosial as Sefton's mustang-grape elixir should rightly be served in the finest blown crystal, not a repurposed jelly-glass from Marisol Gonzales' second-hand shop in Karnesville, from whence had come by donation all of Richard's household china *(actually mismatched melamine, most of it)*, silverware and pots and pans.

"I'm about to serve supper," Richard allowed. "Do you want to join us – there's plenty. I'm testing out a new entrée for the luncheon menu and I would value your honest opinion."

"Sure!" Clovis beamed honest delight. "You fixed it – I'll eat it and gladly, especially since I'm not paying for it, this time."

"Enjoy – it's vegetarian," Richard said, and noted with a sour sense of satisfaction that Clovis' anticipatory expression fell slightly. He went inside the Airstream to take the pasta bake out of the oven to rest, and toss the salad with the cheese crumbles and other additions. The dressing would go on at the very last minute. He emerged from the Airstream to see the other three men deploying folding lawn chairs and jelly-glasses of mustang-grape ambrosia, regarding the medium-distant and sad ruins of the Grant home-place, the massive pile of straw bales and assorted construction donations which lay under the largest of the trees which surrounded the low knoll.

"I really miss the sight of the old place," Richard said. "Dinner will be served in fifteen minutes. I know it wasn't a piece of architectural splendor, but it had a certain eccentric charm."

"It was our home," Sefton replied, morosely. "I built it for Judy with these hands, every bit of it myself. Raised three children in it. Gawd, I wish she hadn't decided against electricity from the county cooperative for the place ... but that's how she wanted it. Claimed that it interfered with the positive energy, she said. So I didn't install electricity in the yurt. I'm not a qualified electrician ... but I could have worked it out. At least, she was ok with propane gas, back then. And hot water from the well. All natural, she said – so that was OK."

"And I thought Clovis here was pussy-whipped," Roman commented, laughing when both Sefton and Clovis rounded on him in indignant denial.

"Your lady is your goddess, man," Sefton protested. Clovis added, "Look, My Little Bride is a firecracker. No denying that, but that's what I liked about her. She didn't take shit off anybody. I spent a hell of a lot of years away from home. Nice to know that your lady and goddess – thanks for that phrase, Sefton – can step in and make stuff happen." Clovis Walcott got that faraway expression on his pleasant, middle-aged countenance which normally descended on it when he talked about his historical reenactor activities. "A woman who can load and shoot, guard your back like a lioness? A pearl above price, gentleman, a pearl above price."

"Amen to that," Richard took up his glass, and raised it in a toast. "To your goddesses, gentlemen. I do not have one of my own at present, but I appreciate the concept. Half of the sky, can't live without them, can't live with them. Alas, that has been my own sad experience."

"Well, Cousin Kate really likes you," Berto dropped that conversational hand grenade with an expression of utter innocence. "A lot – she told Araceli so. I'll bet you could live with her fine. Except she lives in Karnesville, so one of you would hafta move."

"Alas, I am not a man for ... involvement," Richard answered; thrilled, horrified and embarrassed in about equal measure. "I do enjoy the company of Miss Heisel, a woman of inestimable value, but ... I confess that I am not worthy of her. I am driven by my art, to the exclusion of practically everything else. She deserves a companion who can make her happy, and I just do not believe that I could give her that."

"You might give it a chance, Rich," Clovis suggested with a broad smile. "You'd be amazed at what the fair sex can put up with, given half a chance and enduring affection."

"Yeah, you can cook and bake," Berto put in, again with the total lack of guile. "That counts for a lot."

"I built my love a house," Sefton looked morosely into his own glass, which had a bare skim of wine in the bottom. "And now I can't build her another one."

There was a short, depressed silence, during which Berto topped up Sefton's jelly-glass, and the four returned their bleak regard on the ruins of the Age of Aquarius; the grove of slightly-singed live oaks, the void circle of eccentrically-patchwork concrete where the colorful yurt had been. And then Berto – Berto of all people – spoke the earnest words that rocked the world of the Age, and as far as Richard was concerned, set his life on another and completely unexpected course.

"You could build a straw-bale house," Berto said. He had a faraway look in his eyes. "Look … all that straw from Tio Jaimie. You stack it up in bales, making walls, leaving a space for the doors and windows. Just like Lego blocks. Then you plaster it over, seal everything up real good. All natural, all organic. Thick walls, good insulation properties. Naturally cool in the summer, warm in the winter. You gotta make the roof overhang by about two feet for every eight feet in height of the walls, though. That's the hard part; you can't let the damp inside."

"I dunno about the load bearing properties of straw bales," Clovis Walcott mused. "The roof itself would have to rest on something more stable."

"Vertical beams," Berto insisted. "I saw it on one of those YouTube videos. It looked really neat. Wood or steel. Didn't seem to make much difference, I think. All to do with the roofing material. But the lay-out has to be exact."

"Yeah, it would have to be," That was Roman, and to Richard's absolute horror, Roman had the exact same faraway and speculative expression, as the two older men and Berto, the eternal teenager, regarded the site of the ex-yurt. "You got a concrete pad left, don't ya? If it wasn't damaged by the fire, you could re-use it for a new structure."

"Yeah, but it's round," Sefton objected. Berto, now fired with the enthusiasm of a new convert, replied, "So make it round. Make it … a tower, two, three stories tall. You could build at least half of one side with Tio Jaimie's straw, right here and now. But you have to work with dry straw, otherwise it just rots and gets nasty."

"How big is the concrete pad," Roman asked, all practicality, and Sefton answered. "I dunno. The yurt was a big puppy, about thirty-five feet across. The concrete pad is a couple of feet bigger."

"I've got a tape measure in the truck," Roman set aside his jelly-glass. "Let's go take a look, so's we know what we're dealing with from the git-go."

To Richard's horror, his other guests followed suit – and with the pasta bake just out of the oven! "Ten minutes!" he called towards their backs, as the four men strode purposefully up the low rise from the campground. "Dammit," he added to himself, in internal despair. If the main course dish sat for too long, cooling and congealing all the time – it would not be at best. Best is what Richard lived for. Any old glop was not his passion. Berto half-turned and administered a reassuring wave of the hand.

Richard, full of despair, withdrew into the Airstream after pouring himself another full jelly-glass of mustang-grape elixir. The harpies of failure were now flapping about his head, much as they had at the disastrous launch of Carême. And there was nothing that he could do about that, save ride the great wave of disaster, until it crested and broke. *For a brief flaming moment, he comprehended the visage of Kate Heisel, flipping the gears of Chris Mayall's little red compact with devastating competence, looking sideways at him and saying, "I kind of like you, Rich; you quoted Shakespeare to me in a personal way. You are an interesting person... but nothing that I'd be interested in committing to, seriously at this point ... I could change my mind about that, any time."*

He pottered about in the tiny kitchen, laying out plates for the entrée, smaller ones for the salad, sliced up the bread and laid out a dish of room-temperature herbed butter, accompanied by an increasing sense of despair, as the minutes marked by the little retro-style clock hanging over the banquette end of the Airstream passed. Finally, he could not stand it any longer; dinner was comprehensively prepared. He came out with his refreshed jelly-glass and looked towards the site of the ruined Grant home-place, and his heart lifted. They were returning, all four and in good time; but he noted with trepidation that all were in deep conversation, Berto gesticulating with Roman's industrial-strength plate-sized tape measure in one hand. Roman himself was jotting in a small spiral-notepad as they walked. From the enraptured expression on Clovis Walcott's face, he had now been bitten by the bug of professional challenge. In easy hearing of the Airstream, Roman folded up the notebook and stowed it in the pocket of his Carhartt barn coat.

"I think it might be doable, guys," he allowed. "Look, me and the guys don't work for free, but you're a good neighbor, Sefton. I can offer at-cost terms for the skilled labor, if you're good with that. You know – the plumbing and electrical, plus my time as foreman. Pay as much or in kind as you can afford, every month. I can't offer any better terms than that."

Sefton scratched his bristly cheek, appearing more cheerful than Richard had seen him in weeks. "I can live with that. I never wanted to be in debt to The Man, but I reckon I can accept being in debt to you for a while. As long as you can repurpose salvaged materiel as much as possible, or use cedar that I cut on the property for beams and such."

"We know where you live," Roman answered. "Hey, Rich – supper still good? I could eat a horse."

"Excellent!" Richard's hopes for extensive feedback on his new menu option rose into the stratosphere, only to be crushed again, when – once the perfectly-finished pasta bake was plated appealingly and set before the hungry multitude – the hungry multitude wolfed it down without comment. The conversation was all about straw-bale construction, the ins and outs, the various limitations, and advantages. Richard held his peace. Until the Grant establishment was reconstructed and Judy back at home, he was duty bound to feed Sefton at least three or four times a week.

"Roof," Clovis Walcott mused, a far-distant expression on his face. "You know, I might know where there is an old stray grain-bin roof looking for a good home. The Bodies replaced one of their old ones with bright and shiny new bin last year. The side panels and everything else were to far-gone to ask money for, especially after that accident. But the roof was good enough, still. Lightweight, already disassembled … Clem Bodie was hoping to sell it on eBay, but he has no takers so far. Last I heard, he was ready to take the whole thing to the metal recyclers. I'd have to check with him on the diameter, though."

"You could build something like this: Uncle R., can I have your book and pencil for a moment?" Berto was already far-gone in the throes of creative endeavor. To Richard's abject horror, Berto sat aside his plate of half-eaten pasta bake and salad, and began sketching out a rough ground-plan for the replacement yurt. "Make it about thirty feet across – build the south-facing side with beams, to allow for a window-wall and a veranda with a lower roofline, about another eight feet wide, to the edge of the slab… You could have a loft over about half the interior space, utilizing the peak of the roof. So, make the outer wall about seventeen or eighteen feet in height from base to eaves…"

"What do you think of the pasta," Richard asked. Berto replied, in an absent-minded manner. "Oh, fine. Now with a kitchen and a bathroom adjacent along the northern-facing angle …"

"Grouping all the plumbing in one single location," Clovis Walcott nodded his approval. "There might even be scope for a small bathroom in the loft area … and if the laundry closet is backed up against a downstairs bathroom and the kitchen, you could run water into a washing machine, instead of Judy hauling everything over to the campground bathhouse."

"I don't suppose you could talk Judy into solar panels; enough to power some small appliances," Roman ventured. "Or is she still that dead-set against electricity?"

"Likely I could persuade her on that," Sefton was wolfing down pasta bake as if one who had been starving. "Solar-power is like … renewable. She was real mellow about living in Jess's place. I was kind of surprised, myself. Maybe run in a coupla electric lines, quiet-like, an' let her think it it's all from solar-on-the-roof."

"I dunno," Berto looked worried over this element of mild subterfuge. "That would be like … telling a lie, 'r something."

"It's not a lie, son," Clovis Walcott observed. "It's a case of just not blurting out the absolute truth. Is there enough of that for seconds, Rich? I couldn't for the life of me name a blessed thing in it, but it is damned-good."

"Seconds for me, if there's enough," Sefton added; Richard waited on further complimentary comment, but none were forthcoming. His guests were deeply engrossed in the possibilities, as Berto covered several pages of Roman's notebook with tiny, penciled sketches of elevations, detailed diagrams, and sections of tentative floor plan, showing them to an increasingly enthused Sefton for approval.

Twilight masked the site of the eventual straw-bale house, and the sky overhead had bleached to the color of oyster-shell, stained in an apricot shade in the west. Against it, the bare branches of the trees were drawn like angular strokes from an old-fashioned ink fountain pen. The mellow golden interior lights from the door and windows of Richard's Airstream cast the only brightness on the last of the meal. Richard repressed a small and glum sigh. He had counted so much on a rapturous reception from all the gentlemen involved in this stag dinner party. The dish which held the main course was entirely scraped clean, so that was something positive to speak of.

He set it to soak in the miniscule sink, and emerged from the Airstream, to hear Clovis Walcott saying, "All right, guys; I'll take your sketches, Roman's measurements, the measurements of stuff donated so far, and generate a set of construction blueprints ... no, consider it my donation. None of this half-assing it on a project that I've designed. Everything will be right, tight and ship-shape. And," Clovis Walcott stood, tucking the pages torn from Roman's notebook into his own pocket, "If there's any permitting issues, or fees involved, address them to me. I'll be in and out over the next couple of months, but Roman has my cellphone number. I'll have the blueprints in about a week or so." Clovis Walcott cracked his knuckles and added, "This will be fun for me, Sefton. Anyone can get anything done when time, space and funding are unlimited – but the prospect of limited funding, a difficult space and unusual materials is a challenge that I relish. Don't go all noble and deprive me of my fun."

Amid the chorus of gratitude and acclimation from the others, Richard had to raise his voice slightly. "So ... what did you think of the pasta bake dish. Good for the Café, or should I rethink and adjust?"

"Oh, it's fine," Clovis replied, echoed by the other guests in varying degrees of what Richard perceived as profound disinterest. "Yeah, fine. OK, good. I liked it ... but what were those mushed-up green lumpy things?"

"The small dark green objects were capers, the larger pale green ones are artichoke hearts," Richard replied, through slightly-clenched teeth. "But otherwise – it met with your approval?"

"Well, yeah. Everything you fix is good," Berto answered, reaffirmed with expressions of mild agreement from the other men now gathering up themselves for departure.

"Do you have any suggestions … you know, any accompanying side dishes … or anything, really?" Richard made one last plea for useful, meaningful feedback.

"Nope. It was good," Sefton replied, honesty in every line of his battered, Willie Nelson-resembling face. "I'd sooner eat that than Judikins' Lentil Surprise, that's for certain. Thanks, Richard. Ya know, when we get the new place …"

"Call it 'Straw-Castle Aquarius'!" Berto suggested over his shoulder, as he followed his uncle. Sefton grinned. "Yeah, whatever, kid. Judikins 'ull sure be glad to get back. I miss her something fierce … all but her cooking."

"I'll see what I can do," Richard sighed. "I am certain there must be something. Look, cooking on a basic level is only a matter of following simple directions on a page. Follow the directions, at least one finishes with something edible, if mostly uninspired. Inspired is for experts, who know the rules."

"Yeah, but Judikins doesn't acknowledge any rules," Sefton's expression faded into one more expressive of regret. "She's always held the conviction that rules were by The Man, to hold us all down."

"You are The Man, now," Richard sought to comfort his companion in exile, or at least, try and do his bit towards domestic tranquility. "Look; I'll try and come up with some recipes for lentils, and I'll do my level best to school your good lady in them, when she returns."

"If she returns," Sefton looked especially morose, which horrified Richard. Feeding Sefton every other evening or so until the end of time was not in his life-plan, although at this point, Richard would have been hard-pressed to say exactly what his life-plan might be, save to keep the Café open and continue serving caviar cuisine on a canned tuna-fish budget.

"She will," Richard said, and he hoped that he sounded bracing, optimistic. "Get the straw-castle built. A pretty nest for your bower-bird mate. She'll be back, no doubt about it."

"Hope so," Sefton replied, by way of bidding adieu and stumped off towards the bare-bones man-camp trailer at the other end of the campground. Sefton lifted an arm to wave at Roman's battered pickup truck with the "Gonzalez Construction & Renovation Company" logo on the side, and Walcott's black and silver SUV as they departed the Age of Aquarius at slow speed and bumping over every rut.

Richard, seeing that his obligations as a host were done for the evening, decided it was time for him to retire to the trailer. On his way, he noted that Miss Letty's gift plant was looking a bit withered. Mindful of her words, he filled a measuring cup at the sink tap and emptied it into the pot.

Celia Hayes & Jeanne Hayden

Winter 2017 Newsletter

Luna City Chamber of Commerce

5 North Town Square, Suite 4

And check out our Facebook Page

The Mills Farm Spa and Resort holds an open house February 25 in the Dance Hall from 10:00 AM until 6:00 PM, so that anyone interested may look at scale models of the the proposed new Water Park development and expanded hotel facility. Completion of the water park and hotel is planned for 2019-2010. A complete renovation is in the works, in line with a renewed focus on a more wide-spread public appeal. Lucien Dubois, the VPI head of marketing, will be available to answer questions at the Open House from 5:00-6:00

Spring Market

The Spring Farmer's Market and Craft Show will be held April 1-2 from 10-4 on Saturday and 11-4 on Sunday on Town Square. Vendors from all across South Texas will offer their wares – everything from hand-made furniture, clothing, toys and household ornaments, pottery, ironwork and art of every description. Local farmers and artisanal food producers will also be offering their products. The Karnes Company Rangers Living History Association will set up an encampment and display their skills and equipment throughout the weekend. The Luna City Volunteer Fire Department will also have one of their engines on display.

This market has been widely advertised in San Antonio and Austin media outlets and a large turn-out is expected. Overflow parking will be in the empty pasture behind the VFW and the Tip Top Ice House.

Upcoming Events

January 8

Formal dedication of the newly-reopened Parish Hall of the Church of Sts Margaret and Anthony will follow 10AM Mass

February 3

Double Feature Movie night at the Koenig Opera House, starting at 7:30 PM every Friday until June!

March 25

Pancake Breakfast at the LCVFD, 9:00 AM.

All Hands Weekend!

Roman Gonzalez and his crew will oversee volunteers Saturday and Sunday, March 18-19 at the Age of Aquarius Campground & Goat Farm. A briefing and assignment to specific crews will be held Friday, March 17th at the VFW at 4:30. Roman and the guys hope to complete work on the Grant's new home over the weekend. Come on out and show your support for our friends, Judy and Sefton!

Luna City, Texas – Home of the Mighty Fighting Moths

Page 1 of 2

Luna City ISD News

Registration for Kindergarten – 2017-18

Registration will be Friday, March 31st at the Luna City ISD offices on Town Square. All paperwork for the upcoming school year must be completed at this time. Students will receive notification in late April regarding the 2017-18 school year. Parents/guardians should bring a copy of their child's birth certificate and immunization records.

School Library Open House

The Luna City High School Library will have an open house at the Library, from 3-5 PM on Friday, February 10th. Parents are invited to come and meet the library staff, and to check out the wide variety of books, periodicals and reference materials available at the library

Spring Break Senior Trip

Seniors and their chaperones will depart from the school gym at 3 PM Friday April 7th for their five-day long trip to San Antonio and the Hill Country. Signed permission slips and payment for transportation, hotel stay and admission to Fiesta Texas in San Antonio must be received at ISD offices by Wednesday, April 5th. Seniors are limited to one suitcase and on small carry-on bag. Students will be returning on the following Wednesday afternoon at 2 PM, traffic permitting.

School Lunch Menus

Weekly menus for both Luna City Elementary and High School cafeterias will be posted by Thursday of the previous week on the LCISD website, under the tab labeled "Good Eats."

Community Marketplace

Silent Auction and Sale at Sts Margaret & Anthony Thrift Shop

The thrift shop will hold a silent auction of items donated to raise funds for the rebuilding of the Parish Hall. Those items – which range from antique furniture and a vintage designer handbag to signed original art and memorabilia will be on display in a case in the lobby of the Cattleman Hotel. Bids for the items may be dropped into a clearly marked box outside the Thrift Shop. The winning bids will be announced at the opening of the Farmer's Market/Craft Fair on Sunday, April 2.

From Chief Vaughn, Luna City PD

The regular LCVFD training session on Wednesday, March 8, 5 PM at the LCVFD classroom will be a joint exercise with the Luna City PD and representatives of the Karnes County Office of Emergency Management. The emphasis will be on high-water rescue and reaction to flood emergencies.

Weekend Breakfast Special at Luna Café and Coffee

The Full English Breakfast offered every Saturday morning as a brunch special was so well-received during a test period that Richard will offer it every Saturday and Sunday mornings from 10 AM to Noon.

Richard's Full English Breakfast includes bacon, sausages, fried, poached or scrambled eggs, grilled tomatoes, baked beans, fried mushrooms, fried bread or toast with butter, jam or marmalade, and tea or coffee.

Signs and Portents

As near as Richard could see, the rebuilding of "Straw Castle Aquarius" progressed like going bankrupt; at first slowly and then all of a sudden. The slow part stretched through the remainder of January and into February; days of leaden grey overcast skies, chill and dreary, varied with days when a crisp breeze cleared the skies, and the temperatures at night plunged down towards the freeze-point. In the early morning, pale mist rose from the river like a length of silk gauze, tangled among the scrub trees and brush which lined the banks, at the bottom of the tract which formed the campground. Richard moved through the days and weeks of his chosen work, noticing in a desultory fashion when something about the worksite changed sufficiently to be noticeable from a distance.

The pile of donated materiel grew – covered against the weather by a series of battered tarpaulins. Richard could not judge from a distance exactly what this consisted of; probably architectural salvage, since Roman's truck and attached trailer made frequent visits to the Age. But at least one delivery was made by the brown UPS van, which advanced slowly up the lumpy, unpaved lane from the main road. The van overtook Richard, as he was pedaling up that lane, and slowed down as it passed. The driver hailed him from the open driver-side door.

"Hey, Ricardo, can you sign for this delivery if Sefton is nowhere around? I don't wanna haul this heavy shit back to Karnesville, if I can help it, and he prolly don't want to drive down and get it from there."

"Certainly," Richard recognized the UPS driver – generally as a Gonzalez/Gonzales, if not specific as to given name; youngish, round-faced, dark of hair and brown of eye. "Anything to be of help, of course. Any notion of what it might be?"

"Yeah." The UPS driver downshifted, slowing the panel van to a crawl, matching pace with Richard. "I heard it through the rumor-mill – it's a door. Mahogany and hand-carved. No wonder it's as heavy as shit. Somebody sent it to Sefton for the rebuild. Wish that I had friends as generous as that, dontcha know?"

"It's a gift, I expect," Richard replied, with a sigh. If any further proof were needed of the affection and respect in which the Grants were held by the community and their larger circle of friends, this certainly provided it. One thing to be wealthy beyond all dreams of mortal man – another to be so highly thought of that necessary items were delivered, gratis as gifts.

The week after the door was delivered, packaged in a substantial crate, and which took all three; Richard, Sefton, and the luckless UPS driver with his industrial-strength dolly to horse out of the van and add to the growing stack of donations – was a relatively quiet one, as far as Richard could see. Oh, there were a couple of days where Roman's pickup showed up with a couple of competent-appearing workmen who did … things. Things purposefully performed; such as a long trench dug by a baby-tractor/excavator between the hot-well that supplied the campground bathhouse and the prospective straw castle, a growing pile of square frames roughed out of twelve-inch planks, and a couple of moveable scaffolds. On a day shortly thereafter, another specialty-tractor appeared; this one drilling a series of holes around the perimeter of the concrete pad.

"For the porch-posts," Sefton explained, when he appeared for dinner at the Airstream that evening. Sefton carried a gas-powered chain-saw over his shoulder, and smelt comprehensively like one of his goats. Fortunately, it was mild enough to eat outside. And Sefton had previously provided another jug of his own mustang-grape wine, which Richard thought would be good for the rest of the week. "And the beams to support the roof. I been cutting cedar in the thicket. Sorry for the reek. I figure everyone is being so great about donating stuff, I gotta get off my ass and do my bit. Judikins will like it, that we're using cedar from the property."

"Nothing like a good bracing day of deforestation," Richard commented, and Sefton snorted, setting down the chain-saw.

"Sheee-yit," Sefton drawled, giving the four-letter word two, or possibly three syllables. "Cedar around here ain't a forest! It's a damned weed tree. An invasive pest, crowding out the regular native oaks an' cypress trees, sucking up every bit o' water out of the ground. The day they figure out a way to kill those damned things down to the roots is a day that can't come too soon for me. But," he added, fairly. "Ya can do interesting things with the wood. There some local artisans making some real fine furniture and doo-dads out of the stuff, when it's cut into planks and finished smooth. Me, I'm not going so fancy for the porch-posts. Not even going to take off the bark."

"Going for the rustic look, then," Richard said, having gathered as much from Berto's drawings.

"Yeah, something like that." Sefton heaved up a deep sigh. "I sure hope that Judikens approves. She sure can get some weird fancies about stuff."

"Mmm." Richard said, thinking that a noncommittal reply to that was likely the safest one. "I did eggplant parm for dinner tonight. All vegan. I'm certain your good lady will approve."

The pace of construction – or rather, reconstruction – picked up early in March, culminating with the arrival of another trailer late one afternoon, this one pulled by another battered pickup truck with the logo of Bodie Feed and Seed, Inc. on the doors. The trailer was piled high with what appeared at first to be a load of scrap lengths of aluminum, lengths which overwhelmed the trailer. A closer inspection revealed that they were wedge-shaped sections, each about twenty feet long, three or four feet wide at the widest end. A square of red rag waved limply from the narrow ends of wedge, which hung off the end of the trailer.

"Grain-bin roof," explained the driver of the pickup, as he deftly unhitched the trailer at the end of the campground closest to the site for the straw castle. He was not a Gonzales/Gonzalez, but a fair-haired and amiable teenager. Richard assumed that he was a Bodie, as they were the only clan of light-haired individuals in Luna City. "Uncle Clem and Dad 'ull come sometime this weekend with the boom truck and get 'er put together, as soon as the frame is in place. Let Mr. Grant know, 'kay?" From the faint sounds of a chain-saw, born on the light breeze from the thickets at the far end of the property, Sefton was hard at work slaughtering scrub cedar trees for the beams of Straw Castle Aquarius.

"I'll pass on the message," Richard promised. He was vaguely interested in what would be involved in assembling the oddly-shaped slabs of aluminum which to his admittedly untutored eye, looked simply too flimsy to be anything than a trailer-load of scrap metal.

But his eye had deceived him, indeed. On the following Saturday morning, after having fed the good citizens of Luna City (and a fair number of wandering and curious motorists) on a surfeit of fresh-baked cinnamon rolls and the more daring (and hungry) on a full-English breakfast fry-up, he returned to the Age to see a large truck with an extendable boom parked in the campground. The boom had a large … well, it was some kind of tyre hanging off the business end, about ten feet from the ground. The tyre supported a large metal ring of somewhat lesser dimension and from it, the wedges of sheet aluminum were being assembled in methodical fashion by three men in work clothes, laboring away with wrenches at the various segments. One of them was the fair-haired youth who had delivered the trailer. He recollected the others from mornings in the Café, and from his impromptu and fortunately abortive turn on the stage of the Luna City Players last performance: Clem and Durham Bodie, whose wives had been cast members of *Let No True Hearts Admit Impediment*. Richard marveled briefly at the fast work they seemed to be making of it.

"'Lo, Richard," Clem Bodie hailed him, as soon as he wandered up. Curiosity couldn't keep him away. especially as he had observed a wood framework now looming up in the grove. It looked like a circular enclosure for elephants, topped by a network of beams arranged like the spokes of an opened umbrella. A huge stack of hay-bales sat under a bright blue tarp, ready to be assembled. "So whattya think?"

"Impressive," Richard ventured. "And the next hailstorm will cause everyone underneath to be deafened by the experience."

"Well, it is that way with tin roofs," Durham Bodie grinned, standing on the next-to-top step of a short ladder, while his brother worked underneath, one of them methodically attaching, and the other tightening the series of bolts that marched in a tidy line up and down the edge of the joins between roof segments. "But Clovis and Roman are planning an inner ceiling, with plenty of sound-proofing. This ol' roof should be right and tight – water-proof and even fireproof. Good for them next time, eh?" The brothers had reached the inner ring at the peak of the roof. Durham descended from the ladder, and the two moved it to the opposite side, and the outer circumference. "We're rushing to finish this tonight," Clem added, over his shoulder. "The wind is supposed to kick up – we wanna get this sucker finished and tied down while it's still calm. Are ya gonna come to the party, on St. Paddy's Day weekend? That's when the plan all comes together!"

"I guess that I will," Richard ventured, slightly dubious of what being asked of him. "What's happening on that particular day?"

"We put this all together," the youngest Bodie replied, the youth who had delivered the trailer several days prior. "The roof on top, fill in the sides, bring in the plastering … hope to finish or come near to finishing it all in one weekend, even if we have to work around the clock."

"Sounds like fun," Richard replied, his heart lifting. With the Straw Castle of Aquarius finished or nearly finished, Judy Grant would return, and take from him the burden of feeding her lugubrious spouse. And there wouldn't be that yawning absence in his view from the little patio in front of the Airstream.

Ala Carte With Quartermayne

(From Daily Variety – January, 2017)

RoadEats Productions has announced that their roving restaurant show *Ala Carte With Quartermayne* has been renewed for another season. A top-rated cooking and regional travel show, *Ala Carte* stars Allan Lee Mayne, who played quarterback for the Denver Broncos from 1983 to 1992 and parlayed his football fame into show-business, with guest appearances in various popular situation comedies, and an unexpectedly successful turn on Season Two of *Dancing with the Stars*. Genial, food-loving – and who can doubt it, at his fighting-weight of 380 pounds – Allen Lee travels the back roads of America in a luxury maroon and gold-trimmed RV, visiting small towns scattered along major and secondary roads, exploring local cuisine hot-spots, and comparing favorite local dishes. Over the six-year run of *Ala Carte*, Allan Lee has partnered with various co-stars, who serve up commentary and sometimes a side-helping of drama, as they explore the culinary byways of America. In the upcoming season, Allan Lee is set to co-host with British reality TV star and long-established miniseries heartthrob Phillip Noel-Barrett. Production of new episodes is set to begin next month, beginning in in Texarkana, Texas.

Ashes, Ashes, All Fall Down

The whole size of the rebuilding effort really didn't dawn on Richard until late Friday afternoon; visitor's night at the VFW. There was always a good-sized crowd on those Fridays, but on this day, the patch of gravel and stunted weeds which served as a parking lot was swamped by motor vehicles. Two more; a large sedan, and a vaguely-familiar appearing RV pulled into the asphalt apron in front of the Tip-Top, even as Richard was propping his trusty bicycle against a handy tree; a cedar tree, he noted, and wondered how it had escaped Sefton's campaign to harvest lumber. It wasn't on the Age's property, he knew, but according to some rumors passed on by Araceli, Sefton and the other Old Communards had a pretty liberal notion about righteous needs justifying suitable action.

"Hey, where's the meeting about planning for the Age?" The driver of the RV clambered down from his lofty perch: Richard recognized him as an old communard, Sefton's friend Bigbee. More than that; he recognized the RV. "We came as soon as I could get away. I got one of the adjuncts to take my morning class. We aren't too late, are we?"

"Nnnno, I don't think so," Richard stammered. "What meeting?"

"Some big-shot name of Walcott called it; sent out emails and posted it on the Age's Facebook page: *Come one, come all, help rebuild the Age of Aquarius, meeting at the Luna City VFW*. I didn't know that God croaked and left him in charge. But we spent some fine times there, back in the day, so of course we had to drop everything and show up, although I'd have never thought I would be setting foot in a VFW. More like – throw a Molotov and burn it down, but ya know. Things change."

"It's that little pink building, round in back," Richard replied. The day being fairly mild for winter, it looked to him as if the planning meeting was going on in back, having spilled out onto the concrete patio. The main room at the V was practically deserted – only Chris Mayall, wiping down the bar and studiously ignoring the television, which was broadcasting a silent game of American football, while outside the windows at the back, the crowd around Clovis Walcott's whiteboard paid their rapt attention to whatever he was saying.

"Ay, Ricardo! What can I do ya for?"

"Ginger beer, if you have any," Richard said, and Chris grinned.

"Yeah, we got. Just for you, since you said you were trying to dial back on the leaded in a public setting. Fever Tree brand OK with you?"

"Splendid," Richard settled onto one of the battered bar stools with a sigh, and looked out through the window. "Tonight's entertainment, I guess."

"Hey, the Grants are good people," Chris shook his head. He took down a heavy glass beer mug from the back-bar, and set it in front of Richard. In a sweeping gesture, he magicked a tall, frosted bottle out of a refrigerator hidden under the bar, and popped off the metal cap. "Here ya go, Rich. You sure you aren't going to join them, as a public-spirited citizen and adopted son of Luna City?"

"I think not. I know bloody-all about construction, so I can't think what use I might be. And the Café is my primary obligation to the town; Saturday and Sunday brunch is absolutely key. Did you know that we now seat twice as many people for weekend brunch as we did last year at this same period? I just provided the figures to Jess. The daily takings from those two days simply overwhelm that from the other five. She was astounded, I must admit. She says if we continue at this rate, then I may hire two interns for the summer months and offer them a little more than what the Mills Farm Country Kitchen does. Plus," Richard added with completely justified satisfaction, "I'm offering proper chef's training. Mills Farm? That is to laugh; little better than working some ghastly fast-food emporium."

"You're all about class, aintcha?" Chris laughed, popping the cap from another Fever Tree for himself. Richard snorted. "No. I am about quality. Animals eat. Humans dine. There is a difference. I am hoping that when the Grant domicile is rebuilt, then things can get back to the usual mundane state of matters. I like mundane," Richard confided. "I like routine. I depend on it, absolutely. I am a creature of settled habits, Chris. A time and a place for everything, everything in its time and place. I get jittery when things spin out of control."

"Sounds like a personal problem," Chris sounded his usual sardonic self. "But I get it. Rich. Look; you're lucky in having finished up here in Luna City. You got the 90% normality that most folk crave, with the 10% crazy that keeps you from going bat-shit nuts from boredom. So relax, pal. Enjoy the ride. You know," Chris added, after a meditative swipe of the bar-top with the ubiquitous towel. "This place done a lotta good for you. Remember; I saw you at the Café, the morning that the Doc offered you the running of the place. That was what – two days after you got dumped at the airport and Berto Gonzales brought you here, 'cause you handed him a buttload of money to take you anywhere?"

"There are no secrets in this place, are there," Richard acknowledged, sourly. Chris grinned. "Nope, not after about fifteen minutes. So ya see, Rich; this place has done you a pile of good. I saw you that morning, and you were about twenty-four hours past being one of the most flaming-hot crackups that I have ever seen. It's my thought you ought to give something back. It's only fair, you know."

"I can't drive a nail in to save my life," Richard protested. Chris shook his head. "No; you got obligations. I see that. But what about volunteering for more than a single weekend?"

"I already have done a cooking class at the school," Richard pointed out, with justification.

"Well, that's a good start. No, I was thinking; what about being a member of the VFD? That would … well, it would make you a real Lunaite, you see. Establish your street cred, so to speak."

Richard stared at him, gob-smacked. "I don't know anything about fighting fires," he protested, and Chris shook his head again.

"No, but you'd learn. And it would go a good way towards … look, that's how I knew I was one of the gang. When I started going to the Wednesday training sessions. I said that I would be their chief medic. Look at me, Rich, I got that year-round permanent dark tan. No getting away from it: I'm not from here, I ain't a Gonzales with an s or Gonzalez with a z. And I'm not a Bodie or an Abernathy. Mebbe an honorary McAllister, 'cause of Miz Letty, but the rest of it is because I sacked up and decided that I would give back."

"So what was it that you felt obligated," Richard asked. "And I do not understand your crude reference to having 'sacked up.' What did Luna City ever do for you as a non-native son and one of … er – possessing a permanent dark tan? Why did you feel that the citizens of this undoubtedly worthy burg were owed anything at all by you?" He added hastily, "You told me that Doc's late good lady and Miss Letty looked after you when you were … erm, laid up. In hospital, so to speak. Seriously; how did they even know about you?"

"Long story," Chris equivocated. "But the short of it is that early in '03, when we deployed to Iraq, all the rest of the guys in the unit had family sending them letters and things. You know; cookies, candy, baby-wipes, books, chili sauce and CDs. My buddy J.W., he noticed that I never got any letters, nothing from nobody. He wrote and told Miz Alice, and she told Miz Letty, and it just kinda snowballed from there. Folks here in Luna City were good to us, even then. I had so many books that we kept a lending library, and so much pogey bait I was giving it away. And letters – the whole third grade class was writing me letters. I had time at first to answer them. So, when I medicaled out of the Navy, I had no better place to go than come here. Truth was I was more at home here, then I had ever been anywhere else, save mebbe in the Navy."

"I'll give it some serious consideration," Richard allowed, after a moment. The suggestion was mildly appealing, the more that he meditated upon it. Yes, it would cement his standing in Luna City "Being a cook and all, I am acquainted with the elementary dangers of fire. I had never considered … where I come from, the fire service services are professionals; generally we'd prefer to leave it to them, but … it would be like joining a club, wouldn't it? Only I wouldn't have to pretend to enjoy tennis, or golf. And putting out fires – it's of use. You know, like cooking."

"Gives life meaning," Chris agreed with a quick grin. "You never really struck me as a sports fan, anyway."

"I rowed at school, and crewed the Charterhouse sailboat," Richard protested, and Chris's grin broadened.

"Not much in the way of that kind of sport here," he said. "May as well stick to riding that bicycle and hauling hoses. Hey, if you want another Fever Tree, better ask for it now. Clovis is gonna break for about fifteen minutes, so's everyone can get a drink, and then carry on with the briefing."

"He's got a good crowd out there," Richard noted through the windows which stretched across the back of the repurposed old portable classroom which housed the VFW post. "Who's the chap sitting next to Benny C? They look like pals."

"New guy at Mills Farm," Chris cast a glance through the window.

"That's where I recall him from," Richard replied. "He was driving a truck, delivering a trailer to the Age. For Sefton's temporary residence. Their new dogsbody, eh?"

He was diverted from further comment, as it appeared that Clovis had handed the mic and the whiteboard over to Roman Gonzales: from the design man to the practical-construction man. His eye roved over the earnest-faced mass of Lunaites, and alighted upon a blessed and most welcome vision: Judy Grant, sitting on one of the crude picnic benches, with an arm around Sefton, and another around the teenage girl at her side. His heart lifted in sheer, blissful relief. All the stars and planets had aligned, God was in his heaven, all was right with his world, his own tiny, well-organized, and peaceful world. The most appalling cook in Christendom had returned, to bless her spouse with her presence, take up her share of caring for the goats, dogs, honeybees and chickens … all of whom, Richard was certain, had been moping for the last two months, although Sefton had assured him several times that the chickens were just molting. And it was winter, after all.

A Troop in Need

From the Karnesville Daily Beacon, April, 2003 (Archive)

Word comes to us this week from Mrs. Alice Wyler of Luna City, whose grandson, LCpl. James W. Ellis is deployed with the US Marines to the Middle East. LCpl. Ellis wrote to Mrs. Wyler concerning a friend of his, Petty Officer Christopher Mayall, USN, who has no living close relatives. P.O. Mayall is one of the serving medics with LCpl. Ellis' unit and during the whole of their deployment has received no letters or care packages from home. Mrs. Wyler reports that the boredom and miseries of a troop deployment to the Middle East are alleviated in a large part by letters and comforts provided by the home folks for soldiers, sailors, airmen and Marines. Candy, energy bars, books, music CDs, wet-wipes and other toiletries are much appreciated, but P.O. Mayall has no one to send him care packages. Mrs. Wyler asks that anyone who wishes to stand in as family and write and send such items to him, should contact her, and she will provide an APO mailing address for P.O. Mayall. Mrs. Wyler can be contacted through the Lazy-W Exotic Game Ranch, of Luna City.

Raising the Castle

Before first light, Richard was heading out from the Airstream, for a half-day of work at the Café. He did make a mental note to do up an extra pan of cinnamon rolls to bring back with him, retaining some foggy memories of well-stocked craft tables on movie locations, both in his past life, and at the horrible zombie movie last summer in Luna City. He thought that he would be the only person awake on a Saturday morning – but as he walked the bicycle up the rutted lane to the main road, he spotted a pair of headlights approaching, bobbing and lurching as the driver negotiated the vehicular obstacle course. He walked the bike onto the driver-side verge, and the truck slowed. It was Roman Gonzales, with a full-loaded trailer hitched to his equally-laden pickup.

"You're out and about early," Richard commented, after exchanging greetings.

"Gotta get the show on the road," Roman answered. "The fellows are on the way, but I brought out the lights and generator, so we can work tonight as well as this morning. The Colonel says this will all go like clockwork, but I always allow for Murphy to get involved."

"Who's Murphy?" Richard frowned. "Is there anyone by that name in Luna City?"

"Not a person, Ricardo. It's the monkey-wrench in the machine that wrecks the best plan. Murphy's Law: What can go wrong will, and at the worst possible time and at the maximum inconvenience to everyone."

"Ah – Sod's Law," Richard was relieved. "Well, hoping you have banished Murphy and Sod and all their spanners for the duration."

"Miz Grant says she's going to take care of that," Roman grinned from ear-to-ear. "Before we start work, she's going to perform some kind of cleaning ritual, with sweetgrass smoke and incense and all that."

"If you're lucky," Richard replied, "She and the Old Communards won't do the ritual sky-clad." Roman chuckled, in an appreciative manner. "It's a construction site in about ten minutes, so appropriate protective gear must be worn. Still, Ricardo; she's not bad looking, for a woman of her age. Best not tell Conchita I said so, though. See you in a few hours, then."

"I'll bring cinnamon rolls," Richard promised, and Roman laughed. "I'll take it as a guarantee, Ricardo ... say, how is the old Airstream holding up for ya? It's been a while, since you got here."

"Beautifully," Richard answered. "I should say ... well, thank you, and thank your Abuelita... this has been almost the longest I have lived anywhere."

"Time flies when you're having fun," Roman put the truck into gear. It lurched down the drive to the prospective site of the Amazing Straw Castle Aquarius, as Richard wended down the rutted driveway to the site of his daily labors, and sank his attention into them so far as to forget the reconstruction project entirely for a brief five or six hours.

"Did seem that we had slightly fewer diners for luncheon today?" he asked Araceli, who shook her head.

"A little bit of a drop, I think. There were more out-of-towners, than local folks. But breakfast was about the same, although I didn't see many people lingering. Practically everyone was eating and running ..."

"Oh, Christ!" Richard felt his heart and stomach drop into his shoes. *The Carême disaster, all over again! How had he not noticed!*

"Chef – don't take that name in vain! No, it doesn't mean what you think," Araceli chided him, although exasperation vied with concern in her expression. "It's just an expression. I meant they were in a hurry to finish and go. Not that they were heading for the bathroom to throw up or something."

"Don't use it again," Richard commanded, still sweating slightly. "I have nerves, you know."

"I do, Chef ... really, I think most everyone was heading out to the Age. Is that what the extra pan of cinnamon rolls is for? Good idea. Nothing like a challenge, around here; build a straw-bale house in a weekend! Berto is wound up like nothing I have ever seen before. He's hoping this project will count for extra credit. It's the first thing he has ever designed for real, full-size."

"It's a project of substance and value, indeed," Richard felt the knot of tension, located strategically as it was in his mid-section, connecting the back of his neck and the pit of his stomach, loosen appreciably. "In fact, I have been considering such a project myself. I have been thinking of volunteering for the fire-fighting company."

To his dismay, Araceli chortled. "Oh, Chef, I suppose as long as you brought cinnamon rolls to weekly training!" As she observed the expression on his face, her own sobered. "I'm sorry, I thought that was a joke. But you are serious! OK, well, " As Araceli considered the implications, her expression reflected Chris Mayall's sober one. "You know, Chef, that would be a good idea. You'd be ... I dunno – less of a passenger. No, that's not the right word, really. You'd be more of a part, even more than you are already, with the Café and all. Yes." Her expression turned positive, determined. "Go for it, Chef. At the very least, the fund-raising feeds for the VFD would have some amazing options to offer."

"Thanks for the vote of confidence," Richard replied, somewhat sourly. "I was certain you only loved me for my cooking."

"Your cheerful face and optimistic attitude count in your favor, too," Araceli retorted. Richard sighed. "You have the most charming way of taking the piss, Araceli. Yes, I most definitely will volunteer my severe lack of lifesavings skills to the Luna City Volunteer Fire Department. I trust that if worst comes to worst, I will be seconded to a position which affords the least-likely odds of doing damage to myself and a luckless public."

On that inspiring note, he left Araceli to finish closing-up the Café for the day, and departed with a double-batch of just-warm cinnamon rolls packed in a heavy cardboard box between layers of waxed paper, securely fastened to the back of his bicycle. He was not sure of what he was expecting to see when he arrived at the Amazing Straw Castle Aquarius; perhaps a scene of desultory labor, where there might be about a course or two of hay-bales dispersed around the perimeter of the wood framework supporting the circular wooden skeleton of the eventual castle tower. And there would be a half-dozen or so volunteers standing around, watching without very much interest; a vision of sloth and lassitude.

Instead – and he paused by the side of the drive, approximately in the same place where he had stopped in the wee dark hours, to converse with Roman Gonzales – thunderstruck and disbelieving the evidence of his own eyes. The Tower was built, a palisade of golden straw, up to the top level all the way around that he could see, the cynosure of a bustle of activity. The inner roof was completed, more loose straw being piled upon it as insulation, handed up in the basket-full by relays of people passing them up from the ground. Even more straw was being stuffed into the interstices between bales, or between bales and those deep wooden frames marking the voids where doors and windows would be. He thought he had a glimpse of Judy Grant in her white ceremonial Druid robes, a sistrum strung with tiny bells on one hand, and a bundle of gently fuming sweetgrass in the other. The sistrum trailed a tiny musical tinkling, the sweetgrass a visual trail of brief grey smoke – which he thought he could smell, borne to him on the gentle breeze. Judy was also trailed by a teenage girl in a similar robe, a girl who also carried a sistrum and a sweetgrass bundle. The girl was one who had been sitting next to Judy at the planning meeting … in fact, she looked enough like Judy to be a relative. But the structure itself claimed his immediate attention. The whole thing resembled a single shining, straw-golden column, rising like a phoenix from the sad burnt remains of the yurt. The shallow metal cone of the repurposed grain-bin roof hovered in the air above it, suspended from the business end of a boom-lift. As Richard dismounted from his trusty bicycle, regarding this spectacle with awe and amazement, a cool breeze fanned his face, and a shout went up from the driver of the boom-lift truck, as the metal roof swayed and shivered gently.

"Keep it steady! Don't let it get away!"

Now Richard saw there were also ropes attached to the circular roof edge, half-a-dozen ropes trailing down to ground-level, those ends secured in the hands of another set of volunteers, spaced around the circuit of the straw tower, shortening, and tightening their grips as the great aluminum cone was lowered, lowered by careful inches onto the structure. The last few buckets of loose straw thrown on the inner roof, the outer one settled with an almost palpable sigh, crowning the circular golden straw eminence.

"OK! If it's even all the way around, tie this puppy down!" That was Clovis Walcott, with a battery-powered bullhorn in his hand, and an anxious Berto at his heels, armed with a roll of blueprints. At that command, a chorus of high-pitched metallic whines arose from around the perimeter of that metal roof.

"We got her, Durham! Let it go down easy! Stand away, all inside!"

The operator of the lift truck waved, a brief salute, and there was another high-pitched whine, as the cable lifting the metal cone from the center went out over the pulleys. In the next moment, there was a small metallic crunch, emanating from inside the castle. Richard watched, agog with amazement. In a moment, a man appeared in … well, he assumed that it was the doorway to the new and vastly improved Amazing Aquarius Straw Castle. Clem Bodie, expertly maneuvered a large tire on a metal rim, rolling it out into the cleared space. Clem had a large metal disk with a hook attached under his other arm. In the space of a moment, he threaded the hook and disk through the center hole in the tire rim, and attached it to the chain which his brother had obligingly dangled from the end of the lift-truck boom. Clem waved to his brother, in the next instant, the tire went swooping up the chain to the top of the boom.

Richard, having come within speaking distance of Clovis Walcott, remarked, "That is the most remarkable sight."

"Isn't it?" Clovis grinned like a boy, as he turned around and noted Richard's presence. "Talk about improvising a device to move a grain-bin roof. There are some very expensive attachments available to go through the center-circle to move it entire, but why spend the money when you can kluge up a cheap and effective solution?"

"I was speaking of what has been accomplished in a mere few hours," Richard responded and Clovis laughed. "Chef, what we can do, when we put our various minds to it! This was actually the easiest element of this project! Stacking the bales and hammering them all together? A piece of cake. You know, there's a lot to be said for this straw-bale thing. After this, I might add it onto my resume of design skills. You know," and his voice went confidential, confiding, "It has all gone so easily together, I think that Mrs. Grant must be on to something, in walking around with her spells, bells, and smells. We're ahead of schedule by about an hour. Say, are those fresh-baked cinnamon rolls? Yours, from the Café?" When

Richard replied in the affirmative, Clovis continued, "Then I can call a break, with this much done. You know, I would like most of the outside plastering to be done before midnight. There's rain predicted for next week sometime."

"My god," Richard exclaimed. He wanted to get some sleep over the following night; how could that be accomplished with a building worksite hammering away at a distance of a bare quarter-mile! The hammers, the generator-engines, the crude shouts of workmen ... With an effort, he reminded himself that this was not London. That this was, in fact, the country. A strangely civilized yet eccentric country. With an effort, he amended his next ill-considered reaction. "I am certain that ... it will all go swimmingly, Colonel Walcott. Where do you want me to put the cinnamon rolls?"

"Hold onto them. Andy Pryor is going to set up the truck over in the campground. For gratis lunch and supper service to the crowd, you know. Next to you, if you don't mind." He winked very broadly. "In deference to Mrs. Grants' predilection for vegetarian fare. Not shared by most of the volunteers, or even by Sefton, I'm afraid – but why kick clients in the teeth, I always say. Hope you don't mind, Richard."

"Vegetarianism," Richard sighed. "Is an offense against all that is good, meet and salutary. Why, in the name of all that is holy, are humans at the top of the food chain, if we are not to eat meat ... tasty, tasty meat? Tasty, well-seasoned and protein-packed meat!"

"I'm with you on that," Clovis grinned. "Vegetables are what I eat for supper eats, although I don't mind them at all as side dishes. The wonders that My Little Bride and her Dear Mama can do with pickled cabbage ... it is a wonder, indeed. So, what do you think of the Brand New Age and young Berto's concept?"

"Unbelievable," Richard answered, and would have made his escape, as several other people, to include Roman Gonzales, were converging on

Clovis and Berto, doubtless, requiring further instruction now that this momentous phase of the working had been accomplished.

But Clovis added, "Ricardo, I heard that you were going to volunteer for the Fire Department; is that true?"

"Yes," Richard confessed, now with a sinking feeling in the pit of his stomach, somewhat to the left of where his personal knot of anxiety was located. "I've been considering …"

"Good, good!" Clovis beamed. "Excellent. You'll really be one with the community, then."

"How on earth did you know about this?" Richard was boggled. He had only spoken of this to two other people; how could it have gotten all over town in the space of less than a day?

"Grapevine telegraph," Clovis' grin broadened. "I can't be an active myself in the VFD. Business concerns take me traveling afar and on a moment's notice, as you well know. But I applaud the effort, and the public spirit. It would do you good, professionally, and personally in Luna City. You won't regret the personal involvement, Richard, really you won't. Think of it as all to the good of where you live, hey? Sorry – duty calls," he added, as the other top-volunteers completed their advance upon him. Clovis should have looked somewhat harassed, but instead appeared to be in his element. Richard knew the feeling well. At the top of the game, large and in charge.

He envied Clovis on that account. If Clovis had ever had complete disaster fall upon him, would he be quite so insouciant about it all? Fortunes' favorite child, and all … Richard pedaled away from the hillock upon which stood the Aquarius Straw-Bale Castle. Home, his small tidy home, just in time to see the Pryor's food truck backing carefully into the space next-but-one. Young Anson, who had ably assisted in serving up succulent slices of rare roast beef at the theatrical wedding event on the square , was standing at the back, signaling to his father, at the wheel of the food truck.

"Hi, Chef!" Anson shouted. "Hey, what a party, eh? Isn't it great!"

"It is indeed," Richard replied, cheered beyond measure that the other provider of bespoke carnivorous sustenance in Luna City had also been roped into participation. But considering that Andy Pryor was married to Patricia Wyler Pryor, Doc Wyler's granddaughter and presumed heir; not that amazing, given that good lady's public spirit and considerable social pull. Also the fact that Patricia Pryor looked like a much happier and fulfilled Diana, Princess of Wales, could not possibly hurt in the community that was Luna City – removed from the larger world in a sense, but not the least unconnected from it. "I brought a double-baking of cinnamon rolls from the Café," Richard added, as Andy Pryor emerged from the drivers' side of the truck. "I thought you could add them to your table of offerings…"

"Fantastic," Andy Pryor enthused. "Hey, I love the way that you contribute. Pat just told me you are going to volunteer for the VFD! First teaching the class at school, and now this! Awesome …"

"Yes, the way that word gets around," Richard commented. Everyone in town knew of this now. And he would really have to do the deed, else surrender his community membership and manhood card forever. Meanwhile, Andy and Anson dragged out a quantity of folding tables and chairs from the trailer hitched to the back of the food truck, arraying them in formation on the side of the truck with the window from which their various smoked and barbequed delights would be served. They worked without speaking to each other, which to Richard indicated that this was something they had done so often that it was a well-practiced process. Which it was, of course. The Pryors were old hands in the mobile marketplace.

"Small town," Andy agreed. "That's the way of it. I can't volunteer myself, but the boys do, although they can't be full-fledged until they're graduated. They tell me that back in the day before the VFD made a rule, high school boys constantly ditched classes to go fight fires."

"Anything to get out of Latin class," Richard said, slightly boggled. He was further boggled when Anson looked up from unfolding chairs. "Latin? For real, Mr. A; is that what they speak in Latin America? I guess you had to learn it in your school, back in the day. Awesome!"

"Yes." Richard turned over several possible answers to that, and rejected all but the simple affirmative. For the very first time, he entertained doubts about what the younger cohort were being taught in the Luna City public schools. Or possibly it was one of those generational things. He mentally speculated on the means of amending some of this, through the medium of his life-skills cooking classes at Luna City High School. In the interests of cultivating a more haute-cuisine appreciative and more culturally-aware citizenry among the junior set in Luna City, he was committed, heart and soul. As father and son worked, the vast and smoke-blacked cooker unit, sitting on an open platform at the back of the truck with a small pile of cut lengths of wood next to it was already sending up a trickle of smoke and mouthwatering odors.

"I'll put a table by the pick-up window," Andy finished unfolding the last chair. "You can park your cinnamon rolls on it. The ladies of St. Margaret and Anthony are bringing a lot of cakes and cupcakes and Miss Letty promised that the Methodist women are going to do their part; baked beans, casseroles and jello salads, I think. There won't be anyone going away hungry tonight."

"How late are you going to be staying?" Richard asked, with some apprehension. He really favored early nights, since his own work day began before dawn. If this was going to turn into an all-hours party, involving the larger portion of Luna City's responsible citizens – how could he possibly withdraw from the festivities. In a spirit of dour resignation, he hoped that he had not altogether lost his stamina when it came to late night jollification and early mornings.

"'Til midnight, or the Q runs out and the smoker goes dead," Andy Pryor replied, with a cheerful, take-no-prisoners grin.

A New Direction for Mills Farm

From the Karnesville Weekly Beacon
An Interview With New Mills Farm Corporate Director Lucien Dubois

Our reporter met last week with Mr. Lucien Dubois, the recently installed Director for Marketing, Venture Properties International. Mr. Dubois, a long-time VPI employee and experienced facilities manager replaced Susannah Wyatt-Gonzales, who unexpectedly retired last fall to devote time to her family and her husband's extraordinary career as a male model.

Mr. Dubois – "My friends call me Lew," he says, with a hearty handshake. He has come to Karnesville, to the offices of this newspaper for the interview, which is an unexpected courtesy. "I was on my way to San Antonio," he says, waving aside my protest that I would have been perfectly willing to meet with him in his office. "No, don't trouble yourself, *cher*. I have an office, but I am hardly ever in it. I manage by walking around, you see. Even helping out, when such is demanded. Then, one is not so much subjected to the management telling you what they think they want to hear. I look at how it seems to those at the ground-level. All my most innovative developments came from suggestions by regular workers."

"Did you start at Venue Properties from the very beginning?" I asked, and he laughed, shaking his head.

"No; I cut my teeth in hospitality working at Disneyland, in Anaheim, during the summers when I was going to college in Southern California. I finished my degree at the Otis College of Art and Design in 1988. I was going to be an artist, a designer of sets and costumes, you see. But then I read an advertisement. VPI is looking for someone with artistic training, but experience in hospitality and must speak French! So, I think; eh, sounds more certain than waiting around to see if I get a job at one of the TV studios. I went to an interview, and voila! I am hired immediately.

Only then do they say; oh, the job is in France! My wife and I had just a week to make arrangements and pack. But no matter, we say – it is the honeymoon that we never had when we first married. We were just students, and like all students – poor!"

It turned out to be an extremely protracted honeymoon, for VPI had purchased the Chateau Venasque; a rundown and aging hotel property in Provence. The Chateau was beautiful and historic, in a spectacular setting. It was VPI's gamble for a top spot in the international stakes for luxury destination hotels but to accomplish that end, the Chateau itself would have to be extensively modernized and refurbished with attention to the historic fabric and cooperation of the French department of antiquities.

"I started at the very bottom," Mr. Dubois explained, shaking his head and laughing. "Third assistant to the American manager, with responsibility for translating. And it turned out for much design work."

"It sounds as if it was a lot of work," I said, and Mr. Dubois laughed.

"It was, *cher*, but I had the time of my life! We started with bare stone walls, a leaking roof, no heat or electricity, doors falling off hinges, but when we were finished, it was spectacular! The most beautiful hotel in the Luberon! You have seen the pictures, of course. And the movies – but they do not begin to do it justice. Seventeen years we were there, and my wife is saying, 'Enough of the honeymoon, Lew; let's come home. We have the boys by then, and she wants to be in the same time zone as her family. VPI says to me, 'Lew, what about Canada; Castle Mountain is our new resort under construction in the Banff National Park. I say; New from the ground up and my decisions are final? No messing around with stone walls and Ministries of Antiquities? Let me have that place, and how soon? They tell me – as soon as you can! So my poor wife must make do to shift our family, while I fly on the next possible day to take over. Castle Mountain is another huge project but new from the ground up. Built from timber, in the lodge style. Twice as big as the Chateau, and three times as many programs for guests. Skiing in winter, horseback excursions in summer, water sports on the lake … And another success for VPI. But I give credit to my staff for that."

"It sounds as if you had your hands full again," I said, and Mr. Dubois agreed.

"Indeed, *cher* – ten years. And my wife says, she would like to be closer to her family, and our boys are all grown now. And I say; No, not for me the retirement yet, but yes, VPI offers me a promotion this year, to marketing director. Houston is close enough to our family in Louisiana. And then, I think this Mills Farm project needs the Dubois touch. My wife, she agrees. The golden touch, she calls it."

"What does this mean for Mills Farm, exactly?"

"A new focus, *cher*. Mills Farm could be as much of a destination as Castle Mountain. No, the scenery is not as spectacular as Banff – the mountains, the lakes, the old-growth forests! They are incomparable … but the company believes that with the properly improved, enlarged facilities, Mills Farm could rival Castle Mountain as a destination for American vacationers of more …of more modest means. The project fascinates me, *cher*; I have always relished a challenge. In the case of Mills Farm, the challenge is to achieve the goal in a manner which brings the most satisfaction to the greatest number of people. I have always been a manager who manages best by engaging all parties, inspiring them to invest themselves in the mission … the corporation, the workers, and the community. It is a delicate business – but I love a challenge."

When a Plan Comes Together

Strangely enough, the excitement and sheer focused energy which permeated the glade where the Amazing Aquarius Straw Castle took shape by leaps and bounds spilled over into the campground. It proved as exhilarating as any number of substances which Richard had sworn off; he did not feel any of the weariness that he usually felt about sundown on a Saturday. Mellow golden light or the white-hot incandescent variety bloomed like seasonal wildflowers between the scattering of trailers and RVs in the campground. The roar of Roman Gonzales' generator, which powered the light stands focused on the tower, construction tools and someone's ultra-powerful stereo boom-box was muted by distance. Curiosity moved Richard to wander over, late in the afternoon, wanting a close-up look at what had been accomplished for the Grant's new domicile.

He had to admit, dodging among the various volunteers, extension cords and loudly-functioning power tools, that even half-finished as it was, the Straw Castle was a huge improvement over the yurt. The interior was a tall, airy, light-filled space. Half of it; with tall window spaces facing south-west, would be open the full height of the tower. The other half looked as if it would be divided into two levels. Even as Richard observed this, he was dodging a crew setting an old-fashioned cast-iron spiral staircase into place, leading from the ground floor to the mezzanine level. More architectural salvage, he assumed. Another crew was framing in the lower level, while two more men wielded chain-saws with cheerful abandon, carving shallow niches and alcoves into the straw walls. On the outside, the plastering proceeded apace. Already half the golden straw surface was buried under a depressing layer of sludgy greyish plaster.

"First coat!" Roman Gonzales shouted over the roar of a stucco-sprayer. "Has to harden, then the second layer, in twenty-four hours, a couple of weeks to cure it all. I'd like to get the first coat on tonight. Tomorrow we work full-out on the inside. Not promising that Sefton and Judy can move in on Monday, but the bulk of the work will all be done by then."

"Amazing," Richard murmured, then shouted it so that Roman could hear, over the roar of the sprayer, assorted power tools and the generator. Roman nodded, in agreement, anonymous in a mask and goggles. Obviously, this plaster was caustic stuff. Richard knew from somewhere that it contained lime, ordinarily; the stuff used by Victorian murderers to dissolve bodies. Best get out of the way, then. He dodged the other volunteer parties, laying slate tile in what appeared as if it would eventually would be a downstairs bathroom, others finishing an interior dividing wall by nailing in lengths of what appeared to be weathered fence palings, their ends cut on the diagonal and fitted together to make an attractive chevron pattern ... Well, Sefton had asked that building materials be reclaimed and recycled as much as possible. He caught a glimpse of Judy, her face radiant, as she circled with her sistrum and bundle of burning herbs, although absent her young acolyte.

"Look where you step!" Someone roared at him, just as he was about to stumble into a trug of … well, it was something greyish and semi-liquid used in the tile-laying trade.

This worksite was definitely outside of his skill-set. Curiosity appeased, Richard retreated to that which he knew better; the campground, and volunteers gathering under the uncertain lanterns and lights around the Pryor BBQ trailer. A steady trickle of workers had passed under them, availing themselves of heaping plates of barbequed meats and sausage, undistinguished casseroles in which overcooked pasta and cans of cream-of-something soup had played a key role, and gelatin salads in unfortunate and vivid colors, larded with unnatural occlusions such as canned pineapple, cottage cheese and finely-slivered cabbage.

Richard observed such culinary offenses against nature and human taste buds with a restrained shudder. After all, he had seen worse in his time. Much, much worse. His determination to bring the tenets of the higher culinary arts to the awareness of Luna City, and instill them into the next generation of cooks was redoubled at that moment of awareness as well as his resolution to be subtle about it. Nothing was more calculated to put the backs up of the average Lunaite than some outsider coming in and grandly telling them they were doing it all wrong. That understanding was one which he had gathered within his first weeks in Luna City. Flies, honey, vinegar, best means of attraction and capture, et cetera. And it might take some time. Consulting his own awareness on this – he was comfortable with the concept of spending a long time in Luna City. In a bizarre way … this place fitted him, contented him, in a way that nothing else had fitted or contented since … well, since a long time.

When he returned to the Airstream that he considered home, he spotted Sefton at one of the tables set out by the Pryor truck. Sefton, with a middle-aged man who looked sufficiently enough like him that being one of his sons was probably a money-winning guess, and the teenaged girl he had seen earlier, following Judy around – that girl who looked enough like Judy to have been of her kin, never mind that she appeared to be glorying in the too-big-for-her white Druidic robe as least as much as she was enjoying the meal. The three of them were wolfing down plates of Pryor's best mixed-meats barbeque. Having to face Judy's regular fare was enough to make even the most ascetic saint appreciate the sheer gastronomic goodness that was well-done Texas barbeque. Richard had known for all the time that he had lived at the Age that Sefton was an unashamed carnivore, who managed to hide those proclivities from his spouse. But obviously not from anyone else in his family. Sefton looked up as Richard approached; yes, he was hungry. As always, the scent of pure Texas smoked and barbequed meats worked their seductive magic on his senses. He would yield, as he knew that he would, and join Sefton and his family. They were already waving to him, as he collected his paper plate of Pryor-provided delicacies, and a couple of scoops of those donated side dishes which appeared at first-glance to be the least-disgusting of the lot.

"Hey, Ricardo, join us," Sefton invited. "I dunno if you met Junior. He's our oldest boy – works for DynaTen in Fort Worth. And this is Brianna June, the baby of the family." (*He pronounced the city as if it were all one word – Fortworth, Richard noted in passing, and stored it away as one of those necessary local social clues.*)

"Pleased, I'm sure," Richard slid into the empty chair and exchanged an awkward handshake with Sefton Grant, Junior, and then extended his hand towards Brianna June, who took it gracelessly but with innocent enthusiasm, as if she was not much experienced with adult courtesies. "Junior … Miss Brianna. Richard Astor-Hall, master chef, at your service. I manage the Café, and it is my distinct pleasure to be a year-round resident here."

"Yeah, Gee-Nan told us," Brianna answered, with innocently engaging enthusiasm. "She's the shittiest cook in the land! Dad and Paw-Paw said we could eat supper here, as long as we told Gee-Nan afterwards that we only ate the vegan stuff." Richard's turn to be mystified, as Junior chided his offspring with a single severe look and explained, "Mom hates to be called grandma – she insists she is too young to be a grandmother. Bree, be civil – don't say she is the shittiest cook around; there must be worse."

"Not around here, there isn't," Bree answered, a sullen expression darkening her relatively pleasant and unformed features. A certain whine informed her voice. "Dad, I don't wanna live here for the summer, not if I have to eat Gee-Nan's cooking! That Lentil Surprise thing makes me barf – Please, Dad, it looks like dog-poop, the runny kind you can't even pick up in the scoop! You can't make me live out here for a whole summer!" The whine achieved a certain irritating sub-sonic note known only to mosquitoes and resentful teenagers. "I'll die of hunger – I'll turn anorexic! I wanna spend the summer at home, Dad! It's the last summer that Cher and Meryl and I can hang around as besties!"

"That's what your mother and I are afraid of," Junior replied, with a particularly tight-lipped expression. To Richard's admittedly blunted social radar, this suggested that Junior and his good lady did not approve of Cher and Meryl as appropriate companions for their charmingly tactless youngest daughter. God only knew why; anything from affiliation with black bloc revolutionaries to tie-ins with international sexual trafficking, to judge by the mirrored expressions on Sefton and Junior's countenances.

"I'll tell you what, Miss Brianna," Richard nerved himself up to take the first plunge into the pool of culinary instruction. "I will make you a promise. If your father and your Paw-Paw *(Richard gulped slightly over this folkloric designation)* approve, and if you spend the summer hols in this … this natural beauty spot, I will undertake to teach you proper haute cuisine. I may even be able to offer a small wage, as an apprentice at the Café. Miss Abernathy – no, Mrs. Vaughn as she is now – has said that I should be able to hire some junior help in the Café over the summer. Would that give you cause to look upon the summer spent here with more enthusiasm?"

"It might," Bree's own expression turned cagy; oh, yes, Richard recognized the signs, although he had never observed them in of such tender years. Yes, the female of the species learned young, no doubt through some kind of osmosis, the means of driving a hard bargain. "Tt would have to be real cooking lessons, not doing recipes out of some stupid book for kids. I'd have to learn how to really cook!"

"You would learn to cook indeed," Richard recognized surrender when he saw it. "The hard way, the classic methods of haute cuisine. And I would treat you as an apprentice in the kitchen. You would be expected to follow my instructions to the letter, without question. No whining, no excuses, no shirking. I would, in fact, treat you as if you were an adult: not a child, playing with little bits of flour and sugar."

"That would be OK, then," Bree's expression turned magically sunny, agreeable. "I'd like that, Mister ..."

"Chef," Richard replied. "You must always address me as 'Chef' when we are in the kitchen. 'Yes, Chef,' 'No, Chef,' 'Immediately, Chef,' are all of what I would expect to hear from you, when I give you instructions or direction."

"What if I – Chef, what if I have a question?" Bree stammered. "About something?" Richard assumed his most formidable scowl.

"I would expect you to make it an intelligent one," he replied, and relented when Bree appeared abashed. "I would suggest, Miss Brianna – that you find a copy of *Laurousse's Gastronomique*, and begin studying it with attention over the next few months. Even if you decided against apprenticing with me this summer, I rather think you will find the information in it most enlightening, as far as methods and terminology involved in the classic French method. There was an animated movie out several years ago, regarding a rat learning to cook, so do not substitute cinema un-verite for *Laurousse*."

"I won't change my mind, Chef," Bree averred, firmly. "Dad – I'm done. Can I be excused?"

"Yeah, certainly, kiddo," Junior replied. Richard approved silently of the fact that the child asked to be excused, if not of the casual manner her parent gave permission. The three of them sat in silence, as Bree collected up her paper plate and the detritus of her meal. This was another cause for approval, in Richard's view. It spoke well of her potential as far as food service went. Bree deposited the trash in the appropriately-designated barrel, and trotted off, her white robe flapping, in the direction of the Amazing Straw Castle Aquarius. The sun was a brilliant half-orb, lingering on the horizon, attended by a brilliant smear of orange, and an attentively hovering shroud of purple clouds.

Faintly the music from that boom-box resounded over the meadow and the lusty voices of volunteers singing along as they worked; *"Golden living dreams of visions, Mystic crystal revelation, And the mind's true liberation..."* not quite drowned out by the roar of generators and the stucco-sprayer.

"She seems an intelligent and charming child," Richard decided to break the brooding silence at the table. "I am certain that I will be able to teach her something of the method of producing edible meals, over the long hols."

"She is," Sefton affirmed, almost at once. "But Bree is a handful. She takes after Judy in that way. Bright, charming, and willful."

"Tell me about it," Junior stared morosely into his half-empty plate. "Carol and I are at our wits' end, Pop. Having Bree spend the summer out here will be a relief for us both. Those two pals of hers are the worst kind of bad news and we can't keep her separated from them, as long as she's at home." He sighed, very deeply, for a moment appearing nearly as old as his parent. "Cher's parents gave her a car when she got her driver's license! They turn a blind eye towards where she goes and who else she hangs out with. A bad influence – neither of us liked the way those girls were going, but Bree has been best friends with them since middle school. That's one of the good things about Bree; loyal to her friends. It didn't matter much that they were a year older, back then. Hell, Bree's six years younger than Kevin, eight years younger than Young Sefton, so she's used to being with older kids. But the way that those two girls are messing around with bad stuff ..."

"Youth gotta rebel, Junior," Sefton shook his head. "It's the way of it. Ya grow, you spread your wings, embrace those dreams."

"Yeah, Pops," Junior had a hard expression on his face, an expression which would have sat oddly on Sefton's. "Rebel all you want, test the social boundaries until the cows come home, but don't drag <u>my</u> kid into hard-core illegal stuff. Meryl already has a record and not just mean-girl bullying or for skeevy male company on social media. She's into drugs, likely the bad stuff. Dealing, not using. And what they used to call procuring, in the old days. Her parents can afford the high-powered legal talent to keep all that on the down-low and let Little Meryl skate away, smelling like a slightly-used rose. <u>I</u> can't afford one of those expensive lawyers and I don't want my daughter involved in whatever hell-raising scene those two are planning for summer after they graduate. Luna City is far enough away from Fort Worth. Even if they keep up on social media, Cher and Meryl can't just drop in. Yeah, Luna City and your place suits me fine for Bree. You let us all have considerable liberty, Pop; you set the outside limits, but never let us know about them, until we ran slap-up against them. Carole and I have talked it over. Bree needs your system rather than ours."

"Or maybe mine," Richard ventured, and when both men looked at him, in interrogative inquiry, he enlarged on the subject. "Treat them like adults and work them stupid. That works for ... well, it worked for me, mostly. At any rate, an apprenticeship keeps them busy; much too busy for any wrongdoing more energetic than smoking the odd cigarette out by the bins in the alleyway. It seems that she really does want to learn. Which is half the battle, really."

"Thanks, Ricardo – we'll prolly take you up on the offer," Sefton beamed with heart-felt gratitude. "Teach little Bree to make some of those casseroles an' stuff that you've been feeding me all spring, an' maybe Judikins can retire Lentil Surprise for good and all."

"We live in hope, Pops," Junior grinned. "I'm guessing that your new place will be ready for guests by the time the school year is over?"

"Way before then," Sefton; grubby, indifferently shaven, and sprinkled with grime and sawdust, looked decades younger than he had in months. The worry about rebuilding the Age of Aquarius and the absence of his wife had weighed more heavily upon him than Richard had thought. "Romans' guys and the volunteers say they'll have most everything done by tomorrow night. We can move in as soon as the plaster is cured, and the water and electric is hooked up. Next weekend for sure."

"It's right nice, Pops, having a place to come home to," Junior observed with feeling. Richard nodded a silent assent.

Yes, it was right nice, having a place to come home to. And better yet, having friends to share it with, in a place like Luna City.

Celia Hayes & Jeanne Hayden

A Whole New Age

From the Karnesville Weekly Beacon – Talk of the Town Blog
By Katherine Heisel, Reporter and Blogger

The venerable home-place of the Age of Aquarius Campground and Goat Farm commune burnt to the ground last December in an unfortunate sequence of events which resulted in complete destruction of the residence of Judy and Sefton Grant. The Grants, long-time residents of Luna City, were leaders of a ground-breaking commune established in the summer of 1968 by students from UT-Austin. The establishment has survived to this day in the form of a private campground on the banks of the San Antonio River about ten miles north-north-east of Karnesville, offering hospitality to RV and tent-campers alike. The Grants have also maintained a small truck garden, providing local produce and herbs, artisanal hand-made soaps, wild-flower honey and free-range eggs to the local community for over forty years. Their main residence was not insured, and the cost of building a replacement would have been prohibitive for the Grants until their neighbors and friends in Luna City stepped in. Through contributions and volunteer effort from the local community (see story, page 3 of the *Karnesville Weekly Beacon* print edition), an ecologically-friendly, and energy-efficient residence was completed almost overnight.

Using architectural salvage and scrap material provided by local construction contractor Roman Gonzales, straw bales for a token or no charge from local farmers, a former grain-bin roof donated by Bodie Feed & Seed and cedar beams harvested on the property by Sefton Grant, a host of volunteers and friends of the Grants from as far away as College Station gathered on a recent weekend to assemble it all into one magnificent structure.

The initial design for what locals have begun calling the Amazing Aquarius Straw Castle was the inspiration of Alberto "Berto" Gonzales, a second-year student majoring in structural engineering at San Antonio's Palo Alto College. Long-time Luna City resident Clovis Walcott, who has had a long career in major construction projects around the world drew up detailed plans for the straw tower, which is warmed in cold weather by passive solar heat, and a wood-burning stove, and cooled by naturally thick walls and judicious placement of vents and windows, allowing air to circulate freely. Water is provided from the Grant's wells, one of which taps a naturally-occurring hot spring. Electrical power for the self-contained residence is provided by a series of solar panels on the roof, and by an antique but still-functioning windmill.

The tower of stacked straw bales, plastered inside and out so that nothing of their humble building materiel can be seen, with a surrounding first-story covered porch and pergola, occupies the same concrete footprint of the original round Mongolian-style yurt. The new structure offers several advantages over the yurt, as plenty of windows make the interior light and airy, despite the thickness of the walls. Half of the main floor, which opens out onto the veranda through several doors, is a comfortable multipurpose space open to the full height of the tower interior, and to an open-plan kitchen which adjoins the living area. Interior walls divide the remainder into a more private master suite bedroom and bath. The bathroom is small, but luxuriously tiled in leftover grey slate repurposed from an upscale renovation in Karnes City, and fittings salvaged from the same renovation project at no cost. The second level, accessed through a circular staircase salvaged from the demolition of an old retail building in Nixon, contains two small bedrooms sharing second small bathroom. All in all, the new Straw Castle is not only a landmark, but a comfortable living space. It's speedy yet low-cost construction is a testament to the deep fondness in which neighbors and friends hold the Grants.

Judy Grant is most especially appreciative of her new home. She gave this reporter a personal tour this week, within days of having moved into it from a temporary residence provided by Mills Farm/VPI management. The living spaces are sparsely but pleasingly furnished, made functional and attractive by a number of shelves and niches built by cutting shallow spaces into the walls before they were finished with plaster. Mrs. Grant enthused throughout the tour over how welcoming and benign the atmosphere within her new home is, saying that affection and what she termed "good vibrations" radiated from every aspect. "This place was built with love," she kept repeating. "And I feel it, every minute of every day! I wish that everyone might be able to live in such a welcoming space as this … it is a true home to us now, and a marvel beyond words to express!" She was also happy that in utilizing the original poured concrete foundation, a small slice of personal history was preserved. On a day in the summer of 1972, when the original residence was still under construction, the Grant's son and the family dog chased a small goat across the still-went concrete. Out on the verandah, the footprints of a small child, a goat and a dog are still visible.

The Amazing Aquarius Straw Castle can be observed from the campground at the Age of Aquarius Campground and Goat Farm, although this reporter would stress that it is a private residence and consideration to the Grants would be appreciated. Both Mr. Walcott and Alberto Gonzales have extensive picture archives of the details of construction on their respective website and Facebook pages if additional details are required.

Eat for Two

"Jessica, dear," Miss Letty appeared at the table where Jess and Richard were going over the weekly finances for the Café. "I have collected all the necessary documents for filing my income tax return, if you wish to come by the house and go over the forms with me. Any day and time that is convenient for you, dear."

It was a mild spring day, cloudy and chill overnight and in the early morning, but warming by midday, grey and lowering clouds fracturing into fluffy white masses, drifting in a pure blue sky. The oak trees in Town Square had put out ruffles of fresh green leaves, as crisp and delicate as tissue paper.

"Of course, Miss Letty," Jess replied, scooping together the receipts from C&S Wholesale Grocers. Miss Letty was the only person in Luna City who always used her full name. "What about today. Around noon?"

"Perfect." Miss Letty nodded regally. "I shall expect you then."

"I will be prompt," Jess promised. Miss Letty valued punctuality, as did Jess herself. It was practically the very first thing that children attending Luna City Elementary School's kindergarten and first grade learned from the magisterial Miss Letty McAllister. That, and putting away things properly.

At five minutes to noon, Jess's bare-bones yellow Jeep Wrangler pulled up to the old McAllister house, framed in a sweep of brilliant emerald lawn and a bank of rhododendron shrubs in bloom like the cover of an expensive gardening and lifestyle magazine. This year, many of the flowers were tinted blue. Jess was certain they had been more pink-hued in previous years.

"It's an old gardener's trick," Miss Letty explained, when Jess remarked upon it. "Bury a lot of old rusty nails under the plants. I had to rather experiment in previous years, but the results are most satisfactory. Shall we sit outside on the verandah? The weather today is so marvelous, I hate to waste any of it indoors, knowing that summer will drive us indoors for months."

"Of course," Jess agreed. Spring days would soon pass into summer; mild temperature and gentle cooling breezes would give way inevitably into blazing heat, days and weeks of the sun beating down on the earth like a vast hammer on a country-wide anvil, while grass and gardens withered and flowering shrubs like Miss Letty's rhododendrons wilted under the torment. The verandah opened from the old-fashioned parlor of the house through tall French doors, and overlooked the garden. The scent of roses, and the blooming Spanish jasmine which swagged the pillars and railing perfumed the air.

"In the north, those poor people are still waiting for spring," Jess remarked as she opened up her laptop on the wicker table, which together with a couple of bentwood and rattan chairs, furnished the verandah. "And looking at bare trees and sticks where there are bushes. Uncle Harry says that in Alaska, they're still shoveling snow, too. I'm glad that you have all your tax documentation ready – so many of my other clients will leave it all to the last minute. I believe they hope for an asteroid to strike the IRS on April 14th, so they will not have to file a report."

"Quite ridiculous," Miss Letty snorted. "One knows that one must file a tax return, every year, and the date that it is due altereth not nor changeth ever. It is a chore which must be done, without fail, so why not do it, and then return to more pleasant occupations? I'm about to fortify myself with a cup of tea. May I bring you a cup as well, Jessica, or even a spot of something for lunch, if you have not eaten?"

"No, I'm not hungry," Jess replied, and felt her stomach suddenly cramp with a weird kind of nausea. The thought of food was utterly revolting. Something of that interior turmoil must have shown in her face, for Miss Letty, who had been about to step across the threshold into the parlor, turned and regarded her with particular attention.

"Are you unwell, dear? Perhaps we can do this another day."

"No … it's just that I am … I have been feeling rather odd, off and on for some weeks. Maybe I'm developing an allergy to oak pollen."

"I don't think so," Miss Letty replied with great emphasis. She sat in the bentwood chair opposite. "Jessica, child, I believe you are in the family way. Do you want to talk to me about it? You can't go on hiding it from everyone, you know."

"I know." Jess felt her face turning pink with embarrassment. How on earth could Miss Letty have known? "I … went through a half-a-dozen of those pregnancy test kits this week. I bought them at the CVS in Karnesville so that no one else in Luna City would fire up the rumor-mill before I could be certain. How did you know – or was it a lucky guess?"

"I can't really say," Miss Letty looked thoughtful. "It's a gift, I assume. There's something in the face of a woman bearing a child for the first time. Something that I sense, even if it is none of my business. But I can always tell, most particularly if it is a woman or a girl that I know well. How far along are you, do you think?"

"I missed last month," Jess confessed, "And I'm a week late this month – and I've always been regular. You can set the calendar by me, or you could until now."

"You would be about seven weeks along, then. Almost two months. Have you told Joseph? Or even seen your gynecologist?" Miss Letty – the only one aside from Joe's mother when she was angry with him – never shortened his name, either.

"I haven't," Jess replied. "It's just ... I don't know what to do, what to think about it. It changes everything. As long as no one knows, then I can think that it's not really happening."

"Not an 'it' Jessica," Miss Letty reproved her. "It's a baby. Or be one, when it is delivered in another six months or so." She mused, her face thoughtful. "About the size of a dried lima bean at present, if your estimation is correct. In another two weeks, the doctor will be able to detect a heartbeat. There is no going back, Jessica. Even if you chose to not carry through with your pregnancy – and I don't think you would – nothing will ever be the same."

"Of course, I don't want an abortion!" Jess flared. "I just don't know about us being parents! Having children at all – it's too soon, Miss Letty. We only decided to get married six months ago! There were things that we wanted to do together first! Take a Caribbean cruise on a sailboat! Hike the Appalachian trail! Drive to Alaska to visit Joe's Uncle Harry!"

"It's a good a time as any," Miss Letty sounded particularly astringent. "You have been ..." Miss Letty searched for an appropriately genteel expression and finally fished it out from her vocabulary. "Keeping company for five or six years, since Joseph returned to Luna City. If you really wanted to perform those strenuous projects, I believe that you would have done them already. Of course you can do them all later, accompanied by Baby. Such journeys would be most educational for children of any age. No, this is an excellent time for you to have children: you have stable employment prospects, and are still young enough to enjoy the experience."

"But I don't know the first thing about raising children," Jess confessed in misery. "Nor Joe, either. We were both only children. One thing done wrong and the poor brat is ruined for life!"

"Nonsense," Miss Letty snorted. "Children are remarkably durable, Jessica, or at least most are. Believe me, I have had a hand in raising a great many children, though none of my own blood. A very few children are delicate and must be carefully tended like orchids. But most are resilient like hardy weeds. They do not require a perfect environment to thrive, or perfect parents. Which is to the good," Miss Letty added, with asperity. "Even if they don't have anything like what those tedious child-raising books advise. Yet they thrive regardless. Young Mr. Mayall, for example; although he was fortunate in his grandmother and in the foster care system. I cannot say that Patricia Wyler's childhood was anything like the ideal either, what with a notorious philanderer for a father and a silly flibbertigibbet of a mother. Patricia was also fortunate in her grandparents. What I am trying to say, in my blundering way – is that now they are both happy, stable adults in spite of those horrific disruptions to their childhood. Raising your child will be just one small step at a time, Jessica. A kitten or a puppy will want the same things as a baby, and for an equivalent quantity of time: Milk, warmth, a feeling of security and a certain degree of cleanliness. Not much more than that. At least you are not required to bathe the baby by licking it with your tongue."

Jess giggled, obscurely comforted. "That's reassuring, Miss Letty. I suppose that I ought to come to you for advice, when I need it."

"My parenting advice boils down to two concepts," Miss Letty answered. "Do not expect very much from them in any case until about the age of three and a half and thereafter, never make a threat or offer a reward unless you have every intention of carrying it out. That above all. Children of all ages need to rely on constants. Now I think that I should fix you something to eat. Something comforting and easy on your stomach. I know; poached eggs on brown toast with cheese sauce."

"That sounds revolting!" Jess was horrified. Her stomach gave another queasy lurch. "Don't go to any trouble, please."

"No, you and Baby require nourishment." Miss Letty looked particularly austere. For some reason, the queasy feeling subsided. "And I used to fix poached eggs on brown toast with cheese sauce for my brother Douglas when he was feeling under the weather. He had a delicate digestive system, because of his work, you see. And," Miss Letty added over her shoulder, as she went into the house. "I do believe I fixed that dish for your mother, when she was carrying you. She was a martyr to morning sickness all the day ... until I noted that she was nauseated as soon as she became hungry. Counterintuitive, I know, but you will feel better as soon as you force yourself to eat something."

"Thank you, Miss Letty," Jess closed her laptop and looked out at Miss Letty's garden. A jewel-toned humming bird zipped among the orange fire-bush blossoms along the border, squeaking like a rusty hinge in indignation upon noting a human trespassing along the borders of its buffet lunch. *It is most amazing,* Jess thought; *it's a doable situation now that I've talked to Miss Letty. Not a piece of cake, exactly – but doable. It's not this awful doom-like thing hanging over me. Hanging over us.*

She reached into her briefcase for her cellphone, and called up her list of contacts. In a moment, the call went through.

"Hi, Babe – what's up?"

"Nothing much, Joe; where are you?"

"In the cruiser, parked behind that big oak tree a mile south of the turn-off for Mill's Farm. Why?"

"Can you break for lunch and meet me at Miss Letty's? I've got something to tell you. We're doing her taxes, and she's fixing me poached eggs on toast with cheese sauce."

"I've eaten worse," Joe said cheerfully. "See you in five, Babe. Love you."

"Love you back, Joe."

Uncle Harry's Naughty Weekend

"Hey, Ricardo," Sefton Grant said, one afternoon when Richard came up the hill after a particularly exhausting day at the Café, bearing his customary bucket of kitchen scraps for the Grant's eternally hungry chickens. "You're gonna have some company in the campground, soon."

"I am?" Richard hastily reviewed his mental calendar; late March, Ash Wednesday already passed, so there wasn't any scheduled gathering of the Old Communards, or any other projected social gathering until the Beltane festival, more than a month away. "It's not that ghastly Gunnison Penn character again, is it? Your good lady sent him off with a flea in his ear on the day the old yurt burned down. And Romeo Gonzales is living large … in a multi-million-dollar beachfront mansion in Malibu, if the *Daily Mail* can be believed – they have a positive thing for noting property market values. He and Susannah have no reason to come back here, especially here, of all places."

Sefton chuckled. "No, not either of those, but a big party of motorbike enthusiasts are headed this way from the East Coast. And then there's Joe Vaughn's Uncle Harry. It seems that Harry Vaughn woke up a couple of weeks ago, and decided that since spring had finally come, he just couldn't stick another Alaska winter. The old guy must be in the high-eighties now, so I don't blame him. I already feel the cold in my bones, and I'm twenty years younger. If it gets below freezing for more than a day around here, it makes the headlines. Global warming? I say, bring it on. I won't be all that heart-broke."

"You're living far inland, and well above sea level," Richard replied, somewhat acidly, and Sefton chuckled. "Roman and his beachfront place might have something to worry about, in that case. Well, when Harry shows up and if Judikins and I aren't around, show him where to hook up and all. He called me yesterday from Whitehorse in the Yukon Territory, said he was heading this way, but gonna take it easy, take four or five days – maybe longer, since it's still the ass-end of winter up North."

"And how will I know this Harry Vaughn?" Richard asked.

Sefton shrugged. "Alaska plates on the vehicle will be a clue, I'd guess. I seen pictures of him when he played football for A&M back in the early fifties. I reckon you should just picture Chief Joe with about forty more years on him."

"Got it," Richard did indeed. Chief Joe Vaughn of the Luna City PD was a hawk-faced and well-muscled six-foot-something, a traffic bollard in khaki and the terror of those given to excessive speeds along Route 123. Richard had always assumed Joe was *sui generis*, but apparently not. "I'll keep my eyes open. I say; whatever was he doing in Alaska all this time?"

"Thanks, Ricardo. Federal marshal, I was told. Retired there, elected sheriff a couple terms in some little town where he liked the hunting and fishing." Sefton replied, in wistful tones. Through his marriage to Judy, a dedicated vegan, he had long had endured such adventurous and gustatory pleasures being denied him through spousal edict. Although Sefton was not above driving to Karnesville for a fast-food hamburger, as long as Judy didn't know. Of late, Richard had begun to wonder of Judy hadn't been tactfully turning her regard aside, and purposefully not noticing the mileage piled up in the chopped-up VW van-truck hybrid which was their main form of transport. It would not have surprised him in the least to discover that this was so. Long-term marriage had begun to appear to him to be built on a foundation of mutual and tactful disregard of the flamingly obvious.

Sure enough, as Richard pedaled home in the twilight after a training session at the VFD classroom the following Wednesday, he was overtaken by a well-weathered high-top camping van. He was near enough to the unmarked and unpaved road which wandered off through a thicket of scrub off of Route 123 and led eventually towards the Age of Aquarius Campground and Goat Farm. The turn-off was innocent of any signage suggesting the presence of the campground, as most anyone serious or desperate about staying there knew about it anyway. The van bore Alaska license plates, speckled with dust and splotches of dried road mud, and drew a second vehicle on a tow-dolly, this vehicle well-wrapped in a tarpaulin equally road-besmirched. There were also a great many tarpaulin-covered items stowed on top of the van, all secured with businesslike turns of rope and bungee cords. Richard thought that one of them might be a small boat. The driver slowed, rolling down his window.

"Howdy, stranger. Am I getting close to the turn-off for the Grant place?" He was an older man, near to the age of Doc Wyler. He looked like the older Joe Vaughn of Richard's imagining; a craggy, weathered countenance adorned with an impressively droopy mustache of the old-fashioned style popularly called a 'soup-strainer.'

"It is, indeed," Richard answered, warmly. "You must be Mr. Vaughn! Welcome home! I was informed of your arrival. Mr. Grant asked that I should see you to the most salubrious position in the campground, and assure that you were well-settled."

"Salubrious, " the driver chuckled. "That's a real fifty-buck word. You must be that English feller who runs the Café nowadays. Throw that beater of yours onto the back, and hop in. I'm your neighbor for a while, until I get fixed up with a place of my own, here in the lower '48. Harry Vaughn," He favored Richard with a bone-crushing grip, extended through the lowered window.

"Richard Astor-Hall," Richard tried very hard not to wince. "Indeed; I've been very pleased with the situation at the Grant place." Obediently, he wheeled his bicycle around to van door into the back, and horsed it into the cramped interior. There was just enough room. Richard was impressed; a grown man had been living comfortably in a space even more miniscule than the Airstream. "I've rented from them since arriving in Luna City," he explained, as Harry Vaughn let out the gears and steered the van back onto the road again. "The lane into the campground is around this bend, on the left…"

"In my young days, it was called the old Sheffield place," Harry Vaughn grunted. "There used to be a big old house out there. It was all fallen to ruin when I was a young sprout, though. We all used to come out here in summer; best damn swimming hole in all of Karnes County, right in that deep bend of the river. Had some fine times there, back in the day."

"It's still pretty deep, right there by the campground," Richard answered. "Here – turn here."

"Right," Harry Vaughn slowed the van, and the trailing auto, and steered very carefully into the turn-off. Richard was glad that with all traffic from volunteers and donations to the building of the Straw Castle Aquarius, that Roman Gonzales had seen fit to scrape the thoroughfare again with a baby bulldozer and pour a couple of loads of gravel down, rendering the lane considerably less lumpy than it had been for years. Still, Harry Vaughn drove very slowly; past the goat pasture, past the thicket of trees at the turn-off which led farther up the hill and into the grove of oaks which framed the gleaming ivory tower of the Amazing Aquarius Straw

Castle like the supporting-cast greenery surrounding the starring flowers of a bridal bouquet. The old windmill clattered away and the breeze fanned the various colorful banners which depended from the oak branches and the rough-hewn mesquite beams supporting the veranda's tin roof.

"Nice," Harry commented, sounding mildly impressed. "Not bad for hippie goat-farmers. Guess this is the campground?"

"Indeed," Richard said; a campground empty of all but the solitary Airstream and its' sheltering roof at the top end, and the large party of motorbike tourists that Sefton had also mentioned. They must have been unusually brave or rough-adapted motorcycle tent-campers; they had their series of basic a-frame tents set up at the bottom end, in a lee of the bank which overlooked the river. "I live in the old trailer there. Sefton said you can pick any place you like, but the places along the long hedge are the only ones with electrical hookups. I will be happy to assist you."

"Not necessary, son," Harry Vaughn replied. "I prefer the big outdoors and solitude myself. I'll take the slot at the far end from you. I'm good with setting up myself; don't want to put you to any more trouble than you have already taken. Since you already work for ol' Stevie-Boy Wyler, I'm certain you already have enough on your plate."

That, as Richard ruminated later, after he took his trusty trail bike out of the back of Harry Vaughn's van, should have been his first clue that Doc Wyler and Uncle Harry might just have, as the soap operas have it, a bit of old history between them.

The shrouded motor vehicle that Harry Vaughn towed behind his van all the way from Alaska was revealed to be an archaic-appearing convertible enameled in a brilliant shade of red known only to aficionados of custom auto paint jobs and county fair candied apples. Said vehicle, with the top down, appeared at mid-morning, a day or so later, arrogantly claiming the parking spot directly in front of the Café. Richard couldn't decide how the convertible could stand out any more flagrantly; perhaps spotlighted by a pair of floodlights, and serenaded by the Mighty Fighting Moths Marching Band. Richard came out from the kitchen with an insulated coffee beaker just in time to overhear involuntary sounds of appreciation from the regulars at the *stammtisch*, and those lesser customers with a good view out the front windows of the Café.

"*Dios mio* – a pristine '66 Lincoln Continental," exclaimed the senior Jaime Gonzalez, the proprietor of the main garage and repair shop in Luna City. "Papi had one. He sold it almost brand new forty years ago to Harry Vaughn!"

"And who are the ladies accompanying him?" Georg Stein wondered aloud, answered by a sigh from the aficionados of classic motors among the patrons, and one of equal depth from Joe and Jess, sharing a small table at the back of the Café.

"Uncle Harry always was a chick-magnet," Joe observed to Jess, who waved away an offer of a coffee refill from Richard. "I'll get my coffee for the day to go in a minute, Ricardo."

"Just bring me some dry toast," Jess said, in a quiet aside to Araceli. "I just cannot face scrambled eggs this morning. I think I must be coming down with something, or it's all the cedar pollen in the air."

"That's our Abuelita," Araceli replied. She hurriedly delivered Joe's breakfast order; a standing order of eggs, bacon, hash-brown fries and biscuits, which Richard had begun plating in the kitchen as soon as he saw Joe's cruiser pull into Town Square. "And her friend Min Kim – you know, Mr. Walcott's mother-in-law. But I don't know the other lady."

"Oh, Christ, it's my Aunt Moira," Richard sighed, in horrified recognition of the handsome older woman in skin-tight, gleaming black motorcycle leathers and a red scarf which matched her lipstick. Yes; Aunt Moira, his father's eccentric older sister. His father's mysterious, adventurous older sister, a woman of wide foreign travel and yet no visible means of economic support, although that of various government agencies had been strongly suggested. Aunt Moira was scarily adept at throwing knives, foreign languages, and exotic methods of self-defense. In his teens, Richard came to an inescapable conclusion; Aunt Moira must be the distaff Agent 007 for some mysterious M-initialed agency. She certainly seemed to show up, or been suggested to have shown up in various exotic locales, weeks, or months before they featured in splashed-out headlines world-wide. This had happened just too many times over the years to be accounted for by sheer coincidence. Now Richard wished that he had kept up his school-days habit of tracking Aunt Moira's whereabouts and correlating them with blaring headlines. The bell over the café door jangled merrily. Aunt Moira appeared, dramatic as was her wont, trailing long scarf which would have made Isadora Duncan hesitate around open-topped motor vehicles.

"Richard, my dear! So here you are, hiding away in this … this charming little town! Dennis and Gwen have been so worried about you! I visited them in Provence for Christmas – I swear that was the first time I heard about your little … contretemps with the opening of Carême. I was … well, I was otherwise occupied at the time, and so I missed the regular news broadcasts entirely, even though the BBC World Service is received in … that place where I was at the time. However much your parents insisted that they were not the least concerned, and that you were perfectly content, I could tell they were worried! I simply had to come and see for myself, so that I could relieve all of our minds on that score!" She embraced him, as the bell jingled again, admitting Harry Vaughn, with Min Kim on one arm and Abuelita Adeliza on the other.

"Show-off!" That was a barely audible growl from Doc Wyler, who looked up from reading his copy of the *Karnesville Weekly Bulletin* at that end of the *stammtisch* understood by universal acclaim to be his.

"Jealous, Stevie-Boy?" Harry Vaughn observed as he and the ladies passed close. Richard, returning his aunt's embrace with the coffee carafe held out carefully, thought he was the only one near enough to hear. "Suck on it then, tea-sipper." In a louder voice, Harry Vaughn added, "Richard, this charming lady claimed to be your aunt! We had conversation this morning in the bathroom block at the campground, and she revealed all!"

"She is," Richard admitted. To his embarrassment, Aunt Moira kissed him as if he were still twelve years old, while Abuelita Adeliza and Min Kim beamed fondly on the charming scene of family reunion. Doubtless Aunt Moira had left the print of her bright red lipstick on his cheek.

"I am, indeed! And no, I most definitely did not reveal all, you dear man! It was public ablutions and there were other people around! I do wish that I had known that it was you, Richard, living in that precious little silver caravan! It would have saved so much of my time! But I didn't want to be indiscrete with questions. I thought I would just keep mum and attentive to local gossip."

"How did you get here, Auntie," Richard asked, in a lower voice, as Araceli showed Harry Vaughn and his attendant harem to an empty table. "I mean … from wherever you were before, to Luna City?"

Aunt Moira favored him with one more embrace, and patted his cheek – again, as if he were still a school-boy. "Darling, I approached some contacts and hitched a ride with the Bennington Patriot Easy Riders," she replied, in the same manner of a dowager confessing to have hired a cheap private jet for a transcontinental journey. "They are the dearest, most gallant chaps, so rough in appearance, and yet so gentlemanly! They're doing a coast-to-coast-to-coast-again circular journey – an iron-butt run, they call it. I'm riding with Big Boss Daddy, isn't that quaint? He has the most amazing vintage wartime Harley motorcycle with a sidecar, so I travel in relative comfort! So charming, all these back roads and small towns! The wind in your face …"

"The bugs in your teeth," interjected Joe Vaughn, *sotto voice*, and Jess hissed at him to shut up. Aunt Moira continued as if she hadn't heard. "The intense feeling of the open road … one simply doesn't get that same thing from driving in a motor-car, even with the windows open. It just seemed the most interesting and subtle way to travel across the United States! I am so pleased that the opportunity presented itself – although, as soon as they said that they planned to break for several days in Luna City, Texas – a most amazing coincidence. I was most eager to accompany them. It was cheaper than renting an automobile, you see. Since it is not official business, the expenses are all mine, Richard darling … although I am going to splurge a wee bit for our last night here and rent one of the suites in that grand old hotel across the way! It would be divine to actually see one of their ghosts, you know."

"You are traveling across the United States with a motorcycle gang?" Richard asked, through clenched teeth, "In the company of some doubtless nearly-toothless American chavish yob named Big Boss Daddy and his company of leather-jacketed morons." Words failed him. Aunt Moira had quite obviously gone around the twist. He wondered if he could delay her in the Café until he could call Berto's Uncle Tony Gonzalez in Elmendorf *(the proprietor of a hire-car service)*, have a car sent with instructions to take her to the airport in San Antonio and put her on the next international flight – a flight going anywhere. He'd leave it to Uncle Tony's best judgement if restraints would be in order. Just to get Aunt Moira out of this situation in one piece.

Aunt Moira blinked. "Darling, don't be such a snob. Do you have any notion of how much these machines cost? The top-flight ones? More than membership and dues in a good country club, and a lot more fun. Every one of the Bennington Patriot Easy Riders is relentlessly middle-class, or better, though of course, one doesn't ask for specifics. In mundane life, Big Boss Daddy is a professor of nuclear science at a particularly prestigious medical hospital, and Pamela – that is Mrs. Big Boss Daddy – has her own Harley, and eschews the sidecar. She is a martyr to motion-sickness as a passenger, and their dog prefers to ride with her. Really, Richard; how can you possibly believe that I was in any possible danger from these lovely chaps and their ladies?"

"Previous bitter experience," Richard answered with a sigh. Obviously, Uncle Tony Gonzalez's services would not be required. A relief, that: It wasn't like Aunt Moira was incapable of taking care of herself. On reconsideration, Richard suspected that Aunt Moira was better at that than he was. After all, he had arrived in Luna City by sheer bungling on the part of a private charter jet pilot and in a state of near-to-blackout drunkenness. On that occasion, he had thrown his last roll of cash money at Berto Gonzales, waiting outside of San Antonio's Stinson Airport, telling Berto to take him as far from there as the money went. Doing a double-cross-country ride with a group of middle-class motorcycle enthusiasts was the height of good sense in comparison.

He retreated to the Café kitchen, his refuge and pool of sanity in hard times. Everything orderly, organized, and under his command. The breakfast rush soothed his troubled soul; the scent of brewing coffee, bacon and sausage crackling on the grill, the rich yeasty scent of a pan of cinnamon rolls that Araceli was pulling from the biggest oven. He breathed it all in, feeling calm and focus bathing his senses. Enough of the human insanity. He had a café to run and paying customers to feed; the challenge of providing caviar cuisine on a canned tuna-fish budget.

He did notice that Harry Vaughn and his table of older ladies did seem to be having a jolly time of it over breakfast. Aunt Moira was conversant in Korean, which was no surprise. So was Harry Vaughn, which was. And both had such a sufficient grasp of Spanish to send Abuelita Adeliza into fits of laughter, while Doc Wyler scowled at them over his copy of the *Bulletin*.

Back in the kitchen, he queried Araceli over this anomaly. "I'd have thought that Harry Vaughn and Doc would have been best pals; same generation, growing up here in Luna City and all that. Instead, if I am any judge of human relations, which no one has ever claimed that I am – they appear to hate each other. Any notion of why? I ask that I can avoid stepping into it unawares. I am on good terms with both gentlemen, and I'd like to maintain that situation."

Araceli shrugged. "Honestly, Chef, I don't really know."

Joe Vaughn had followed Richard into the kitchen. He was filling up his duty Thermos with coffee from the big kitchen urn preparatory to going on duty. He topped off that Thermos with a splash of cream and replied, "Two alpha bulls in the same field, Rich. They would see each other as rivals."

"You speak from experience, of course," Richard could not resist adding, rather snidely, "You would know, as a not-inconsiderable alpha bull yourself."

"Ya got it, ya flaunt it," Joe returned snide for snide. "As you would also well know. See, Uncle Harry and Doc, they were the two big teenage studs in a small town, yea on these many decades ago. Uncle Harry got his growth early, like I did. He was big enough, fast enough, aggressive enough; he got tapped as quarterback for the Moths the first season that he was in high school in 1939. OK, so maybe the team was desperate for talent and they cut corners as far as eligibility went. That was the same year that Doc was a senior. Doc was small and wiry, just as he was back then. There are pics of the 1939 Moths in the foyer of the high school, as proof that I'm not BS-ing you. Doc played kicker on the '39 Moths team and Uncle Harry was quarterback. He was the star, and Doc was just on the team."

"I don't follow," Richard said.

Joe sighed, "OK, small words, then. Doc was the only son of the richest man in Luna City in 1939. He was the only student who had his own car. Not all that unusual now; but in that day, it was outstanding. Doc should have been undisputed king in the local social set and in the sports set, but he wasn't. That was all Uncle Harry's fault. Or so it was, according to my grandfather; Uncle Harry's much older brother.

Grandpop was a bookish sort, distantly amused by the whole thing. Grandpop was more a pal of Miss Letty's brother, the professor."

"Ah," Richard thought he could see it clear. "A geriatric willie-measuring contest."

"That's about the size of it," Joe answered, laughing coarsely. "Look, Rich; you should know small towns around here by now. People in them have their quirks. Trouble was – not just Doc's senior year got messed up by Uncle Harry. Doc went to UT once he graduated; that's the University of Texas in Austin. Uncle Harry went to A&M; Texas Agricultural and Mechanical. Where he was in the Corps of Cadets and played football."

"I fail to follow," Richard said. "Should I pound my head against the nearest solid wall, until that statement eventually makes sense?"

"No, because nothing but drywall would leak in, and I'd be in for a couple of hours of Jess bending my ear over the cost of repairs, as well as potential damage to your noggin. You haven't ever followed college sports in the Lone Star State. I get that; UT and A&M maintain the most ferocious rivalry known in these parts. Not a grad of either school myself, so I'm agnostic. I see it as pretty damn juvenile, but I was in the Army before I was twenty, fast-roping into hell in Mog, not going to collegiate pep rallies. Nothing like life and death to put a school football rivalry into proper perspective."

"Ah, I see now," Richard ventured. "Liverpool and Man United, Tottenham and Arsenal, Newcastle and Sunderland. War to the knife and knife to the hilt; a knife preferably in the back of your opponent?"

"Correctamundo," Joe nodded as he capped his Thermos. "But that wasn't all. You gotta see some other implications, Ricardo. Doc graduated, went to serve in the Army Air Corps at the ass-end of the big war; Double-ya-double-ya two, in the expectation of serving eventually in the last push against Japan. So, yeah, that was Doc's war service and he volunteered for it with eyes open. A bad risk for getting life insurance, you gotta admit, considering the overall casualty rates. But Uncle Harry, he was in the infantry in Korea. Caught that all full in the neck, including defense of the Pusan Perimeter. Got a couple of solid decorations for actions on the front line. Out of decency, I've never asked Uncle Harry for the gory details and never will. Again; Uncle Harry comes out of his war all covered in glory, while Doc was just doing time in service in his. It still must chap Doc's ass how Uncle Harry topped him in just about every way that matters to a young stud."

"A geriatric willie-measuring contest with bells on," Richard acknowledged. "Extra-loud, clangy bells. Thanks for the background 'gen. I rather like both gentlemen, frankly. Do you have any suggestions as to keep from getting drawn into the … erm – contest?"

Joe shook his head. "I'd advise tact, diplomacy, and strategic deafness with regard to cutting remarks made about the other in your presence. Sorry pal; best advice I can offer. I like both of them, too. Grandpop always got along great with Doc, so they say. And Doc gave a damn-fine elegy at his funeral."

With those encouraging words, Joe departed with his Thermos, ready for a day of defeating petty crime, speeders and other minor malefactors in Luna City, leaving Richard to contemplate the cultural minefield at his feet, still wondering how best to navigate it. Unbidden, the old saw about how when two elephants fight only the grass suffers, sprang to mind. This was not a heartening insight, and he firmly squashed it back into the depths of his subconscious.

"So, what do you think?" He inquired of Araceli, when the breakfast rush passed, and the café emptied of those who had paying employment or entrancing hobbies to draw them away from the fresh hot coffee, cinnamon rolls and made-to-order omelets in the hours of early morning.

"They've been married official for nearly six months," Araceli replied, with a mischievous look. "So I think she is pregnant. That's how I first realized … when I couldn't face a breakfast of anything but dry toast."

"What?" Richard was shaken to his core. "My god, how can that be – they've only just met for chrissake, and she must be sixty if she's a day."

"What?" That was Araceli's turn to be deeply shaken. "Who are you talking about, Chef? I meant Jess. She and Joe must be starting their family now that they are properly married."

"I meant … someone else," Richard stammered. Araceli shot him one of her trademark sideways looks, as she loaded the industrial dishwasher with the last load of used plates and cutlery. "Oh, your Auntie. Give it a break, Chef. She's likely forgotten more about romance than I ever learned."

"Bugger romance," Richard answered. "It's dirty weekends that I'm talking about. At least the middle-class motorbike morons are off tomorrow, so there is that. I suppose that I should be grateful."

"She's probably forgotten more about those, too," Araceli answered, smartly, and shot the final basket of dishes into the washer. At that point, Richard concluded there was no more to be gained from continuing that topic.

The Bennington Patriot Riders

The Bennington Patriot Riders is a New England-based motorcycle club principally *(but not exclusively)* composed of military veterans and family members, and loosely affiliated with the national Rolling Thunder, Inc. organization. The club was originally founded post-World War II, but saw an influx of new members in the early 1970s. It is registered as a non-profit organization, and supports several military-oriented charities such as the Blue Star Mothers, Soldiers' Angels, the Fisher House Foundation, the Red Cross, and others. Their colors are blue and gold, and their club patch features a representation of the Bennington Battle Monument.

The Bennington Patriot Riders participate in national events such as the annual Rolling Thunder Ride for Freedom or Ride to the Wall, a massive motorcycle rally held annually in Washington DC, on the Sunday of the Memorial Day weekend. Members gather silently in the Pentagon parking lot, and at the stroke of noon, fire up their machines and slowly process to the Vietnam Memorial. The Bennington Patriot Riders also take part in a yearly transcontinental road trip. In even-numbered years, they cross from Montpelier, Vermont, to Portland, Oregon via the upper mid-West states, and down the Pacific Coast to San Diego. From there, they cross to Houston, New Orleans and to Jacksonville, Florida, and then up the East Coast and back to Montpelier. In odd-numbered years, they reverse the itinerary; traveling south first, and then west across the southern states. The exact route varies every year, as do the places where they pause in the journey, which generally takes two weeks.

The Patriot Riders prefer to travel by secondary roads rather than the major interstate highways. This long-distance ride is scheduled for early spring, and usually draws forty to sixty participants.

With His Foot in His Mouth to the Kneecap

Opening the Café every day meant that Richard was awake and wheeling his bicycle away from the Airstream even before the Grants' roosters began tuning up their morning serenade and long before the Bennington Riders roused themselves for an early-morning start. He had been given to understand that the motorbike enthusiasts were to break camp and come to the Café for a hearty breakfast, before assembling and hitting the road en masse. Aunt Moira had said something to that effect, which reminded Richard that perhaps an additional pan of cinnamon rolls ought to go into the oven. He did notice, as he pedaled silently past Uncle Harry's van, that the red convertible was not there. He thought little or nothing of that, in the rush of the morning routine, assuming Uncle Harry must have stayed overnight with Joe and Jess.

It gratified him all over again, the sight of the Café filled every morning for breakfast; the first wave of diners on the run, like Roman Gonzalez and his work crew, yawning and clad in paint-splattered work clothes and steel-toed work shoes, wolfing down hot cinnamon rolls and mug after mug of coffee on their way to a worksite, or teachers at the schools in a similar rush. Then there were those dawdling in a leisurely fashion, retired or semi-retired like the Steins, Doc Wyler, or Hiram Abernathy, whose businesses did not have to be commenced at the crack of dawn. Then, as the bell rang in the elementary school playground across Town Square, women who had walked children or grandchildren to school drifted in to meet their friends for a coffee. The breakfast crowd usually tapered off after 9:30, only to pick up for luncheon two hours later. This morning, the additional twenty or so Bennington Patriot Riders *(twenty-one, counting the little fuzzy dog in his own leather jacket, helmet and goggles)* swelled the breakfast rush into spilling out into the tables set on the wide sidewalk in front. As far as Richard could see in the front, when he made his customary pass through the front of the house with the coffee carafe, it was all motorcycles; well-chromed, gleaming motorized mastodons, standing alone or leaning together, or against the lamppost and the railings which enclosed the outdoors tables and chairs.

Their owners' leather jackets all gaudily bedizened with colorful patches reminded Richard rather of pictures that Gran had shown him in old magazines, pictures of WWII American bombers with murals of spectacularly and improbably-endowed women on their aircraft. Which brought him around to consider Doc Wyler and the decades-old feud with Uncle Harry … *hang on, was that Uncle Harry? Uncle Harry, coming out of the front door of the old Cattleman Hotel, across the way … and hand-in-hand with … Aunt Moira? Walking close together, together in an intimate way which suggested that the two had not been sharing holiday snapshots. Richard's heart sank.* Uncle Harry's unmistakable candy-apple convertible was parked on the square opposite the Cattleman.

"Is that your uncle?" he asked Joe Vaughn, sitting with Jess out at one of the sidewalk tables, where they had been driven from their usual table by the influx of motorcyclists. "And his automobile?"

"It's his, all right," Joe replied. Likely behind his mirrored sunglasses, he was squinting. His voice sounded deliberately casual. "It was parked there by the Cattleman from about 9 PM on, according to Milo, and was still there when a patrol from the county sheriffs' department did a courtesy sweep through town at 2 AM."

"Oh, my god," Richard said, for at that very moment, under the antique glass awning over the Cattleman Hotel's front entrance, Uncle Harry and Aunt Moira turned towards each other, and exchanged a passionate kiss. "They've spent the night together, and ..."

Joe removed his sunglasses and regarded Richard with sympathetic patience. "I doubt they were eating cookies and drinking cocoa. My considered judgement is that your aunt and my great-uncle spent the night in pleasant conversation interspersed with episodes of 'hide the salami' – several rounds, if they had the energy for it. They say that age does adversely affects prowess."

"Not so far," Jess added with a perfectly lewd snicker, and Joe said, "Silence, wench. Rich, think of it as a rite of passage; observing clear evidence that your elders do indeed have a sex life. Can carry on like hormone-crazed teenagers, on occasion. A cringe-making thought, I know, but it's the world we live in."

In the silence which followed this simple observation, the temporary lovers broke apart, and strolled, still hand-in-hand around the corner of Town Square towards the Café. Richard sighed. "I'll do my best to think of it in that way. Joe, Araceli's plating your usual. Jess, are you still of the dry-toast-only breakfast inclination?"

"No, I'm fine this morning," Jess replied. "Scrambled eggs and bacon, as always, Rich. Can we go over the accounts, once the morning rush is done?"

"Certainly," Richard answered, with a certain feeling of relief. Things might be – should be – *must be!* – back to normal in the Café. Aunt Moira was leaving with her motorcycle mob, God was scrambling back up the ladder into heaven, and all would soon be right with his world. He topped up Joe and Jess's cups, and dodged back into the kitchen to relay their orders to Araceli.

When he emerged again with a refreshed carafe, the Bennington Patriot Riders were assembling on the sidewalk and in the street, trickling out of the Café in the direction of their machines as if some kind of dam had been broken. They went, wolfing the last of their breakfasts, purchasing a goodly number of cinnamon rolls to go *(and he was glad that they had baked that extra tray, for the Café would have been cleaned out of them, otherwise)*, the tiny dog in his comical helmet and leathers being boosted up into his bespoke and sheltered perch, on the back of one of the flashier machines. Said perch boasted an additional tiny windscreen. Only in America, Richard observed; but after all this time in in Texas, he had sufficient wit to keep that thought to himself.

Aunt Moira flung her arms about him, in exuberant affection, exclaiming, "Richard, darling, Big Boss Daddy and Pamela say it's time to … as they say, hit the road! I'm sorry we couldn't spend more family time together, but since the main purpose of this flying visit was so that I could assure your parents of your well-being, you will forgive me? Ta for now, dear! Now, promise me that you will call your mother and Dennis more often, won't you?"

"I will, Auntie," He replied, and she departed in more than her usual tempestuous fashion, trailing the brilliant scarlet scarf as she donned motorcycle helmet and tucked herself into the boxy and low-slung sidecar. Richard was also reassured to see that she tucked in the scarf likewise. Town Square filled with the thundering chorus of motorcycle engines, a mighty, heart-thumping, window-rattling diapason, as the Bennington Patriot Riders roared away, two and three abreast, until the street was empty and ordinary silence settled on the Square. The ensuing silence was nearly as deafening as the racket had been. Richard stood among the sidewalk tables, carafe in hand, still faintly shaken from that final embrace.

Harry Vaughn stood there also, watching the last bright tail-light and polish-gleaming chrome fender vanish around the corner of the Cattleman Hotel, which street led into the outskirts of town and the turn-off on Route 123, slightly to the south of the Tip-Top Icehouse, Gas, and Grocery. Harry Vaughn shook his head, and observed in an ordinary voice,

"That's one splendid woman, that aunt of yours."

"I know," Richard replied. "And if you are a gentleman, don't ever say so to me again."

"Understood." Harry Vaughn replied, and if there was a broad and lascivious grin on his lips, the drooping mustache efficiently veiled it. "Say, Rich, there's an old friend of mine that I'm meeting this morning…"

"Say no more," Richard said. "The Café is the place where everyone comes to meet in Luna City, sooner or later. Wait for your friend at the regular's table, if you like; the big one at the front window"

"That kind of place is one of my favorites in the whole wide world," Harry Vaughn agreed, with another one of those slightly mustache-veiled smiles, and Richard warmed to him on that account. It would be a long time, Richard thought, before Aunt Moira came to town again.

He was pleased to note that Benny Cordova was taking breakfast at the Café on this morning. As operations manager at Mills Farm and a corporate loyalist (if a somewhat devious and twisted loyalist) Benny would have had his breakfast appetites satisfied at the Mills Farm Country Restaurant. But instead, he was a Café regular. And Richard recognized the man with Benny; him with a battered and agreeably craggy, middle-aged face, the face of a man who did lots of physical work in the open air. The man was the one who had driven the truck delivering the man-camp trailer to the Age, the trailer in which Sefton had lived in during the time that the Straw Castle was being dreamed about, planned, and constructed – a trailer from which they had only moved in the last week or so. Benny's constant patronage was a compliment, Richard was certain. His cuisine at the Café, not to mention the bounteous cinnamon rolls and the legendary weekend full-English breakfast must beat the Mills Farm Country Restaurant into a cocked hat. And he did this on half the budget. *(Richard had lunched once at the Mills Farm, and been there for the movie-launch party and was not impressed in the least, having run a comparison of what he and his party had been served with his own estimation of costs incurred thereby.)*

Now, he greeted Benny Cordova breezily, in the casual way of old acquaintances: "Benny, old chap, how splendid to see you this morning! I say, I hear that you have a new boss to work for some Froggie poofter named Lucien Dubois! That will be an interesting change from Ms. Wyatt, I dare say! Any interesting 'gen on him at all? But never mind interesting bits, we'll settle for scandalous gossip."

In a fraction of the next second, the expression on Benny Cordova's countenance went from 'friendly and collegial' into 'poker-faced and neutral.' Richard sensed instantly that he had stepped in it. Stepped in it epically; catastrophically, even. Benny Cordova cleared his throat as the craggy-faced individual regarded Richard and replied in a mild tone of voice, in which the accent was clear, yet not quite that of the French that he knew best.

"Well, then '*cher*, that would be myself. Lew Dubois, from Arnaudville on the Bayou Teche. Not a Froggie and not a poofter, either, unless my wife of thirty years has been seriously misinformed."

At Richard's back, Harry Vaughn commented in a voice so dry that it could have shriveled the water from several bayous, "This is Richard Astor-Hall, the manager of the Café; his talents include haute cuisine, restaurant management, and being able to speak clearly with his foot in his mouth all the way to his kneecap."

"Can I fetch you some coffee, Mr. Dubois? I'll bring some strychnine for myself, or arsenic, if you would prefer." Richard moistened his lips.

Yes – stepped in it, epically. "I apologize for speaking so out of turn; part of my artless charm, it would appear. I thought you were merely one of Mr. Cordova's custodial staff."

Fortunately for him, Lew Dubois did not seem to take easy offense, or be of the grudge-nourishing type, for he gave a genial chuckle. "Think nothing of it, '*cher* Richard. It is true that I prefer to manage by walking around, and getting my hands dirty."

"The difference between Lew and Miz Wyatt is the difference between night and day," Benny Cordova observed. Oh, good, he had not taken offense either. Now Harry Vaughn drew up a chair at their table and settled onto it with a mild 'oof!' which suggested weariness … no, Richard winced from considering the reason for such. "Lew and I are old pals," Harry Vaughn added. "From when he was running that fancy Banff resort."

"Castle Mountain, yes," Lew Dubois nodded. "That is VPI's largest and most successful operation in Canada. It was my honor to be a part of that success."

"I'll tell Araceli to take your orders," Richard said. "While you wait, may I offer you some coffee? I've begun experimenting with roasting the beans here, in house, and grinding them freshly every day."

"*Parfait*!" Exclaimed Lew Dubois. "I see that you quest for that perfection in every matter – even as simple a one as a morning coffee! I like that! I am a man who looks for that perfection also."

"But of course," Richard poured, breathing an invisible sigh of relief. "Would you prefer hot milk? Or cream – there is a pitcher of cream on the service table…"

An effable expression of pleasure crossed Lew Dubois' slightly battered countenance. "Hot milk, *s'il vous plaît*. I am immediately at home in this palace of gastronomic delights …"

Within earshot, Doc Wyler grunted, "First time those bastards at VPI ever stirred themselves – that's one for the records!"

Richard thought he heard Jess, lingering over her breakfast after Joe left for his working day, fighting crime in Luna City, hiss a suggestion at Doc that he try at least to be civil. But he was too relieved that his monumental gaffe hadn't done any lasting damage.

"I shall be extravagantly honored, M'sieu Dubois …"

"Oh, I am Lew to everyone," Lew Dubois waved a dismissive hand. Richard sensed that the other man was dialing up his rough-cast charm to the highest possible degree. In aid of what? Yes, this man wanted something of Luna City; a matter of benefit to Mills Farm, obviously, but if Lew Dubois' project was also to the benefit of Luna City … well, that was a matter for debate, was it not? And was Uncle Harry, Joe Vaughn's long-time-law-enforcement professional uncle, supporting or in opposition of whatever it was that VPI was planning? He would need more information, Richard decided; information of a non-partisan nature. He would have to talk to Chris Mayall and Sylvester Gonzales, the next visitors' night at the VFW. What Chris didn't glean from casual conversation over the bar, Sylvester, the computer and gaming nerd, devotee of all means of enabling surreptitious surveillance, would have collected through means that Richard was pretty certain were mostly illegal. He still shuddered to think of how he and Sylvester laid hands on the script of that wretched movie project backed by the despicable Phillip Noel-Barrett. In the meantime, Araceli was just as well-situated in the Café for picking up useful local gossip.

"Half-a-dozen fresh cinnamon rolls for table 4," he said, upon returning to the kitchen. "Gratis. A peace offering," he added, when Araceli raised an interrogative eyebrow. "I stuck my foot in it, when I asked Benny Cordova about his new boss at Mills Farm – the French poofter. Who was sitting right there. I thought he was one of Benny's workmen."

Araceli looked ceilingward and muttered something under her breath in Spanish. "Chef, I have to say you have a gift …"

"People have often said that," Richard agreed. "I gather that opinions are split, regarding said gift being for good or ill. Nevertheless, I have apologized, and that apology has been handsomely accepted by all. But I still want to know; what is going on with this at Mills Farm? Explain it in simple words, if needs be, Araceli, but there is something in the wind. They have plans, and I need to know whether 'tis nobler to jump to one side or the other, or just keep my mouth shut."

"Your mouth shut would be a wise opening move," Araceli piled a serving platter with six warm cinnamon rolls, aromatic with the fragrance of spices of the Far East, dripping with freshly-made and still-oozy simple frosting. "I take it you did not read Kate's story in the *Bulletin*? Really, Chef; try to keep involved. It would save you so much trouble. OK, I'll tell you what I know after I take their orders. Benny will want his regular order; fried ham, eggs over easy with the yolks still slightly runny and crispy hash-browns. I'll take care of it, Chef."

"Thanks, Araceli," Richard said to her back, as she went briskly through the swinging door to the front of the house. Richard slapped a ham cutlet on the grill, and a handful of seasoned grated potato – the eggs would go on at the last minute and be ready when Araceli returned with the other orders. She was never wrong about the regulars. Such was life in a small town, such was service in Café which catered to everyone in town on weekdays.

He had Benny's order plated, and Harry and Lew Dubois' orders well along. Araceli took Benny's breakfast onto her tray, saying, "The word is that Mills Farm wants to get away from identifying so much with Old Charley. I think it's beginning to sink into their tiny corporate minds that Old Charley might not be the best image to brand their place with. And there's more than just that. You could have read all this in the *Bulletin*, you know; or on Katie's *Talk of the Town* blog."

"Indulge me then," Richard sighed. "It has been my experience that what gets into print is usually only a faint simulacrum of the true reality of a situation or event. In fact, I believe – and Miss Heisel is an exception in that she is utterly free of any intent to deceive – that the main intent of most news media is to misdirect, obfuscate and outright lie. They have their story already written before the dust settles. All they want are the appropriate words and pictures to adorn and support their particular corporate take on the subject. I prefer to get my information like I do my coffee; straight from the urn and unfiltered. Prepare to brief me in full, if that is not a contradiction in terms." He swiftly plated Harry Vaughn's cheese omelet, added a side of spiced-apple compote, and Lew Dubois' sausage, scrambled egg and biscuits. I trust your information, and even more, your insights into the matter."

"Flattery will get you nowhere, Chef," Araceli sniffed and whisked the two plates away. When she returned, Richard was scraping the grill clean, with one eye on the clock. The old-fashioned spring bell on the Café's front door jingled a little less frequently. The post-breakfast slowdown was beginning. This was the best time for a heart-to-heart, between Araceli dashing out now and again to ring up departing customers, and sorting out trays of china and silverware for the dishwasher, while Richard began prepping for the luncheon crowd, although he did have that daily confab with Jess Abernathy – Jess Vaughn, as she now was – on his to-do list.

"OK," Araceli reported, in her usual businesslike fashion in the first interval. "The gossip grapevine has it that VPI top-management wants to totally revamp Mills Farm into a huge waterpark resort. Swimming pools, slides, water-rides … and to enlarge the guest facilities. Katie says that a big new-built hotel facility for guests in in the works, according to her sources. Which … sorry, gotta go, Chef," she added, as the bell chimed.

After the short interval, Richard demanded, "Well, wouldn't that be to local advantage? A new and enlarged element; not only for the local building contractors, but for employment generally, upon completion?

Packing the punters in is the name of the game. The sweet, sweet lolly, the dosh …"

"The what?" Araceli frowned.

"The money," Richard explained with heavy sarcasm. "Filthy lucre. Bags of swag."

"It would mean something, sure," Araceli replied. "But you see, Chef – we kind of like Mills Farm the way that it is."

"Nothing remains the same," Richard observed, seditiously. Araceli scowled in a dangerous manner. He looked towards the rack of long kitchen knives, reassuring himself that she was not standing too near them.

"Look, Chef, you asked for my unvarnished account and my opinion on the matter, and this is it: Yes, we might make a mint of money off enlarging Mills Farm, but what would it mean in the long run for Luna City? No one really wants to be an adjunct to Disneyland-Karnes County version. People are in two minds about it all. We can see the benefits … but we can also see the downside, too. I expect that is why Mr. Dubois is here to oversee the beginnings of the project. Or even – and that's what Katie gathered, although she didn't put it into her final story – that he might be inclined to fashion it into something more locally fitting. Her words, not mine. He's their big location-manager guy, with a solid record behind him. We talked about this last Sunday. Joe said that it was his opinion that Lew Dubois had been nominated to walk point and take the local fire."

"I don't remember that," Richard interjected, as the front bell chimed yet once again.

When Araceli returned, she said, "You were out on the lawn, showing Matty how to dribble a soccer-ball properly. Like Beckham, you said."

"I am a lamentably-poor imitation of Beckham," Richard replied. "As my school sport was rowing. So. I missed a relevant conversation last

Sunday at your regular at-home, while teaching your son a highly useful life skill. Continue."

The bell chimed again, and there was a brief pause, while Araceli tallied up a final charge for a departing customer. When she returned, she carried on as if there hadn't been an interruption. "We were all talking about the waterpark project; Joe was the most against it, because it would bring in too many of what he called 'the dirtbag element.' Roman and Berto were the most in favor; Roman believes that it would all be a plum project for him, since he is already in good with their people for maintenance and repair contracts. And Berto just thinks that a big fancy waterpark would be ultimately cool."

"What did you think about it all, then?"

"It would be a change," Araceli replied. "A big change if it really happens. They're looking to buy more land for the expansion. The three property owners with acreage that borders Mills Farm are Doc Wyler – who wouldn't sell under any circumstances to VPI, Great-Uncle Jaimie … he has the last bits of the original Spanish grant, and he <u>might</u> be persuaded to sell off some of his pasture land by the river. And then there's the Grants. I don't think Judy could be persuaded to sell out entirely, but they might part with a couple of acres, if they were offered enough. Jess says that financially, it would make sense for them."

"Judy Grant and the concept of financial good sense are not even on speaking terms," Richard said. "But Sefton might be persuaded." He felt a bit of a chill at that thought. No, he didn't relish serious change in his living situation any more than any other Lunaite. The last few months had been traumatic enough.

"Doc Wyler wouldn't," Araceli promised, confidently. "He wouldn't walk across the road to piss on Mills Farm if it were on fire. But he and Great-Uncle Jaimie are both really old." She suddenly sounded a lot less confident. "Patricia doesn't hold grudges the way that Doc does. And Great-Uncle Jaimie's sons don't either. And they don't care about owning a tract of land the way that Great-Uncle Jaimie does. The last of the Gonzalez league-and-a-labor from Spanish days; that's a sacred trust for him. Not for his sons."

"So, if VPI is really serious about long-term plans like this, then all they have to do is wait and deal with more agreeable heirs. How long … three, four years. On the bright side," Richard made a determined effort to be cheerful. "Well, anything can happen, I suppose. Sufficient unto the day, eh?"

"That," Araceli still looked worried. "Speaking of sufficient … we're down on our supply of cinnamon rolls. Hadn't we start a new batch today?"

"Agreed," Richard nodded, thinking – *At least that is a matter which we can do something about.*

Rivers Run Through It

A number of rivers of note meander across the state of Texas, most of them impressive in stretches although nothing like the scale of the mighty Mississippi-Missouri; three such rivers, the Rio Grande on the south, the Red in the north, and the Sabine in the east form all or a portion of the state borders. The Colorado and the Brazos span the state entirely, from the north-west borders to the coast of the Gulf of Mexico. The Canadian crosses west to east across the Panhandle region. Notably, the Brazos and the Rio Grande were navigable for considerable of their length by commercial steamboats in the early days, although low water in dry years sometimes hampered such regular traffic. Other rivers were channeled, deepened, controlled, and dammed to facilitate traffic on inland waterways. Generally, the farther into the heart of Texas one goes, the chances that the nearest river will be used only recreationally are commensurately greater.

Such is the case of the San Antonio River, which watercourse skirts Luna City on its southern margin, before passing the Age of Aquarius Campground & Goat Farm, and then Mills Farm, several miles farther downstream. The San Antonio River, which rises in Bexar County from a number of smaller spring-fed streamlets was the original reason for the Spanish to plant missions and a small settlement along its banks. The river was improved even in the early days with channels to provide water for agricultural purposes and for domestic needs. By the mid-19th century, the San Antonio River provided power for a vast grain mill operation on the south side of town, water for a pair of breweries on the banks, and as now – for recreation. The river was not one of those navigable by larger craft for very much of its length.

Being subject to seasonal fluctuations and apt to suddenly flood after prolonged rainstorms farther upstream, the San Antonio River can sometimes be a difficult neighbor for those who live along its' banks. This is also true of many another of the smaller Texas rivers. There is a good reason for houses in riverside locations to be constricted on tall foundations, or on tall pilings. The river, which for years might have been a gentlemanly placid and waist-deep trickle between steep banks, meandering over a wide stretch of polished gravel, water-scoured bedrock, and small thickets of rushes … will drink deep of a sudden heavy rainfall, and go mad.

The Rain It Raineth Every Day

"It's like a lovely English summer day in Bickley," Richard observed sourly at half-past eight, as the Café door opened and shut, admitting a gust of wind, a splash of rain blowing in on it, and Joe Vaughn, immense in a bright yellow rain-slicker from which water ran in sheets. The Café was half-empty, the reason for it obvious through the streaming windows. The bandstand and the trees in Town Square were barely visible in the dreary grey downpour. "They never told me that Texas had a bloody monsoon season."

"But they did say something about how, if you didn't like the weather here – to wait five minutes and it would change?" Joe shed his dripping slicker, grinning broadly at Richard and the handful of patrons; the Steins, Jess, with the elder Abernathys, Harry Vaughn, and a scattering of strangers passing through Luna City at the start of what would have been the prime breakfast hour. Richard was annoyed; he had a pan of cinnamon rolls cooling. At this morning's dismal rate of consumption, half of them would be no good for anything but ... *perhaps he could work up a means of using stale cinnamon rolls in something. Like a rich and raisin-laden bread pudding...*

"I've been waiting since first thing this morning," Richard was cross. He had been caught in the first downpour on his bicycle commute, and soaked to the skin by the time he arrived at the Café. Fortunately, he kept several changes of dry clothes in the cubbyhole closet next to where the brooms, vacuum cleaner, mops and buckets, and stock of lavatory paper for the WCs were stored. But his socks still squelched in his clogs – he hadn't thought to keep dry socks on hand as well. "It's been more than five minutes since then, and bloody nothing has changed."

"Yes, it has," Joe's grin was ear-to-ear. "It's rained even harder." He leaned down to kiss Jess on the cheek. "Morning, Babe; morning, Babe-ette-to-be. And the forecast is for even more rain. The river's running pretty high already." Joe's expression turned from jocular to something more serious. "We've had to barricade off some low-water crossings already – y'all already know which places I mean. It's gonna be a soggy Memorial Day weekend in Luna City, I'm afraid. Specially if we have to close the bridge, like after the big flood in '98. I've already got a call from the Emergency Management folks in Karnesville, telling us to stand by."

"Guess we'd better move up the training session," Martin Abernathy observed. "And make it into a briefing. Make it 3 PM today – LCVFD classroom. All hands and responsible citizens attend. I'll send out the word."

"Good," Joe nodded. "I'll have my guys in as well. I don't think it will be as bad as '98 – but you never know. I wasn't there, and you were. Hey, Ricardo – my usual. Thanks."

"So, what happened in '98?" Richard ventured, before heading kitchen-wards.

"It rained," Joe answered. "A lot. Not here so much, but away upstream."

"So much in some places that it topped out the rain gages," Martin Abernathy said, from the table where he sat, having overheard Richard's question. "But hardly a drop here, mind you. At least we had fair warning, when it all came pouring downstream." He looked morose. Richard thought it best to retreat to his kitchen, redolent with the scent of bacon, of cinnamon rolls fresh from the oven. He thought of the view over the bend in the river at the bottom of the campground. He couldn't imagine that bend of lazy green water flowing in a furious torrent.

"Araceli, my sweet – what happened here, in '98?" he demanded, when Araceli brought the latest breakfast orders.

"My senior year," Araceli retorted smartly. "I went to the prom with Patrick. And Patricia got engaged to Andy Pryor. Abuelo Jesus passed away … no, wait. That was the year before."

"Weather-wise," Richard barked. "Not with your personal life."

"Oh, you meant the flood?" Araceli took up the plated orders and vanished into the front of the house. When she returned, with an empty tray, she continued as of there had been no interruption. "Yes, There were dead cows stuck in the thickets and trees by Mills Farm. Washed down from how-knows-how-many miles away. The smell of them stuck in the trees was just horrible. Tio Jaimie got some of his cattle returned from Beeville, though. Did you know that cows can float and swim for quite a good distance?"

"I did not," Richard allowed, through slightly-clenched teeth. "But the Olympic swim-team possibilities of cows are not what I wish to discuss. I was asking about the flood, itself. I did not know that the river itself could pose such a risk."

"Only when it has a lot of water in it," Araceli reposted. Observing Richard's exasperation, she relented and enlarged upon the topic. "It was a hundred-year, maybe a two-hundred-year flood. I mean, just look at the banks, and then at that little bitty trickle of water in normal years. But anyone can see, or ought to be able to see, that those banks were carved out by high, fast-moving water. Miss Letty's house; why do you think that's on such a tall foundation? Her place is the oldest house in town, and I'd like to have a hundred-dollar tip for every bad flood that old house has seen and ridden out. They built them smart in the old days."

"I am certain that they did," Richard allowed. "So there was a substantial flood in '98. Good to know."

"Well, the curious thing about it was that it didn't actually rain much here at all. All the rain from a bunch of heavy storms fell in the Hill Country, around San Marcos and New Braunfels. So much rain and it fell so fast that the water filled up all the rivers and the dams to overflowing …"

"I am acquainted with the general concept," Richard acknowledged. "So, all that water eventually moved downstream. How badly did the river flood at Luna City?"

"Way over the banks," Araceli said. "And a foot or so over the bridge on 123. Miss Letty's house was like a little island. So was the Grants' place. They're on that hill, which is higher than you would think. Now, the Tip-Top had water inside halfway to the walls. Uncle Jesus had time to sandbag the garage and move most of his stuff to higher ground, but there was a foot or so of water all through the lower part of Luna City, south and east of the Square. But at least, we had plenty of warning. The thing is that if it rains very, very hard, as hard as it has been raining today over someplace like Floresville or Lavernia, then we could have a flash-flood, with hardly any warning at all."

"Mayor Abernathy is going to hold a meeting this afternoon at the VFD," Richard said. "To address that very possibility, I assume."

"You should go to it, then," Araceli said, and Richard sighed.

"I suppose that I ought to – it was supposed to be the ordinary training sessions. I was just acquiring a grasp of the fine art of hose-handling," Richard added, with feeling. Yes, man-handling one of the heavy high-pressure fire hoses was a full-body-contact sport, like wrestling an immensely strong python with a stubborn streak. There was a knack to it, apparently; a knack which he had slowly developed over the last few months, although he had nearly been knocked cold by a thrashing hose that first time. Chris Mayall had been humorous about Rich's resulting black eye for weeks. He had yet to go out on a call of any sort save as observer but he had been issued a helmet, a battered turn-out coat and a pair of gloves for training purposes.

"How are you liking it?" Araceli asked, and Richard shrugged. "It's more amusing than I thought it would be. And I think it really seems like I'm one of the regular chaps, but I hate to think that someone's life might depend on me in a crisis. I'm really not the heroic sort of chap. I'm not even interested in looking like I was a hero."

"Never mind about all that," Araceli riposted. "It's your cooking that we look to you for, anyway. Still, we should sort out what to do, in case of a flood here in the Café."

"I thought you said the water never came near to Town Square?" Richard protested, and Araceli looked exasperated.

"Give a thought to sandbagging the door, at least." She replied. "And to moving perishable stuff to a higher level. Ask for advice at the meeting."

"Sufficient until the day," Richard said, and left the matter at that.

Cattle Call

Luna City's volunteer fire department was housed in a large metal-sided barn of no particular architectural charm, three blocks east of Town Square. Together with the Luna City PD headquarters next door, this put them both on the edge of town by the northernmost and newest of the two roads that led from off Route 123 and into Luna City proper. *(Miss Letty's and the Tip-Top were located at the southernmost, closest to that bridge which spanned the river.)* The rain had let up by then, although from the grey and threatening appearance of the sky, the weather gods promised additional precipitation. Richard pedaled along, carefully avoiding the standing puddles, and reminding himself to bring some dry clothing on the following day, lest he be caught again. Really, despite being an Englishman born and bred, he had a cat's dislike of being first soaked to the skin and then enduring a day inside an air-conditioned building. Nothing, he was convinced, was apt to make a person more ill than being wet, and sitting under a vent blasting cold air down upon him.

The somewhat scratch parking area around the police and fire department, an area composed of about fifteen percent crumbling macadam to eighty-five percent gravel and hard-pressed and mostly dead grass was entirely full, for the first time in his admittedly limited experience. A jumble of vehicles, most of them the usual selection of pickup trucks which he had come to see as the normal transportation option in Luna City, were parked without regard to order and reason.

Well, that was one advantage to a bicycle. He wheeled it around to the side, where a couple of heavy timber picnic tables and a rusty barrel-shaped BBQ unit sat underneath the customary oak tree which was a constant in Luna City, and leaned the bike against the nearest table. The side door was already propped open, with Chris Mayall's young medic-apprentice volunteer lurking just inside. The name of the apprentice momentarily escaped Richard, although the boy had "Gonzalez" embroidered on the front of his dark-blue uniform shirt. Richard privately admitted to a sense of wistful envy. Just by being born with that surname in Luna City meant that the lad was instantly more one of the local elect than Richard would ever be, Charterhouse and Cordon Bleu education notwithstanding. The classroom beyond was empty – and it was nearly the appointed hour.

"Hullo, young Jaimie," he said, having wrenched the boys' name from his recalcitrant memory. "Where is everyone? I thought that time for the regular training session was moved up – not the location."

"They moved it into the bay, with so many people," Jaimie replied. He was still young enough to be excited by a whiff of potential catastrophe. "There's Cousin Horatio from the County, and the forecast is saying there will be more rain over the next few days. I guess this will be the command post, for a while."

"Joy and rapture unrestrained," Richard answered deadpan and walked down the narrow corridor from the door, past the empty classroom on one side, past the offices on the other, and the dormitories for the duty firefighters on the other, and into the soaring space which housed the various engines. There was more space in the barn than engines to fill it. The area beyond the pump and ladder trucks, the brush truck and the ambulance had been transformed, with ranks of folding tables and rows of chairs. An immense map hung on the far wall. As he came around from the last engine, someone was rolling out a video cart with a large television on it. The map drew his attention first, though; a detailed, large-scale map of the river, it's many tributaries and watershed as it rambled through Karnes County. Through the VFD training sessions, he had become well-acquainted with Luna City, and those outlaying parts covered by the volunteer firefighters, but this was a much larger map. He took a seat in the rearmost row of chairs; the bustle of activity around the tables made him profoundly uneasy. He exchanged a nod with Sylvester Gonzales, dapper as always in retro-nerd fashion – this time in khaki slacks and a vintage and vividly-colored Hawaiian print shirt – who seemed to be overseeing the set-up of many telephones, one at each place along the first table. The telephones and attendant cables were being unpacked from a couple of lidded plastic tubs. Richard knew or at least recognized most of those present, and sifting in as the hands of a clock hanging on the wall above the map inexorably advanced towards the hour of three. He almost didn't recognize Miss Letty, unaccustomed to the sight of her in a slate-grey uniform-cut women's suit, adorned with a shoulder patch and ARC lapel insignia. Nothing like an old emergency-service warhorse scenting a disaster, Richard thought to himself and immediately his inner good-manners angel booted him for being an ungallant prick. Still, he thought the old dear had better not try to wrestle an active fire-hose. Although Chris Mayall, who was sitting in the folding chair next to her, would doubtless prevent her from doing anything so reckless.

There was only one man present who was a stranger to him. Since the name-plate on his unfamiliar uniform bore the surname of Gonzalez and the familial resemblance to those Gonzalezes and Gonsaleses of his acquaintance was quite marked, he thought it likely that he knew of that man by repute, if not by first name among the clan.

"That's Cousin Horatio," Jaimie whispered, as he slid into the seat next to Richard. "You know … he went and joined the Coast Guard out of high school, but now he's with the county sheriff's department. He knows all about boats and things. They call him all the time for stuff involving river rescues and that."

"Shush!" That was Jess, sitting in the row of chairs ahead of them. And there was Joe Vaughn, striding up to stand before the stand microphone, in his office as chief of police for Luna City.

"Hey, ladies and gentle-grunts; thanks for taking the time from your busy day to come to this briefing… Hey, is there any rep from Mills Farm? No? Well, they have their own resources. I'd have thought they would be there, 'cause of their riverside properties. As you should know from watching the weather, it's been a rainy spring. This week's forecast calls for even more rain. We've been advised to activate our emergency response team, in the expectation of catastrophic flooding from the San Antonio River and possibly various local creeks over the next few days. I know that it's only a precaution, and no one is getting really panicked at this point," and Joe favored the gathering with an especially serious look. "But there is a holiday weekend coming up. A lot of out-of-town folks traveling to the coast, just visiting a place like Mills Farm – I really wish they had sent someone to this meet, since flooding is forecast … back on topic; folks staying for the weekend with friends in the country are those who prolly don't know the lay of the land…"

"He's got a point," Jaimie whispered. "If we live here, we know where all the low-water crossings are, all the places that flood out …."

"Shush," Richard replied, for he was strangely unsettled in recognizing a newer arrival; Kate Heisel, in her oversized drooping tan trench-coat, cat-footing around the perimeter of the gathering. The sound of her camera and brief flare of the flash attachment riveted his attention, although she seemed more focused on the immense map, and the tables with telephones already laid out. When she turned and aimed her lens at the assembled multitudes, he swiftly bent down to re-tie a boot-lace. No need to borrow trouble, even if he liked and trusted Kate Heisel in a small way. Even if she had said to him, on one memorable occasion, *"No one here gives a waffle-fried damn that you used to be Rich Hall, the Bad Boy Chef,"* Kate's one picture of Romeo Gonzales had gone international-viral, once it had been posted on the Karnesville Weekly Beacon website for publicity purposes for the Luna City Players performance of *Let No True Hearts Admit Impediment*. That it all had come out rather well for Romeo was irrelevant to Richard: Once a photograph taken by Miss Kate Heisel was loosed on the internet, control was out of her hands, despite the best intentions of all concerned.

He didn't entirely come up for air with regard to his shoelace, until Miss Kate herself came and settled into the folding chair next to Jaimie, returning her camera safely to her camera case.

"Hey, Rich, long time, no see?" she whispered. "Are you a volunteer now? Cool beans!"

"Well, I live here," Rich whispered back, disregarding the faint hushing sounds from either side. "What brings you here?"

"News, silly; activating the emergency response command post is certainly newsworthy. Any time there's a million cars parked outside the VFD there's bound to be something of interest happening. I really came down for the cattle drive."

"Cattle drive?" Richard was glad that his voice didn't squeak. A small rustling commotion among the audience as Chief Vaughn introduced Lt. Gonzalez from the Karnes County Emergency Management office covered Kate Heisel's reply.

"For sure," she whispered. "There's going to be about a hundred-fifty head of Lazy-W cattle moved from a pasture on low ground moved from a low-lying pasture across the river into the Wyler Ranch, proper. Too many to truck, and too late to do anything but walk them through town. A real cattle drive – I wouldn't miss it for the world!"

"When is this going to happen?" Rich whispered back.

"In about twenty minutes," Kate replied, sotto voice. "My … um … friend is going to call me when they get close to crossing Route 123."

At his side, Jaimie Gonzales exclaimed in a normal voice, "No shit, Katie? I wanna see this!" to an enraged hiss of hushing from those nearest to them. At the microphone, Horatio Gonzalez broke off his introductory remarks to frown and address his juvenile kin.

"Is there something you wanted to share with us all?"

Unrepentant, Jaimie stood up and replied in a loud voice. "Yeah! Cousin Kate says there's going to be a real-live cattle drive through town!"

Richard noted several things at once: Jess sinking down in her seat, Joe clapping on his wide-brimmed white Stetson and taking out his cellphone, and most of the assembled volunteers assuming expressions of lively interest.

"So where they gonna go? Whose' herd? How soon?" was the boiled-down essence of those questions which came thick and fast. Kate Heisel stood up, and finding her small height a disadvantage, stepped up onto her chair. Which being of the folding persuasion, was a perilous perch. Richard gave her a hand up, beating Jaimie to it by a short lead.

"It's one of the Wyler herds," she explained, and the timbre of her voice suggested something of embarrassment. "It's an emergency. My informant has it that Lazy-W ranch management wanted it done and fast, so as to reduce panic …"

"A hundred and fifty cattle in the streets of Luna City? That will reduce panic all right," Joe Vaughn observed, within the pick-up range of the standing microphone, so that his remarks were perfectly clear. "Katie, why don't we know about this?"

"I thought that everyone had been informed," Kate replied, in perfectly reasonable tones.

Joe Vaughn heaved up a deep sigh, from the depths of his soul. "All right, people; here is our very first flood-related emergency situation. All hands to battle-stations. How long do we have before the herd hits, Katie?"

"Twenty minutes, I think." Now Kate sounded positively rattled. "Joe, I was sure your people already knew!"

"Well, we do now," Joe noted. "OK, briefing's suspended for the moment. Who's in charge of the cattle drive, Katie? Doc Wyler?"

Kate nodded, concentrating on safely dismounting from a folding chair. Richard thought, fleetingly, that she may have leaned on him more than was absolutely necessary in doing so – but this was Kate, Kate of Kate Hall, as long as her camera lens was not pointed in his direction. Meanwhile, Joe was rapping out crisp directions alternately into his cellphone, his radio, and to the volunteers taking their places along the table.

"They'll be taking them along Oak from 123 and the south side of Town Square, past the elementary school, and over to Cypress and north to the Wyler Ranch. You better alert Jerry at the ISD. The elementary school is already dismissed for the day, but they'll be going past the high school just at 4:00. Just call everyone along those streets and alert them to what is going on. Cameras are optional, I guess. But shovels and wheelbarrows will be absolutely necessary afterwards."

That was the last that Richard heard, over the hubble-bubble. Oddly enough, most everyone else appeared to think this was something exotic and exciting, worthy of notice, nearly as much as Richard did. They were vacating the fire department barn in a rush, all those whose services were not immediately required. Someone among the VFD staff on duty had obliged by raising the two garage doors. Miss Letty, calm and magisterial as always, refused Richard's assistance in joining the throng.

"My grandfather saw herds of cattle trailing through the streets quite often. Quite a nuisance it was at the time, he always said. The manure was useful, for gardens, of course." She fell silent for a moment, and then added, "I suppose it has been years since you young people have seen such a thing, save in movies or on television."

"It has, Miss Letty!" Katie chirped. "It's why it's news!"

Miss Letty snorted. "Sensation, Katherine. Pure vulgar sensation."

"Sensation is my bread and butter," Kate replied, not nearly as put down by Miss Letty's obvious disapproval as Richard thought he would have been. "Vulgar or not. It's something interesting, and new ... or newly-new. I'm off, Miss Letty; my job. You know, that professional understanding that puts a meal on my table and pays for the gas in my car?"

"I know, dear," Miss Letty unbent sufficiently to offer a smile. "You young girls have so many opportunities, these days. I'm not at all certain that some of them are for the betterment of our sex, but still ... you have them."

"I know," Kate smiled in return, a smile that lit up her relatively ordinary face, and extraordinary blue-green, beryl-colored eyes. "And I'm not entirely lost to decency, Miss Letty. I do keep some newsworthy confidences."

"And if you like, Miss Kate, I can offer a meal this evening," Richard heard himself saying, to his utter horror. "At the Café, if you would like." *Where in the name of all that was holy had that come from?* Richard wondered, but Kate favored him with a blinding smile, and Miss Letty with an expression of wintery approval.

"I'd like that," Kate said, and then went off at a trot in the direction of Oak Street which crossed from 123 into the regular – or somewhat regular grid of Luna City. That ridiculous oversized trench-coat flapped behind her like a loose sail. At the corner, she turned, and cupped her hands to shout, "See you after the trail drive, Richard!"

"So," Miss Letty observed, after another short interval, in which they and the others had drifted down towards the Oak Street corner and spread out along the mostly-unimproved verge. *(Sidewalks in Luna City didn't begin for another half a block or so.)* "How does the spider plant that I gave to you for your patio fare?"

"It's still alive," Richard replied. "Sending out a couple of small shoots. Baby spiders, I do believe. I hope they don't choose to crawl indoors and begin spinning webs."

"Excellent," Miss Letty appeared amused. She and Richard came to the corner, where a low wall of cut limestone adorned the roadside. Years ago and in a fit of municipal enthusiasm, a previous mayor had caused it to be built and adorned with cast-metal letters spelling out the words, "Welcome to Luna City – The Biggest Little Town in Texas." One of the g's had fallen off, and the last letter s was loose and tilted sideways. All the letters had bled dark smears of minerals down the pale stone, but the grass was clipped neatly around the wall.

Miss Letty took a large handkerchief out of her handbag and spread it on the level top. "I believe I shall sit and watch the excitement from here, Richard. And walk home if the meeting is not continued. I must say that it was good of you to take such an interest. The school cooking classes, the VFD and now Emergency Preparedness."

"I don't know if I'm all that much an addition to the strength," Richard confessed. "I can barely manage a hose without knocking myself silly. And I do not drive. Really, all I can do is cook."

"You have other skills, I am certain," Miss Letty assured him. Richard was distracted; Kate was there, her camera out and at the ready, standing at the verge where the grass gave it up in favor of a scattering of chippings and the tarmac road.

"I can ride a bike and row a boat and that's about the limit. Look; I think the cattle are nearly here." Richard shaded his eyes with one hand. The road out towards the river and Route 123 jogged slightly, so he could not see very far. A horseman came around the bend, then another, their hooves clattering on the tarmac. To the west at their back, the clouds were mounting up in the pale sky; creamy mounds of cloud edged with fiery gold, sweeping shadows and light across the distant line of pale green hills dotted with dark green stands of oak. It was an unexpectedly theatrical setting, one which Richard pedaled through twice a day without noticing any outstanding aesthetic merit. At that very moment; whether it was the clouds, the anticipation or whatever the setting was almost epic-movie perfect. David Lean would have given his left testicle to get it on film in one uninterrupted take.

The first horseman was the perfect movie cowboy; a tall, fair young man, slouching easily in the saddle of a Palomino horse, a golden horse with a dark mane and tail. The horse seemed to have a sense of occasion which the rider lacked; strutting along as if on parade, and there the mass of cattle following, tossing heads and red hides, shouldering each other as they followed.

"Santa Gertrudis," Miss Letty remarked. "Stephen has a prize-winning herd of them. Also of Angus and Hereford. And a number of original Texas longhorns. Those, I believe, he keeps in the main pasture. The horns, you see – a hazard."

"Amazing," Richard breathed, and Miss Letty asked, "How so?"

"I usually see them as sides and quarters, already prepped."

"Ah. You have an appreciation for where your chops and burgers come from," Miss Letty's sarcasm was restrained, which Richard appreciated.

"Well, of course. I like a good feed and I am not a vegan. Just interesting to me to see a year's worth of good beef dinners on the hoof, as it is."

"Visions of steaks, stews and ragouts are dancing through your head?" Miss Letty had a wry turn of humor which Richard had really not observed to date.

"Yes," and then Richard's good humor turned all … well, to something. Kate with her camera dashed out into the road, in the path of that first horseman. Yes, of course the spectacle would be irresistible; a spirited horse, a handsome young rider in all the accoutrements of a classic cowboy. But that wasn't the part which turned Richard's attitude in the directions of sack, ash-cloth and discouragement. It was that Kate – his Kate – blew him a kiss on her fingertips.

And the cowboy on the Palomino laughed and returned the gesture.

This evening was not going to turn out well.

Disruptions and Eruptions

"Why, it's Bodie Madison," Miss Letty observed. "Caroline Bodie-Madison's oldest boy. He spent summers here, although the Madisons live in Beeville."

"He looks quite the dashing young hero," Richard replied sourly.

"I believe he follows the rodeo circuit, when he is not working for Doctor Wyler. Riding and roping are his events. Jessica tells me that he does moderately well at it."

Richard eyed the horseman with loathing. He did not recall ever having taken such an instant dislike to someone before, unless it was Phillip Noel-Barrett. On second thought, it had taken at least a week or so for Noel-Barrett's essential foulness to manifest itself, but Richard had never claimed to be an acute observer of the human condition. Now the Palomino went past the spectators on the wall; Richard whispered "Tosser!" under his breath. Miss Letty couldn't have heard, he was certain, for the cattle were following, a column of lumbering red, piebald, black, and fawn-colored backs spilling from around the far bend in the road. They came on, bunching five and six abreast, some at a trot, others pausing to stare with mild bovine concern, sometimes lowing in protest.

The sound of their hooves on the paved road was a thunderous clatter, punctuated by inarticulate shouting and whistling from their mounted escorts. The riders were in constant motion, their horses pirouetting and dashing hither and yon, patrolling up and down the column, rather like someone attempting to control a rolling trickle of mercury by stroking it judiciously with a feather to make it go in the desired direction.

He was briefly aware that Doc Wyler halted his own horse as the passed them, saluting Miss Letty with a touch of his right hand to his hat-brim; Doc Wyler and the odious Bodie were the only ones of the riders wearing what Richard thought to be proper cowboy headgear – all the rest were bare-headed, or wearing billed caps, many with commercial logos on them. He was vaguely offended by this; one should dress appropriately for the occasion; no matter <u>what</u> the occasion.

"I hope they can keep them together," Miss Letty gathered up her handbag and the handkerchief upon which she had been sitting, when the last of the cattle and horsemen had gone past. "It sounds as if it is going to rain again." She looked at the western sky, where purple-tinged clouds had closed up tight against the sunset, although an occasional beam escaped through shifting gaps. "I suppose that I should be getting along."

"Allow me to walk with you," Richard suggested. "Let me get my bicycle…"

"If it will not be an inconvenience for you," Miss Letty replied, just as Kate Heisel reappeared from the thinning crowd. The last of the Wyler outriders had already disappeared, leaving only the evidence of fresh deposits of manure on the road that they had ever passed that way.

"Richard, I'm sorry – I have to ask for a raincheck on supper tonight." She gasped, pink with exertion and excitement. "Doc Wyler has arranged for dinner at the ranch for all the hands and volunteers … and I have to get the rest of the story tonight and file it with Acey … that's my editor. It's my job and I have to leap on it, right away. You don't mind, do you? I mean, tomorrow evening would be perfect, if that's all right."

"Certainly, Miss Heisel," Richard answered, little caring that disappointment made him sullen. "Do what you need to do. I'll be where I need to be."

"Thanks, Richard!" Kate smiled, a flash of relief brightening her expression. "I'll see you tomorrow evening then."

"Fine." Richard had no idea of why he sounded so grudging, unless it was the sight of Kate blowing a kiss to the dashing cowboy on the spectacular horse. It couldn't possibly be that he had anticipated impressing Kate with that he did best – cooking a splendid, personally-crafted dinner for the only woman that he had spent a night with in almost two years. Never mind that the two of them had passed that night sleeping chastely in separate beds. It was a night and in the same bedroom, which ought to count for something.

"Katherine is a very able young woman," Miss Letty remarked. "Mr. McClain reposes a great deal of trust in her, not only for her reporting, but for her photography. She also seems to be quite adept with this 'social media' matter which I hear so many younger people talk so much about."

"She does make things happen," Richard said, thinking of how the Luna City Players last production had been turned upside down when her photograph of Romeo Gonzales went viral.

"I am certain that you two will have a perfectly splendid supper," Miss Letty sounded absolutely certain of that. Richard doubted it, even doubted that there would be a meal at all. "I hope that the rain doesn't spoil everything for you two."

"It's not the rain spoiling everything," Richard grumbled. Miss Letty sighed. Richard felt that she looked sideways at him, and might have considered saying something but tactfully forbore. In silence, they walked the three short blocks, past the untidy sprawl of the Gonzales Auto Repair and Body shop. Beyond that business, Luna City raveled out to widely spaced houses; houses with their attendant sheds and garages, a few small enterprises, interspersed with thickets of brush and small trees.

They took a short-cut of a well-trodden path which came out behind the VFW, and around to the Tip-Top, where Miss Letty thanked him for his companionship, and made no comment on his brooding silence. There was no traffic on 123 at that moment, but Miss Letty looked both ways carefully and walked briskly across to where the old McAllister house sat, serene behind the white picket fence and the bronze historical marker on a pole, which designated it as the oldest residential structure in Luna City. *(There was one older such in existence, constructed of adobe brick, save for a few traces, it had melted back into the hard clay soil of which it had been made around the year 1808 or thereabouts, not to be rediscovered until an archeological excavation in the 1960s. The Old McAllister House, constructed in 1857 of thick quarried blocks of limestone, was square and sturdy enough for a fortified castle, and not in any imminent danger of melting.)*

Still in a depressed and surly mood, Richard considered going into the Tip-Top and purchasing a couple of bottles of the most drinkable of the cheap wine on the shelves. Anything with a cork, as opposed to a screw-cap, would be considered quality tipple at the Tip-Top. Although there was always the stuff in a box … the finest *vin du cartonnage* around, and he was certainly in a mood to drink to excess. He was about to go in, when Roman Gonzales's pickup truck pulled into the gravel parking lot, and Roman rolled down the window.

"Yo – Ricardo! Glad we spotted you. Look, man, the storms are rolling in tonight. Joe and Horatio have passed the word; either sandbag your place at the Age or evacuate."

Richard gaped at him. Harry Vaughn emerged from the passenger-side door. "Look, son, the campground is just at flood-stage level. I've already driven the convertible to high ground, Roman was just giving me a lift to go back and get the van. Throw that beater of yours in the back and let's get moving. Time's a' wasting."

"But I just came from the briefing," Richard gabbled. "They said there wasn't much danger of a flood to speak of. It was only precautionary."

"So it is, son, but I got a bad feeling about these storms blowing in," Harry Vaughn replied. "My rheumatiz an' bunions are aching to beat the band. No matter what the smart fellows at the Weather Channel say, the rheumatiz and bunions have never lied to me yet."

"Get in, Ricardo," Roman urged, "Time's a-wasting and the daylight is going." Such was the conviction in both their voices that Richard sighed, tossed the bike into the back of the pickup, and scrambled up after it. Roman spun out of the parking lot so fast that he scattered a spurt of gravel after.

He had a splendid view of the San Antonio River as Roman's truck crossed the bridge over it. His heart sank down to the level of his shoes. The river was a mere four or five feet short of the level of the road, higher than he ever could have imagined. The tops of trees and bushes growing along the sandy banks were now but green and leafy blobs, waving desperately in a pale-brown torrent which had submerged all but the topmost branches. *How had that come about?* He rode this way every day, coming and going from the Age to his place of employment and never had he observed the river at his place to be any more than a desultory trickle connecting a series of shallow pools, amid rocks and sweeps of gravel and tortured thickets of reeds and brush. The truck bumped down the unmarked driveway to the Age of Aquarius. The rain had not done all that much to return that unpaved expanse to its' natural state, thanks to repeated applications of gravel over the course of reconstruction. *Having lost the first Age to fire, were the Grants about to lose the second to water?* That was a dispiriting thought.

Roman pulled next to Harry Vaughn's parked van, whose owner leaped out a great deal more spryly than Richard would have thought possible. Harry went to the driver's side of his van without a backwards look. Roman wheeled around and backed up his truck to the Airstream. When he parked, and cut the engine, Richard scrambled down from the back.

"I don't know what the emergency is!" Richard gasped, as Roman emerged from the cab. "I just came from the meeting and everyone assured me, solo and chorus that these are just precautions."

"Look, Ricardo," Roman said patiently. "Sure, just precautions – but better safe than sorry, OK, *hermano*? Between Harry Vaughn's bunions and Judy Grant's spirit advisors, not to mention the KSAT-4 weather forecasters <u>and</u> Abuelita, everyone has a bad feeling about the next couple of days. You saw how the water's risen in just the last half a day? You stay here, you might be OK. If I haul this old tin tiny house up to the Grants you'll be safer still, but you might not be able to get to work in the morning. <u>If</u> you do, guarantee that it will be pissing down rain on you, every foot of the way. You, Ricardo, are an essential utility in this town, not to mention being Abuelita's favorite Food Channel crush so you get the luxury treatment. Hop in, make sure that everything is bolted down, and I'll haul this oversized vintage tin can to wherever in Luna is OK with you as long as it's above the high-water mark."

"And the Straw Castle…" Richard began, until Roman cut him off short.

"Like I said; I park you there, likely you won't be able to get to work tomorrow unless you have a boat handy. Harry does – you don't. The Grants have already begun inflating that patent flood-barrier thing that their boys sent them, so taking the trailer up there is not an option for much longer. Where do you want me to take your little tin-can-cottage?"

"To the Café…" Richard acquiesced. It seemed there was no choice. He grabbed Miss Letty's gift plant from where it hung from one of the roof supports, went into his little tin cell, ensuring that all the cupboard doors were latched, and that plant and dangling baby plants, the teapot and his mug were safely stowed away. When he emerged again, Roman was attending to the tires of the old Airstream with one of those small compressors. The Airstream was already hitched up to Roman's truck.

"I don't think this thing has been moved in thirty years," he said, red-faced with exertion. "It'll be a bumpy ride and thank your patron saint that we don't have to take it very far, or go very fast when we're doing it. We're off as soon as I uncouple the utilities. Good thing we made certain the connections weren't all corroded shut when we fixed this up for you."

"Everything inside is secure," Richard said, thinking that everything was happening all too fast. He hated disrupting his routine.

"Good," Roman detached his compressor and hefted it into the truck bed, next to Richard's bike. "Hop in, we'll make this quick."

"One more thing." Richard hastily folded up the two lawn chairs which adorned his patio, and the plastic flamingo with the sign depending from its neck: *Bienvenido a casa*! Yes, tacky and an offense against good taste in garden décor, but the pink plastic flamingo on wire legs was a gift of the Gonzalez-Gonzales clan, and damned if he was going to lose that as well.

There was no place to put the flamingo but in his lap for the short, slow and tense journey down to the main road, over the bridge and past the Tip-Top and Miss Letty's. Twilight was falling, along with a gentle misting of rain as they trundled past the Tip-Top. Richard momentarily regretted not going in for that *vin du cartonnage*. It looked as if the Tip-Top was still open, too.

"It's just the leading edge of the storm," Roman remarked, as he flicked on the headlights. "On the weather radar, this sucker looks like it is stalled over Bexar County, just thinking about moving slowly north-east. Ricardo, man, I'm glad to have you and your crib moved to higher ground. It's gonna get bad tomorrow. You want me to park your place in front or in back?"

"In back, if there is room enough." Richard answered. "And there are a couple of electrical outlets by the back door. I suppose I can thread an electrical cord out through a window or something."

"I got plenty of extension cords, if you don't," Roman chuckled. "Nothing like a good short commute to work, Ricardo! Means you can sleep in tomorrow morning – a whole half hour."

"I imagine so," Richard added this relocation of his home and the cancelled dinner with Kate to his list of simmering resentments. He liked the bike ride in the pre-dawn hours, although he knew Roman was correct about doing it in the pouring rain. It would not have been a pleasant experience. He sourly hoped that Kate was having a rotten time at Doc Wyler's supper for his cowboys. *She could have been having dinner with him!*

"Right. Have you settled around in back in no time!" Roman sounded quite chipper, now that his good deed for the day was nearly accomplished. "Abuelita will be will be happy when I report in. I hafta say, I wouldn't have got any peace for weeks from anyone, especially Abuelita, if we had left you at the Age."

With the practiced dexterity of someone who did this kind of thing daily, Roman stopped his truck in the alley behind the Café, stopped it just in front of the little garage in back of Stein's Wild West Round-up, cranked the steering wheel all the way over, and backed the Airstream at right angles onto the crumbled pavement square which made up the mews area behind the Café. This was a small area sheltering several industrial-sized wheelie bins, and a pair of timber-framed raised beds in which flourished Richard's selection of home-grown herbs. Roman performed this with such dexterity that the Airstream slotted neatly in between the herb beds and the wall of the building next to the Café. This would provide Richard with a view of his herbs and the pocket garden that the Steins maintained in the back of their shop for the duration of his stay.

"All righty then, Ricardo!" Roman let down the support which balanced the trailer when it was parked, and unhitched it from his truck with the same alacrity with which he had attached it. The folding lawn chairs were already leaning against the trailer. Richard stuck the plastic flamingo's legs into the nearest herb bed. "Pleasant dreams – sleep tight and don't let the bedbugs bite. See ya in the morning. I prolly won't have any jobs to get to, the way the weather is shaping up, but if they want me to help fill sandbags, I wanna have some good coffee in me before work starts."

"In the morning, then," Richard replied, with a noticeable lack of enthusiasm. Roman fished around in the massive tool locker in the back of his truck, and handed Richard a long coil of extension cord.

"Hook this up to one of your GFI outlets, and you're good to go," he said, as the rain, which had been a mere and half-hearted drizzle, became slightly more aggressive. Roman waved from the driver's seat and roared off, leaving Richard with the extension cord in his hands and depression in his heart. He really wished that he had gotten that *vin du cartonnage* at the Tip-Top while he had the time. There was a jug of Sefton Grant's peerless mustang wine stashed in the trailer, but that was too good a vintage for the purposes of getting stinking blotto on, so moderation was therefore forced upon him. Probably just as well.

High Water

The rain it fell, fell in Biblical quantities during the early part of that night, drumming in a gentle but regular manner on the tin roof of the Airstream, sluicing off the adjoining roofs, water flowing in streams along the low places and gutters of Luna City. Richard slept lightly, although more deeply than he expected, after having the place which was his home wrenched like a precious jewel from its' customary setting and transplanted to another place. After dining on a solitary serving of sole almandine, and one or two glasses of Sefton's marvelous mustang elixir, he retreated to his bed, tired and in a no more than slightly mellow condition, only to be awakened sometime in the wee hours by his cellphone ringing imperiously. No, not to be denied, although he did try ignoring it. No such luck – it began ringing again, not three minutes later. Richard crawled from bed, fumbled his way to where he had left his trousers hanging from a hook in the narrow closet, and fished out the cellphone.

"Mum, it's … two in the morning here," he squinted at the faintly illuminated hands of his alarm clock.

"Sounds like a personal problem," Joe Vaughn drawled, sounding so normal that Richard didn't detect the urgent undertone in his voice at first. "Ricardo, sorry to wake you at this hour, but we got a bad situation here. We got to call in all volunteers, and at this moment, you are one of 'em. That is, one of them that we haven't already called in."

"What's happened," Richard's heart sank right into his shoes, or would have, if he hadn't been barefoot. "It's not something on fire, is it? I'm barely trained."

"High water," Joe Vaughn replied. "And we're tapped out, boat-wise. Look, I'm on my way already, with Uncle Harry and his. Get dressed. Something heavy, with long sleeves, boots and gloves if you got 'em. I'll brief you when I get there. Five minutes."

Approximately four minutes later, his phone rang again.

"I'm outside your place," Joe said. "Where the hell are you?"

"Leaving a note for Araceli to open in the morning, and carry on until I get there," Richard replied. He locked the back door of the Café behind him, seeing the impatient flashing lights of one of Luna City's SUVs parked out in the alley. For once, it had stopped raining, and the moon peeped coyly from behind the shifting clouds. By that fitful light, Richard could see that it had a small boat-trailer hitched onto it.

The passenger-side door opened, and Harry Vaughn called to him. "Get in the back, son. We got us a serious matter of life and death."

"Pull the other one, it has bells on," Richard replied, his hopes that this was some kind of jape fading as Harry Vaughn snorted.

"I shit you not, son, this is real. You're good with boats, they tell me."

"I rowed for my school and crewed the school yacht as well." Richard answered. "Years ago, but I guess you could say I'm good with boats. What does this have to do with … oh, no. I thought you had people to deal with this. The county people, with their fancy rescue boats!"

"Are all called out, all across the county," Joe didn't take his eyes from the road in front of him, as his radio crackled again. "The nearest of them is at least forty minutes out from the situation and the rest are even farther. Yeah, put her through," he said into the radio. "We've just collected Richard; we're on our way to as close as we can get. The upper bridge is under water," he added over his shoulder to Richard. "Elmendorf and Lavernia got slammed by the storm in the last few hours … Ma'am," he said into the radio. "Hold tight, stay calm – we've got a boat on the way. ETA … no more than twenty minutes, I promise."

"Hurry, please hurry." The woman's voice shook. To Richard, it sounded as if she were doing her best to keep terror at bay. "The first floor is filled with water … we're in the large upstairs bedroom, the one with the big window looking northward."

"That's where they'll be coming from," Joe reassured her. "That's good. Stay with us. Do you have any flashlights … can you show a light, Miss … what is your name? I'm Joe – I'm with the local police department. You hear me OK?"

"Susan," the woman replied. "Susan Hartman … No, I don't think we have a flash – but I do. A little one, on my keys. Oh, please hurry! There are things, things in the water hitting the house. My husband thinks it will come apart at any moment…We're in the dark, there aren't any lights, the power went out, hours ago!"

"We're coming as fast as we can – just hold on." Joe reassured her. "If you can find your keys, start showing the light in about … ten minutes. Flash it for five seconds, every minute or so. How many others are there with you, Susan?"

"This was supposed to be a holiday weekend!" Susan wailed. In Richard's experienced estimation, she was about two seconds from achieving total hysterical meltdown. But to his vague astonishment, Susan did pull herself together. Her voice sounded much calmer in her next words. "There are seven of us and our dog. My husband and I, our two sons and a daughter. My sister Ellen, and her baby. Oh, please come … the whole house is shaking!"

"I understand, Susan." Joe had better control of his voice than Susan did, even at the mention of a baby. "OK … I have your cellphone number. Go ahead and hang up … no, don't worry. One of our guys is going to call you right back. He'll stay on the line with you, all the way. Take a deep breath, Susan – keep calm. All of your lives depend on keeping calm…"

Over the crackling radio came Susan's voice … "My husband – he's a strong swimmer. There's this rope. He's going to try and take it to … no, Todd!" That ended on a scream. The silence, save for the crackle of the police radio was an agony, as Joe Vaughn threaded the water-washed streets Luna City which lay to the west and south, adjoining the river. To Richard, it looked as if Joe was heading towards the meadow and parking lot on the riverbank behind the VFW. Only, under the shifting silver moonlight – the river was coming to join them. Harry half-turned in the seat, and enlightened Richard in a whisper.

"She's calling from one of the Mills Farm cottages – the one down by the river-edge. I reckon the water came up all of apiece and caught them asleep. Lew says they called all their guests early on, but these folks didn't answer their land-line, they lost power, and then the line got carried away. Why in the deep blue blazes they didn't pay any mind to evacuation warnings; out-of-towners, I reckon."

"Susan!" Joe fairly shouted into his radio. "Susan, talk to me – what happened just now! Susan – are you there?"

"I am," her voice sounded desolate, pitiful. Richard could hear a dog barking in the background, and the shrieks of children, frightened children. "Todd … he was taking the rope, we can see the riverbank. So close. I can see lights, there is someone there. But there was a big tree … it took Todd. It was moving so fast in the water! I heard him shout, I'm sure I did. And now the rope is just hanging there in the water." Her words ended on a sob, as Joe drove into the now-flooded parking lot behind the

VFW and the Tip-Top, and turned in a half-circle. There was just enough moonlight that Richard could see water pooling around the VFW building, with barbeque drum and picnic table-top like islands in waist-deep water.

"Susan," Joe commanded, as he set the parking brake, an expression on his face as grim as Richard had ever observed. "Listen to me, Susan. Focus on the here and now. We're coming for you. Todd will be OK; the odds favor him – you said he was a strong swimmer…" Joe nodded to Harry, and held the radio away from his face. "Get the boat launched now, gentle-grunts. I'll stay on the line with her until you're ready."

Still disbelieving the situation which he had gotten himself into, Richard clambered out of the back, splashing into water up to his knees. Harry was already at the winch which held the prow of his boat steady – the boat which had been loaded onto the top of his van for the long drive from Alaska. It was a lightweight, shallow-draft fifteen-footer of rather battered aluminum, with two seats and a small motor about the half the size of the Café's Hobart mixer mounted in the stern, already dipping blades cautiously into the floodwater.

"Can you back 'er up a little more, Joe?" Harry called. "Not quite deep enough."

The SUV jerked, and backed a little more, until water came up almost to the rear bumper. "Now we got 'her!" Harry shouted, frantically spinning the winch. "Shove from your side – that's it! She hardly draws at all – crack open a six-pack and ride for miles on the foam."

The boat slid off the trailer and bobbed freely, as light as a feather on the dark water. Richard scrambled in, rolling without any grace over the gunwale and landed painfully on the pair of oars, a pile of life-vests and other gear thrown into the bottom. Uncle Harry arrived a split-second later over the other gunwale.

"Good to go!" Uncle Harry shouted, and Joe waved from the window of the police SUV. In a moment, the lights had vanished in the direction of the faint lights of Luna City.

"I suppose that some point, you will tell me what is going on," Richard demanded, "And where we are supposed to be going? And why the blue blazes am I involved?"

Uncle Harry drawled, heavily sarcastic, "You ain't figured it out yet, son? We're heading down-river to Mills Farm for an extra-high-water rescue. You're with me for three reasons; you're a volunteer fireman, you know boats, and nephew o' mine flat-out ordered me not to risk it alone. Set the oars in those locks and get to it, son; time's a' wasting."

"That engine is purely ornamental, then?" Richard snapped.

Uncle Harry's voice dropped, to a dangerous whisper, as Richard sat there, obdurate. "'Fraid it is, son – most times, anyway. Cranky old beast, always takes a while to fire 'er up, after a long time sitting."

"Nice," Richard observed, heavy on the sarcasm. "Very, very nice. I am extraordinarily fond of being press-ganged in the middle of the night into a bout of fruitless chivalry, in a boat with a useless engine."

"Call it chivalry or not," Uncle Harry replied, an ice-cold edge in his voice. "But tell yourself that it's everything to do with not sitting on your aspidistra, when a woman and a bunch of children are screaming in mortal terror because the house around them is about to fall apart and you might be able to get to them in time to save their lives. And if you can't get to them …" Uncle Harry's cellphone suddenly cheeped, the sound loud against the water lapping the sides of the boat. "… in time, at least you can look at yourself in the mirror and know that you tried. Now, pick up those oars, son, or I'll knock your block off with one of them, ninety-two or no."

Richard gaped at him for a moment; no, the old codger was entirely serious. He fitted oars, and positioned himself on the center bench. Oh, god – this was not going to go very well. The oars were almost too short, the boat was all the wrong shape for efficient sculling, and he would have to depend on Harry for navigation, since he would face the stern to pull at the oars with more energy. Nonetheless, within a minute or two, he had edged the boat into the main current, out on a ghostly river under the elusive moon, and from that moment, it was only a matter of keeping it on a straight heading, silently and swiftly going downstream. Thank God, the rain had stopped. He was taken back at how wide the river had become, how deep, and powerful the current was, like a rip-water tide, drawing them on and on, in their cockleshell of a tin boat.

"Miz Hartman," Uncle Harry drawled into his cellphone. "You doin' OK then? We're in the water and on our way, don't you fret none about us. We'll be at your position in two shakes of a lamb's tail… just hold on … a mite to your left, Richard, that's a tree that looks pretty solid. No, just talking to my partner now, Miz Hartman. That's good. Little more to the left, Richard. "

Richard could not hear Susan Hartman, save as a series of squawks and squeaks on Harry Vaugh's cellphone, which to him was something of a relief, since it meant he could concentrate on sculling: lean forward, dig the oars deep in, brace, pull… and lift. Repeat. *Lean, dig, brace, pull, and lift*. He was sweating, in spite of the chill before ten minutes had passed. He could hear Harry talking, throughout – stalwart and soothing, assuring Susan of their progress, holding his cellphone in one hand, while he fiddled with the recalcitrant and aged outboard motor with the other. Prime with a bit of petrol, adjust the choke and throttle, after each adjustment, administer a skillful and violent pull of the flywheel cord … and nothing, through a good half-dozen cycles of this process.

To his mild surprise, they were soon gliding around the bend in the river, below the Age. Richard had never seen it from this angle before; the Amazing Straw Castle Aquarius, tall, pale, and proud, among the stand of guardian oaks. A few dim lights shown from the upper windows, so at least the Grants were safe, although he could see those lights and coy, transient moonlight reflecting on the dark water which lapped around the hill upon which it stood.

"Miz Hartman," Uncle Harry said, at last, as they swept around that last bend before Mills Farm began on the western bank. "I b'lieve we are in sight of your position. Go ahead and begin flashing that little flashlight of yours … got it! Look – I will shine a light from this here little boat, but I'm going to have to break the telephone connection, once you see us. But keep flashing that little light of yours, let it shine, shine, shine, just like the song we used to sing in Sunday School. You hear me, ma'am? Good. Tell me that you see this…"

A bright light stabbed into the darkness over Richard's head; Uncle Harry had one of those massive water-proof battery spotlights, which to Richard's night-accustomed sight shone as brightly as the sun.

"Be bloody careful with that thing!" he hissed, temporarily blinded by the brilliance of it all. Uncle Harry took no mind, but spoke into his cellphone. "All right, Miz Hartman – just a few more minutes. I'm going to hang up my phone now that we're in sight. We're going to come up right below the window where you are, so you all be ready to hand the children down to us first. All right, Miz Hartman, we're nearly there … good."

Richard cast a quick glance over his shoulder; yes, he could see a tiny flicker of light in a darker shadow ahead, a dark and regular shape of walls and a peaked roof; another island in an impossibly wide stretch of turbulent water. In the silence between strokes of the oars, he heard the faint distant roar of a generator, and worked out that they must be coming from the main establishment at Mills Farm, high on the hills above the river. Like the Age, this was a familiar view, but from the other direction. Uncle Harry nestled the battery spotlight in the pile of lifejackets and bent to fiddling with the outboard motor again. The engine caught with a roar on the first pull. Uncle Harry shouted in pure triumph and gestured to Richard to ship the oars, which he did with grateful relief.

"Take this and shine it on the house," Uncle Harry commanded, handing Richard the battery spotlight. "Good! Looks like there is a bit of porch roof, lower down. I'll bring 'er right up next to it. I don't by god want to tie up, since the whole place looks ready to go, so you'll have to help them down from the window and into the boat."

"How many will this hold?" Richard asked. Uncle Harry grinned.

"Max capacity six adults; we'll be right on the limit. Good thing you don't have to row any more, son."

"Thank you so much," Richard took the spotlight, and crouching low, scrambled to the prow. Yes, somewhat dangerous, standing up in a moving small boat, as Uncle Harry jockeyed the boat to and fro, sliding crossways to the current so as to bring it sidelong against the porch roof, the lower edge of which was under water. Even as Richard trained the spot on the dark square of a window, in which flickered the tiny glimmer of a pen-light sized flashlight small enough to attach to a ring of keys, there was an ominous cracking sound, for all the world like a massive tree branch breaking. The roofline was no longer quite as square against the sky as it had been a moment before. A woman screamed, and the whole structure seemed to lurch. A pale figure moved against the house wall; a sobbing child in footie pajamas lowered from the window by the wrists, feet dangling eighteen inches or so from the roof.

The boat bumped solidly against the porch roof. Richard abandoned the spotlight, and launched himself from the boat onto that slanting roof, landing on his hands and knees. The roof seemed to flex and buckle, sagging at one end.

"Got you!" he gasped, lowering the child the rest of the way. The kid – a boy, judging by the hair-cut – struggled frantically, screaming "Mommy!" Richard called up to the pale face in the window, "Send down the next one!" He grasped the back of the boy's pajamas like a cat handling a kitten by the scruff of its neck and tumbled him into the boat. The porch roof sagged even more. There came another of those ominous cracking sounds. The second child, a slightly older boy, made an easier transit down, since his bare feet nearly reached the roof below. Richard shoved him into the boat. As he did that, he was nearly knocked off his feet by the sudden rush of a large yellow retriever, leaping down from the window.

"Pepper!" called the older boy. The dog bounded into the boat and sat there, tail wagging as if he had done something clever. Now a girl about the age of Araceli's daughter Angelica straddled the windowsill, a woman's pale face hovering behind her.

"Come on, girlie, easy does it," Richard reached up towards her, as she brought her other leg around. "Come on, I'll catch you."

She nodded, reaching down; either she jumped, or her mother pushed her. Richard caught her full weight, which nearly toppled him backwards into the boat. He didn't even set her down but dropped her bodily into it after the boys. The porch underneath him rocked as badly as the boat did. Now for the women, having gotten the children ... oh, blast – the baby.

The first woman, hardly more than a teenager herself, was already scrambling from the window. Richard steadied her, as the porch – no, the whole structure shifted, to the tune of another series of those ominous cracking sounds. The outboard engine roared, and Uncle Harry shouted, "Shift it, son, the whole place is about to go!"

"In the boat!" Richard shoved her towards it and turned towards the window, where the last woman – Susan, undoubtedly – stood with a wailing infant in her arms. "No time! Drop the kiddie, I'll catch!"

No time, no time, although the moments seemed to stretch out endlessly, as endless as a summer day in Bickley; Susan held the infant over the windowsill, leaning down as far as she could, and let go. Richard, otherwise an agnostic, sent up a prayer for a hitherto unrevealed skill to whichever deity happened to be listening. The wailing, soaking-wet morsel dropped into his arms. Richard tucked the baby into the crook of his elbow and reached up towards Susan, who came scrambling over the windowsill. To his utter horror, the porch roof dipped under as it ripped bodily away from the wall, rocking underfoot like a fun-house floor. The roar of Harry's outboard was lost in a storm of breaking lumber, as the house shimmied violently, and the three of them tumbled into the boat. The baby didn't even pause for breath, but continued sobbing.

"I've certainly had days like that, old chap," Richard commented to the infant, as the younger woman took it from him. Like her offspring, she was also sobbing. She was trying to say something to Richard, but such was his state of mind, and her emotion that he couldn't make it out. At their backs, the house timbers gave one last almighty cannonade as they broke free from whatever foundation had anchored it in place. It tipped to one side and was gone, as if whisked out of sight by some almighty force, leaving the boat rocking in the swift current. Richard, feeling as if he had been pummeled in a spin-dryer filled with boulders, retrieved the spotlight, and slowly stepped between the sobbing children and two women stammering their incoherent gratitude. He could barely hear them, over the rumbling outboard, and the violent river current slapping the boat sides. It did not escape his notice that Harry regarded him with mild approval.

"Good job," Uncle Harry didn't mince words, or even spend much time on them. "I knew I'd need a man good with boats. Nice catch, too. You ever played football? Real football."

Richard had never thought Americans were much for understatement. Rather the opposite, really – but Uncle Harry might almost have been English.

"Piece of cake." Richard raised his voice to be heard over the outboard. "No, footie was never my sport. Now what?"

Uncle Harry scratched his jaw, and replied after a theatrical moment of thought, "With this current and no engine, I didn't put too much hope in getting back to where we launched from, so I planned on a secondary retrieval point, a piece downstream. Got the engine going now, but we're pretty loaded down. So, secondary it is. At the bottom of Jaimie Gonzales' place. Pretty good little meadow, nice slope to it, access road through the ranch above water – just another mile or two downstream. You wanna call Joe, let him know everything is copacetic?"

"Of course," Richard replied. "But I … left my own cellphone behind. In a hurry, you see. Saving lives and all. "

"Here," Uncle Harry fished in the pocket of his battered Carhartt jacket, and handed Richard his own cellphone. "You call. He's on my contact list. You know how to work one of these?"

"I was born sufficiently close to the end of the century to be familiar with the technology," Richard answered, in a particularly acid tone of voice. Uncle Harry's cellphone was the same model as the one which he had tossed into the river, the morning after arriving in Luna City. Swift work to scroll through the contact numbers and auto-dial, hearing Joe pick up.

"Harry – Jesus F—king Christ, where the hell are you?" Joe said, straight-away. He answered on the first ring, whereby Richard knew that Joe had been waiting on tenterhooks for a call from that number.

"It's me, Joe," Richard replied. "On your uncle's cellie. We're OK. Piece of cake, actually. We got them all out from the house. All but … Mr. Hart-something. He went out before we got to them, trying to swim a rope to dry land."

"We got him," Joe replied. "Battered as hell, but he'll be OK. Came ashore, and Lew Dubois' folks picked him up. Meet you at the secondary?"

"Perfect," Richard answered. Only then did he break out in an ice-cold sweat, thinking how close he had come to slipping from the sagging porch roof and into that dark, furiously-rushing water.

Celia Hayes & Jeanne Hayden

Dramatic High-Water Rescue!

From the Karnesville Weekly Beacon
By Katherine Heisel, Staff Reporter

An extended family vacationing at Mills Farm over the Memorial Day weekend were rescued from high floodwaters along the San Antonio River early Saturday morning by two volunteers from the Luna City Volunteer Fire Department. Todd and Susan Hartman, their three children, Emily (12), Jeffrey (8) and Nicholas (3), along with Susan's sister Jennifer King and her infant daughter Kendra (4 months) were spending the holiday weekend at Mills Farm. The Hartmans and Mrs. King, all from Corpus Christi, were staying in the luxury Riverside Cottage, built on pilings with a small private dock in a secluded location at the river's edge. Mills Farm management revealed on Monday that electrical power and the land-line to the cottage were severed sometime in the early evening, just before the Karnes County Emergency center began warning residents of immanent flooding along the banks of the San Antonio River throughout Karnes County. In the rush of alarms over imminent flooding, the presence of the Hartman party was overlooked. Mr. and Mrs. Hartman had turned off their cellphones and gone to bed early, unaware that significant amounts of rain had already fallen in the area of Lavernia and Floresville. By the time that they were awakened after midnight, by rising water rushing into the ground floor, knocking over furnishings, and breaking windows and doors, they were already cut off from dry land. They retreated to the upper floor, together with their golden retriever, Pepper, and Susan Hartman frantically called the Luna City Police Department.

The local disaster preparedness center had already been activated *(see related story, p. 3)* but all three Karnes County rescue launches had already been dispatched to other emergencies by the time that Susan

Hartman's call was put through. *(see related stories, p. 3 and 4 for other accounts of high-water flood rescues during this last weekend.)* None was closer than forty-five minutes. In the Riverside Cottage, the water had risen nearly to the second floor, and Mrs. Hartman reported that the building itself was shaking. "I didn't see how we could make it out," she said to this reporter. "Things were crashing into the sides of the building, and the river was flowing so fast! There was no way that Todd or Jenny or I could have taken the children and swam through it."

There was only one boat available at short notice – a fifteen-foot aluminum launch owned by Mr. Harold Vaughn, a long-time law officer, recently returned to Luna City after three decades' residence in Alaska. With the cooperation of his nephew, Chief Joseph Vaughn, Chief of the Luna City PD, and a single LCVFD volunteer, Mr. Vaughn took to the water in an attempt to rescue the Hartman family before it was too late. Mr. Vaughn, aged 92 *(but as fit as a man thirty years younger)* spoke briefly to this reporter, and downplayed the desperate gamble that this effort was: in the pitch dark, on a flooded river, choked with fallen trees, trash and debris bought downstream by the high water. "It's like the Coast Guard says: You have to go out. You may not come back – but you <u>have</u> to go."

And go they did, launching that small boat with an erratically-functioning outboard engine, on a flooded river in the dark. Mr. Vaughn began talking with Susan Hartman on the cellphone once they were on the water. "It was so enormously comforting," Mrs. Hartman said to this reporter, when interviewed at the Karnesville Medical Center, where she and her family were taken for treatment after their rescue. "We were so desperate – Todd, my husband, he took a rope and tried to swim to shore. But he was struck by a floating tree and carried away. The children and Jenny and I … we were certain we were going to die, right then and there. But Harry – Mr. Vaughn, he kept talking to us, encouraging us, telling us to be calm, what to do when they got there. He told me to shine this light…" Mrs. Hartman held up a ring of keys with a tiny flashlight attached. "So that he would know where we were. I was never so grateful for anything in my life as I was, once I saw Mr. Vaughn's boat."

The launch was just barely large enough for the two women, three children, the baby – and Pepper the dog, who leaped cheerfully into the boat. Susan Hartman handed down the children from a window over the first-floor covered porch to the unnamed LCVFD volunteer assisting Mr. Vaughn. The volunteer, who wishes to remain anonymous, placed the children in the boat, and assisted Susan Hartman to safety, just as the house began disintegrating under the power of the flood. "Another two minutes would have been too late!" Susan Hartman told this reporter, as she and her sister and the children were released from the Karnesville Med Center, having suffered nothing worse than brief exposure to the cold and wet. "We are so grateful to Mr. Vaughn and the volunteers who were able to rescue us in time. We owe them everything."

Todd Hartman, a corporate lawyer who suffered a punctured lung and other injuries in his attempt to obtain help for his family, has indicated that he intends to bring suit against Mills Farm and parent company Venture Properties International for neglecting the safety of their guests.

Luna City Volunteer Fire Department
Established 1878

Safe Ashore

Following Harry Vaughn's example, Richard shed his coat and the pullover sweater under it, for the two women and their children had nothing on but pajamas, and were barefoot besides. It was cold, on the water, even at this time of year. Harry's Carhartt jacket went around the two small boys comfortably. They clung together, still shivering and wet, while the baby wailed, a thin and constant shriek of protest at the cruelty of existence. The sky paled towards the east, and Venus hung like a jewel, almost brighter than the thin sliver of moon.

"The kiddywinks isn't hurt?" Richard asked, belatedly concerned about how the baby had been dropped from the window into his arms. "You'd best put on the life-preserver, too."

"No," the younger woman answered, although the strain around her eyes could be seen plainly now that it was getting light. "She's just frightened, wet, and miserable."

Not the only one among us feeling that way, Richard thought to himself. Susan Hartman said, sounding almost normal, "It's when they are silent that you have to worry." Richard had already passed on the news of her husband being found, bruised and bloody, but alive. He wished that he, or Uncle Harry and Joe had added blankets to the gear thrown hastily into the boat but considering the haste in which this expedition had been organized, they were lucky to have thought of lifejackets. Harry deftly piloted the heavy-laden boat around obstacles, fixed, floating or undetermined. There was no possible means of going against the current, not with the boat loaded to slightly over-capacity. Richard took up the battery spotlight and directed it at the turbulent water waters ahead. In this way, they picked their way along the swollen river, until Harry's cellphone rang.

"It's Joe," Harry called. "They can see us now. We're almost there."

Around one last bend, a stand of tall native bamboo standing in water to half their height made a landmark. Beyond it, a soggy meadow opened out, revealing two Luna City PD's utility vehicles, one with the trailer backed into the water, the VFD's ambulance and a farm pickup truck parked a little beyond on drier ground. Several people stood by, ankle to knee-deep in water; Joe and Chris Mayall among them. Uncle Harry pointed the boat at the shore and ran until the prow grounded in the mud. Richard scrambled out, as did Harry, little minding that they floundered in mud and water well over their knees. The boat lightened, they were able to pull it farther in, at least to only ankle-deep water, with the aid of those volunteers who came rushing forward.

"Here we are, ma'am," Uncle Harry gallantly helped Susan step over the side. "This will be the reception committee."

"Bless you," Susan's teeth were chattering with cold and delayed shock. Chris Mayall flung a blanket around her shoulders. "Bless you all. We'd never have made it, if you hadn't come in the nick of time."

"Think nothing of it," Richard replied, as Uncle Harry rumbled, "All in a day's work, ma'am."

"You look like you could do this justice," Joe produced his Thermos and a pair of mugs and poured a cup of coffee for each. Richard wrapped his fingers – fingers sore with sculling, aching with cold – around his.

"Ambrosial," he could only say, and Joe chuckled.

"Of course – it's yours …"

"So's this," Chris Mayall drawled, returning Richard's sweater and coat, much the worse for wear. "Put 'em on, you look cold. You all want some Motrin to go with it?" Joe chuckled; this was an ongoing jape of some sort, which Richard didn't quite grasp.

The women, children and baby had all been swiftly bundled into the ambulance, swaddling in dry blankets. Nothing remained but to load Uncle Harry's boat onto the trailer; all done, as swift and efficient as it had begun. The vehicles convoyed down the ranch road, the ambulance in the lead, and the ranch pickup lagging behind to close any gates.

"All but the debrief, of course," Joe added, as the ambulance lights vanished around the next bend in the unpaved ranch road.

"Seriously?" Richard complained. "We went out, we got them, and came back. Isn't that all that matters."

"Not to officialdom," Joe chuckled, knowingly. "Or to the media."

Richard shuddered. "Please, Joe; keep my name out of it all. I'm a private person, a modest, quiet-loving person." Harry Vaughn snorted derisively at that. "All I want is to go home, wash up, and open the Café this morning. Is that too much to ask?"

"Sorry, pal," Joe said. "Talking to Horatio is mandatory … but I'll let him know that if there is any media interest…"

Harry snorted again. "There will be, Joey. There will be, count on that."

"Then you can play the reporters like a violin, Harry. Just let them know that your second volunteer wishes to remain anonymous, if anyone asks. Seriously, Ricardo; I'll let everyone know you wanna keep a subterranean profile. My word on it."

"Appreciated," Richard said in gratitude. Sufficient unto the day – although it did turn out that he had to wait at the firehouse for an unconscionably long time, waiting for Horatio Gonzales to return from supervising another high-water rescue, farther up-country. After a while, he wandered outside, into the cool foggy dawn of another day.

Armed with another mug of acceptable coffee, he found Chris and Joe, lounging at the picnic table, and contemplating the contents of a temporary corral set up with metal traffic barricades underneath the tree. The residents of the corral regarded the humans with mild interest in return; an enormous, mastiff-like dog, a very small pony, a hand shorter than the dog, an even smaller goat, who baa-ed pathetically at Richard in a manner which reminded him of Che – one of the Grants' Nubian goats whose adoration of Richard was as inexplicable as it was embarrassing – and a tiny white and grey bantam chicken, perched on the pony's withers.

"Where did those creatures come from?" Richard couldn't help himself.

"Dude, I have no idea," Chris answered. He sounded as punch-drunk from exhaustion as Richard felt. "They just turned up. Flooded out, I guess. Someone found them down by Gonzalez Auto last night and brought them here. Guess if no one claims them, they go to the Grants."

"They seem real friendly with each other. It's like the set-up to a joke," Joe said. He also sounded exhausted. By Richard's calculations, they had maybe six or seven hours of sleep between the three of them out of the last forty-eight. "A horse, a dog, a goat and a chicken walk into a bar... and the bartender says, "Hey, why the long face?""

"If they sign a cat to the act," Richard ventured into the exhaustion-fueled silliness. "They can tour as the Bremen Town Musicians."

"I saw the Bremen Town Musicians open for System of a Down at the Whisky-a-go-go on the Strip in the late 90's," Joe reminisced in exhausted affection.

"You a fan of metal? Righteous!" Chris said. "Not my style, but ... righteous, dude."

"Now, if they sign a cat who can wear boots," Richard might as well go with the flow, much as he had done in the wee hours in Uncle Harry's tin boat, "They can lock up the Disney fans. And if the cat can sing in tune ... better yet." The three of them regarded the potential musical group through bleary eyes.

"Anyone know a talent agent?" Chris asked, after one of those long pauses.

"I do," Richard confessed. "Or I did. But the bastard has dropped me, through lack of interest, months ago. Alas, I am not really *au courant* with the celebrity scene, these days."

"Sorry, dude," Chris raised his mug of coffee, and Richard answered with a sigh, "Don't be. It's hardly worth the attention of a sensible person. Ghastly people, in the main. The dosh and the benefits were nice enough, but in the end, it wasn't worth what I had to do to keep on getting them."

"Well, you've landed on your feet here," Joe said. "And Uncle Harry promises that he'll walk tall and gather any media interest to himself about your little adventure, so you won't have to worry about being door-stopped by a camera crew. Don't forget; we saw how you reacted the last time that happened."

"Your secret mission is safe with us," Chris assured him with a leer. "Although if she really tried, I'll bet Kate could worm it out of you."

"You bastard," Richard said without heat. "Here I thought you were asleep in the back seat, during that drive from Marble Falls, not eavesdropping on a personal discussion between the two of us."

"Hey, I ain't been dropping no eaves on anyone," Chris guffawed at his own wit. "But she likes you, dude; she really likes you. I can't for the life of me figure out why you keep backing off, like she's made of plutonium. If any woman had been giving me the quiet come-hither the way she has been doing with you, I'd have hit it, months ago."

"Back in the day when I was single, I'd have made a move five minutes after being introduced," Joe nodded agreement.

"Miss Heisel is too fine a woman to even consider in that sense," Richard insisted. "In any case, my own lamentable past experience with the fair sex disqualifies me, as much as I am fond of the old bit of whatever. I have no taste and worse luck. Besides," he added with a bit of the simmering resentment from the day before. "She was supposed to have dinner with me last night at the Café, just the two of us. But she went to the Wyler Ranch instead. Oh, she claimed it was her job, posting a story about the cattle drive, but I know the real reason. It was a hot date with that tosser on the fancy horse; Bodie Madison."

"Bodie Madison?" Joe raised his head, alertly. "Young guy, first with the cattle yesterday, on a Palomino. You sure she was going on a date with him?"

"I am," Richard insisted with indignation. "She blew him a kiss, after taking his picture. It's perfectly obvious they are more than just good friends? And I am glad that you find this amusing," he added, for Chris was folding up in helpless laughter, while the dog, the pony, the goat and the chicken looked on in bemused curiosity.

"You have to admit, it is pretty funny," Joe was chuckling. "You being certain-sure that Kate stood you up for a date with Bodie Madison? The Bodie Madison, the rodeo rider?"

"She did," Richard insisted, and Chris conquered his amusement long enough to comment, "Dude, Bodie rides more than just bucking broncos!" before dissolving into uncontrolled mirth again.

Joe made a heroic attempt to control his own amusement. "Ricardo – Bodie's gay. Everyone knows … or I thought everyone knew, or at least suspected and were polite about it. He and Kate are old friends; were friends since the first grade in school. You had nothing to worry about. Matter of fact, ol' Bodie is likelier to make a pass at you than at Kate."

"Well, thanks for that." Richard replied, sourly. "Strangely; not all that reassuring. But still – thanks."

A La Carte With Quartermayne Heads South!

Headline, San Antonio Express News – Entertainment Section

The Food Network's top-rated series, *A La Carte With Quartermayne*, is on the road in Texas, for the sixth season of that popularly acclaimed cooking and travel show. Word from the producers is that former football star, quarterback Alan Lee Mayne and his traveling companion, former BBC import series heartthrob Phillip Noel-Barret are heading south, after completing filming of an episode in San Antonio, featuring a throw-down between two local restaurants specializing in genuine Mexican street food – La Gloria Icehouse at the Pearl Brewery, and Erick's Tacos on Nacogdoches on the north-east side outside the Loop. Which of the two contestants won the contest will not be revealed until the show is broadcast in the fall of 2017. Episodes already in the can, so to speak, for the season include similar contests in Amarillo, Abilene, College Station, Giddings, and Lockhart.

Sources within the show production team have revealed that the final contest will be a nail-biter between Mills Farm Country Restaurant, the house restaurant at Venture Properties International's destination resort of Mills Farm, and a small local restaurant in Luna City. Phillip Noel-Barrett, Alan Lee Mayne's co-host and co-producer for this season, will only say that the final reveal will involve an extra fillip – the resolution and unveiling of a solution to an abiding mystery in the world of celebrity television chefs.

Broadcast of the sixth season of *A La Carte With Quartermayne* begins September 15th.

Table For Two

Relieved to be assured by Joe and Chris that he had absolutely no reason for fearing that Kate Heisel's romantic attentions had been diverted by the handsome – and flamingly gay Bodie Madison, Richard did feel himself to have been a complete and immature prat in his reaction to Kate rescheduling … well, it wasn't a date, really – he assured himself, as he walked back to the Café. (*Why had he acted like a jealous teenager, then? That was a question that he refused to consider when it came to his interior interlocuter.*)

Late in the morning, he and Uncle Harry had finally been debriefed and roundly congratulated by Horatio Gonzalez on the daring rescue of the Hartman family from Mills Farm's Riverside Cottage.

"But I hope to hell I never have to ask that of y'all again," Horatio allowed. "It's a hell of a risk. It paid off this time, but next time, an amateur crew might not be so lucky."

"Luck had nothing to do with it but the timing," Uncle Harry growled. "Ricardo here, he kept his cool and knows his boats, and I know mine, by god. Don't sweat the small stuff, Horatio. The truth is, just about everything day to day <u>is</u> small stuff."

"Always good to hear from the voice of experience." Horatio stood up, thereby indicating that the briefing-interview was completed. "Thanks again, boys. You done good."

"Piece of cake," Richard replied and made his escape, still slightly pixilated from lack of sleep. The morning rush at the Café would be long over. He hoped without much conviction that Araceli had not been too terribly inconvenienced by his absence over the morning. Well, the nice thing about having the Airstream temporarily out in back of the Café was that he could slope outside for a quick forty winks. The downside to that was that now everyone looking for him had only a short distance to go. The distance out to the Age of Aquarius Campground and Goat Farm tended to discourage casual visitors.

The high water overnight didn't appear to have badly affected the historic part of Luna City; a lot of small branches knocked down from the oak trees in Town Square, and a Plimsoll-line of small debris added to various gutters, once the water which had brought that debris to a certain point. Richard went around through the back, eyeing the Airstream with a certain degree of longing – or at least, the bed which it contained, and from which he had been summoned so abruptly. A small furred thing meeped at him, and vanished with alacrity behind the dust-bins as he walked past and through the back door. Probably one of the Stein's cats, he thought … although they were sheltered, spoiled and as far as he knew, never went out of the Stein's back garden.

"Chef!" Araceli shot the last basket of dirty dishes into the industrial dishwasher. "Where on earth have you been! We were worried sick when you weren't answering your phone!"

"Didn't you get my note?" Richard was slightly boggled by this reception. "I left a note – I'm certain I did …"

"You did!" Araceli replied, afire with indignation. "And I thought you'd be back from wherever in time to deal with the morning rush, but you didn't answer your cellphone, and you weren't in your trailer! We were frantic! Where were you? Katie called the police and the VFD, but all that they would say was that you were out on a rescue call!"

"You were?" Richard couldn't help himself. "Worried about me?" Yes, he sounded smug, and Araceli's expression darkened in a dangerous manner.

"Yes, we were, Chef!" she fairly spat. "You weren't answering your phone and then we heard it ringing in the trailer! You didn't take it with you! Chef, that's purely irresponsible!"

"I was on a mission of mercy," Richard replied, hoping to placate the fury. "It's just not something I want to talk about ... but seriously – you were worried about me? I am touched. Honestly."

"Well, of course we were worried!" Araceli planted her hands on her hips. "It was flooding all over the place last night, just about everyplace south of San Antonio and you don't know the country very well at all. And Katie was frantic, because she really was looking forward to a special dinner, but she absolutely had to file that story. When she heard that you had gone out on a high-water rescue she began to cry. Yeah, she locked herself in the bathroom so that no one else would see her... well, it was four in the morning. Really, Chef, can't you show a bit of consideration?"

"So this is my fault," Richard sighed. "All right, whatever it was, I apologize. Deeply, sincerely, from the bottom of my heart. Is that sufficiently abject?"

"It's not just me; it's Katie you should really be apologizing to," Araceli sniffed, but Richard sensed that she was appeased. "And you should make dinner for her tonight the most amazing meal you have ever fixed."

"It will be," Richard promised, stifling an involuntary yawn. "And even more amazing if I can stay awake through all courses. What should I prepare, do you think?"

"Something that she would never have tasted before," Araceli looked thoughtful. "Something fabulous and classic French that you learned in

Paris. Something like what you would have done at that Carême restaurant place for all those celebrities and rich people."

"Out of what we have on hand this very day," Richard mused. "Tall order ... but there's the thing about challenges..."

All exhaustion miraculously banished, Richard sallied forth into the walk-in cooler, to make an assay of the contents, not neglecting to inspect the contents of the tiny refrigerator in the Airstream, wherein languished some choice impulse purchases from his last foray into the Costco in Karnesville the previous week. Yes, a small, whole, fresh free-range and totally organic chicken, some relatively fresh sole fillets, tinned truffles, imported foie gras, and a larger tin of caviar from his emergency stash against the days when Luna City felt too down-market and rural for words. There were fresh eggs in plenty in the Café's walk-in cooler, tomatoes, lemons, cream, even a large bunch of leeks ... He lost himself in a veritable orgy of prep-work. A continental-style French dinner, of several courses, scaled down for an audience of two demanded his absolute attention and dedication, not the least because he was performing it all himself, with the assistance which classic French cuisine ordinarily required.

"You know, people will think that you're dangerous when you are talking out loud to yourself," Araceli remarked. "Especially when they see all these knives around." She was putting on her coat and taking up her handbag and umbrella. The hands of the kitchen clock read 3:00.

"Hmm ... what?" Richard startled into awareness. "Don't do that. It breaks my absolute concentration."

"It's the end of the day for me," Araceli explained patiently. "Everything is ready for tomorrow, in case you haven't noticed. So, what time should I tell Katie to be here?"

"Seven of the hour," Richard sighed. "I know – desperately early for the established and traditional time. But any later, I'd be falling asleep into the dessert course by the end of the evening. Alas, we don't have anything on hand to even remotely pretend to be a proper cheese course, so we'll have to skip over that. I'm tremendously disappointed; the cheese course at Carême would have been amazing. Picture a rolling cart of assorted gourmet cheeses from across France and England, with crackers and thin-sliced toast to accompany … Supermarket cheddar on a Trisket cracker will so not serve."

"Chef," Araceli cleared her throat. "You're wandering. But it's OK. You want this to be a success, I get that. Your art, and you're gonna get back to exercising it, just this once. What should I tell Katie to expect?"

"Oh, right." Richard focused, with an effort. All this work was to impress Katie, Miss Kate Heisel, his super-dainty Kate, Kate of Kate Hall. "It's a simplified adaption, of course. Very few of us in this modern day have the stamina for the full programme. Which only really works if one has only a bite or two of each dish. First course – an *amuse-bouche* – a touch of something to tickle the appetite. Just a few little bites, carefully composed. *Ouvres en gelee* – or to put it in crude English – poached eggs in aspic jelly. I poached some eggs from the Age laid by Mrs. Grant's bantam hens. Lovely little bite-sized eggs. They are glazed in aspic, ornamented with slips of leek and tiny tomato flowers, served on a bed of aspic cubes with the appropriate garnish."

"It actually sounds kind of revolting," Araceli commented. "But if that's what you have all finished in the cooler – that looks amazing. Too pretty to eat, almost. The aspic cubes look like yellow diamonds, and the eggs look like those fancy jeweled Imperial Russian Easter eggs."

Richard sighed. "Araceli, my sweet unsophisticated innocent – I can see that you clearly prefer your poached eggs with the Benedict treatment: drowned in Hollandaise, with a wodge of ham on a soggy muffin. I have such hopes for teaching you more elevated tastes!"

"Well, don't mind me, Chef, for not being a food snob. I just cook the simple stuff and sling it out for paying customers who want breakfast and lunch. So, what else does Katie have to look forward to, this evening?"

This was why he like Araceli, and Kate. They didn't wither under the rough side of his tongue when he waxed sarcastic. Richard appreciated that.

"Well then there is the soup course. I just went with a simple veal consume. Simple, clear, pristine, a brief splash of Madeira. Not the top-flight stuff, I am afraid – merely supermarket quality. At the last possible minute, I will add narrow strips of sliced crepes to the soup. A symphony of sophisticated flavors, alternating with something plain to rest and clear the palate. It's the same with the salad course – which comes after the main dish. I know," Richard sighed again when he got to this part. "This so contra-local-custom. I so hope that eventually I will be able to train Americans out of it. My mission, and I have accepted it whole-heartedly. After the soup, there is the fish course. I am preparing *Paupiettes de sole Duglèrè*; small slivers of sole, gently oven-poached in fresh tomato puree and a splash of *fumet de poisson* – that's fish stock to you and served with a *veloute* sauce. Each one is a tiny tender bite, the essence of the sole and the sea. White wine to accompany all the courses, though. In classic service, there is a different wine with every course. Alas, the cellar here is not quite what I would wish it to be."

"We don't have a cellar, Chef, and you have no hope of getting Katie drunk," Araceli said, and Richard glared at her. "It will be white wine throughout, although I might propose some brandy in the post-prandial coffee. Now for the main course; *Poularde Derby*, an invention of Escoffier – you've heard of him, I trust? A roast chicken stuffed with rice, truffles, and vegetables on the side. I had to go with ordinary root vegetables – carrots and parsnips and celery. That will be followed by a salad of spring greens, dressed with a simple dressing of lime juice, olive oil and fresh herbs. Nothing heavy. As for dessert, I changed my mind about preparing lemon mousse. I have instead prepared a crème Saint-

Honoré with little almond macaroons and sauced with a concoction of my own invention, involving some of those divine little mandarin oranges that were on sale in season last week at Costco. If you will be so kind as to tell Miss Heisel that this dinner will be a leisurely affair … don't snicker like that, Araceli, it makes you sound like a prep-school girl with a dirty mind. Excellent food should be appreciated and savored, not bolted in ten minutes."

"I'll definitely let her know that the rest of her evening is completely blocked out," Araceli promised. "Should I tell her to come around the back, since the Café is closed for the day?"

Richard nodded, "Seven o'clock. The back door will be unlocked – likely I'll be going back and forth between the kitchen and the caravan all afternoon."

"All right then," Araceli took herself away and Richard once again buried himself in performing those culinary arts which he loved the best, hardly aware of the afternoon hours fleeting away. Grey twilight fell, slipping between the shifting clouds. At least, it had stopped raining sometime during the morning.

It was dark in the Café with the sun gone, and with the shades pulled down all the way over the windows. Richard set the smallest table – the one closest to the door into the kitchen with two place settings, even to the extent of several forks and spoons in various sizes. Buried in the farthest corner of the storage cupboard, he unearthed a dusty box of pale wax tapers, and picked a lavish handful of white flowers in the grassy verge of the lane which ran behind the Café. A splendid crop of them had sprouted there. Araceli, or someone had told him that they were called rain-lilies and always sprouted and bloomed within several days after rain. He regarded that handiwork with some satisfaction; plain and understated, but suitable and seasonal. Several times, as he went back and forth between kitchen and caravan, he thought that the cat observed him warily from behind the wheelie bins. But everything was in order. He took a moment in the caravan to don a clean shirt and chef's apron – blast, it was ten minutes of seven, no time for any more elaborate ablutions. He emerged from the caravan, just as Kate straightened up from attending to something small, something small, feral, and elusive behind the wheelie bins.

"Hello, Richard," she said, and if she was slightly pink in the face it must have been from bending down. "Do you know that you have a cat, hanging around the Café?"

"Must be one of the Steins'," Richard replied. "They spoil the wretched things, let them wander everywhere."

"This one doesn't look spoiled at all," Kate said. "It really looks quite small and wretched."

"No matter," Richard grandly extended his elbow. "Do you have an appetite, my Kate of Kate Hall?"

"Starving," she confessed, and added as they walked into the kitchen. "Oh. My. God. That smells amazing! You must have been working for days!"

"Hours, merely," Richard said. "Your table awaits, madam."

"You are eating with me?" she shot him a sideways glance from those amazing beryl-green eyes.

"Of course. I'm starving, as well. I have not eaten anything since … I think it was one of those horrid glazed doughnuts, on the table at the VFD early this morning when we returned from … never mind. Ordinarily I wouldn't have touched the ghastly thing. Allow me to take your coat, Kate."

"Of course," Another one of those beryl-green sideways glances, as she slid that oversized poplin trench-coat off her shoulders. Under it she was wearing one of those prim businesswoman skirt suits. "So, what do you have planned for the evening, Richard?"

"Fine cuisine and sparkling conversation," Richard answered, firmly. He put the coat onto one of the brass hooks of that enormous old-fashioned coat, hat, and umbrella-rack. "Those alone. They deserve our complete and undivided attention."

"Oh, good," Kate smiled in what looked to be unabashed relief. In the back of his mind, he was vaguely disappointed, as he pulled out the chair for her, at the little, candle-lit table for two. *He had a reputation as a heartless roué to uphold, after all.* "Anything great is worth taking your time to appreciate!"

"A glass of wine, to accompany the first course," Richard commanded. "And to lubricate conversation." He brought out two filled glasses from the kitchen, and putting one in her hand, set the other by his place and sat down. "This is one of the most splendid white wines I have ever tasted. Sefton creates the most wonderful ambrosial vintage from the toughest and most unpromising wild grapes imaginable. He has promised me an unstinting supply of it, in gratitude for keeping him fed all spring while Judy was away and for promising to teach his granddaughter – whose name at present escapes me – to properly cook when she comes to stay at the age for the long summer hols. The Café has done so very well this last year that Jess says that we can afford to hire summer help. I plan to formulate the summer experience as the beginnings of a proper kitchen apprenticeship..."

"Brianna," Kate supplied, with a gently ironic expression. "Brianna – that's the name of the Grant's granddaughter. Shall we drink to your future as an educator, then?"

"Yes, of course," Richard answered hastily, and they clinked glasses together. "So, how went the information-content gathering business today? Anything totally fascinating to report?"

"Well, you were part of a last-ditch heroic effort on behalf of a whole family about to be carried away in the highest flood in decades," Kate answered, with a wry twist to her expression. "But you want to be modest about it, so my opportunity for an exclusive interview is shot to all heck. Cousin Horatio put his foot down, said that you wanted to be anonymous.

Good thing that I respect the wishes of private citizens. That and Cousin Horatio would see that my life in Karnes County was made miserable, if I decided that I wanted a huuge scoop, instead of respecting the wishes of an individual. Also, I prefer to like looking at myself in the mirror every morning." She fetched up a deep sigh. "I guess that's why I am unfit to be a provider of news on the national level. I'd feel … I dunno, slimy. Making a career from exploiting the emotions of ordinary people on the very worst day of their lives? There's something unsavory about being an emotional vampire, you know? Sucking up tragedy and spreading it all over the front page in 12-point type. I'd rather do the little stuff. The local stuff. Because people really have to know about things going on, you see. There <u>was</u> one big story that I broke back in Chicago when I was an intern. Front page, but I hated myself afterwards. Not all the seas incarnadine…"

"If it is any help," Richard consoled her. "I wasn't really a volunteer on the occasion to which you refer. I was brow-beaten into participation. Harry Vaughn threatened to strike me about the head and shoulders with an oar if I didn't do as I was ordered. He's extraordinarily fit for a man of his age, did you notice?"

"He is," Kate grinned, wide and unabashed. "He cuts quite a swath among the older ladies, doesn't he?"

"You've no idea," Richard answered, hoping that Kate's interest would skate over the recent visit of Aunt Moira and the Bennington Patriot Riders. "Are you ready for the first course, Kate of Kate Hall?"

"I thought you would never ask!" she answered. Richard took one more sip of Sefton's marvelous vintage and went off to bring the first course to the table.

"Now – remember, this is the first of seven courses," he warned her, as he set down the small white dish, in which four small ornamented and aspic-coated cold poached eggs lounged voluptuously on a bed of chopped aspic cubes. Kate looked at them with a dubious expression as he slid two of them onto the topmost plate.

"They're almost to pretty to eat," she ventured, much as Araceli had done.

"The principle is that all the senses should be delighted," Richard said. "The eyes and the nose as well as the tongue. This is why a proper luncheon in France takes two hours. Every creature eats but only humans dine. Go ahead – have a taste."

Obediently, Kate sliced one of the eggs in half with the edge of her fork, and lifted a bite to her mouth. Richard quailed inwardly; what if she didn't like it at all? The little harpies of impending disaster flittered briefly in his imagining, but Kate only chewed and swallowed, a thoughtful expression on her face.

"It has an interesting flavor," she allowed. "I've never tasted anything quite like it before. I think I like it – you know, growing up here, the best of the food you eat is … you know, pow! Spicy-hot, bright – unsubtle. Good, but unsubtle."

"Savor it slowly," Richard advised with relief, as the harpies of disaster flicked out of existence. "We have all the time in the world tonight. Have a sip of wine. Take your time."

"I will," Kate nibbled at the rest of her eggs in a leisurely manner, as Richard did at his.

"So you know about my day," he said, as she scooped up the last golden diamonds of aspic. "Half of it spent on a flooding river, in a boat with a furious OAP threatening to wallop me with an oar; it was rather like the galley scene in the old *Ben Hur* movie; *Row well and live!* The other half chained to a hot restaurant stove, preparing this dinner. You … well, Araceli said you were looking forward to it so much. And I want …" Richard floundered. No, he didn't know what he wanted when it came to Kate. Marvelous and subtle woman, she came to his rescue.

"To dine," she offered, brightly. "My day was on steroids, because of all the flooding. Your family rescue at Mills Farm wasn't the only touch of drama, you know. There was a man in Floresville caught in three feet of water and carried away in his car, and he climbed out of it and into a big tree, and called KSAT in San Antonio, while he was waiting to be rescued. They broke into their regular programming to give updates." She regaled him with several more episodes of flood-related drama, while he took away the first course plates and the empty serving dish, and brought out the small soup tureen *(unearthed from the farthest corner of the Café's closet of plates and odd serving dishes)* and ladled a serving into each bowl.

"It looks like noodles – like *Abuelita's* broth with *fideo*," Kate said, upon looking into the bowl of rich brown broth.

"Not *fideo*," Richard said. "But fresh crepes, slivered into lengths and floated into the broth at the last minute. Want some bread to go with it? I am perfecting my own sourdough bread recipe. Although I haven't inflicted it on the Café patrons, yet, but I have high hopes for this particular starter."

Kate lifted the first spoonful of that rich broth to her mouth. "Oh, my god – Rich, that's fantastic!" she cried. "You know there are women who would sleep with you, just for this … but …" she added hastily, "For me, the jury is still out."

"I know," Richard sighed, heavily. "There are women who <u>have</u> slept with me for food. Or associated fame. I'd like to think I have moved beyond that."

"You have," Kate twinkled that beryl-green look at him. "You are now running a little café in a small town that no one in the big world has ever heard of. You know, I used to have to tell people that I was from San Antonio. Because they have heard of that, at least. It was too long to say I'm from Karnesville, or from Luna City, and then have to add that it's an hours' drive south of San Antonio, and then you take this little side road and look out for the oak tree in the middle of the road."

"I'm from Bickley, myself," Richard replied, attending on his own plate of soup. "A more prosperous and boring London suburb can hardly be imagined. Still – nice place. My parents did well by me, although they did have to give up considerable of their hopes for me making a career at first."

"So did mine," Kate allowed, generously. "Dad sighed when I said I wanted to specialize in journalism. He said it was a straight journey into living at home forever, and wouldn't I consider a STEM major … that's short for science, technology, engineering, and medicine? I did do some marketing and IT courses, so I wasn't completely unemployable upon graduation. And I did score a job with a big-city newspaper in Chicago. Although I've always suspected that the offer came because I was a minority woman, if you bend down and squint sideways at my resume. I'm still a bit embarrassed about that."

"Should have done food service," Richard said. "Jobs everywhere, if you don't mind getting your hands greasy, but the pay usually isn't all that and a bag of chips."

Kate giggled, and for the rest of the soup course and into Richard serving up the *Paupiettes de sole Dugléré*, they compared impossible supervisors, incredible coincidences, and improbable job-related horrors. Upon tasting the first bite of the sole, she half-closed her eyes in delight.

"My god, I can't believe how good this is! You cook like this all the time, and I'd come to supper here every night. Your restaurant – the one on London, that would have been amazing!"

"Alas, it was not to be," Richard took up his own fork, after helping himself from the serving dish. "I've tried to be philosophical, but it still stings. I had so much riding on the success of Carême. I'd sunk about everything I had into it, called in every favor that everyone owed me; it was my escape from being essentially a performing monkey on this or that television show, you see. Constant travel, passing judgement on other people's cooking. My own restaurant … it's a brutal grind, most times – but it was my choosing."

"So, what happened," Kate ventured, and hastily added. "Look, if you don't want to talk about it, you don't have to. I know that the first night was an absolute disaster, but Abuelita and I always wondered why. Part of my own mental makeup," she added with a quick grin. "Mom swears that my first-ever spoken word was not Mama, or Papa, but 'why?' What set it all off?"

"No, it's all right," Richard replied, although it really wasn't. The opening of Carême was an enormous, degrading failure of the sort that Chris Mayall described as an 'emotional sucking-chest wound.' But this was Kate asking; his gallant, fiercely independent Kate. "It was, as everyone knew – opening night. My god, the media presence was overwhelming. The dining room was packed with international A-list celebs. Models and movie stars, politicians, a couple of international tycoons and even a Russian oligarch or two. As you can imagine, I was wound up pretty tight that night, what with the intense pressure. Front of the house greeting them personally as if they are my oldest, dearest friends, then back in the kitchen, overseeing ... you know, I'm a perfectionist. I wanted everything to be just so..."

"You're bending your fork," Kate reminded him, dispassionately. Richard looked down at his hands. Yes, he was. He made himself to set the fork down, and relax that grip.

"Yes. Well. Everything – and I mean everything – depended on that first night. And I think I would have pulled off the first night in spectacular fashion, but for Roger what's-his-name, one of the junior cooks. A spoiled little git who fancied himself as a man about town. He had just broken up with his latest conquest. She was some society debutante; the sort of girl who gets her picture in *Country Life* and she was there with her new boyfriend, and her parents, or his. I can't recall which, at this point. I suppose one of the waiters told him she was there. He was at insufferable sort whom most other chaps hate on sight. Any of the front house staff would have been happy to turn the knife in him." Richard brooded over his own serving of *Paupiettes de sole Dugléré,* until Kate prodded him by saying, "And then he put – I can't recall, some kind of emetic in everyone's soup?"

"No, just the soup for the party at her table," Richard sighed. "And when they all began vomiting, ten minutes later, it spread. A case of mass hysteria, where everyone else in the place gets sick, or faints or something. It's happened before, I have been told. But in this case, the massed media were there to record the whole debacle. I don't remember much of the rest, really. That was the point when I lost it all. I believe that my New York publicist organized an intervention; shoved me on a trans-Atlantic flight with orders to his minions to collect me at JFK, hire a private jet for Los Angeles and decant me into some private and massively expensive looney-bin until all the fuss died down. Instead … I finished here. Can't say I mind, really."

"We certainly don't," Kate smiled, a brilliant and joyous smile. "Count it as one of those fortunate accidents. You're better off cooking for folks in Luna City, then for all those people in London – even if you can't do a simply splendid meal like this every day. I'm certain there are dozens, hundreds of trained chefs in London, and restaurants the equal, almost the equal, of Carême on every corner. But here in Luna City, you're unique. Special."

"Likely that I am," Richard sighed. The thought of Carême – beautiful, lost, doomed Carême – still hurt. Kate's smile widened.

"Ours. One of ours. And you have a restaurant, of sorts. OK, so it's a coffee shop and luncheon sort of place, unless there's something special going on in town. Abuelita adores you, and you are the first choice of every Gonzalez or Gonzales in Karnes County for a special event. It's your second chance."

"That's what Chris said, last year," Richard suddenly had appetite for the fish course again. *Carême was the lost dream, gone beyond recovery. This was the here and now.*

When he brought out the main course; the small roast chicken, adorned with carefully sculpted roast vegetables, glazed with butter and their cooking juices, Kate clapped her hands; Richard thought that she regarded both him and the main course with approximately the same degree of rapturous anticipation.

"I can see why French cuisine is so popular!" she exclaimed. "This is wonderful, Richard! I would never have the time to do this every evening, but I love it for tonight, for special. Are you going to teach Brianna to cook like this? The kids in the high school adult survival class, too?"

"Not much that I can teach in a week or so," Richard acknowledged, ruefully. "But I did offer a two-week curriculum next year. And it would be to do a roast chicken and then how to do a different dish every night with the leftovers. Finishing with a brief course in making soup with the bones and remains. The trouble is that an appreciation for haute cuisine has to be taught early. Otherwise, it's just for special occasions on a Saturday night. Meanwhile, everyone is diving to Karnesville for hamburgers, or fixing ghastly casseroles with a can of cream-of-something soup. Or even...Lentil Surprise."

"I get your point," Kate giggled, most enchantingly, and then fixed Richard with that thoughtful, beryl-green gaze. "But what if you could ... apply your cooking lessons a little more widely. I just had the most splendid idea."

Oh, shit – Richard thought, his heart abruptly sinking

"You could do a cooking show," Kate exclaimed. "A cooking show for children – have a little website with recipes and do YouTube videos and post them. Lots of people are doing it these days."

"A splendid notion, Kate," Richard replied, with heavy sarcasm. "And entirely wreck the privacy that I have attained here. Hey, boys and girls, gather 'round; here's Rich Hall, the Bad Boy Chef, back again and badder than ever, all ready to teach you the secrets of fine French cuisine!"

"I didn't mean that you would do it as yourself," Kate said, patiently. "You could be a character, in a mask and furry gloves, like Captain Kangaroo, or even a puppet like Kermit the Frog. You could be ..." Kate's countenance lit with missionary zeal. "Captain ... Captain Kitten! Call it 'Captain Kitten's Kitchen.' Everyone likes cats. You wouldn't have to use your own voice, even. You would just ... write out the lessons and recipes, put on a cat-disguise and demonstrate them. I can set you up with a website, or even just a specialty page on "Talk of the Town." You did say that in France they start off teaching them young, to appreciate the finer things. Well, instead of pushing junk food – you could start showing them how to ... well, not things like this, not quite. But simple things that kids could do, rather than just bug their parents for a Happy Meal with a stupid plastic toy. Make it simple, fun ... I would have adored being taught how to decorate poached eggs like this when I was about eight. I would have made a mess in the kitchen and I don't think Mom would have been OK with that, but I would have gotten better. You're already teaching that class at the high school. A series of videos and a blog would be the next logical step."

Her enthusiasm was disarming. Richard began considering all the reasons why not; the time that such a project would consume, the infinitesimally small chance that it would bring the dreadful imposture of the Bad Boy Chef back to the awareness of the public ...

"A small step," he allowed, but the notion took hold of his imagination, began sprouting, putting out leaves and tendrils, like one of those fast-growing tropical plants on sped-up film. "I would have to do it at several different levels," he mused thoughtfully. "One set for smaller children. You know, that wouldn't involve sharp knives, or hot hobs ... and a set for the older lot. It could be done, you know. I could do it ..."

"I knew you'd see the possibilities!" Kate glowed with satisfaction, and for the remainder of that course and the salad which followed upon it, Richard expounded and enlarged on the topic; what could be taught easily, the simple sauces and dishes, and Kate enthused and urged him on. He could not recall when he last felt so optimistic and energized; a lifetime ago, surely – about the time that he won that wretched cooking contest. And he had wanted that prize, wanted it so badly that he would have given practically anything for that win, disregarding the words of Gran, who often said, "Be careful of what you wish for, Richard – for you may get it."

Through the salad, and onto the heights of the dessert course, they went with renewed vigor to the mountain-top, the above-oxygen-level of crème Saint-Honoré – Richard feeling like he should have planted a small flag on top, and looked around at the lesser heights in triumph. He had constructed an amazing dinner, and spent … good lord, it was past ten o'clock … hours of an evening with a woman whose company he enjoyed, and yet both of them still clothed, and chaste; certainly, a first in his often lamentable but superficially-enjoyable experience. He poured the final cup of coffee – with a splash of brandy in it – with a feeling of regret. The evening was over. Perhaps he would have other evenings with Kate, but this was the first; the Mount Everest of their mutual attraction and regard.

"D'you want more coffee, Kate?" he asked, at last, and Kate shook her head.

"I won't be able to sleep a wink, if I do," she answered. "Richard – this was lovely. Everything I had hoped for. Shall I call you tomorrow, sometime?"

"I'll be disappointed if you don't," Richard said. "Do you have the number for my cellie?"

"No," Kate reached into the front pocket of her trench-coat, which Richard had retrieved from the old-fashioned rack and settled it on her shoulders. "Let me add it … oh, crapula – I have a message. Sorry, it's from a contact – I absolutely have to listen to it this minute."

She raised the cellphone to her ear, and walked away a few paces, through the darkened Café. He could hear nothing but faint squawking emanating from Kate's cellphone, but nothing worried him about it. Kate's business, after all. He gathered up the last few dishes and silverware from the table, pinching out the candle flames as he did so, and carried them into the kitchen. Araceli would expect to find the front of the house almost pristine, when she came in tomorrow for breakfast. Richard tidied away the few leftovers, and left the used dishes and silverware to soak in a sink full of hot, soapy water. He intended to show Kate out through the back door, when she was ready to leave, and then retreat to the Airstream with visions of her cooking education programme dancing in his head. A quiet and short interval, perhaps with a consultation with *Larousse*, leading to pleasant dreams and ... well, who could know from then?

He came out into the dining room again, to find Kate, with a stricken look on her face, as she put the cellphone away.

"Richard ... I have to tell you. I have bad news – the most appalling news. I don't quite know how to say this, but ..."

To be continued...

A Fifth of Luna City

A Sky Full of Stars

"Richard ... I have to tell you. I have bad news – the most appalling news. I don't quite know how to say this, but ..."

That was Kate, his super-dainty Kate, her face expressing a mixture of horror and regret. Only his own sense of shock and possibly his own gentlemanly upbringing belatedly coming to his rescue – miraculously coming down from the heights of his prolonged classical venture into French cuisine on her behalf – kept him from blurting out his initial reaction: *"Jesus, Kate – you can't be pregnant! We've never even slept together!"*

Instead, he just looked at her as if pole-axed, and said, "Well, tell it to me, Kate. I've had a long day, starting with being bullied in an open boat by an OAP with a bad attitude, and coming close to drowning in a flooded river. Frankly, I don't think there is any more bad news you can tell me."

"Well then," Kate drew a deep breath. "My informant is one of the techies involved with *A La Carte with Quartermayne*. It's a traveling TV food show. If you don't know anything about it, Abuelita does, and so does everyone else who watches the Food Channel. They're coming to Luna City at the end of summer, for a food showdown…"

"No, absolutely not," Richard was stone-faced. "I will not participate in one of those travesties. I will not be a performing monkey on a lead for the entertainment of the masses. Again. If I see a TV camera within half a block of me, I will turn around and go home. I've been there, Kate. It's Hell. I've learned my lesson – and won't do it again."

"No, it's not for the Café," Kate swiftly reassured him, those amazing beryl-green eyes huge with sympathy. "The showdown will be between the Pryor's Meats and BBQ, and the Mills Farm Country Kitchen. But the co-host of Quartermayne this season is someone that … well, you know. And according to my informant…"

"Your spy in the enemy camp," Richard amended, dryly.

"Whatever. You and he have a long history – Phillip Noel-Barrett."

Richard broke out in a cold sweat, despite the residual heat in the kitchen. "Stone the crows, not him – that unregenerate tosser! What malignant plan is that unmitigated arse-monger up to now? Nothing good, I'll warrant. And those Quartermayne berks better be on their guard, because if he does half the damage to the immediate vicinity as he did with that wretched movie…"

"I see that you remember him fondly also," Kate commented with just the faintest touch of acid. "It looks like he will be up to some nasty tricks with regard to yourself. In a moment of …"

"Alcohol-fueled frankness," Richard supplied and Kate grinned.

"Exactly what I assumed. He is planning to reveal you as the Bad Boy Chef – not resting serenely sedated in some expensive loony-bin but working happily away in an obscure little town café. My contact says that Noel-Barrett is practically slavering at the chops in his eagerness to do you a bad turn."

"He always was a malicious little git," Richard sighed. What a way to finish an evening – a beautiful evening, which had topped off a very long and fraught day. "I'll do my best to stay out of the way, Kate. I don't want to be outed, much less by Pip Noel-Barrett. I like it here. I like the Café, my little caravan, Luna City and all. I don't want to leave. But I cannot go back to the old life. I won't go back. It wasn't good for me. I know that now."

"Don't worry, Richard," Kate shrugged her outsized overcoat over her shoulders once again. Her face bore an expression of adamantine determination, fearsomely like that of Abuelita Adeliza Gonzales when that formidable lady put her foot down. "We'll see that you are kept safe, doing what you love to do, and doing it in Luna City. You have friends here, not just me … although Acey McClain – he's my boss, you know? At the *Beacon*. He might just begin to wonder about where my loyalties lie, if he ever hears about this caper."

"Thank you, Kate," Richard wondered if he was being honestly grateful for the very first time in his so-called adult life. They stood very close, at the back door to the Café, near to the vast pot-washing sink and the industrial dishwasher, which smelled very faintly of dishwater and drains. But they stood so close, as he intended, somewhat reluctantly, to see her out – and he detected the perfume that Kate was accustomed to wear. On an impulse, he leaned down – not very far down – and kissed her, intending the kiss to land in a brotherly, even an avuncular manner. But the minx turned her head at the last second, and it landed on her lips. For a brief eternity, he was lost – Kate, his wonderful Kate of Kate Hall, his super-dainty Kate, before whom all his previous passions, or whatever they had been – were momentary shallow flirtations. Until she pulled back, grinned at him and said,

"That was a kiss to set all records, Richard – perhaps one day, we'll set another one like it. But I have to go now. 'Celi will wonder where I am. If I don't get on my way this instant, she will call Joe to go and get me – and Jess will be furious. Good night, sweet prince; blessed angels see the to thy rest. I have to go."

"Indeed," Richard gave a wistful sigh for the night that might have been – but no, it wouldn't have been right. He and Kate had worlds enough and time. The thought of a wrathful Joe Vaughn, the Luna City chief of police, bashing down the door of the Airstream to haul a weeping and half-dressed Kate into the cruiser was a thought to banish all erotic fantasies, right then and there. "Do you want me to walk you to Patrick and Aracelis'? It's not far."

"No, *mon cher* Richard – you must be exhausted after all this. I'll be all right. We're in Luna City, after all." She stepped neatly out of his half-hearted embrace and opened the outer door. Outside, a shy quarter moon rationed silver light on the back of the Café and the buildings adjoining it on Town Square. A few small lights from the back windows of the Stein's place, and from the rooms over the small businesses in the other direction, rented out on BnB to those who wanted a small-town Texas experience, cast a dimmer and more golden light. "Oh, look – your cat is still here."

"I don't have any pets…" Richard insisted obstinately. "It must be one of the Steins' perishing little beggars. Wretched things – they pee all over the carpet inside, and crap all over the garden outside."

Kate peered at the small, shadow-shape lurking in the depths of the hedge between the Stein's garden – a garden groomed to a state of perfection with a Teutonic devotion to detail, in vivid contrast to the space of crumbling macadam interspersed with weeds and rubbish bins behind the Café. That space was currently interrupted with the Airstream, and a couple of timber-framed raised beds, in which Richard nourished cooking herbs and a crop of exotic salad greens.

The small shadowy shape mewed at her. It sounded commanding, rather than querulous and pathetic, as Richard would have expected a lost or temporarily discommoded cat to sound.

"It's too small for Beethoven, Bach or Mozart," Kate observed. The Stein's musical trio were sheltered, spoiled, well-fed and of considerable size. "Annise would never let them outside in this weather anyway."

"The flood brought in all sorts of animal flotsam and jetsam," Richard sighed, thinking on the outsized dog, miniature pony, bantam hen and stray goat, confined in a makeshift corral by the VFD. "A stray, I suppose."

"Be kind," Kate said, and in the shadows behind the Café, Richard was sure that she was smiling at him. "Give the poor little thing some of that lovely chicken, or whatever. Good night, Richard – sleep well."

"I will, even if lonely," Richard sighed. Quite suddenly, the burden of total exhaustion fell upon him, a burden which rocked him to his knees. "Honestly, I couldn't have done justice to the occasion if you had even wanted to spend the night with me. I've got some pride left in me, Kate."

"I know," Kate blew a kiss in his direction, and departed without another touch of her hand or lips, walking swiftly to the bottom of the desolate patch which was the Café's back garden. Richard thought that she turned and waved at him, before she vanished around the corner of the Stein's garden-shed/garage.

The evening was over. On the whole, it had been a success beyond his dreams, Richard thought, as he turned out the lights in the Café, and sent the last of the dishes and glasses into the commercial washer. A long day, and a hard day; a supper with Kate, and space enough and time to meditate upon where their mutual attraction should go. Bad news about Pip Noel-Barrett's malicious intentions … but that was consummation months in advance. Sufficient unto the day were the evils thereof, as the school chaplain used to say. Today's troubles were enough for today.

He got out one of the folding chairs from the Airstream, and sat beneath the inconsistent moon, with a glass of Sefton Grant's marvelous elixir, contemplating the day, in all of it's exhaustion and glory, obscurely grateful that he didn't have to get up on the bicycle and pedal all the way back to the Age of Aquarius. Because of the flood and the good offices of Roman Gonzalez, the Airstream caravan that he called home had been temporarily moved from the campground and small farm where it had sat for at least three decades. His daily commute was reduced to a matter of fifteen steps … and the cat suddenly interrupted these meditations. It emerged from the dividing hedge and sat not five feet from him.

"Mrrow?" It said. Startled out of his reverie, Richard answered.

"What's that, old chap?"

"Mrroow!" replied the cat, one eye reflecting the pale moonlight. "Mrroow!" it said again, with added emphasis and air of cold command, which well those passions Richard read.

"All right, then!" Richard set aside his glass, and went into the Café kitchen, to the walk-in cooler, where reposed the container with the last of the chicken from his glorious supper with Kate. He brought out a small bowl, filled to the brim with some-barely cooled shredded chicken and crumbled bits of pate, and carefully locked the back door after him – wondering why he bothered at all, since Luna City was one of the most casually law-abiding places that he had ever set up residence in, however temporary. He set the dish down, and the cat fell upon it with every evidence of glutinous pleasure. When it had polished the dish clean, it approached Richard, still nursing half a glass of Sefton's mustang white, and sat at his feet. A small pink tongue polished its' whiskers, one swipe a side, as the cat assumed the expectant posture of one of those ancient Egyptian statuettes of cats.

"Mrroow," it commented, sounding slightly less commanding.

"You're welcome," Richard replied. "But no, I don't care if you want some wine to go with supper. This is all mine."

"Mrroow!" The cat sounded slightly disappointed – as if it had hoped for that but was sporting about being turned down. Seen now in the dim interior light shining through the Airstream's screen door, it stood revealed as a small brindle animal, with one eye as pale and lifeless as the moon overhead, the other dark and brimming with feline mysteries. Richard was no great judge of cat-flesh, but he thought it was a young animal, despite the blind eye. It regarded him steadily with the other eye, as Richard communed with his glass of wine, coming down from the mighty cloud of terror or exertion expended during a day only a little longer than what he had been accustomed to in his early days as an apprentice chef. Since he didn't have Kate to talk to, he directed his remarks to the young cat.

"Rough day for you too, Ozymandias-King-of-Kings? Look upon your works, oh mighty, and despair. Nothing remains … but a hell of a lot of flood water."

"Mrroow," the cat commented, sounding rather forlorn.

"Sorry about that, old chap. Just worked out that way. Global warming, you know – but in Texas they call it 'the weather'. Still a bit disconcerting, especially if one has an aversion to drowning."

"Mrroow," Ozymandias-King-of-Kings agreed. Richard sank the last little bit of Sefton's prize white mustang grape wine. When he had drained the glass of that last mouthful, the brindle cat was sitting at the foot of the step to the Airstream, regarding him expectantly. "Mrroow?" That last had a kind of tentative, yet commanding sound to it. Richard marveled again, at the depth of feeling that the beast could put into a single sound. The Librarian of the Unseen University had nothing on this cat.

"All right, you conniving little beggar." Richard sighed, and opened the screen door; instantly, Ozymandias-King-of-Kings hopped up into the Airstream as if it was his by rights. He-She-It strolled through the brief sitting area and kitchenette, sniffing at the odd item in a way that suggested judgmental skepticism, but marginal acceptability as to conditions. And then hopped up onto the disturbed bedding at the foot of the single double bed at the back of the Airstream, licked itself several times in businesslike fashion, curled into a neat circular form among the blankets and dropped into whatever was for a cat, deep, deep slumber.

When Richard performed his late-night ablutions, resumed the pajama trousers which were his customary night things, and took his own place in the bed, Ozymandias only burped – or perhaps farted – briefly, purred for a bit and fell back into deep slumber nearly as soon as Richard did.

In the Editorial Offices of the Karnesville Weekly Beacon

"Kate! Katherine Miranda Heisel! When we you going to tell me about the TV show cook-off in Luna City! Get in here, Kate! Now!" Acey McClain, chief editor, head-writer and general manager of the Karnesville Weekly Beacon bellowed from his tiny office, which occupied prime second-floor real estate in the 19th century brick building which had housed the Beacon since it was first established as a daily newspaper at the end of the Civil War. The managerial office was not, as was traditional in larger publishing concerns, a superbly situated corner office. It did command a single tall window, a window which afforded a not particularly appealing view of a Valero gas station, an auto-parts store and a small frozen yogurt franchise recently opened by a hopeful retiree capitalist from Dallas-Fort Worth.

"Really, Chief," Kate appeared almost before the dust dislodged by editorial fury finished sifting down from the superannuated ceiling fans. "You don't have to shout. And only my Mom calls me by all three names. Take a chill pill – I was going to tell you at staff meeting, anyway, but since you ruined my surprise…" She settled into the guest chair before Acey McClain's monumental executive desk, a relic of the Cleveland administration, took the #2 pencil from where it had been thrust through the sloppy bun of her dark hair, and opened her narrow reporter's notebook.

"Surprise? Kate, nothing surprises me these days. I was last surprised by a rattlesnake in my granny's outhouse, sometime in the Fifties."

"Eighteen-fifties, Chief?" Kate licked her pencil-point and delicately took the piss out of her supervisor. "I didn't think you looked anywhere near that old. You really must work out."

"Keep a civil tongue, Kate," Acey scowled. "Granny didn't get electricity in the house until 1936. Indoor plumbing took a hellova lot longer. Your surprise?"

"Well, it's my scoop, and the … friend who told me about it will absolutely lose his job if word leaks out about it any sooner, but the planned local cook-off to feature in the finale of the latest season of *A La Carte with Quartermayne* is definitely going to be in Luna City, between the Country Kitchen restaurant at Mills Farm, and Pryor's Meats and BBQ. According to my friend, it's gonna be focused on real, down-home Texas BBQ."

"My money is on Pryor's," Acey grunted. "Their smoked brisket is awesome. Mills Farm is just crap for the tourist trade passing through."

"Mills Farm doesn't do a bad meal," Kate argued. "But they are full-time food-service professionals, they have heaps of corporate backing, and Pryors' is only open on weekends if you are lucky. I think that the Quartermayne people are planning for one of those David-and-Goliath show-downs."

"Well, I know who I will be rooting for," Acey leaned back in his chair. "But I'm surprised that they didn't opt for setting the showdown between the Country Kitchen and the Luna Café and Coffee. I hear that the guy who runs it now is a real French-trained chef; I'd have thought he'd give his left nut to be on *Quartermayne*."

Kate was shaking her head already. "Nope, Chief. He's a pretty modest guy in some ways; swears up and down he is so <u>not</u> a performing monkey on a lead. If he spots a TV camera anywhere within half a block, he will turn around and go the other way."

"Camera shy, huh?"

"Camera abhorrent, more like." Kate turned to a fresh page in her notebook. "So much for my surprise, Chief. Now, I did a little leg-work about Mills Farm…"

"You went snooping," Acey McClain grinned widely. "Good for you, Kate. What did you find out?"

Kate sighed, in dramatic fashion. "Snooping is <u>such</u> an ugly word, Chief. I did no such thing. I just talked to Cousin Teddy, the guy who plays Old Charley. Did you know that his wife makes the most awesome butter cookies? Old Scandinavian family recipe of hers. I gained a pound just smelling them, fresh from the oven. She's from Minnesota: I'll pass on some for Christmas for sure. I made nice and asked to speak to Lew Dubois; you know what he was doing? Bussing tables in the Country Kitchen! But it was a slow day, so he took off the rubber apron and gave me ten minutes of his time. Now, he's a character, for sure. He spends one day a week, he says, working someplace at a ground-level job. Management strategy, he says – keeps him in touch with the working peeps. I wanted to ask about the new focus for Mills Farm. Cousin Teddy likes being Old Charley. He's out of a gig, if the new marketing program and water-park enlargement is adopted for Mills Farm. Cousin Teddy says he'll look like heck in swim-trunks."

"What about the lawsuit," Acey McClain folded his hands and leaned back in the battered leather executive chair which was essentially his very personal throne. "The lawsuit," he elaborated, when Kate just blinked in polite bafflement. "Over the Memorial Day weekend flood." Acey had a personal interest in following injury lawsuits, as his personally-broken scoops with regard to cases of spectacular corporate negligence had been professionally quite rewarding during his day as a big-city beat reporter.

"Oh, that!" she answered. "It's going nowhere, Chief. The injured party, Mr. Hartman, specifically claimed that he had not been warned by Mills Farm of the flood danger, when he checked in with his family. You remember; the family who were rescued by the old retired federal agent from Alaska, in his cranky old boat, just before their weekend cottage was swept away in the high water? Well, yeah; it turns out they <u>were</u> warned when they checked in. The clerk told them so; specifically told them to keep their cellphones on, since there was a flood emergency warning out for residences along the river over the weekend. And the place they were renting was on the river."

"I fail to follow," Acey frowned and steepled his hands. Kate sighed again, deeply, and elucidated.

"He was, in fact, such a demanding and confrontational a-hole when he booked in, that the check-in clerk recorded the whole thing on her own cellie – mostly because he was being such an a-hole. She was afraid that he would report her to management, so she did her own recording." Kate explained. "That recording is now in possession of the Mills Farm attorneys. Lucky for them, isn't it? The clerk is my cousin Bianca; she's doing a course in hospitality management ..."

"Lucky for her," Acey straightened his chair and regarded his ace reporter with a searching expression. "Does she want to go into a career as a journalist? The kid has the right instincts."

"Eh ... no," Kate reported with mild regret. "Bianca has no career ambitions, other than to meet her Prince Charming, marry and have half-a-dozen children with him. Nice kid – but read too many romance novels. And she's fixated on…"

"Never mind the personal life of your cousin," Acey slumped in his chair. Really, sometimes Kate disappointed him with her lack of enthusiasm for the journalistic jugular. "What was so damning about your Cousin Bianca's recording that it would sink the whole lawsuit?"

"The part where she advised him to keep their cellphones on and charged because of the rain, and he told her to … um … fornicate off, they had come to Mills Farm for a relaxing weekend, not to be panicked by some sub-moronic working-class pleb, and it was management's responsibility to assure their guests' comfort and security anyway."

"That would do it," Acey nodded, in sad agreement. "He's not a local, is he?"

"Transplant from the east coast, to his firm's Corpus Christi office," Kate consulted her notebook. "And the recording will go over real well, with a Texas judge, especially since two local volunteers subsequently risked their lives to rescue his family, after he chose to be a total and irredeemable a-hole and ignore Cousin Bianca's advice."

"Ah … winning friends and influencing people wherever he goes," Acey McClain sighed, a sad sigh fetched up from the depths of his soul. "Some guys just have the talent. Gotta hand it to them, Kate; I should send him a copy of Dale Carnegie, not that it will do him any good. So, anything else about Mills Farm, since they are the story o' the moment? Any more of your exclusive with Lew Dubois? Now, there's a guy who obviously read the book."

"Not really, Chief." Kate frowned at her notebook. "But I kind of get a feeling that he isn't really on board with the grand corporate scheme, for the massive water-park to compete with Six Flags, or Schlitterbahn. Nothing I can really put into words, or make a story of. It's all … subtle stuff, you know? I think Mr. Dubois has his own notion of what Mills Farm might be … ought to be, could be. And he is a guy with juice, you know what I mean? Not quite enough juice to force them into a U-turn ... but sufficient to bend things his way, if he puts his mind to it and works behind the scenes. On the ground-level. There's no story here, Chief – not yet, but I think that there might be. I just want to keep my feelers out. There'll be a good story in it down the road. It just may take some time."

"All right, Kate," Acey looked at his own computer monitor – yes, it looked as if there was enough going on locally for the next issue, and the issue after that as well. "Keep me posted."

"There is one little news treat for you," Kate folded up her notebook and absently thrust the pencil back into her hair. "Rich – who runs the Café? He's gonna work with me, setting up a little 'cooking for kids' feature on the Beacon website. *Captain Kitten's Kitchen*, it's gonna be called; little videos and recipes – he's really keen on teaching kids to appreciate good food. And he does good food..." Kate's expression was momentarily reminiscent and gluttonous. "He fixed me supper, last weekend, Chief. It was ... oh, it was the absolutely best meal I have ever eaten. And I grew up eating my Abuelita's holiday meals."

"Sounds a great idea, Kate. Keep me posted." Satisfied, Acey McClain turned his attention back to his own computer monitor, momentarily baffled by the challenge of downloading an email attachment and saving it to his own documents. He could have asked Kate, but she had already walked him through this several times. And she had work to do.

"Will do, Chief." Kate escaped, before her supervisor, boss, and senior editor could ask any more searching questions about Richard, and the proposed Quartermayne food challenge, and her own decidedly split loyalties.

And a Caravan Full of Cat

Richard, having slept the sleep of the deeply exhausted after a full day of rowing a small boat on a flooded river, waiting to be debriefed by the head of the emergency services center, and spending the afternoon and early evening in constructing a classic French menu with an eye toward impressing Kate Heisel at least as far as the door to the Airstream, did not wake early for once, as was his usual custom. He slept until the sun was full up, in a watery blue sky studded with drifts of pure white cotton-candy clouds, a sky limited by the walls and roofs of downtown Luna City.

He might have slept for much longer, save for an uncomfortably full bladder and an equally uncomfortably heavy weight on his chest, a moving weight which persisted in thrusting a whiskered muzzle in his face, and demanding, "Merroow!" in such emphatic tones that he absolutely had to pay attention. Especially when the heavy weight bounced somewhat lower on his supine anatomy…

Richard vented himself of a few heartfelt remarks as he vented his bladder into the appropriate receptacle, while Ozymandias-King-of-Kings smugly took over the warmest portion of the bed where Richard had lain, kneading the bedclothes with slit-eyed satisfaction.

"You conniving little beggar!" He concluded. Ozymandias-King-of-Kings regarded him with that towering air of smug superiority which only cats and certain aristocrats easily command. It came to Richard as he hastily dressed for work that he and the cat had one quality in common; an adamantine determination to have their own way in all things, large and small. Still, he felt a certain amount of grudging affection for the beast. No, he would not turn it out to cope for itself, after all. It would be pleasant to have something glad to see him at the end of a day's work – even if it were only that he had opposable thumbs and a tin-opener. He had kept Miss Letty's gift plant alive all this time; perhaps he could try his luck with higher forms of life.

It was light outside, although the Airstream and the gardens behind the Café and the other buildings ranging that side of the Square were still in shadow. Richard added a couple of more curses, under his breath – since Ozymandias-King-of-Kings was already looking at him with one of those looks, as he opened the door and stepped out into an unexpectedly cool morning. Still, humidity hung in the air like the remembrance of a bad hangover. It was hours past his usual time to be up and opening the Café for morning breakfast. By now, only the late lingerers at the *stammtisch* would still be there; the Steins, and perhaps Doc Wyler and Miss Letty. But with the bridge still flooded, and construction crews like Roman Gonzales's workers all sidelined by high water, likely there hadn't been much regular business anyway – well within Araceli's ability to cope.

When he went to the back door of the Café, the cat followed him in – as confidently as if he had been expected, as an honored guest, no less. Richard didn't notice at first, but Araceli did.

"Where did that nasty thing come from!" She demanded, shooting a basket of dishes into the industrial dishwasher. "Shoo! Get out of here!"

Richard wondered if he had something unsavory on the underside of his shoe, or perhaps his trousers. "I don't know, I thought I put on a clean pair," he protested, and the brindle cat sat just inside the door, tail neatly wrapped around its paws, chin lifted as if it were passing judgment on the Café kitchen. *'Not anything like what I'm accustomed – but will have to do,'* said Ozymandias-King-of-King's superior expression. "Oh, that," Richard twigged, "Well, erm. It's a kitten. A cat, maybe. It was hanging around outside, and it looked … well, hungry. A bit lost, too, so I fed it last night, and let it into the caravan. I suppose it's expecting to be fed again."

Araceli's sigh was one heavily exaggerated for effect. "Chef, once you feed it, it's yours. I suppose you've given it a name already."

"Erm … I have. Ozymandias-King-of-Kings. Ozzie for short."

"Mrrooww!" Ozzie commanded, imperiously. Richard began rooting around in the cupboard of odd dishes at the very back of the kitchen next to the broom and mop cupboard for something suitable to feed the cat from, while Araceli continued, "Chef, you know you can't have cats and dogs in the food-prep area – the health department will have a cow."

"They have a cow? A bad example for the rest of us, I must say. I would have thought that a cow was even more unsanitary, the way they let fly with their poo whenever they feel the urge."

"You know what I mean," Araceli scowled, as Richard fetched out another cat-sized serving of cold chicken and pate from the cooler, left from the night before. He had found two odd dishes, stuck at the back of the odd-crockery cupboard. "Chef, you can't have that animal indoors, not in here."

Since he was in diapers, nothing had ever made Richard more obdurate than anyone telling him that he couldn't do something – but in this case, Araceli was correct. Silently, he filled one dish with minced chicken, and the other with water, and carried them out the back door, bidding Ozzie to follow him. Ozzie made a show of leisurely grooming whiskers and paws, before strolling out after Richard and the dishes; an irritating show of what the cat expected of his human servitor.

Richard left Ozzie scarfing down cold chicken as if he had been starving for weeks, and re-entered the Café. "All right; sorted. Anything else you care to know? I imagine that Kate regaled you with every tiny detail of last night, including the fact that nothing happened which would not stain Abuelita Adeliza's cheek with the slightest blush."

"Don't be so sure of that," Araceli replied, smartly. "Some of Abuelita's stories are so raunchy they would make a stone saint cover their ears and beg for forgiveness. But Katie had a wonderful time; she went over every single bite of your special dinner until Pat and I were so hungry we went to the kitchen and polished off the leftovers from our supper. Pat was watching the water level at our place all last night – we had water up to the bottom step, but luckily, that's as far as it got."

"There is a good reason that houses in certain localities are all built on tall foundations," Richard agreed. "I apologize for missing the morning rush, Araceli. I was just that exhausted from yesterday. All of it. I swear, I have not crashed and burned so comprehensively since ... well, I can't remember."

"Not a problem," Araceli thawed slightly. "There weren't that many for breakfast this morning anyway. Mostly the VFD – they cleaned us out of baked goods, though, right down to the last tray."

"Well, then," Richard was reassured, at this hint of the regular routine reestablished. "A double-batch of cinnamon rolls, and the same of croissants, Just the ticket, eh? And make a tray of the rolls in that orange-nutmeg-flavor variant. They have proved quite popular, you will have noticed. Kudos indeed, my sous-chef. That is what you will be, over the summer."

"A promotion?" Araceli perked up. "Does that mean a raise?"

"Alas, no," Richard sighed. "Just the honor of the thing, plus tips. Although I will speak to Jess about a small increase in your basic wage, on general principles. I have been informed that I may take on two student apprentices over the summer, and I intend to school them severely in the methods of classic kitchen management."

"Sounds interesting," Araceli, who had been employed at the Café since she was herself a teenager, sounded as if she were guardedly invested in the prospect of turning the place into a tiny and unheralded gourmet hot-spot. "Are your apprentice prospects anyone that I might know?"

"Possibly." Richard was already dumping ingredients for basic sweet-roll dough into the massive Hobart mixer. "Robbie Walcott, and Brianna Grant. Young Robbie was the stand-out in my survival cooking segment at the high school this spring, and the good colonel has given his blessing to the prospect of his son being brutally schooled in the good old-fashioned manner of a professional kitchen. Must be all that military blood; they have a thing for cold water, harsh treatment, and men in funny hats yelling personal abuse at one." Richard began cracking eggs into a smaller bowl, and paused to look thoughtfully at his second-in-kitchen command. "You have begun studying *Larousse*, haven't you? I assigned it to Robbie and Brianna; you should at least be familiar with the concepts …"

"It's on my bedside table reading stack," Araceli replied smartly. "Right under *Fifty Shades of Grey*. Give me about a week or so, Chef. What about the other apprentice? Is she one of Sefton and Judy's grandkids?"

"Indeed," Richard sighed. "She has apparently fallen in with bad company. Her parents despair, since they can't keep her away from them, once school is let out for the summer hols." He smirked, briefly. "In the days of my tender youth, I was the bad company whom careful parents desired to keep their spawn from associating with, lest I lead them into temptation. How things have changed! Now, I am their last, best hope. I promised to teach young Brianna how to properly cook. Considering that her grandmother is absolutely the very worst practitioner of the art that it has ever been my misfortune to encounter – and I survived as a student at a British public school, I'll have you know … well, she is a charming young lady. Honestly, I have to begin somewhere."

"Katie told me about your plan to start an on-line cooking class to teach kids," Araceli nodded. "*Captain Kitten's Kitchen*, she said it would be called. She was all excited about it – Katie is all about new media. She learned a lot in college. If you want, you can use Matty and Angelika for your series – they were all keen about it. They like coming here, you see. And they like you, too."

"Children have appallingly unformed tastes," Richard sighed, and Araceli grinned. "They've been helping me out here after school for years. Katie said you wanted to do two levels of cooking – one for the younger set, and one for the older teenagers. I suppose that I can ask Robbie and Brianna for the olders. After all – they will be your peons in the kitchen for three months."

"You have read Larousse!" Richard exclaimed, just as there came a commanding scratch at the back door and a loud 'Merroow.'

"Your master calls," Araceli added, with what Richard thought was a totally uncalled-for turn of sarcasm. As he moved toward the door, Doc Wyler appeared in the kitchen, empty coffee cup in one hand, his veterinary medical satchel in the other.

The irascible owner of the Café, the Lazy W Exotic Game Ranch and just about everything else of value in the vicinity observed with mild interest as Richard opened the back door. "I see you have a cat, Rich – or should I say that the cat has you? Dogs have masters, cats have staff, or so is the saying." Doc Wyler filled up his mug at the coffee urn; such was situated just by the archway between the kitchen and the Café proper, for the convenience of those, like Joe Vaughn and Roman Gonzales, who loaded up their Thermoses prior to heading off to their workaday tasks. Doc Wyler was also qualified as a veterinarian; now he regarded Ozzie with keen-eyed professional interest. "You can't let that beast have the run of the Café, you know. But otherwise – a good vermin-hunting specimen, or would be. No depth perception with a single eye, you know. Good hunters need that."

"You don't recognize this creature, do you?" Richard asked, with fading hope, as Doc Wyler shook his head. Setting down his coffee mug and satchel, Doc Wyler scooped up Ozzie with the deftness of long familiarity with members of the animal kingdom. Richard halfway expected a spit, snarl, and claw-slash of objection, but instead the perverse beast merely uttered the faintest of a "Merroow!" and lay across Doc Wyler's forearm as if it were a boneless leopard melting against the branch of a lonely tree in the veldt. There was no further objection, even when the brief examination got rather more intimate.

"I don't recognize your little friend," Doc Wyler answered at last. "But then I don't do much small-animal stuff. Never did, except for when it came to friends and their beasts. But you got yourself a two-year old neutered male, otherwise in good health save for the eye. Looks like a birth defect, or a very old injury. No scarring that I can see. And well-fed. Maybe displaced by the flood, in which case, he may have come from a long way away. Here – you hold him for a minute." Handing Ozzie to Richard, the old veterinarian rummaged in his medical bag.

"What are you going to do?" Richard asked, in some trepidation, as Doc. Wyler jabbed a small syringe into a vial and drew out a careful quantity.

"Rabies shot." Doc Wyler replied. "Don't look so worried, son – he won't feel a thing. I got it down to a science."

Indeed, he had; Ozzie barely twitched when the jab went in; Richard reflected that anyone who had been doing what Doc did in the way of veterinarian practice ought to be damned good at it, given six decades of experience. Meanwhile, Doc produced another bottle and shook out a small white pill. "You want me to give him that!?" Richard protested, as Ozzie flexed a single paw, fringed generously with claws and growled deep in his throat. "What is it?"

"Droncit, 'case he's picked up some intestinal parasites," Doc Wyler grunted. "Never mind, I'll do it. Just keep a good hold on him."

It was over in a flash; Ozzie thrashed once, and got a good slash with his back paw which raised a thin line of blood across Richard's forearm, but Doc Wyler had pried the cat's mouth open with one deft hand, popped a pill halfway down Ozzie's throat with the other, clamped the cat's mouth closed and gently rubbed the throat while Ozzie complained and thrashed some more. "I told you to keep a good hold on him," Doc Wyler added, when it seemed that the Droncit pill had indeed gone all the way down. Ozzie grumbled some more, but seemed inclined to stay in Richard's grasp. Perhaps that was because it put the cat closer to major blood vessels. "You might want to show him to the Steins. They're cat people, and they might have an idea of where he belongs."

"I've never seen him around the Café before, so I think he belongs with me," Richard replied. "I've rather gotten fond of the little beggar. My Gran always had a cat or two around her place, and I got on with them."

"You have a lot in common," Doc Wyler closed his medical bag and snapped the catches. "Remember – always wash your hands after handling animals. But do show him to Anni and Georg. Someone fed him, saw that he was fixed, he ain't feral. Likely a pet."

"Yes, mine," Richard said to Doc Wyler's vanishing back.

The Steins, when presented with an armful of squirming Ozzie, cooed in admiration and friendship, but confessed to unfamiliarity.

"No, we don't recognize him," Annise Stein said, with confidence. As she and her husband kept three luxuriously spoiled specimens of the feline ilk in their shop, and Annise fed a colony of semi-tame or feral cats whose chosen hunting ground was Town Square *(or the various enticing dumpsters at the back of those businesses and residences which lined the Square)* she spoke with authority. "Although I would speak with Judy Grant. She also loves cats. Perhaps she may know of where this little fellow belongs."

"I would," Richard sighed. "Alas, we are temporarily marooned here until the floodwaters subside, so Ozymandias and I are stuck here with each other until then."

"You have named him?" Annice Stein beamed. "And fed him twice? Then he is yours, assuredly. Cats, they will make their own choice when it comes to these things. Do you have a proper potty for him? You know; a pan of litter for him to make poops in?"

"I don't," Richard acknowledged. "And I don't suppose that I want him using my herb beds."

"Then I shall provide," Annice glowed with approval; Richard thought it was almost as if she were the chief of an orphanage, seeing a promising child adopted into a satisfactory home. "You will allow – we are neighbors, of course. And … food. We have a sack of very expensive dry food – alas, it makes our Mozzie, poor Mozzie – throw up. We cannot feed it to ours, and until the water subsides we may not go to the grocery in Karnesville! So – I will bring around through the garden, when Georg and I are finished with our *kaffe*. Ah, we are cast on our own, until we may drive to Karnesville for our groceries…"

"There is always the Tip-Top," Richard pointed out, and Annice made a scornful face.

"A petrol-stop, and so expensive! But we in Luna City, we shall make-do, as you Americans say…"

"I'm not American," Richard protested and Annice gave a girlish giggle. "You speak English – you see. And I think that you are … what is the phrase? You are one in sympathy. The *gleitschaltung*, as we say. In a kinship, a way of thinking."

"Interesting thought," Richard – at first rejecting the notion with all fervor – thought better of it, almost at once. "But I think, my dear Madame Stein – I am more a Lunaite, than anything else. As are you and your good husband. Luna City rules OK, as we say."

"Certainly," Annice agreed with another one of those twinkling smiles, scratched Ozzie's ears, which attention the cat accepted graciously as only his due. "I shall bring around the necessaries in fifteen minutes."

"You heard her," Richard told the cat, as he walked back through the kitchen, and out the back door into the little area at the back – now filled with the silver caravan, along with the pair of raised herb beds and the selection of wheelie bins. "She said she would be around with the proper kit to see you settled. So be a good Captain Kitten, and we'll have you settled, *rickki-tick*. And by the way – I will have a job for you. Or at least – my sweet Kate of Kate Hall will. Behave yourself until then, OK? More chicken will be your reward."

"Merrow!" Ozzie blinked, and took himself off in a businesslike manner, although Richard left the door to the Airstream open, before he went back to work in the kitchen.

He had only himself to blame for the slaughtered mouse that Ozzie left, secreted under the topmost bed pillow, and which he only discovered very late of an evening, when he crawled into the Airstreams' double bed. Ozzie looked at him with slitted eyes, when he went and dumped the thing in the trash, shuddering with revulsion as he went.

On his return, Ozzie had taken the warmest and most-central place in the bed.

"Damn your eyes – er, the one eye," Richard said, as he shoved Ozzie aside. "Why the hell can't you be Kate?"

After the Flood

From the Karnesville Weekly Beacon – Katherine Heisel, Staff Writer

Clean-up from the unprecedented flooding of the San Antonio River which struck over the Memorial Day weekend began last week as soon as the river subsided into its regular channel. Floresville, Falls City, Karnesville and Goliad all felt the effects of unusually high water to one degree or another, but the community of Luna City caught the worst of unseasonably heavy rains falling across the upper basin of the San Antonio River. For three days, high water cut off all access save by shallow-draft boat to Luna City itself, as well as the resort destination of Mills Farm, just downriver. Cattle and other livestock had to be moved from low-lying pastures along the river bottoms to higher ground, resulting in the first officially-recorded cattle drive through the streets of Luna City in nearly a hundred years. *(See pictures, page 2, this issue.)* Water flowed nearly three feet over the top of the Hernando Gonzales Memorial Bridge, which carries Route 123 over the San Antonio River on the eastern flank of Luna City, according to Luna City Police chief Joseph P. Vaughn, and inundated businesses such as the Tip-Top Ice House, Gas & Grocery, Gonzales and Sons Auto Body and Engine Repair with up to a foot and a half of water. Water even came close to the offices of the Luna City PD, and the LCVFD firehouse, although never in sufficient depth to hamper regular operations. Most businesses and residences on the eastern side of Luna City sustained only minor damage to gardens and outbuildings, since most – like the historic McAllister House – were constructed on high foundations.

The worst effects of the flooding were felt at Mills Farm, where high waters carried away two riverside holiday cottages, a utility building which stored rental watercraft for the resort, and a boat-dock and waterside pavilion. Those structures were completely destroyed, according to Venture Properties International, whose senior marketing director, Lucien Dubois, spoke to reporters on Tuesday following the flood. Damage is estimated at nearly a quarter of a million dollars, according to Mr. Dubois. He emphasized that rebuilding will commence as soon as possible, and regular operations of the popular event venue and destination resort will resume as soon as Route 123 opens for regular traffic. Mr. Dubois did emphasize that the two guest cottages will be rebuilt on higher ground overlooking the river. He declined to comment on how the catastrophic flooding will impact VPI's expansion plans for a water-park and upgraded recreational facilities, saying that he cannot speak authoritatively on that subject until he has conferred with other board members.

Luna City's other popular recreational venue, the Age of Aquarius Campground and Goat Farm, has already re-opened for business. Isolated as it is, on high ground in a bend of the river, the campground and the newly-rebuilt residence of Sefton and Judy Grant suffered no worse damage than being cut off by high water flooding the access road to the campground to a depth of four or five feet. The Grants, who claim to be entirely self-sufficient with their truck garden and chickens, augmented by a windmill and solar panels, say they rather enjoyed their period of isolation from the outer world.

In the Office and On the River

"Lew, Mr. Norberg is holding for you on line two," the hard-pressed senior executive secretary said, as Lucien Dubois passed through the outer office. It was mid-morning at Mills Farm, the Texas show-place of Venue Properties, International

"Thanks, Ramona," Lew shed his hard-hat and reflective vest and dumped them casually on one of the chairs lined up in formation in front of the secretarial desk. "I'll take it in my office. I wasn't expecting him to call until 4 … did he reveal to you something of particular urgency in calling at this moment?"

"He didn't say," Ramona answered, wondering what she should do with the vest and hat. "I'll hold your other calls." Of course: Harry Russell Norberg was the CEO of VPI; all other calls were automatically a lower priority. Ramona concealed a small sigh of regret. Working for Mr. Dubois was so very different from working for the previous manager of marketing. Miss Wyatt may have been a difficult woman as a supervisor, but she was predictable, and most always to be found in her office. Mr. Dubois … well, Mr. Dubois could be practically anywhere during an ordinary a working day. In just a single month Ramona had used up nearly an entire telephone message logbook. At this very moment, a stack of message slips sat on Mr. Dubois' desk – and that was for this day alone. And it wasn't even noon.

Lew Dubois closed the door to the inner office, and took up the telephone receiver. "'Allo, Harry – I wasn't expecting to talk to you until later."

"You know me, Lew; no time like the present. I had a short meet-and-mingle with some big shareholders this morning, and they put the expansion plans front and center for the day. Can't get any peace of mind until I confabbed with you over them."

"You know my feelings on that score, Harry." Lew Dubois drawled, the deep Louisiana accent coming out as thick as blackstrap syrup. "I've never made any secret of how I feel about changing our marketing focus so drastically."

"You haven't," Harry replied, "And I respect your honesty. The truth is that I halfway share your doubts. But with half the directors and some of the biggest investors on board with the whole project as is, and convinced that all VPI has to do is to convince local property owners that money is no object …"

"But since you saw my last memo on the matter of land acquisition," Lew was already shaking his head. "Unless two of the three possible are agreeable, the project cannot be built as designed."

"I know, I read the memo, Lew. You were brutally realistic in your assessment; all three are opposed, one of them adamantly. I suppose that Mrs. Grant could be brought around to part with an acre or two, but that is hardly enough. And the flooding last month – the news coverage shook some support among the directors."

"Pictures taken in the immediate aftermath of disaster always make the situation look even worse than it really is," Lew agreed. "By the way – I assume that Mr. Hartmann has chosen to settle quietly, once he spoke with VPI's legal section."

"Oh, yes," Harry's sense of satisfaction was palpable, even over the telephone. "Kudos to your duty clerk and manager, by the way. That was very well done, handling a difficult customer. He was amazingly less belligerent, once that he was informed of the existence of that recording. I think you can draw a line under that matter, Lew."

"Good. I have bigger fish to fry." Lew chuckled. "Something to make a better feast for our shareholders than a mere water-park. But I have a little more work to do before sharing it with even you, Harry *mon vieux*. It is in my mind a different vision for Mills Farm, for which I have been laying groundwork here and there. I go today on an excursion with an old friend from my days at Castle Mountain – he has retired here to Luna City, where he has family."

"You have a better idea for Mills Farm than the water-park?" Harry sounded intrigued, which pleased Lew no end. "I'd like to hear more."

"This afternoon; I shall have pictures to send you – and I will sound out my old friend … as well as some of my new ones, regarding the possibilities. I am making progress, my friend; more progress than I had thought possible, given the past relations between VPI and the good people of Luna City."

"Ah, that," Harry mused, sounding regretful. "We – that is – our predecessors in the corporation did get off to a very bad start with the locals, back in the very beginning. Well, it's good that you are mending fences, my friend."

"My *grand'mere* used to say that one caught more flies with honey than with vinegar," Lew agreed. "But one must make the effort with the honey, of course."

"You're doing a splendid job, Lew," Harry assured him. "Brief me when you return, this afternoon; I must admit that I am intrigued by the possibilities that you are exploring. I can't talk you into giving me a hint?"

"My lips are sealed until this afternoon." Lew replied. "Four hours. Give me four hours."

As he set down the receiver, Ramona rapped politely on the closed door. Per the privilege of senior staff, she opened it without waiting for a reply and looked around the doorjamb. "You have three new messages, Mr. Dubois."

"Leave them on my desk, Ramona; I'm going out on the river with Mr. Vaughn."

"Shall I tell people when you'll be back in the office?" Ramona's secretarial heart sank, anticipating an afternoon of explaining Mr. Dubois' absence, taking messages, and putting out various small metaphorical corporate fires.

"Four-thirty, at earliest, Ramona – after five at the latest. Anyone who has my private cellphone can call me on it directly. If the matter is most urgent, refer them to Dan in Houston. See you tomorrow, then."

He shrugged on a battered and faded old barn coat and an almost new baseball cap with the logo of Mills Farm embroidered on the front, and departed, whistling tunefully to himself as he walked through the marvelous, summer-enhanced kingdom that was Mills Farm. An emerald swath of velvet-smooth lawns, colorful plantings arranged with perfect asymmetry to enhance the period cottages, carefully tended flowering shrubs and towering oak trees.

He paused to speak with Benny Cordova, the day-to-day manager of Mills Farm, a man with whom he had developed an easy working relationship.

"Out on the river, Benny my old; I want to do a *soupcon* of research for what I think should be the new face of our enterprise."

Benny – slight, tough, middle-aged and the only local employee of Hispanic background not related by blood or marriage to the Gonzales/Gonzalez constellation – was in Lew's confidence, and had been from almost the first day. Now Benny grinned. "Last touches on your renovation plan, chief?"

"*Certainement, cher. El Grande Queso (This was Bennys' term for the CEO of VPI, which Lew had adopted as a means of solidifying rapport with Benny – a capable and solidly loyal employee)* is intrigued with what I have hinted to him of my scheme to renew and enlarge Mills Farm. This evening, I will enlighten him, and in the following days, prepare him with materiel to support my vision over this hideous water-park monstrosity."

"Good luck, chief," Benny nodded, with wholly sincere respect. "If anyone can do it, you can."

"Thank you; but if my plans do come to fruition, you and the other staff will have taken a large part in bringing it about." Lew knew the value of a solid management team at any level, and of paying heartfelt compliments to those members of his team. He had not gone from being a temporary low-level employee to a senior director in a major international hospitality corporation by ignoring such details.

He waved to Teddy Gonzales, in his role and work attire as Charley Mills, seated on the antique but functional Farmall tractor; Teddy was harrowing a small fenced patch of land which would be planted in late-harvest glass-jewel corn, for the edification of visitors and the eventual autumn decoration of Mills Farm. Past the weathered gray ramble of the Dance Hall, and down the winding patch past the sweep of the open-air amphitheater, where two groundskeepers were trimming the grass around the half-circle raised stage at the bottom of the slope. They waved to Lew, and he waved back, calling them by name. He skirted the edge of the golf course, the acre of specimen garden, sending up the scents of lavender and sage into the air, past the graveled parking lot at the Country Restaurant, waving again; this time to the young pot-walloper horsing a wheeled fifty-gallon trash can out from the back of the kitchen to the dumpster, calling him by name and making a friendly jest with reference to pearl-diving.

On past the worker's parking area, across a farther sweep of lawn, and down to where tumbled stones and a couple of thick wooden posts slanted awry from the shallow water, with one heavy beam still connecting them. This was where the riverside cottage had stood, with a little private dock, from which it had been swept away in the Memorial Day weekend flood. Save for Harry Vaughn and a volunteer from the Luna City VFD, two women and four children might have been swept away with it, swept away and drowned in the turbulent floodwater. Which was another reason for Lew Dubois to be heartfelt grateful to Harry Vaughn. Losing a family of paying customers would certainly be a horrendous blotch on the VPI escutcheon, let alone the human tragedy – a matter with which Lew Dubois had experience. With luck, Harry Vaughn would assist Lew Dubois in going three for three on a grand project. Lew had just enough vanity to be ambitious in that manner, enough confidence in his own judgment to insist on his way, and enough experience to get it … one way or another. Now Harry Vaughn and his light metal cockleshell of a motor-boat idled in the shallows, just at the end of where the precarious wharf ended in waist-deep water.

"You are on time, *mon vieux*!" Lew called, over the rumbling of the outboard motor, and Harry called in reply, "On time is an old habit of mine, Lew. Hop in, I'll take you for a spin. Show you the sights outside of your corporate Potemkin village."

"Don't disparage Potemkin villages," Lew said, as he nimbly walked over the narrow beam, until he reached the point where he could step down into the small boat. "They are my living – and a profitable one, at that – although not as profitable as those which the Kingdom of the Mouse built." *(By which he meant the Disneyland destination resort franchise, compared to which VPI was as a small, exclusive boutique.)*

"Damn few are at that," Harry Vaughn snorted, as Lew took a seat in the center of the small tin launch. "Can't see the appeal for myself. But thousands do, apparently …" he added some pithy remarks on what he thought of people who spent hundreds to walk around in a fully-sanitized, expertly designed and immersive stage set interspersed with the occasional thrill ride. Lew let those comments pass over him as he let the river pass by, knowing as he did that most people on vacation wanted to have the real world edited, hemmed, and smoothed over, at least to some degree. Those who wanted the real world at raw full-strength were few and far between. In his realm, a lot depended upon the skill of those doing the editing.

"I thought we would drift downstream for a bit," Harry said, as he let the engine to a low rumble, just enough to keep the boat on course. "Show you the bottomlands … this is mostly part of the original Spanish grant to Don Manuel Gonzalez y Gonzales. Just about everybody with that name around here are descendants and all of them kin but damn if any of them can tell you how, lessn' it's within the last hundred years or so."

"So, Jaimie Gonzales is the current owner of all this." Lew mused thoughtfully. "A descendant of the original Don Manuel?"

"More or less. They're not real certain of how he spelt that last bit of his name." Harry Vaughn agreed. "Crappy handwriting on the original paperwork. He had a league and a labor on this part of the river, back in the old days. That's about four and a half thousand acres. Most of it got sold to Capt'n Herbert K. Wyler, just after the War Between the States, and other bits and pieces ever since then. But Jaimie's stubborn and family-proud. You'll pry any of his land out of his cold, dead hands. Now, the Wyler patch starts on the east bank, just about opposite of Mills Farm, and runs up to the city boundary of Luna City. I'll point all that out to you when we get to it. Likely VPI couldn't get anything but the time of the day and a kick in the aspidistra from ol' Stevie-boy Wyler. He's family-proud, too. The contrary old bastard is as tough as nails and likely will live another fifteen years just to spite VPI."

"This I knew," Lew mused, as the small boat powered downstream. The water was still high, and sufficiently deep in the center, enough to accommodate Harry Vaughn's boat. "The thing that I am contemplating, *mon vieux* – access along the riverbank. A bridle-trail for horses and bicycles, landing places for canoes and kayaks, at various points along the river, beginning at Luna City. And leases for hunting, to our guests."

"Not certain with Stevie-boy," Harry Vaughn grunted. "But Jaimie may be agreeable. There's prime hog-hunting lower down. Wild pig, fattened on acorns and pecans. Ask Andy Pryor about how good those hogs can be, dressed out. And there are more of them than are fleas on a mangy dog, so there ain't no bag limit on them, either. But the Grants won't budge on the hunting. Judy Grant is foursquare against anything that hurts animals." He gave a small snort of disgust at this heresy. "But they wouldn't have nothing against boats and kayaks. Or even horses, crossing their patch."

"I cannot open such negotiations with Mr. Pryor until after the food challenge," Lew admitted. "Because we are contestants in the barbeque contest. It's an ethical matter. But ... he would, I think, not be amiss in an agreement to process game for our clients. These small towns – I must go carefully. Feelings in such places are delicate. The bonds of connection so complicated and strong. I know that, to my bones, being an outsider in so many places. I must proceed with all delicacy, and you are my guide – we are friends of many years. I trust that you will guide me in those ways which will best serve us all. This place, this project requires special care. I am convinced in my heart that the water-park expansion is ill-advised, even impossible. But to dissuade VPI from the folly of pursuing it, I must offer something better, more attractive, unique." He fell silent, as the motor-boat puttered along, around several bends, always where the water ran the swiftest, clear and green, where strands of water-weeds followed the current, now a sullen brown from sediment stirred up by the recent floods. Stands of oak, cypress and cotton-wood trees lined the banks, interspersed with open meadow, and the occasional field of coastal rye grass. Now and again, they passed a scattering of cattle, and several times startled long-legged white egrets, stalking though the shallows. Lew kept his cellphone in hand, occasionally taking pictures of the most attractive country vistas

"It goes on like this for several more miles," Harry Vaughn idled the engine within sight of a particularly tall stand of trees. "All the way to where Route 80 crosses over toward Helena. See enough?"

"I think so," Lew agreed. "Now – back toward Luna City. I have a question to which you may know the answer – who owns that old hotel, now? That splendid old pile on the Square?"

"The Cattleman?" Harry let the boat drift sideways, until he could turn the engine and gun it against the current for the return journey. Both men remained quiet for some minutes, while the riverbank slid past. Finally, Harry spoke. "Used to belong to the Bodies, who own the feed mill in town. Now it's the property of the city, and the Historical Society. There's four suites all done up for visitors on the second floor. Listed on some internet B&B service, so we got visitors coming through now and again, paying enough to keep the lights on. I've stayed there myself a time or two. Ain't anything like it was when I was a young sprout, though." He sent a shrewd look at Lew. "You VPI folks tried to buy it once – to knock down and move it all to Mills Farm, lock, stock and barrel. You figure on trying again?"

"A method much less drastic, *mon vieux*," Lew replied. "My plan incorporates a lease of the property, on terms mutually advantageous to both Luna City and VPI. We complete renovations, and maintain it as a hotel."

"You be anticipating a whole bunch of new visitors, then?" Harry scratched his jaw, an expression of extreme skepticism on his craggy countenance. "This here Luna City is not the Kingdom that the Mouse built and neither is Mills Farm. You'd never get enough guests to fill a quarter of those rooms."

"Ah, but you see – under my expansion plan for Mills Farm there would be." Lew leaned forward, his own face alight with enthusiasm. "It is in my mind to offer riverine excursions – canoes and kayaking on this very river! Imagine it, *mon vieux*! And pony trekking, hunting, swimming in a naturally-formed pool, a campfire ring and group singing around a blazing fire! A thousand times more authentic than an artificial water-park, with ridiculous chutes and ladders. So very plastic, so plebian! Nothing like we have always marketed Venue Properties – luxury experiences for the discriminating traveler. Can you see it in your mind? The old-world experience, here in Texas – but a genuine reflection of place! The ambiance of a perfect small town like Luna City! So many Americans, they do not wish to travel to Europe now; the expense, the hassles; they wish rather to enjoy a quality experience, and this – this is what I envision for the new Mills Farm!"

"Nice work if you can get it," Harry Vaughn ventured, after some thought. They were at that moment passing by Mills Farm; the manicured acres, the perfectly-positioned buildings, the soaring trees.

"I will have it," Lew nodded, in perfect assurance. "I have done for VPI two of their finest resorts. One began as a ruin of stones and brambles, the other as a pile of logs; with this, I am not starting from the very beginning. Now I would see the river between Mills Farm and Luna City. I wish to send pictures to the person whom I must first convince of my wisdom…"

"Your CEO?" Harry Vaughn grinned, a grin partly hidden by his enormous, old-fashioned mustache.

"My wife," Lew also grinned. "She is an artist, you understand – a designer of sets and stages. She will provide me with something I may show to my fellow directors, and to our shareholders … now this prospect is a most interesting one. I have never regarded it from this angle. Is it part of the Grant establishment?"

"Yup." Harry Vaughn idled the boat engine so that Lew could snap another picture with his cellphone. "The best swimming hole along the whole river is just around the next bend. This bit was overgrown with cedar since I can remember. Too hard to get to by land, but the water is nice and deep. The old Sheffield place was about halfway up that low little bluff, but it went to rack and ruin about the time I was in short pants. Used to be a tramp lived in a cave up in there for a while after that, but he was the only regular resident for forty years, until Judy and Sefton turned up with their parcel of crazies."

"A boathouse," Lew mused. "Here, where the river is deepest – of the old-fashioned kind, *mon vieux*. If we cannot find one to purchase and move here from elsewhere, then my wife will design one …"

"If you can convince Judy and Sefton," Harry Vaughn cautioned. "Best not mention your plans for hunting…"

"No fear," Lew snapped off a couple of more pictures of the wooded slope, and the nearly invisible gullies which threaded it. "I will be the soul of diplomacy. And this little tract borders Mills Farm already, does it not? They strike me as parties who will be agreeable to selling this sliver of land; they are often short of funds, *n'est-ce pas?*"

Harry Vaughn snorted. "They are not sensible with money, since they see it so very rarely. But my nephew's wife is their CPA – all but their keeper, in financial matters. And she is no fool, so don't even think of being anything less than straight with her. Small-town girl or not, she'll have your balls for breakfast if you have any intention of cheating her clients in a real estate venture."

"Such a thought never entered my head," Lew protested. "My dealings with Luna City must be all entirely open and above-board, as they have been with all my ventures. I am that rarest of creatures in the corporate world – a fair and honest man. It is a curious thing, *mon vieux* – in possessing the reputation of being of scrupulously moral character, one is hardly ever offered the opportunity to be otherwise. It spares me a great deal."

"Especially wear and tear on your memory when it comes to testifying before a grand jury," Harry Vaughn replied, with a cynical chuckle. "Always be honest, I used to say. Saves remembering the details of the lies you told."

"Exactly," Lew Dubois put away the cellphone. "And now – it is Friday afternoon. Guest night at the VFW. Will you join me in some casual networking? I wish to sound out others regarding my proposal for the renewed Mills Farm."

Harry Vaughn chuckled, deep in his chest. "You are one crafty sombitch. You don't miss a trick, do you?"

"Of course not," Lew returned. "That's why they pay me the big bucks - *beaucoup d'argent*."

Reveal

In the kitchen of the double-wide home on Oak Lane, Araceli Gonzalez-Gonzales sang softly along to the radio, tuned to KTKO in Beeville, to *Tennessee Flat-top Box*, as she stirred the batter for lemon-butter pound-cake cupcakes. "In a little cabaret, in a South Texas border town …" Araceli and the radio could barely be heard outside of the kitchen. The double-wide was a small one, the dividing walls thin, and her husband Patrick was fast asleep in the darkened master bedroom. Pat worked nights, driving a tanker truck for a company working the shale oil formation in South Texas. This was a Saturday afternoon in early summer; the heat outside at the sizzle-on-the-blacktop worst by late afternoon. Araceli and Pat's children, Angelika and Mateo came inside after a morning of helping their mother with the outdoor work of mowing the lawn and pulling up weeds in the bed of cosmos flowers and multi-colored salvia plants which lined the yard – a yard defined by a waist-high chain link fence.

That fence was nearly the first improvement that Pat made to their home when Angelika was a baby. There had never been very much traffic on Oak Lane, almost the last residential street before Luna City raveled out into cultivated fields, pastures, and stands of live oaks – but eventually the narrow street wandered out toward the main road. The first thing which could be said about Araceli's children, was that she was fiercely but unobtrusively protective of them. The toddler-aged Angelika was a fearless wanderer. In the living room adjoining the tiny kitchen, Angelika curled up in a battered old Barcalounger, absorbed in a thick Harry Potter adventure. Eleven years old, going on twelve, with a round, solemn face and long dark hair done up in loops of braid and tied with ribbons, a fastidious and intelligent child. Her seven-year-old brother sat at the kitchen table, building a complicated Lego brick starship.

This room – indeed, the whole double-wide was a shabby place, especially in comparison with other homes in Luna City, and yet it was comfortable and immaculately clean. Nothing in it matched particularly, or would ever be the subject of one of those interior decorating features. But Araceli and Pat's friends were repeatedly drawn in, made welcome, especially on Sunday afternoons, when Pat served up barbeque from the massive grill and smoker parked out in back. No guests at Pat and Araceli's Sunday afternoons worry about rings from the bottoms of cold soft drinks or beer bottles leaving marks on the furniture, or guacamole dip spilled onto the sofa slip-cover. Araceli will just sigh and run it through the washing machine.

There was a heavy, old-style television stowed away in a console cabinet as the central feature, under a framed painting of the Virgin of Guadalupe, in her starry cloak and wreathed in a golden halo and a wealth of pink roses. A constellation of family pictures crowned the top of the cabinet; baby pictures of Angelika and Mateo, of Araceli and Patrick on their wedding day with their attendants – the girls in aqua blue dresses, the young groomsmen solemn in their rented formal suits, a hand-tinted studio portrait of Araceli's grandparents, Abuelo Jesus and Abuelita Adeliza, her younger brother Berto in his high school graduation cap and gown, Araceli in hers – seemingly solemn and thoughtful. In spite of all encouragement to the contrary, Araceli had already made up her mind as to what she would do after the finished high school.

"Mama, are those for tomorrow?" Mateo asked, as Araceli deftly poured batter into a twenty-four-pan cupcake tin, each hollow lined with pretty yellow cupcake papers.

"They are, *hijo* – but you may lick out the bowl when I'm done. I need to have one for everyone who is coming tomorrow."

"Why?" Mateo sneaked a lick at the beaters of the stand mixer.

"Stop that, Matty – the beaters are for your sister, you're getting the bowl. Because this is the way that are going to announce Miss Jess's new baby to all our friends tomorrow – whether it is a boy or a girl."

"With cupcakes?" Mateo frowned in puzzlement. Araceli slid the cupcake pan into the oven and shutting the oven door on a gust of heat.

"I'm going to make a sweet cream cheese filling for the inside of the cupcakes – strawberry for a girl, blueberry for a boy, and then frost the top. People will have to eat the cupcake to find the answer." Araceli explained. Mateo's expression lightened.

"You must know if it is a girl or a boy. Are you going to tell us?"

"I do know," Araceli pursed her lips. "But my lips are sealed. It's a secret until tomorrow. But since I will cut a little bit out of the middle of the cupcakes to leave room for the filling, we will have those for our dessert tonight. OK?"

"OK," Mateo agreed philosophically – he had the bowl with the last bits of batter to console him, after all. When the bowl was nearly cleaned of all smears of buttery, sweet, lemony cake batter, Mateo put it in the sink and returned to his Lego starship. At that moment, his father emerged, yawning, from the bedroom.

"You didn't leave any for me, *hijito!*" Patrick complained; bleary-eyed, his hair ruffled from heavy sleep, after a long night spent jockeying a heavy tanker truck along narrow country roads in the dark. Araceli spared a quick affectionate kiss for her husband; stocky and thick-shouldered. Pat had the same rounded features as his daughter, but his hands were those of a mechanic – ridges and fingernails never quite scoured clean of oil and grime that comes from working with engines. Pat and Araceli had known each other all their lives and married for the last thirteen years – married the week after they graduated together from Luna City High School.

"I left the beaters for you, Papi!" Mateo claimed, and Araceli chided him.

"They were for your sister." From across the room, Angelika looked up from her book.

"I don't want them," she said, all seriousness. "I read that you shouldn't eat batter and cookie dough that has raw eggs in it."

"Oh, pooh – those are eggs from your grandmother's hens," Araceli replied. "There's nothing wrong with them. It's eggs from the market that you need to worry about."

In the meantime, Patrick poured himself a large mug of coffee. Still in bathrobe, tee-shirt and pajama trousers, he settled at the table next to Mateo. Araceli smiled at them both; this is what she wanted, against all expectations, since she was fifteen.

Araceli was that most curious of modern women; one who never really wanted anything more than to be a wife, mother, and homemaker. She was a quiet rebel and nonconformist. All through her schooldays, everyone assumed that she would go to college, even if she had to go live with the uncle and aunt in Elmendorf and take on a profession. Her mother urged her to be a science teacher, the guidance counselor at the high school looked at her grades in science and mathematics and recommended all kinds of professions – everything from software developer to chemist.

Araceli smiled and nodded, and kept her own counsel, as she had since she was Angelika's age, the oldest of a family of four, and the maternity nurse put her baby brother Berto in her arms, and her mother said, *"Do you want to take care of your little brother, 'Celi?"*

"Oh, may I, Mama?" Araceli breathed. That was the summer that she was eleven years old, and from that day on, Berto was her living baby doll – cuddled, fed, tended, and amused by a doting older sister – to the point where their mother hardly had to lift a finger until school began again. It was a family legend, that when Berto first went to kindergarten, the formidable Miss Letty McAllister had asked him who his parents were, and Berto had replied, *"Mama, Papi, an' 'Celi."*

After that summer, Araceli was never in any doubt that babies and children were what she wanted; a family with a proper house, and husband and all. Just like *Little House on the Prairie,* the reruns of which television show was her very favorite. Only with electricity and cars. It was perfectly fine that most of her friends insisted they wanted to work at something glamorous in the city and live in a fashionably-decorated apartment and eat in restaurants every night of the week. Even her best friend, Jess Abernathy said she wanted that, even though Jess really wanted to be a world-championship barrel-racer in the rodeo. Araceli knew instinctively that her modest ambition was something considered terribly retrograde, old-fashioned, even something to be scorned.

She bided her time and waited. She waited until she and Patrick were eighteen, done with school. Abuelita Adeliza approved, even if Araceli's parents were appalled. Abuelita was of the old generation, and this was expected for a girl; the white dress and veil, the wedding Mass said by Father Bernardo, setting up modest housekeeping with a bunch of miss-matched and hand-me-down cheap furniture. Another stepping-stone in the progress of a life. She did go on working at the Café; secretly, Araceli quite enjoyed the Café. A job was just a job, something one did for a few hours a day; real life was making a home, a home for herself and Pat, and then the children. If the job facilitated that – all to the good. That's what a job was for, something that underpinned and supported that real life, the life that gave quiet contentment and fulfillment to everyone – even those friends who only knew it in the retelling.

"What's for supper tonight, 'Celi?" Pat had nearly finished his coffee. So scrambled, his working days; supper was his breakfast, his supper was a brief meal eaten in the early morning before he went to bed. Araceli checked the progress of the cupcakes through the glass window set in the oven door.

"Lasagna," she answered. "I'll start it baking as soon as the cupcakes are out of the oven. Last of the batch that I made and froze. If you aren't in the lasagna mood – I made a bunch of meatballs from Anna-Maria's recipe. They're in the big freezer."

"Lasagna's fine." Patrick grinned at her and Araceli grinned back. Utterly content; tomorrow they would host a good array of their friends. A whole brisket side was already soaking in Pat's secret special marinade. Sometime tonight or in the early morning, he would start it slow-smoking in the massive BBQ. That purchase had been his first and only indulgence when things started picking up in the shale oil fields, and he landed the job which so far – had been the best-paid of his life. Likely that he would never have a better-paying one, but Araceli did not mind that very much. She had never intended or wanted to marry a rich man; a hard-working, sober, and honest one was what she wanted. All that she had ever wanted; of those building-blocks was a happy life built, in Luna City.

Luna City Autumn Newsletter

Fall 2017 Newsletter

Luna City Chamber of Commerce

5 North Town Square, Suite 4

Check out our Facebook Page

Mills Farm Country Garden opens their Halloween Pumpkin Patch on Saturday, October 14th, in the field adjacent to the Texas Specimen Garden. Bring the little ones, and pick your very special Halloween pumpkin, plus enter for a drawing to be held every Saturday at 12:00 noon to the 28th for a set of pumpkin-carving tools and a $25 gift certificate for the Mills Farm Country Store. A costume contest will be held on the 28th at 4:00, so put on your scariest duds and come on out!

A La Carte With Quartermayne Cooking Challenge

The Luna City VFD chapter hosts the cooking showdown between Pryor's Meats & BBQ and the Mills Farm Country Restaurant from 3:00-8:00 on August 24. For a small donation, all are welcome to come on out, sample the competing dishes, and vote on the winning signature dishes. The word is that Pryor's and the Country Restaurant will prepare smoked brisket and whole roasted pig, with accompanying sides. This event will be filmed for broadcast on the popular Food Network series A La Carte With Quartermayne, hosted by former Denver Broncos quarterback Allen Lee Mayne. Participants must be aware that they may appear in background shots. Anyone interviewed on camera will be asked to sign a release allowing that footage to be used in the final program. Come on out and show your appreciation for good old Texas BBQ, and give a hearty Luna City welcome to Allen Lee and his crew. All donations will be turned over to local and military-oriented charities such as the Salvation Army, and Soldiers' Angels.

Luna City, Texas – Home of the Mighty Fighting Moths

Upcoming Events

August 24

The cast and crew of *Ala Carte with Quartermayne* will be filming locally for a showdown pitting Pryor's Meats & BBQ against Mills Farm Country Restaurant.

September 11

A ceremony of remembrance for 9/11 will be held at 9 AM at the flagpole in front of the LCVFD/PD facilities.

September 16

The Luna City Players present the classic comedy *The Man Who Came to Dinner* at the Koenig Opera House. Performances are Saturday evenings at 7:30, with a Sunday afternoon matinee at 12:30 through the end of the month.

Hurricane Season Begins in Late Summer

Lunaites are encouraged to prepare for violent winds, heavy rain, and power outages.

Luna City ISD News

Mighty Months Marching Band Practice

Moths Marching Band practice will be every Monday afternoon from 3-5, and every Thursday morning from 6-8. Coach Garrett has distributed music for new selections; band members are to be familiar with their parts before the start of practice.

Life Skills Course – For Fall Semester

Richard from the Café has agreed to teach the 'survival cooking' portion of the life skills class again. Parents of sophomores scheduled to take the Life Skills Course must note any food allergies on permission slips, as food will be prepared and consumed as part of the class. Adverse reactions will merit transportation by the fastest means possible to the Karnesville Med-Center for treatment.

Emergency Shelter Exercise

As part of a drive to improve local emergency preparedness during the upcoming hurricane season, community volunteers will be setting up an emergency shelter in Luna City High School's Hernando Gonzalez Gymnasium during the third week in August.

LCISD PTA Hamburger and Hot Dog Stand

Volunteers are needed to run the PTA-sponsored hamburger and hot-dog stand by the Moth Field stand during all home games. All volunteers must take the food-handler safety course offered on-line at http://courseforfoodsafety.com/ in order to participate in this fund-raising activity. Food poisoning is no laughing matter. The course is available for a small fee and an hour of your time.

Community Marketplace

Proposed Model on Display at Mills Farm

A detailed scale model of the proposed water park expansion of Mills Farm will be on display in the foyer of the Mills Farm Country Restaurant throughout the months of August and September.

From Chief Vaughn, Luna City PD

Engineers from TxDot have begun repairs on the Rte. 123 bridge over the San Antonio River. Spring flooding undermined the bridge footings on both sides of the bridge. Until work is completed, all traffic will be routed over a temporary single-lane bridge. Traffic lights at either end will regulate traffic flow. Chief Vaughn asks for courtesy and good sense on the part of all until repairs are complete, and everyone can go back to being careless and inconsiderate drivers.

Captain Kitten's Kitchen Series!

Richard at the Café beings a cooking series for kid as part of the Talk of the Town blog. Kids and teens will learn classic French cooking through a series of demonstrations and recipes, beginning in July. Check the Talk of the Town Blog for new videos, kitchen tips and recipes for kids of all ages.

Captain Kitten's Debut

Barely a week after Roman Gonzales came around and returned the Airstream to its' usual place in the Age of Aquarius, Kate Heisel's small late-model VW Bug came bumping up the freshly-regraveled road from town. Richard was luxuriating in having everything that he had become accustomed to getting back to normal. The campground was entirely deserted – just the way that he liked it. Sprouts of new grass cast a haze of rich green across the still-soggy meadow, the windmill up the hill at the Grants' clattered away, and the dying sunlight in the west gilded stands of oak and cedar with an edge of gold and made the Amazing Straw Castle gleam as if it were made of ivory. Miss Letty's gift spider-plant, newly fringed with runners from which depended tiny new plants, hung again from its' accustomed place on the awning that sheltered the Airstream and the square of concrete blocks that made Richard's patio. Ozzie the cat played in a desultory manner with a stray chicken feather blown by the breeze on a patch of concrete made warm by a day of sun.

All was in its place again, and all was right with his world. In the pasture beyond, the enormous dog and small pony – accompanied as usual by the small chicken riding on its withers – wandered as they liked. No one had claimed the oddly-assorted trio after the floodwaters receded. As expected, Judy Grant incorporated them all into hers' and Sefton's menagerie of lost and formerly abused creatures.

He watched the little VW approach with a pleasant frisson of pleasure: Kate, who demanded nothing from him but undemonstrative affection and the occasional excellent meal, a level-headed, independent woman, to whom tantrums and blackmail – emotional or otherwise – were completely foreign emotions. She parked the VW and got out, tugging an enormous plastic bag spangled with the Walmart logo with some difficulty out of the back seat. He thought that he should kiss her, a comradely peck on the cheek without asking for anything further – and no, she did not.

"Hey, you," she puffed. "All back to your usual haunts, I see. It was kind of nice, having your little trailer out in back of the Café, though. Everyone knew just where to find you at any hour."

"Well, my Kate of Kate Hall – that is why I preferred to return here. It's quiet and I need my quiet, my open spaces. You know, Kate – I've come to doubt that I am really a city sort of chap after all. I've become accustomed to open spaces, an unimpeded view of the sky. Peculiar, I know."

"You're becoming a Texan," Kate giggled deliciously and then giggled more at the expression that Richard was certain he had on his face.

"Perish the thought, Kate. I'm an outlander here, always will be, I'm afraid – fond as I am becoming of it all. I'll never be 'of' here …"

"Yes, you will," Kate allowed, in an air of generous sympathy. "You'll be like the Steins, or Chris, or even Clovis Walcott. You'll be 'of' here, you just aren't <u>from</u> here. No one holds it against you – you just got here as fast as you could. I see that your Captain Kitten apprentice is all ready for his close-up… aren't you, Ozymandius-King-of-Kings," She cooed, leaning down to scratch Ozzie's brindled head. "Who's the best and most photogenic kitten in the world, then? Who's ready to take the internet by storm? You are, darling Ozzie! Just be adorable, and you'll be a star in no time." She added a bit of baby-talk, while Ozzie – shameless at being admired – wound his lithe self around Kate's ankles *(fetchingly revealed and made curiously enticing in stockings and sensible, low-heeled shoes worn with her equally sensible skirt suit)* and leaned into her hand, begging for more, more, and more.

Richard observed this with a degree of disgust. "You shouldn't have to talk to him that way, Kate – he understands perfect English."

"I'm just buttering him up," Kate retorted. "I have to encourage him, in front of the camera – although he is the most awful ham… Besides, I need him to wear a sort of costume for the shoot, and sometimes animals are a little hinky about the whole prospect."

"I can't think why …" Richard began, and then Kate set down the bulging plastic bag and removed five objects from it. "My dear Kate, have you taken leave of your senses."

"It will be fantastic," she assured him, in deliberately soothing tones. "See – this cat head and the furry mittens are for you to wear for the video shoot when you demonstrate your kid-friendly recipes. You wear that white chef jacket and that white toque… and see, Abuelita made a little set for Ozzie …"

"I will not abase myself by dressing up like one of those ghastly mascot animals," Richard insisted; the cat head was of brindled plush-covered fake fur, with upstanding ears, topped with a crisp white toque, intended to slip over the wearer's head. "Wherever did you get this horrible object, Kate?"

"They have them at Walmart," Kate replied, seemingly unmoved by Richard's horrified reluctance. "They call them 'maskimals.' I bought one, and Abuelita fixed it up to look like Ozzie, with the toque and all.

You only have to wear it for the medium shots," she added with calculation, and Richard shook his head.

"I won't do it, my Kate – and nothing you can say or do will make me." (*Not even offering to seduce me would seal the deal, Richard added silently.*)

"I suppose that I can ask Bree or Robbie, then." Kate, the irresistible force meeting the immoveable object, was not the least dismayed. "All they have to do is to stand up behind the table and demonstrate the recipe. You don't want to do a voice-over narration?" she asked, sounding unnaturally tentative for her usual forthright self.

"Hell will freeze over first," Richard assured her. "I'm the behind-the-scenes creator in this, don't you forget." Kate shrugged. "I'll find someone to do it, then. Lew Dubois even offered – he thinks it is a keen idea, teaching kids to appreciate fine food. He's even arranged for Mills Farm to be a sponsor of the website. Cool, huh?"

"Sub-arctic," Richard agreed, in mild sarcasm, which seemed to fly right over Kate's head.

"Let's see how Ozzie does with his part," she said, taking out her huge and eminently serious camera from the oversized purse which served as her portable office. "Ozzie, darling kitten-cat, are you ready to play dress-up?"

"Mrrroow!" Ozzie replied, coming again to twine himself around Kate's sensibly-shod feet. To Richard's astonishment, Ozzie permitted Kate to scoop him into her lap, button the miniature chef's jacket around his forelegs and fit the small toque over his ears. He did swipe at the toque, knocking it rakishly askew over one ear, and bounded toward the steps into the caravan.

"Now what?" Richard asked, and Kate – suddenly businesslike – took up her camera and followed.

"I take a million snaps of Ozzie being cute all over the place, and post the best of them on your new website," She suited actions to word, as the camera *click-click-clicked.* Ozzie posed and stretched, Kate going to her knees to get a cat-level angle. "We can do some inside, if you don't mind. I've got some decent lights."

"All right," Richard agreed, secure in the knowledge that it was Tuesday, and Conchita Gonzales had already performed her weekly miracle of bringing order to the bachelor squalor which otherwise reigned increasingly as the week rolled around until the following Tuesday. He had a small pot of minestrone soup and kettle on the hob, and the table set – but only for one – and the scattered utensils from his meal prep still scattered on the miniscule counter-top and around the sink.

"Just take a moment," Kate said, her attention focused wholly on her camera, on the miniature spot and reflective screen as they focused on Ozzie. "He's a total natural, Richard. No matter what he does, he strikes a good pose and it's cute."

Now Ozzie hopped onto the banquette seat, and surveyed the table setting; Kate's camera again went *click-click-click.* Ozzie jumped entirely up on the table, then to the narrow counter-top, where he posed before the window – the window offering a view of the western sky approaching sunset – before turning his attention to the hob, with the pot and kettle on it. Kate followed, her concentration absolute on the cat in the white toque and coat; Ozzie patted the wooden spoon on the holder next to the hob with one paw, leaned over and seemed to sniff the plume of minestrone-scented steam rising from the pot. Richard tried to stay out of the way, and to not distract woman or cat from this all-important task. Finally, Ozzie leaped down from the cooktop, and sauntered around the edge of the accordion door which led to the miniscule sleeping area. Kate followed with her camera and portable light-stand.

Richard breathed a silent sigh of relief that the bed was properly made, the patchwork counterpane smooth and tight and the pillows in their snow-white covers plumped up … bed and pillows so inviting, so soft and cozy, the evening light falling gently through the window over the narrow chest of drawers. Kate set her light on it, and adjusted the reflector as Ozzie curled up in the center of the counterpane. The toque fell to one side; Ozzie blinked sleepily at them, yawned a tooth-fringed cat-yawn and went to sleep in the swift fashion of cats, while Kate's camera *click-click-clicked* some more and Richard lingered in the doorway – still trying to stay out of the way. Kate finally closed up her camera and shut down the light.

"That is so perfect," she breathed. "<u>He's</u> perfect. Wait until I post the first series of pictures. He'll be as famous as Cousin Romeo. As famous as Grumpy Cat. And don't worry about the voice-over, Richard. I knew you didn't want to put yourself forward with this. God, with that awful Noel-Barrett breathing down your neck again … well, I should have thought this all through."

"Never mind, my lovely Kate," Richard thought that he apologized in the most noble manner. "This is your project as much as mine. I'll work behind the scenes … may I offer you glass of wine and a bit of soup for an early supper? It's nothing like I fixed before …"

"That was special," Kate twinkled at him. "This is just a working day for both of us. Sure; a jug of wine, a loaf of bread…"

"And thou beside me, singing in the wilderness," Richard capped the quote. "Save me, Kate – you are an educated woman. It's only a plain vegetable soup, but if you want to share it with me …"

"Just a bite," Kate took out her laptop, as Richard set out another place setting on the table. As he busied himself with meal preparations, she was already reviewing pictures of Ozzie, cropping and enhancing the best of them. It was a strangely agreeable feeling – Kate at work, himself pottering around with the soup, stirring in the last little bits of mashed-up, garlic-infused pork fat and pouring two glasses of Sefton's peerless mustang grape wine – the red version, this time.

He had left the outside door propped open, only the screen door latched; the spring flood had brought out floods of mosquitos, all too ready to batten on human flesh. It had also brought out fireflies, brief bright flashes of miniature lightening in the twilight, hovering above the grassy meadow where the goats and the pony grazed. He had sliced up the loaf of good French-style bread of his own making, and was about to dish up the soup when footsteps crunched on the patio outside, and someone knocked tentatively on the screen door.

"Hey, Chef – are you busy? It's Bree. Bree Grant – you remember me from the house-raising?"

"Miss Brianna," Richard answered, more warmly than he would have greeted any other teenager. "Of course, I remember, since you are coming to work at the Café this summer. Not having second thoughts about it all, are you?"

"Hi, Bree!" Kate looked up from her laptop. "No, we're not busy – although we are about to sit down to dinner. Are you ready to start work soon?"

Richard opened the screen door to admit Judy and Sefton's granddaughter; a charming and willful child of just barely sixteen, who resembled Judy so much in character and appearance that her own parents had despaired of keeping her from bad company in Fort Worth over the summer. They had consigned her to the eccentric care of her grandparents for the duration. Richard, despite his own deep misgivings regarding his ability to manage freedom-addled teenagers, had volunteered to initiate Bree Grant and Robbie Walcott into the mysteries of haute-French cuisine through a summertime apprenticeship program.

"I am, Chef!" Bree replied, with a happy beam which melted into woe as soon as she spotted the pot of minestrone, keeping warm on the burner. "That smells so good. I wish I was eating that instead of Gee-Nan's tofu-barf. Grampy says I can't learn to cook soon enough, but he doesn't say that where Gee-Nan can hear."

Kate and Richard exchanged a brief look; Richard's heart leaped within him. *Oh, yeah – that's what couples had! A whole vocabulary of silent looks and expressions with which to communicate in a relatively private manner.* He had often observed such exchanges, but never been part of one. The tiniest of nods from him, and Kate saved her final photo edit.

"You want to have a bite with us? It's just a little home-made veggie soup and bread," she offered, in a wholly natural manner, adding with an infectious Kate-grin. "There's a bit of pork in it, I think – and I cannot absolutely guarantee that the broth is entirely vegan."

"Strict vegetarianism is an offense against all that is good and holy," Richard, still standing before hob and sink, reached down another bowl from the tiny cupboard above them, and produced another miss-matched set of silverware. "Break bread with us tonight, Bree – at least it will take the taste of your ... grandmothers' cooking out of your mouth."

"If you're sure that I'm not intruding," Bree slid onto one of the banquette seats, still looking with huge, apologetic puppy-dog eyes at Richard, as he set down the additional bowl and silverware. The space in the Airstream was too confined for more than one person to remain standing in the tiny kitchen and dining-table end.

"You are not," Richard answered, echoed by Kate. "In fact, this dish will be one of your initial assignments, so I hope that you have been applying yourself to the volume of *Larousse* that I assigned to you. I'm going to add it to the regular Café lunch menu in due time. It's on page 922 of the classic edition – minestrone. Fancy Eytie word for vegetable soup is what it amounts to. But the key to a satisfying soup is always the broth ... and alas for your grandmothers' ethical principles regarding eating our dumb chums – the best broth for this and other soups depends on a refinement of beef bones ..." he continued in this vein, until he noticed that Bree and Kate were exchanging certain looks, and realized that he was gesticulating with the soup ladle. "Sorry," he concluded. "It's one of my bug-bears. The formulation of a proper rich broth – and I demand the best for the Café customers – it's one of those things, ladies."

He explained at some length on the proper formulation and construction of rich meat broth, until Bree asked, "Can we eat now, Chef?" – again with the huge, begging puppy-dog eyes.

"Yes, I think it's time, Rich." Kate added briskly. "And when we are done, I'll show Bree the pictures of Ozzie that I've been taking for the cooking series. I'm going to pick out his profile picture from the ones I took just now."

"I liked the one of him riding on the back of my bicycle," Richard busied himself with filling the three bowls of soup – it was easier that way, in the limited space in the trailer.

"How cool is that?" Bree breathed, wide-eyed. "A cat riding on your bike! How does he manage that?"

"There is a rack on the back, and I strapped a small crate to it, to carry things back and forth with me," Richard explained. "And he just hopped up into it, the first morning that we were settled back here. I think he just likes the hunting around in back of the Café. I thought of leaving him here during the day, but he's a damned stubborn beast."

"Gee-Nan and Grampy say there are coyotes all around here, even in the daytime," Bree nodded soberly. "And they will kill cats – they put theirs inside at night and let the dogs run free. The dogs keep them away from the baby goats, too. It's super-cool that he wants to go with you all the time. He must really love you."

"I think that Ozzie just wants to closely supervise his chosen servant," Richard said, glumly. "I have opposable thumbs and a tin-opener."

"Or the great goddess Bastet just decided that Richard needed a special guardian," Kate grinned. "And sent him Ozzie."

"I prefer to think he appeared because you needed me to have a cat for your cooking website scheme," Richard slid into the open end of the table and banquette seat, thinking how very pleasant it was, this kind of company; weirdly like a family having supper together, rather than a date with Kate.

"Friends in high places," Kate answered, with an expression of solemn smugness, and they fell to eating, while outside the last orange bits of sunset faded into dark indigo, and fireflies flickered like tiny lightning bolts in the twilight.

Local Legends: The Scar-faced Tramp

From the Karnesville Weekly Beacon – Talk of the Town Blog
By Staff Writer Katherine Heisel

Besides the enduring legend of the Aqua Dulce Ghost Riders, and the ghost of Old Charley Mills, his pet alligators and his lost treasure, there is one more local legend haunting the area around Luna City. The legend of the Scar-faced Tramp is not as well-known or as widespread as the first two, being purely a local matter. In brief, a patch of woods on the east bank of the San Antonio River is supposed to be the particular haunt of a raggedly dressed tramp with a hideously-scarred face. That property was once the site of the Sheffield residence, an extensive mansion which fell into ruin and eventually was demolished as a safety hazard around 1930. That tract and the woods where the tramp was most often seen are now the property of the Age of Aquarius Campground and Goat Farm; the present owners say they have never heard or seen anything out of the ordinary, and profess to know nothing about any such person.

This reporter spent some time and effort trying to trace the origins of the legend; only a few of the oldest residents of Luna City knew of the Scar-faced Tramp, among them my own grandmother, who claimed to have seen him when she was about five or six, and been so frightened that she ran home screaming and crying. The Scar-faced Tramp was a tall man, as tall as a tree, and a huge white scar which hideously distorted his face. He had long straggling gray hair, and shuffled when he walked. My grandmother told me that when she came home, still crying, her own mother chided her for being so badly frightened, saying that the Scar-faced Tramp was only a poor hobo, living in the woods and subsisting on handouts and doing a little handyman work for people now and again. Miss Leticia McAllister, the oldest person in Luna City said much the same: a homeless itinerant, who lingered in the area for a few months.

This particular man was gone from the area by the spring of 1936 – at least, he was never seen in the area again. There were many such during the Depression, says Miss McAllister. They came looking for work, but there was little to be had, and in any case most local folk were only a little better off.

The legend of the Scar-faced Tramp seems to have merged the local memory of one particular itinerant with any number of similar stories which became current at a later date; most particularly that of the hook-handed murderer who was supposed to haunt lover's lanes. At least, one can be certain that certain stories do have a basis in real life, however thin.

Baby Dreams

Midnight, and Jess dreams.

She dreams of a hot dry desert, a desert where the winds blow dust as fine as talcum powder. But overhead, the sky is harsh and blue, and the world around here is the color of dust. Dusty green, dusty brown, dusty beige, dust without any color at all. Dust the color of tents, of motor vehicles, veiling the uniforms that they all wear, smudging their faces. He wears goggles over his eyes, stepping down from a Marine Corp. Humvee, shoving them up to his forehead as he does, the grin across his face making a cheerful boyish mockery of the strapped-on body armor, weapons and helmet which add to the male bulk of him.

"Jessie, darlin'!" he says in her dream, the quicksilver grin from ear to ear. The guy that she has loved since they were both eleven, the two of them horse-mad and given freedom of the Wyler stables and paddocks. "Fancy meeting you here, in the garden spot of the near east. We gonna go dancing tonight, or should we just sent out for pizza and watch an old movie?"

"Jamie, you nutcase," she exclaims, wishing that they could embrace and kiss exuberantly – but they cannot, as there is a war on, they are both in uniform and there are people around, most of them male and of much higher military rank than Jess the reservist. He kisses her anyway, a brotherly peck on the cheek, and she whispers, "How long can you stay?"

"Just long enough to top up," he answers. "MarDiv's on the move. Can't say anything more, even if I did know. Op-sec."

"Of course," she says – her heart sinking within her, but her voice as calm, stoic as a Spartan woman. "Be careful out there, Jamie."

"Always," he answers, but he simmers with suppressed excitement. She casts around for something to say, some brief gesture to make. "I got a care package from home last night – Pops sent me some Moon Pies that didn't get too much melted. You wanna take some with you?"

"Whatever you can spare," His eyes gleam with anticipation. Moon Pies are his favorite sweet. The first summer that Jamie spent at the Wyler Ranch, it was their special excursion to ride out to the Tip-Top Icehouse, Gas & Grocery to buy Moon Pies with their allowance money, and to eat them by the riverbank, dangling bare feet in the cool river, while he tried to frighten her by telling long-ago stories of the scar-faced tramp who lived out in the woods below the old Sheffield place.

"Wait right here," she commands him; Jamie grins again.

"Yes, ma-am!"

She runs to the quarters that she shares with the other Air Force woman officers; spare but more comfortable than a shelter-half over a slit-trench. But when she returns with half-a-dozen Moon Pies, Jamie is not where she left him; a moment of panic – where did he go? Oh, there – already back in the vehicle, leaning out the driver-side window, waving to her. She passes the Moon Pies up to him; the engine already turning over, no time, no time, only a hasty word of thanks from him, she forms the words "I love you" with her lips, and then the line of drab-tan vehicles rumbles away, sending up another cloud of dust, and they are gone, anonymous in the featureless desert.

That was the last time she ever saw Jamie, in anything but dreams and memories. The air conditioner unit is an older one, and when it clicks on it does so with a wheeze and a rush of cooler air. This wakes Jess or brings her up to the edge of wakefulness. The summer in South Texas is as hot as always; Jess and Joe both sleep best in a cooler room, and so the air conditioner runs all night. Her hands feel numb, and her wrists ache a little; a weird side-effect of pregnancy. She rolls over and settles in to sleep again. Joe's arm goes around her, in that new position; an automatic gesture, for he is soundly asleep.

In the small hours of the morning, Jess dreams again.

In that new dream, she is eleven years old; it is her birthday and Pops – widowed and grieving the loss of Jessica's mother not two months before – has promised her a special birthday present. Jess swings her feet as she sits at the breakfast table, wondering what the present can be, since it was not wrapped in paper and tied with ribbons, like the gifts from her grandparents.

"Tell me, Pops!" she begs again, and Martin Abernathy smiles, teasing her in a way that had been in abeyance for months, all the time that her mother was so sick.

"Can't tell you, Jessy-bell. It would ruin the surprise. I will tell you one thing, though … it's bigger than a bread-box!"

"Pops! That's no fair! What is it?"

"A surprise," Martin says, and Jess pouts a little.

"Pops, you can be so provoking!" she exclaims. That is a word she heard her mother say, now and again. Jess knows what it means but has never actually said until now. Martin's amusement dims, just a little, like a candle flickers in a sudden gust of wind.

"Part of my happy inconsequent charm, Jessy-bell," he replies. Jess is not quite certain what 'inconsequent' means, although she knows the other words. She would question her father more, but for the sound of a large pick-up truck, bumping down the long gravel drive past the house. The house where Martin and Beth set up housekeeping is on the edge of Luna City, in a small post-war bungalow built on a large lot with a corral and a large shed at the back; a shed divided into disused horse stalls, where Martin keeps the gas lawnmower, and Jess the bicycle that she rides to school, where she must wear thick glasses to do school work and the other children tease her by calling her "Jessie Four-Eyes."

The truck tows a horse trailer; both trailer and truck adorned with the logo of the Wyler Lazy W Exotic Game Ranch. Everyone in Luna City knows the Wyler brand, and knows Doc Wyler by sight. Jess is no exception; he is an important man, even aside from being the veterinarian. And why should Doc Wyler be driving around to the back of the Abernathy house? They don't have any pets. Jess does not know the boy with him, who climbs down from the passenger side of the truck and stands looking at Jess, standing on the back-door stoop. The boy is her age; wiry and with a grin that lights up his face. If he were from Luna City, she would know him, and if he is the same age, they would be in the same grade at school. It is a puzzle; Jess cannot resist questions and puzzle-solving.

"You best come and meet your birthday present, Jessy-bell," Martin comes up behind her, resting his hands on her shoulders. At first, Jess does not comprehend. *What present?* But Doc Wyler is opening the back of the horse trailer and leading out the horse in it by the halter, with many soothing words. The horse is a chestnut quarter horse with a white blaze on its nose, small even for a quarter horse; a young gelding who dips his muzzle into Jess's hands and blows out an alfalfa-scented gust into her shirt-front.

"Here you go, young lady," Doc Wyler gives the halter-end to Jess. "His name is Stinker, on account of being painfully surprised by a skunk when he was a colt, but I reckon you can call him anything you like. He was sired by a champion cutting horse, his mama was showed by my daughter Pamela in dressage events, but he growed up a mite dwarfish, so your father thought he'd be a perfect horse for you."

"Mine?" Jess could not comprehend at first. *A whole horse, a real horse of her own? Only twice in her later life was Jess Abernathy rendered completely speechless.* At last, she finds words. "Oh, Pops – he's beautiful! And mine, really all mine?"

"Yes indeed, Jessy-bell – all yours." Martin squeezed her shoulders in reassurance. "Your …" his voice broke, just for a second. "Mom said that you should have one, when you were old enough. I reckon that you are, this very day. He'll live here; out at the back – but you have to take responsibility for him. You must ride him every day. Give him a good brushing, make certain that he has good feed, is watered every day, put away in the shed at night …

"We brought along one of Pam's old saddles," Doc Wyler was saying. "Should serve well enough. Jamie, you want to get it from the truck? You haven't met my grandson, have you? Pam's son. He's going to spend the summer with us. Jamie, this is Jess and Martin Abernathy. Martin and his folks keep the hardware store on the Square."

"James Wyler Ellis, Junior," the boy put out his hand and shook Jess'. "But mostly Jamie. Pleased to meet you, miss. Mr. Abernathy." His grip is firm, adult, his gaze direct.

"Hi…" Jess is at a complete loss and stares at the ground. She likes boys as friends, but this one is a stranger. But she begins to like this one, when he offers to help saddle Stinker. And she likes him even more, when he promises to come over the following day on his own horse. And he doesn't know any of the other kids their age, since he is only visiting for the summer. Jess barely notices the satisfied look that Martin and Doc Wyler exchange over their heads.

Jamie spends every summer at the Wyler Ranch, until he drops out of college in the second week of September 2001 and enlists in the Marines.

The bladder complained. Jess sighed and slid out from the bed, from under the embrace of her husband and the tangle of bedclothes, obeying the call of nature. The bedroom was comfortably cool. That being done, she crept back into bed, curling herself spoon-fashion against the bulwark that was always and forever Joe.

Jess dreams again. She has been living in Arlington for three years and working as a traveling CPA.

She has just completed a demanding temporary job in Corpus Christi, another starting in San Antonio – and a too-brief weekend at home in Luna City between them. A good reason to rush, in the little yellow Wrangler with two suitcases and her laptop carrier thrown into the back seat. Oh, to be at home for a couple of days in the spring, when the fields around Luna City are ablaze with yellow and red Mexican hat, purple field verbena and blue and white buffalo clover, which everyone calls bluebonnets, and esperanza splashes flaming yellow in all the hedges … and that is flaming yellow, red, and blue lights on Route 123. Jess, absent-minded and thinking of nothing but home – after months away, sorting out other people's financial woes – does not think at first that she is the driver at fault.

Until the police car flashes headlights emphatically at her. And she is the only driver on 123 at that moment. Jess is a law-abiding person – as a licensed CPA, she can be nothing less, not without escaping severe penalties. She signals an obedient right turn, comes to rest on the shoulder, half on grass and half on asphalt. The police cruiser rests in similar position behind her. Jess waits, heart hammering with apprehension. The economic penalty she can easily cover, the absolute humiliation of a traffic ticket within a few miles of Luna City is humiliating. The cop gets out of his car, Jess observing in the rear-view window; he is tall, muscular, well-built, walking with an Alpha-male swagger; she estimates his age as in the late thirties, and approves – setting aside all other considerations. A nice bit of man-flesh, all told. Clean-cut, not run to seed in the least. Mirrored sunglasses hide his eyes, as he approaches her Wrangler. Jess sighs and rolls down the window.

"Good morning, ma'am. Do you know how fast you were going?"

"Over the speed limit, obviously officer, or you wouldn't have pulled me over." Even in dreams, Jess has a smart mouth. The officer sighs; a bit on the theatrical side, Jess thinks. She also thinks that he looks familiar. He has sergeant's stripes on his sleeves and the nameplate on his tan uniform shirt is a clue. "Vaughn."

"I know you!" she exclaims. "Joe Vaughn! You were the quarterback with the Moths, when I was a freshman in high school."

"Yes, ma'am; varsity, senior year. May I see your identification, please?"

Resigned, Jess reaches into the enormous handbag/briefcase which serves her as both. It's been fifteen years and a lot of water under the bridge, but no one could forget Joe Vaughn, high school hero. Besides, he took Jamie's older cousin Patricia to the senior prom. The all-American golden couple, back then. *He probably believes that I'm trying to charm him out of issuing a ticket*, Jess thinks, as she hands him her drivers' license.

He takes off his mirrored sunglasses to look at it more closely, and exclaims, "Now I remember; you're little Jessie Four-Eyes! Used to hang out with Pat's cousin Jamie all the time. Gotta admit I like the improvement; makes all the difference in the world."

"Lasik surgery," Jess winces. That nick was something she had managed to bury, along with all the usual adolescent humiliations heaped on the plain but clever of the female of the species. Still, she is not immune to male admiration, especially from one who had been well out of her reach, back then.

"So, what have you been doing with yourself since then?" Joe is still holding her drivers' license; Jess doesn't quite have the nerve to take it back from him.

"This and that," Jess replies. "The usual; college, a turn through ROTC and the Reserves, now I'm working for the Manfred Group out of Arlington, but I hope to set up my own office in a couple of years. Too much time on the road. Sorry; I guess I do have a bit of a lead foot. I'm home for this weekend. I didn't know that you were back in Luna City. I thought you were still in the Army."

"Was," Joe finally returns the drivers' license. "Short version is that I blew out my right knee, the other isn't in much better shape. The Big Green machine called it a disability and wouldn't allow me to reenlist, so I hired on with the Luna City PD once I was home. So …" He hesitates and then takes the plunge. "You're gonna be home this weekend; wanna meet for a burger or something? Talk over old times?"

"That would be nice," Jess is flattered. For the big man around the high school campus, the teenaged Joe Vaughn wasn't nearly as much the insufferable asshole that he could have been. He is improved now in a good way, and Jess approves wholly. Now he scribbles in his notebook. Reading upside down, she realizes with mild dismay that it is the ticket book.

"I still gotta write you a ticket," he confesses, with a touch of embarrassment. "You were going 85 and the limit on this stretch is 70. I can't make exceptions. For anyone. Matter of principle with me, I guess. That's my cellphone number. I'm living in my grandparents' old house on Oak Lane. Your pop has the number for the dispatcher; they can get ahold of me any time if you're still serious about that burger." Joe seems a little apprehensive; as if he thinks she isn't interested at best and despises him at worst, for just doing his job without fear or favor.

"Or something," Jess accepts the ticket with mixed feelings and a smile.

"You can pay it at the city offices during the week," Joe says, kindly. "Or go online anytime. See you … um, Saturday work for you?"

"Sure." Jess has decided that she will go out with him, even if it is only as far as the Dairy Queen in Karnesville, just to be assured that she has left Jessie Four-Eyes in the distant, dim, and painfully adolescent past. "See you around."

"You too." He grins, obviously relieved. Jess sets the Wrangler in gear, and as she drives toward Luna City, she sees the cruiser pull a U-turn, and vanish in the opposite direction.

Jess wakens from that final dream; there is dim daylight behind the curtains of the bedroom, but that is not what has disturbed her sleep, or the complaints of a stressed bladder. No, something else, a funny tentative flutter low in her abdomen. It happens again – no, not a bubble of gas working through … but independent, deliberate. Something not of her body.

"Joe?" she whispers; they are still lying spoon-fashion in the bed; she is tucked into the curve of his body. "Are you awake? It's nearly morning."

"Mmm. Sure, Babe. I'm awake." He mumbles indistinct and sleep fogged. "What's wrong?"

"Nothing," she answers. "I just felt the baby move."

Real Texas Barbeque

From Texas Highways and Byways – June 2017 Issue

It's just fitting, since Texas is so large a state that there is not just a single style for smoking and grilling meats, but several different regional variations. In less-blessed climes, barbeque is done by just throwing your choice of animal flesh on the grill on the back porch and allowing it to char slowly over the coals or propane flame. Our staff have even encountered *shudder* recipes for marinated and grilled slabs of tofu, although it is unclear where and by whom these abominations were produced and consumed.

Barbeque here in Texas means mainly beef, although pork, turkey, chicken, and sausages may make an appearance. Cabrito – or goat and mutton – makes an appearance in the borderland Hispanic variant of *barbecoa*. Then there is the east Texas variant; marinated beef cooked slowly over hickory wood until the meat falls from the bone and served with a thick, tomato-based sauce. In Central Texas barbeque means beef or other meats rubbed with spices and cooked slowly over pecan or oak wood, and in the south, a popular method features cooking over mesquite wood – an acquired taste. Otherwise, South Texas style preference generally is for a thick sauce and moist meat.

That being explained, we turn to a brief examination of the commercial origins. It appears that a great many of the old established independent barbeque places began as meat markets in the century before last. It became the practice of the proprietors, in the days before large deep-freeze and cooler units, to smoke and slow-cook all those leftover or unsellable bits at the end of the day, thriftily providing them as ready-to-eat morsels the next day rather than let them go to waste.

In the main, Texans new and old have high standards when it comes to making barbeque themselves, and adamant concerning the virtues of all those places which provide it; from chains like Bill Miller with outlets everywhere, through enormous single-standing locations like the Kreus Market in Lockhart and the Salt Lick in Driftwood, down to food-trucks towing their own smokers and setting up wherever there are hungry people. Aficionados will drive any number of miles to sample the glories of an independent barbeque outlet … and other aficionados will also pay interestingly substantial amounts for grills and smokers of every description, and for specialty woods to bathe the chosen meats in the flavored smoke. Statewide BBQ cooking contests draw competitors by the hundreds, and hungry fans by the thousands. During the summer months there may be three or four different such contests happening every weekend in one part of the state or another.

Real down-home Texas BBQ will even feature this upcoming season of the Food Network's popular travel and cooking show, *A La Carte with Quartermayne*. The tiny town of Luna City will host a BBQ showdown between a pair of local eateries late in August. We at this magazine confidently predict that no matter which of them is the winner – everyone partaking in the event will go away well-satisfied and licking their fingers.

Kitchen Work

"The work day in a restaurant kitchen starts early," Richard had told his young prospective apprentices, halfway wishing that they would reconsider the whole thing. "Very early – as in before the crack of dawn; 5 AM to be precise."

"Well, that's all right," Bree Grant chirped. "Gee-Nan and Grampy's roosters tune up just outside my bedroom window, hours before sunrise, and Grampy gets up early to feed the goats."

"And on those days when we serve supper at the Café – which will be those Friday and Saturdays around the holidays and special events," Richard continued, hoping to dampen some of that juvenile optimism, as it made him feel very old, "Your work day will end at ten o'clock. Midnight if you are not on top of the game. Otherwise at around 3 PM, when everything for the following day is sorted."

"That's all right," Bree was unquenched. "Anything to get out of eating Gee-Nans tofu and lentil barf."

"Wait until you have spent a week scrubbing dishes, pots, and pans," Richard warned. "That tofu-barf might start to look awfully good to you, then."

"Never," Bree looked obstinate. Richard scowled. "Let me remind you; I am to be addressed as Chef. I will address you as Grant and I will not be contradicted. About the only thing I want to hear from you is a request for clarification, and it had better be a necessary request, let me tell you – is 'Yes, Chef – immediately, Chef.' Are we clear?"

"Yes, Chef," Bree nodded. Richard, obscurely pleased that she did not quit on the spot, said, "Good. See you tomorrow, Grant. Bright, early, and 4:30 sharp."

"Yes, Chef." Bree glowed happily, and Richard sighed for the resilience of extreme youth.

Bree was, in fact, waiting for him the next morning, when he opened the door to the Airstream. She was sitting on the old picnic table at the next camping-spot over, with her own bicycle leaning against it.

"Good morning, Chef!" she exclaimed, as Richard rolled out his bike, and Ozzie hopped into his basket on the back. "Is this early enough for you, Chef?"

"Grant, don't talk to me and expect a civil answer until I've had twelve more inches of hot British caffeine in me."

"Yes, Chef," she answered, still irritatingly sunny.

To his mild astonishment, Robbie Walcott was sitting on the back stoop of the Café, waiting for them. An elderly Volvo sedan was parked in the space by the trash bins – obviously, he had driven himself. The Volvo was dented here and there, and splotched with rust and off-color primer paint; obviously the main transportation vehicle for the younger Walcotts.

Like Bree, Robbie was annoyingly cheerful. "Hi, Chef, Hi Bree. I didn't want to be late on my first day. Dad always says if you are on time, you are early…"

"He would," Richard unlocked the back door, and flicked on the lights in the kitchen; spick, span, and scrubbed tidy. "Well then, Grant, Walcott; by the time this summer is over – and if you last, you will be qualified to start in any restaurant in the land as a line cook. An extremely inexperienced one – but a line cook, none the less. I expect you to know where everything – every plate and pan, every ingredient, every tool – is in this kitchen by the end of today. Perishable storage is to the right – walk-in cooler, and freezer. To the left, non-perishable. Through here – the main kitchen. Every item of cookware here has a designated place, and by the end of the day, be in it; clean, polished and ready for continuing use. Am I clear so far?"

"Yes, Chef!" they chorused obediently. Bree bounced up and down on her trainer-shod feet. "I have a question, Chef – what are we going to learn, first?"

"Ah," Richard smiled, dangerously. "How to wash dishes. And scour pots. And take a turn at peeling veg and taking out the garbage. Still keen on learning classic French cuisine, the old-fashioned way?"

"Well, yeah, of course, Chef," Robbie answered first, earnest and slightly baffled as to why it should be any other way. "Dad says that the right way to learn a job from the ground up is to start with the dirty stuff. And to handle a ration of crap. It's a form of hazing, Dad says. A necessary ritual initiation required to become part of an elite unit. Otherwise it just wouldn't be the elite if just anyone could power through and carry out the unit mission. Dad says otherwise it's participation trophies all the way around, and that's no way to manage an elite organization. Not if the organization wants to go on being elite. Dad says…"

"Enough," Richard held up a hand. It pained him to admit, even if only to himself, that Clovis Walcott – that is, Colonel US Army Retired Clovis Walcott – had a point, albeit one pounded in with a sledgehammer. "You don't need to tell me what your father says, again."

"I really want to learn to cook, Chef," Bree announced, her lower lip sticking out, mutinously. "Cook the right way, and anything that isn't tofu-barf. And I'll wash pots and take out the garbage, if that's the deal. What comes next, when we know everything there is to know about dishwashing and peeling potatoes? When do we really start learning to cook."

"In good time, Grant, and in stages," Richard smiled ferociously. "When you are sufficiently experienced at pearl-diving, then you move on to plating up cold salads, appetizers and desserts. Not actually making them – just putting them on plates in an attractive manner. Once you are adept with the cold foods, you will move on to plating the hot foods – side dishes, stews, or casseroles. Because this is a small establishment with limited menu options, I plan to combine those duties with managing the fryers. Should you succeed in not setting a massive fire which burns the place to the ground and actually dishing up edible servings of fried items, then it's on to the sauté station. Ah, my innocent little novices – the sauté station will be the making or breaking of you. Lots of different foods, cooked in hot pans, all at the same time. Here again – because it is a small place, with a limited menu, I have combined it with the broiler-grill station; chops, burgers, hot sandwiches, sautéed fish. Attention to detail, unflappable in the face of distraction – that is what this station demands of the aspiring apprentice cook. In between breakfast, lunch, and dinner, I also plan to familiarize you with the mysteries of baking breads and sweet rolls, edible garnishes, and making soups and sauces. In larger kitchens, those are the province of dedicated specialists – but here in the Café …"

"You double up," Robbie nodded, quite without guile or sarcasm.

"Indeed," Richard continued. "What normally would take four or five years is being crammed into the space of three months ... by the end of summer, should you last that long," he added, parenthetically, "You will have the barest, slightest inkling of how to cook properly. And one more thing. Hygiene is of primary importance. You will wash your hands upon starting work, after using the facility, after handling raw food, eating, or touching your hair, face, clothing, coughing, or sneezing ... in fact, go and wash your hands now, just on general principles." He sighed again. "Every day, a clean apron – they are hanging up in the closet by the back door. Dirty ones go into the bin at the end of the day. The same for clean towels. The laundry truck comes once a week. But for now, *mes enfants* – go wash your hands and put on your aprons. The workday begins."

"It has surprised me no end," Richard confessed, not a week later, when Kate Heisel came out to the Age of Aquarius. Over the previous month, they had fallen into a habit; on Monday afternoons, after Richard had gotten a good night sleep after a weekend of eighteen-hour long days, and the *Weekly Beacon* had been put to bed, of Kate coming out to the Airstream for a light early supper, a progress report/strategy session, and a cuddle. Unfortunately, the scheduled cuddle was with Ozzie, who made no secret of his perverse adoration of Kate. Now the cat was curled up in Kate's lap, as she lounged in the banquette seats in the caravan, her sensible shoes kicked off and a glass of Sefton's marvelous mustang grape elixir at her elbow. Richard was fixing *trout almandine* on the tiny gas stovetop, sauced with a concoction of cream, lemon juice, and parsley to accompany a dish of carrots caramelized with a bit of butter, ginger, and brown sugar.

"What has?" Kate asked, reasonably. The first two videos for Captain Kitten's Kitchen had been shot, edited and posted, one with Mateo and Angelika, one with Robbie and Bree – all demonstrating simple dishes and techniques.

"The apprentices," Richard answered. "Grant and Walcott; I have been brutal with them, my Kate of Kate Hall. Brutal, sarcastic, and demanding. Run them off their feet, hounding them every second, like a species of human sheepdog, snapping at their heels. Do this – wash your hands – no, you imbecile, attend to the recipe card as it is written – and to what end?"

"Yes, what end?" Kate gave Ozzie a lingering caress, and Richard scowled at the sauté pan in which the sauce for the trout, fresh from the coast, was thickening nicely.

"To no end! They are cheerful, obedient ... every dish and pot in the place has been scoured to the nines – three times! The prep-work for the following day has been done – even before I ask for it! They say, 'Good morning, Chef!' and 'What can I do now, Chef?' The walk-in cooler is cleaner and more neatly-arranged than I have ever seen it! Guests can hardly set down an empty cup or a dirty plate, and Grant or Walcott is around to whisk it away. I am baffled, my Kate – baffled beyond words."

"You shouldn't be," Kate grinned and held up her glass for a refill – which Richard was happy to do – seeing that it only was a half-step from cooker to refrigerator, and then to table. "You're flattering them, Richard. You're doing the courtesy of treating them like adults and not pulling your punches. Kids that age crave being treated like adults, not like delicate little children-orchids. And," she added, taking a sip of Sefton's glorious elixir. "That is what kids of that age want, more than anything else. To be treated as if they are grown-ups, to have real responsibility. Doesn't matter if you're the harshest, most demanding bastard on the planet. You're being real and absolutely straight with them. And you are teaching them important things. Bree wants to learn to cook, in the worst way ..."

"Agreed with that," Richard sighed. "She's impulsive with the recipes, without a sufficient grasp of the rules required to break them successfully."

"But she wants to learn," Kate continued. "So does Robbie. Now, he strikes me as being one of those kids who adores a challenge."

"They certainly have it now," Richard agreed, and Kate giggled.

"Reminds me of working on the school magazine when I was in high school."

"I didn't know there was such a thing in Luna City," Richard racked his brain and came up empty, and Kate giggled again.

"No – I went to school at St. Scholastica's in Karnesville. The guy who taught the journalism class which produced the magazine was a crusty old Jesuit, who made his vows equally to God and the *Chicago Manual of Style*. He was as brutal to his students as you are to your apprentices – but we all adored Brother Gerald. He had high standards. When you finally succeeded in pleasing him, you had accomplished something, and you knew it was good. It was rough at first," Kate admitted generously. "Getting back a story that you had slaved over covered with so many red marks it looked like an ink-bottle had exploded was a definite kick in the ego. And eventually, learning was achieved."

"Life, alas, is full of kicks to the ego," Richard poured himself another glass of wine. "Best learn to handle them and move on."

"Speaking of moving on," Kate gave an extra-thorough head-skritch to Ozzie. "Have you picked up any stray talk about the Mills Farm expansion?"

"Thou woundest me, Kate – that you would treat me as an informant, lurking around the tables, picking up gossipy tittle-tattle around the Café for your news stories!"

"I wouldn't do anything of the sort!" Kate protested, although she had flushed rather pink. "No, I was just making conversation. If I wanted the straight scoop on that, I would go directly to Lew Dubois. I'm just a small-town newspaper reporter and a weekly at that. I had just been talking to Great-uncle Jaimie last week – and he was going on about signing a hunting lease agreement with Mills Farm. He was so pleased –

and it was all because of Lew. He came and talked to Uncle Jaimie a good few times, all dressed in a dirty barn coat and muddy boots, explaining what it was all about… Uncle Jaimie was pleased as anything. He's been next-door-across-the-river with Mills Farm since forever, and all he ever got out of them by way of outreach was Benny Cordova buying him drinks at the VFW now and again. Uncle Jaimie must be about the only property owner in Karnes County who doesn't have a gas lease on his land."

"Anti-fracking?" Richard stirred the sauce for the trout and scattered parsley. "Supposed to cause earthquakes, you know."

"No, just no one ever explained it to him that it wasn't like the movie *Giant* … an oil well spewing finest grade-A crude in a humongous pool over all of his pastures. Uncle Jaimie would rather not deal with all of that. He's a guy from the last century – no, strike that. The century before the last. A hunting lease is fine with him. Give him a break, Richard, he's in his eighties. And … can I have another, Richard? I have a cat in my lap."

"Seeing that it's my cat…" Richard obliged, and topped up her wineglass. "Do continue, my Kate. The main entrée is nearly ready. What else is going on with this strangely diplomatic Dubois character?"

"Well, he has also managed to sweet-talk Judy and Sefton into sale of half an acre of their lad, with about sixty feet of river-frontage. Which is a mere sliver of what they do have, so I don't think that is any great sacrifice. Which pleases Uncle Roman no end, because it means Judy and Sefton can repay him a good chunk of the costs for their new home … and he has a potential contract to build a new facility for Mills Farm – a riverside boat house, Uncle Roman says."

"So Roman Gonzales profits coming and going," Richard topped up his own wineglass. The sauce was coming along nicely. "Nice work, if you can get it. Maybe I should have gone into carpentry and construction."

"Too seasonal," Kate replied. "And there's at least as much demand around here for good cooking … oh, speaking of which – I'll be a bit late next Monday, I'm afraid. Last-minute town council meeting, and it may run long."

"Oh?" Richard felt his heart sink several centimeters. He hated having a routine disturbed. "What brought all this on? You couldn't just skip it, could you?"

"I can't," Kate explained with careful patience. "It's my job, so I have to go – as boring as town council meetings normally are. This one is special, though. Martin Abernathy sent out the meeting agenda to everyone who usually attends, and even posted something on the Chamber of Commerce's Facebook page. The first order of new business is to discuss a bid to lease out the Cattleman Hotel to Venue Properties."

"And this is significant? The place is a huge white elephant. The municipality can barely keep the lights on at the best of times." Richard was well-acquainted with the bedraggled Belle Époque splendors of the Cattleman Hotel, as it took up half a side of Town Square. It once had been a quite splendid establishment, but its best days were now at least half a century in the past. There was a small museum in the old lobby, opened two days weekly by the Luna City Historical Commission, which maintained an office on the second floor. There were a handful of suites available to adventurous travelers, and a splendid and old-fashioned bar open with great fanfare on Founder's Day weekend. Otherwise it served as a lumber room and overflow storage for the city, and most of the third and fourth floors had been abandoned to dust and slow decay.

"Too true," Kate nodded in agreement. "Oh, thanks, Rich – that looks delish! I know – everyone loved the old place. I mean, half the elder citizens have fond memories of going to parties in the ballroom, or having supper … and everyone was up in arms when VPI first set up Mills Farm, and they wanted to buy the whole place for a dollar, disassemble it and rebuild someplace else. Before I was born, but Great-uncle Jaimie and Abuelita still spit fire when they talk about it. The VPI manager at the time – he thought that he could just waltz in, drop some money on the table and rip out part of the heart of Luna City. Although," Kate added, as Richard set down his own serving on the table and slid onto the banquete; Kate obligingly shifted her feet to allow him room and continued. "I think the Bodies were pretty slick, gifting the place to the city, way back then. It was a dead weight to them, and the tax advantages should have been obvious. Keeping the Cattleman open cost more than it would ever bring in, and that doesn't even consider the costs of repairs and renovation. I'll have the skinny on that after the meeting next Monday, anyway." She took a delicate bite of the fish, and Richard was distracted by the expression of sheer gustatory delight which passed over her face. "I could eat this every night, Rich... are you going to offer this as a *prix fixe* option some weekend? Look, I don't mind being your test subject. I'd beg to be ... hey, you catch your own fish!" she reprimanded Ozzie, who had reached out a paw with the speed of light, aiming to snag the next bite from her fork.

"The little blighter will have his own fish, my Kate – just dump him off your lap," Richard savored his own first bites, and Kate protested.

"No, he's our star kitten. Can't we indulge him, just a bit?"

"Bad for his character," Richard answered. "Trust me – I know this from first-hand experience. Enjoy your own supper, my Kate – I have prepared a special sweet for afters. But you don't get your sweet until you finish your supper and veg."

"Cruelty in the extreme," Kate protested, but her eyes were merry and full of affectionate laughter, and Richard considered once again how very content he was with this new life; his café, his caravan and most of all, his Kate.

Celia Hayes & Jeanne Hayden

A Ala Carte With Quartermayne Showdown

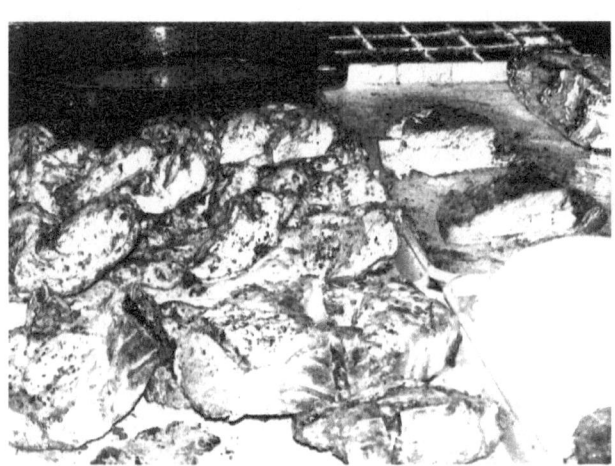

A La Carte With
Quartermayne!

—

August 24

4:00 – 8:00 PM

—

At the Luna City
VFW Post

—

Good Eats and Fun
for the Whole Family!

—

$5.00 Donation at
the door

AUGUST 24
BBQ SHOWDOWN

Head to head – two great local eateries!

Pryor's Meats & BBQ meet Mills Farm Country Restaurant in the great BBQ showdown of the season! This event is to be videotaped for broadcast on the Food Network's popular food and travel show A La Carte with Quartermayne, hosted by former Denver Broncos QB Allen Lee Mayne. Come on out and meet Allen Lee and his co-host Phillip Noel-Barrett, and cast your vote for the best BBQ in town!

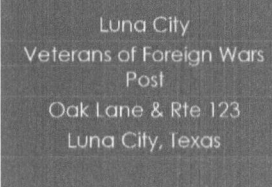

Luna City
Veterans of Foreign Wars
Post
Oak Lane & Rte 123
Luna City, Texas

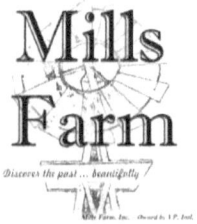

Hot Time, Summer in Luna City

"Hey, Ricardo – are you all ready for when Allen Lee's showdown hits town?" Berto Gonzales asked, with all the guileless subtlety of a concrete block through a plate glass window. The two were partaking of barbeque hospitality at Araceli and Patrick's double-wide house-caravan, on a Sunday afternoon in late summer. Berto, twenty-one and absent a devious bone in his body, looked taken back when his older sister hissed a warning at him, and Richard curtly replied.

"I certainly am, in that I intend to take no part whatsoever in that carefully-arranged travesty. For my money, Pat does the best smoked beef brisket around …"

"Thanks, Ricardo," Pat acknowledged the compliment with his mouth full of lemon meringue pie – the contribution of Jess Vaughn from one of her grandmother's famous recipes – and a murmur of approbation from everyone else present; the Vaughns, Araceli, Berto, Kate Heisel, Sylvester Gonzalez *(clad in a fetchingly retro chino trousers and a vintage Aloha-patterned shirt)* and Chris Mayall.

"Alas, since Pat is only a private citizen and not the proprietor of a restaurant, he is not even in a position to compete in this ..." Richard racked his considerable vocabulary of invective for a suitable expression of contempt, "this pitiable sham of a travesty for the amusement of the numbskull masses."

"But you are," Berto persisted, all dogged and clueless innocence of how heavily he treaded the minefield. "I just don't see why you aren't competing ... or even just helping out with the judging. You're a big-name professional chef! Abuelita is furious that you haven't even been considered to be part of the program – she's your biggest fan!"

"I realize that, and I honor your dear Gran for her fan-worship," Richard's deep sigh was one of depression and weary acceptance of fate. "But I don't want to have anything to do with that bloody program, as long as Phillip Noel-Barrett is a part of it."

"Why? I thought he was a friend of yours?" Berto asked, while Sylvester and Chris exchanged a glance and a burst of short, cynical laughter.

"He is not a friend of mine," Richard admitted, through clenched teeth. "He is one of the most corrupt, unmitigated celebrity tossers to slither on this earth. We were associates, at one time – an association which I heartily regret, ever since he publicly boinked one of my ex-girlfriends before she even became my ex-girlfriend. This resulted in the most purely risible sex-tapes ever released on the internet. But that has nothing to do with my present animus against him. It's just that he is apparently determined to drag me back into the white-hot spotlight of publicity. And I am reluctant to go there ... tell them, Kate." Richard waved a hand toward Kate. Unless it would compromise your informant..."

"No, of course..." Kate set aside her plate of pie, having scarfed down the last few mouthfuls. "The word is that Mr. Noel-Barrett is going to out Richard, as part of the program – make a big, flashy scoop of telling the whole world where he is and what he is doing now. You all know that he used to be famous, right?"

"I don't see what's so awful about that," Berto mused. "You'd get all kinds of new customers coming to the Café. That would be a good thing, wouldn't it?" From the expressions of exasperation on the faces of the others – all save Patrick, who never watched anything but football on television, and of late, not even much of that – Berto now realized that he had said exactly the wrong thing.

"They'd be the usual kind of celebrity ---" Richard added a very short, obscene descriptor. "They wouldn't give a damn for the cuisine, for the Café. They'd be coming to gawk at this year's equivalent of the Elephant Man. I like my privacy here, Berto. Like the great Garbo, I want to be left alone, to practice my art and pass that art on to others."

"Many may say that," Kate elaborated, "But few really mean it. Richard is one of those who truly mean it. Noel-Barrett is just planning this out of spite and vengefulness."

"So, what are you going to do when the circus comes to town?" Joe asked, scowling. "And before you answer; whatever it is, I've got your back. Less'n it's a felony. A misdemeanor I can maybe look away from, depending."

"I have tried very hard not to think about it at all," Richard confessed. "It's two months from now, and anything could happen. Sufficient unto the day, y'know. I had just considered avoiding the prat and his film crew entirely."

"Small town," Jess said. She lounged comfortably on the sofa, with Joe's arm around her, her head on his shoulder. "He knows when you're at the Café, every day. Shouldn't be too hard to find you at the Age and turn up with a camera crew."

"You could stay at my place," Chris offered, and Jess shook her head.

"But you still need to be at the Café," she pointed out. "Even if you stay in the kitchen, there's nothing to stop them from staking out the back entrance. All they need do is get a good clear video of you – and bam! You're outed on TV as the fugitive Bad Boy Chef, film at eleven."

"I didn't want to think about it," Richard admitted. "Maybe I should just go away for a couple of weeks."

"Why should you have to do that?" Berto, while sometimes slow on the initial uptake, did have a facility for eventually getting down to the nut. "I mean, this is Luna City."

"Why, indeed!" Araceli got up from her chair. "Chef shouldn't be put to the trouble. It's that jerk Noel-Barrett who ought to be suffering. Jess, is there any pie left? I'm gonna have another sliver, to hell with the calories. You want some more?"

"Help yourself," Jess replied. "Unfortunately, Baby gets the hiccups when I eat anything acidic. Strangest thing, I've ever felt."

"I used to think that Angelika was doing the can-can," Araceli laughed. "You haven't lived, until you've been kicked in the belly-button … from the inside. You should talk to Doc Wyler about this, Jess. Maybe there is something he can do; he owns the Café, after all. And he was furious about how he was gulled by Noel-Barrett and his Hollywood pals over that stupid zombie movie. Tia Conchita was afraid he would burst a blood vessel when he found out that it wasn't going to be a serious historical epic."

"Doc is the last resort," Joe explained. "Only to be used when all other avenues have been explored and exhausted."

"I think we have come to that point," Kate argued, and Jess nodded reluctant agreement. "I'll talk to him tomorrow, and see what he suggests."

"Maybe I could just go away for a fortnight," Richard said. "I hate to be of trouble to any of you."

"No trouble, Ricardo," Berto replied. "This is your home now, isn't it?"

***

Richard was certain that Jess had forgotten speaking to Doc Wyler, and was making plans to ask for a fortnight's vacation from that worthy, and to ask Roman Gonzales or any Gonzalez with a large pick-up truck if he would tow the Airstream to anywhere else for a fortnight. There was a perfectly acceptable caravan site at some distance. A nearby location for Texas, a moderately far one by English standards; at a state park at the edge of a pleasant reservoir lake which surely would make a suitable refuge for himself and Ozzie, for the duration of the period that the television shoot would be in town. But when he took up the matter on a Tuesday morning – the day when he was accustomed to meet with Jess and Doc Wyler – the old veterinarian and rancher shook his head. He was at the other side of the regulars' table, what Georg Stein called the '*stammtisch*' with his single cup of coffee, and his copy of *Veterinarian Monthly,* or whatever his magazine full of medical conundrums regarding our dumb chums was called. Coach Garrett shared the table, as this was the summer holidays and practice mornings for the Mighty Moths Marching Band wouldn't start for another month. Lew Dubois, because it was his prerogative as senior management for VPI, and it wasn't as if Benny Cordova weren't perfectly capable anyway when it came to day-to-day management.

"Request denied, Richard. Too much at stake during those weeks. Can't have the Café slacking off, just because you don't have the balls to face up to your personal *bete noir*. Look," and Doc Wyler fixed Richard with a particularly piercing gaze. "There will be a lot of business coming through town, just because of that TV shoot. You need to be on top of all that."

"I wasn't aware that I had signed my life over to the Café, regardless of events," Richard replied, and Doc snorted.

"Yes, you have, although you haven't acknowledged it, yet. Look," and Doc Wyler made a brief wave over the *stammtisch.* "This is your place. Where you have made your stand, poor pathetic bastard as you are.

Will you fight for it? Or will you let it go; all that you have worked for, put your heart into. Will you run away with your tail between your legs, or will you fight for it? The question – the *Gretchen-frage* – is yours to answer. Where do you stand, Richard; what do you want and what will you fight for?"

"To pop Pip Noel-Barrett right in his peerless profile," Richard snapped, goaded into absolute frankness. "If ever there was a more punchable face than the countenance of that smug, smarmy git… and then to see him leave town with <u>his</u> tail between his legs."

"I can arrange for it to happen that way, son," Doc Wyler folded up his reading glasses and squinted at Richard. "For you not to be outed by that smooth-talking fraud; a couple of telephone calls to the right people, and I can make that television broadcast go away. Easy-peasy. Take me five minutes, and it's done. But I've always been a firm believer in people needing to stand up for themselves. I'm not in the business of being a public crutch; a pain in the patoot for me, not good for you. If you are serious about pasting your old pal a good one, I reckon we can settle this this the old-fashioned way, the way that it used to be settled when I was a kid in high school."

"And what was that?" Richard demanded, and Doc Wyler grinned, an expression quite devoid of mirth.

"When two boys were spoiling for a fight, Coach – or maybe the principal himself – would have the two of you strap on boxing gloves and take it out behind the gym. Couple of good punches, a bloody nose or two, and the whole thing would be sorted. Are you up for sorting out your old pal, Richard?"

"I don't know anything about boxing," Richard mused, although the notion was strangely attractive.

"Not a problem." Doc Wyler raised his voice. "Coach – a moment. Can you give Richard here a little of your time? He needs to practice with the gloves for a little grudge match out behind the barn."

"Sure thing, Doc," Coach Garrett didn't appear the least surprised. "Come around to the field-house this afternoon. Give me a call first, though."

"Now see?" Doc Wyler turned his attention back to Richard. "When that smarmy movie-star pal of yours gets to town, you go up to him and tell him to his face that you want to settle it for good and all – with the gloves, out behind the barn, just like I said. Tell him if he doesn't, then he is a nut-less wonder and a laughingstock here in Luna City; an even bigger laughing-stock than he was before. Agreed?"

"Agreed," Richard frankly quailed at the thought of going all fisticuffs in with Pip Noel-Barrett, but the thought did have certain appeal. And he himself was in topping physical shape, through having to go everywhere on the bicycle. Doc Wyler must have thought so as well, for he buffeted Richard heartily on the shoulder, and added, "Looking forward to it, matter of fact. You'll let me referee, of course. That lying little twerp got away from here before I could settle his hash up close and personal. You wouldn't deprive me of the pleasure of being a vindictive old bastard, wouldn't you?"

"Wouldn't dream of it," Richard contemplated having Doc Wyler as a personal enemy and mentally shuddered. Fortunate for Luna City in general that the old man generally used his considerable powers for good.

"Good – hate to lose your services as a cook. You've really brought this place around, and I don't like to see my investments piddled away. Matter of fact, you've done so well, we'll look at hiring some more staff for the place. You won't forget that, when you confer with Jess, will you?"

"More staff?" Richard was gob smacked. "That would be … smashing, absolutely smashing. I'd like to train up another line cook, of course. And open for supper service more often."

"Excellent plans, son," Doc Wyler grinned, shark-like. "I know you're going to stick around and follow through on them."

"Certainly ..." Richard started to say more, but just then a certain splintering crash from the kitchen and a short cry of distress immediately following wrenched his attention away.

"Best go see what's happening in your kitchen, son." Doc Wyler turned his attention back to his veterinary journal.

Report on Luna City Town Council Meeting

From the *Karnesville Weekly Beacon* – Sept.4, 2017
Katherine Heisel, Staff Writer

The mayor and a majority of elected Luna City town council members held a special meeting last Monday evening in the city council chambers. The public was invited to attend by Mayor Martin Abernathy, to fully discuss and solicit feedback from interested parties on an offer formally tendered to the city by Lucian Dubois, the Director of Marketing for Venue Properties, Intl. Mr. Dubois proposed that VPI's local affiliate lease the Cattleman Hotel for a period of ten years with first option on an extension of another ten years, for a yearly payment of $128,000, as additional lodging for the popular Mills Farm Resort. Planned expansion of the facilities at Mills Farm, to include water sports, kayaking expeditions on the river, as well as guided horseback tours, and local hunting is estimated to triple the numbers of guests at Mills Farm when the expansion is completed in 2020. In addition, Mr. Dubois proposed that upon the lease of the Cattleman being accepted as proposed, that Mills Farm would undertake renovations of the 132-year old facility in order to bring it up to modern standards without compromising the historical nature of the building.

Objections were raised from the floor over the proposed lease. The four-story tall Cattleman Hotel contains approximately 16,000 square feet of guest rooms, offices, kitchen, and commercial space, and $8.00 per square foot per year is far below the going rates elsewhere in Texas. Similar commercial/residential structures charge twice or even three times that amount. Mr. Dubois countered that such costs were for new or recently renovated space in major urban areas and pointed out that his estimation of costs for completely renovating the Cattleman could easily top a million to a million and a half. He provided such a written estimate from Roman Gonzalez, of Gonzalez Brothers Construction, LLC, and from several San Antonio constriction firms, all of which agreed with Mr. Gonzalez' estimation.

Leticia McAllister, representing the Luna City Historical Society, spoke in favor of accepting the VPI proposal, stressing the historical value of the hotel to Luna City and candidly acknowledging that there was no possible way that the Historical Society could fund the necessary repairs and renovations required to bring the Cattleman to anything like up-to-date code and the expectations of modern hotel guests. City Treasurer Curtis Bodie, Jr. confirmed that the present cost of upkeep and utilities for the Hotel are just barely met by rental from the Historical Society for their offices, and the income generated by the second-floor suites available for rent. Any out-of-cycle costs, and unexpected repairs would have to be met by a local bond, or an increase in local taxes.

After several hours of discussion, the town councilors voted unanimously to formally accept VPI's offer, beginning in the 2018 fiscal year. There were no further objections from the floor, and the meeting concluded at 8:55 PM.

Dinner at the Walcott's With Entertainment

"Richard!" Exclaimed Clovis Walcott, one mid-morning at the Café. "A moment of your time, if I may … how's Robbie doing, by the way? Satisfactory, I hope. You know, when Belle goes off to Julliard this fall, it will just be him to keep My Little Bride and Min Kim company."

"He's doing quite well," Richard answered, with a somewhat guarded expression. His two apprentices were indeed doing very well; much better than he had expected initially, considering the accelerated and short-cut nature of his cooking course. "He has been able to handle the sauté station and the grill with no more disasters than I would normally expect. He keeps a very cool head under pressure. Quite rare for a boy of that age…"

"Well, it's good practice, for when My Little Bride is on a tear," Clovis chuckled, and Richard smiled uneasily. Sook Walcott, the most determined and demanding tiger-mother in all of Luna City did have an unenviable reputation for throwing earsplitting tantrums upon the slightest provocation. Richard entertained the sneaking suspicion that Clovis took a perverse pride in her reputation; he certainly didn't seem to be as hen-pecked as one might have thought. "Glad that Robbie is having a good summer experience, but that wasn't what I really wanted to speak to you about. We were wondering if you would do another one of your splendid suppers at our house … For the usual consideration, of course."

"Certainly," Richard answered, although every fiber of his being screamed *"Oh, hell no!"* He had done two lavish catered dinners for the Walcott manse, both of which had tiptoed along the knife-edge of disaster for very different reasons. Ultimately a rousing success on both occasions, the experiences had left his nerves in tattered shreds. It was as some malign spirit under the Walcott roof had an abiding grudge against Richard and a desire to torment him. "What would be the reason for the occasion, Colonel?"

"Two reasons, actually; a send-off for Belle to college, and a celebration and send-off for me. My firm is launching a huge project in Dubai, and I'll be over there for the next six months to a year, overseeing the groundwork and initial construction."

"That sounds … interesting," Richard ventured. "The reenactors group will certainly miss you."

"Can't be helped," Clovis replied, with slight expression of regret. "This is too big a project to cut corners on. The Karnes Company has plenty of good officers – they'll do just fine without me. As for the supper; it will be about a hundred guests, between Belle's school friends and my associates, so probably a buffet service would be most efficient. Open bar, of course; I talked with Chris last week at the VFW, so that's sorted. Tell you what – I'll send you a budget, your people come up with a list of menu selections, and we'll see what we can work out."

"Excellent," Richard's spirits rose, somewhat. Clovis and Sook entertained often, although not often at their home. Payment for Walcott catering events were generous enough to serve as a balm for the nerve-shredding. And besides – Richard had to confess to himself – he did love the challenge of something a little out of the ordinary.

A hundred people; the Walcott's lavishly equipped kitchen, a kitchen almost to restaurant standard. Most items would be prepped in advance. A consult with Araceli would be in order. Of course, she was thrilled at the prospect. So were Grant and young Walcott, who had the advantage of complete familiarity with his own home, and now with Richard's methods in the kitchen.

"The tiny Scotch eggs as one of the *hors d oeuvres*, for certain," Araceli got a pencil and a long pad of legal paper from cash desk. The four of them sat down at the empty *stammtisch*, to brainstorm after the Café closed for the day. "They're the thing that everyone remembers from your suppers."

"Much as I wish they wouldn't," Richard confessed with a shudder, recalling his eventual escape from Susannah Wyatt, high-powered corporate marketing expert and sexual stalker extraordinaire. The memories still made him wake in a cold sweat sometimes, never mind that she had now been married (apparently blissfully) to Araceli's cousin Romeo Gonzalez for months. "Right then – the Scotch eggs. A veg – oh, mushroom caps filled with feta cheese, mini-pita breads spread with spiced *labneh* cheese. Mini-crab cakes with a remoulade dip. All carried around on trays, as per usual. See if Blanca and Beatriz are available. We've worked with them before, and I trust them."

"Check," Araceli made a note. "They're both working summer jobs in Karnesville … but if this supper is scheduled for a weekend in August, they should be free, still. I'll call Uncle Roman and Uncle Jaimie. If they aren't free, I'll find someone. Don't worry about serving staff, Chef. What about for the buffet itself. Salad, fish course, main, and sides. Then sweets."

Richard consulted his memory of last week's purchasing expedition to the enormous Costco store in Karnesville. "Mixed green salad … no, spinach salad with caramelized pecans and dried cherries. A sweet-sour poppy-seed dressing. Cold poached salmon – the thing about that is it can be done ahead, and just kept cold. No further fuss. Your challenge, Grant and Walcott ... search *Larousse* for some appropriate sauces to go with the salmon ... and create some garnishes, keeping in mind what we were working on last week. I noted that summer squash is in season now. Steamed green summer squash with a ratatouille dressing. Something with corn, as well. You two look at *Larousse* and make suggestions. I'll tell you if they are no good and why. For the main buffet ... herb-crusted roast beef tenderloins. I saw some very attractive items along that line on sale at Costco. A sauce to go with – leeks, mushroom and parsley."

"If it's beef, they'll be looking for potatoes," Robbie Walcott summoned the confidence to speak without being spoken directly to.

"I know," Richard nodded. "And I do not want to go through the trouble of wrapping a hundred or more potatoes in aluminum foil to bake... strike that, I don't want you to go to the trouble, not when we'll be working on the dessert table. A nice rice pilaf, I think. With subtle spices and vegetables. Seasonal, of course. With luck, we can do it just beforehand, and put it out on the buffet table as is. And fresh-baked rolls and thinly sliced baguettes, with sweet butter. Now, for the desserts; a choice of seasonal fruit tarts. Tiny pecan nut tarts. Fresh seasonal fruit with flavored syrup, and ginger-infused *Cream Anglaise* to sauce. All prepped beforehand. I suppose if we purchase the beef and sausage from Pryors' they will arrange the use of their refrigerator van, as before."

"On it, Chef," Araceli replied, smartly making a note on the pad. "I'll speak to Patricia; we have a rehearsal for *The Man Who Came to Dinner* this evening. As long as we have a driver available, I'm sure Patricia will let us use the van. Not Berto, I'm afraid. He's not available."

"Why not?" Richard was mildly indignant. Berto was one of those that he liked and trusted and was a professional driver besides.

"He's out in California, visiting his girlfriend," Araceli replied. "Likely be there for a few weeks. There's a red-carpet award event that she wants an escort for, and Berto said he'd do it."

"Just when we need him," Richard sighed a deep, theatrical sigh, and began doing the calculations for additional supplies, and calculating the costs of a buffet supper for a hundred. His good fortune that Grant and young Walcott were far enough along in training – and what is more, willing to work hard – to be a substantial help on this occasion. Really, it would be a kind of final examination for them. With Araceli organizing the wait-staff, Chris at the bar, himself in the kitchen with Grant and young Walcott … nothing could possibly go wrong, this time.

* * *

On the appointed afternoon, the Pryor's refrigerated van pulled up to the gate of the Walcott's residence; a towered and terraced edifice of gray stone which managed to look as if a rampant medieval French chateau had impregnated a Beaux-Arts villa and abandoned the resulting bastard offspring on a tall hilltop across the river and a little to the north of Luna City. The private drive beyond the gates spiraled around the hill several times before arriving at the crest, and a graveled forecourt which commanded an imposing view. Much of the usual view was blocked now by a vast white party pavilion, gaily hung with streamers, garlands and balloons, which took up most of the hilltop lawn and terrace, and appeared to be connected to the house. In the heat of a Texas late summer, it even appeared as if the pavilion was air-conditioned. Well, Clovis Walcott knew how to get things done for the comfort of his guests. Young Anson Pryor at the wheel of the van, and assigned to carve and serve the roasts for the evening, yelped in alarm and fairly stood on the brake, as a trio of large black and tan dogs burst into the forecourt, barking and growling like the very hounds of hell.

"What the bloody hell!" shouted Richard. Robbie Walcott's aging Volvo sedan, which had followed them up the hill, pulled alongside as Richard rolled down the passenger-side window.

"Oh, hey, Chef – I forgot to tell you about the guard dogs. Dad was worried about Mom and Halmeoni and I being all alone out here while he was away, so he went and got us some trained guard dogs. They're OK. They'll be locked up in their kennel before the guests get here." He shouted at the dogs, "Loki! Odin! Thor!" and added some words of command in another language, whereupon the savagely-barking trio magically ceased barking and morphed into ordinary dogs, albeit very large, thick-furred black and brown Alsatians. They wagged their tails, and sank back onto their haunches, regarding everyone with friendly eyes. Richard could only imagine that they were sensing the odor of food, and this sudden affability was highly developed cupboard-love.

"I assume that we are to go around to the kitchen entrance?" Richard ventured into the silence.

"Well, yeah – Yes, Chef. Of course." Robbie put the Volvo into gear, an action which Richard had never quite understood, and began to roll up the window. "I'll see you in the kitchen, Chef. Park the van by the back door, Anse. I gotta put the Old Beast in the garage; Dad wants us to leave enough room for the first guests."

"Ok – cool," Anson Pryor also set the van into gear, with an air of competent authority; a vision of boy mastering machine, which Richard feared in his heart that he would never be able to equal. For some reason, probably to do with his parents being savagely protective *(and much good had that done them!)* he had never learned to drive. Or learned well enough to get a license. Until his arrival in Luna City, this inability had never mattered much. There was always some form of public transport, and latterly, his status as a cooking super-star earned him the convenient courtesy of a driver, or at very least, a taxicab. Being a non-driver in rural Texas was an extreme social handicap, however. Araceli and Kate had often, of late, hinted that he really should learn to drive. So far, he had resisted.

"This is gonna be so great!" Robbie Walcott enthused, even as he helped Bree Grant horse a large wheeled cart up the back steps and through the doorway; a cart stacked with covered containers of either prepared vegetables, meats and fruit, or baked breads, tarts, and required equipment that Richard knew the Walcott kitchen could not provide. This was the third trip between van and kitchen; both apprentices were even more enthused than ever before, although Richard had not thought that possible until this very moment. "When summer is gone and school starts, I'm gonna keep on cooking! I'll bet Mom will let me do supper every night!"

"I'll probably have to, anyway," Bree sighed. "Mom wants to run for the school board or something dire like that. Dad and I might wind up eating take-out pizza every evening. Your parents' place is fantastic." She added, with a slight touch of envy; Robbie answered,

"Mom likes to live large. Halmeoni, too. When Halmeoni was born, her folks were refugees. They had to live in a leaky old shack, but she says that they were ancient Korean nobility, back in the old days, and accustomed to better. When Mom and Dad designed this house, Mom sort of went ape. She wanted everything she had ever seen in a fancy design magazine, or in a movie; half-a-dozen and gold-plated, too. I guess it's nice enough, but it always seems a bit empty, unless Mom and Dad are having a party."

"Good that you have the dogs, I guess," Bree said, cheerfully, and the conversation might have continued in that vein but for Richard reminding them that they were there to work, and not to gossip.

The set-up for this party was as different as could be from the previous occasions. The first had been a formal party with service *a la Russe* for forty in the opulent dining room of Chez Walcott, the second an intimate family meal served in the cheery yellow breakfast room adjoining the kitchen. This set-up was something more like the wedding banquet buffet set up on Town Square for the presentation of *Let No True Hearts* by the Luna City Players in the previous year. Richard thought that he even recognized the party pavilion set up as an extension of the vast white and gold formal living room, or at least, the work crew adding the final finishing touches. Who by the general appearance and resemblance to Pat and Roman, must be Gonzales or Gonzalez cousins. This, Richard knew, was a certain bet in Luna City.

"Hey, Ricardo! Hi, Chef! Bringing us some coffee, *hermano*?" the two guys attaching fairy lights and hanging white and gold garlands and bunting called down from their respective ladders, and Richard replied,

"Sorry, chaps – didn't bring the big urn with me."

"Too hot now for coffee, anyway," the younger of the pair acknowledged without any rancor. "And we still have all those dinky tables and chairs to set up, soon as we finish with the lights and day-kor."

"I'll have one of my staff bring you some ice-water," Richard promised. *Dear lord, what had gotten into him lately, that he was driven to be courteous and considerate to the ordinary working stiff?*

"Thanks, *hermano*," The older Gonzales/Gonzalez waved, one hand full of white plastic zip-ties. "We're almost done here … Look out, Ricardo, here she comes!"

"What … oh…" Richard looked around, discovering that the chatelaine of Castle Walcott, advancing threateningly upon him, a tiny imperious figure in tee-shirt and yoga pants.

"Riiichard! Why you waste time with help! Not in kitcheeen!" Five foot nothing, maybe a hundred pounds dripping wet, Sook Walcott was a potent force; perhaps because she could shriek at a decibel level normally owned by peacocks and Wagnerian sopranos. It was all to the good, Richard felt, that her sons and daughter had inherited the more placid and even temperament of their sire.

"My dear Sook," Richard summoned up the ragged remains of his social charm. "We are such close friends, are we? I may call you Sook, then? I am merely ensuring that the venue for this evening is arrayed to the highest standard. This – and the adjoining reception room is where your guests will commingle and dine. I wished to confer with the gentlemen setting up the scene of your social triumph … now, I would say that we should have the serving stations to the right and left … yes, here and there. Mr. Mayall will have the bar in the … receiving room. And when supper is ready – on the dot of… what was it? 6:30? Then your guests will have a lovely, and scrumptious meal served to them, and then be able to go out into this marvelous pavilion. Where they may sit and nibble at the collation that we – including your son – have provided, while watching the sun set in the west … and later may come and partake of the dessert table. It will all be memorable, dear Sook. You should not concern yourself, not in the slightest. This event will be memorable …"

And it was – but not in the way which Richard had envisioned.

What's In a Name

Some enchanted evening, across a crowded room ...

Afternoon light poured into the pavilion, as golden as honey; the view from across the terrace of the Walcott mansion was toward the west; a gentle rolling green landscape of green pasture and meadow, quilted with hedges of hackberry, and thickets of oak, and the tall green stands of cypress, pecan, and poplar along the rambling margins of the river. A faint smudge on the north-western horizon hinted at the presence of the big city – San Antonio, more than an hours' drive distant from Luna City. Hinted at concrete acres, city lights, multi-leveled freeway interchanges, tall buildings looming over narrow crowded streets.

Joe Vaughn, a glass of champagne in each hand, lingered by that view, thinking of all the places that he would rather not be, wistfully grateful that he was not in them. There was only one place he would prefer to be at this moment, but ... eh, the Walcotts threw great parties.

"Next month we're gonna have to get us a baby-sitter, when we want to go anyplace by ourselves," he remarked to no one in particular.

"That close?" replied a familiar voice; Patricia Pryor, her footsteps and the silken rustle of her artfully gathered pale blue gown barely heard over laughter, music, the bustle of a convivial gathering well-along. Joe turned with a grin. "Five weeks, Pat. Don't know if I'm ready for it, but Jess certainly is."

"She'll do fine," Patricia affirmed, briskly bracing. "You both will – you'll be fantastic parents. One step at a time. Once you're past the 2AM bottle, it's downhill all the way. A straight road in easy stages until they're accepted at a good college and then the heavy lifting is done. Like Belle," Patricia gestured with her elegant chin toward Belle Walcott, slim and dark in an amazing pink confection that Joe reckoned didn't have enough fabric in it to serve as a pillow slip.

He groaned faintly. "I'm glad ours is a boy. I don't envy the Colonel – she's a beautiful girl. In his place, I'd be all *'got a shovel and a .45 and a dirtbag like you would never be missed'* to every guy who ever looked at her cross-eyed. I know what guys are like," Joe affirmed in all earnest and Patricia giggled.

"Don't think I haven't forgotten all those afternoons after practice, when you drove me home to Paw-paw's…"

Joe swore, briefly. "Damn, Pat – I thought you had!"

"Never," Patricia nudged him, and Joe protested. "Hey, you almost made me spill that!"

"You drinking for two now?" Patricia jeered, secure in the knowledge of being old and affectionate friends. "Just like Jess eats for two? As an honest cop, you'll be pulling your own self over for driving under the influence, for certain, Joseph P. Vaughn!"

"Naw … Jess is driving. I forgot that she can't drink at all, these days. Two sips and she's sicker than a dog. I didn't want to see the Colonel's good stuff go to waste. My duty an' all, Pat."

Joe and Patricia contemplated the sunset vista in silence for a few moments, easy in the silence with each other. They had a history together, a history of two paths which had diverged when they themselves had been just a year or two older than the pretty girl in the brief pink dress.

"You ever regret anything, Pat?" Joe ventured after that silence.

"Regret?" Ever theatrical, Patricia softly sang the chorus of Edith Piaf's *Non, je ne regrette rien.* "No, Joe, sweetie – Noting regretted much. We were kids, and then we grew up. You weren't burnt up much over the Dear John I sent to you. You weren't, were you?" she pleaded, momentarily anxious, and Joe chuckled.

"The one you sent while I was deployed to Mog? Seriously, I had much more important shit to worry about. Seemed kind of trivial at the time. So, my home-town girl had broken up with me, to marry a guy she met in college? Didn't seem quite real to me at the time, Pat. Never really did. Just a phase I had outgrown; no harm, no foul. After a while, when I had time to think about it all, I was kind of relieved. It needs two people to hold up a relationship, one lifting at each end."

"An established habit," Patricia nodded, in perfect understanding. "We just got tired of lifting at the same time. We were lucky in that, Joe. I've seen what happens when one party got tired, and the other couldn't let go. Ugly. Dysfunctional. Sad. All of that by turns. In giving up the way we did, we both of us had a second chance. You wanted to see the world … and I had already done that before I came to live with Paw-Paw and Miss Alice. I wanted safe and normal, you were the one who wanted excitement, adventure and reached for it with both hands."

"Got that right," Joe sighed. "Heaping servings of it all. Mog. Bosnia. The 'Stans. Iraq. I just couldn't see you living in a crappy little apartment on the economy, or a dump in the enlisted family housing area, waiting for my next deployment. Not your style at all, Pat."

"I'm just a simple little country girl at heart," Patricia agreed, and Joe chuckled. "No one looking at you tonight would agree, not in that dress. Country girl my ass."

"This old thing?" Patricia put on a mock-modest expression. "I'll have you know it's vintage Oleg Cassini! Jackie Kennedy had one just like it, only in green – lucky me, I wear the very same size as Miss Alice did, in her prime. Paw-paw gave me all of her old things, after she passed. He couldn't bear to see them moldering away, and he didn't want to give them away to strangers."

"Miss Alice was quite the lady." Joe raised one of the champagne flutes. "Here's to her."

"To Miss Alice," Patricia raised hers, and they both drank. After a moment, she mused. "I don't think she ever got over losing Jamie. She and Paw-paw had dynastic ambitions; Jamie would marry Jess, uniting two of Luna City's important families, and then inherit a major interest in the ranch. All handed neatly on to the next generation, you see. I would marry you, or maybe one of the Bodies … it all sounds dreadfully feudal, but Miss Alice and Paw-paw meant well for us all … for everyone."

"I can't really object to how it all turned out in the long run," Joe acknowledged. "Andy's a lucky man, and your boys are great kids. I hope Little Joe turns out just like them."

"They will," Patricia affirmed. "Although Anson sometimes has the attention span of a fruit-fly, and Andy isn't much better – plus the dirt that child tracks in! He's like a real-life, walking talking Pig-Pen. I haven't the heart to yell at him, though. He's the one who most reminds me of Jamie." Patricia stared at the cloud-shrouded glory of the sunset over the western horizon and if there were tears trembling on her tastefully mascaraed and made-up eyelids, Joe tactfully avoided taking notice of them.

"Jess and I did have a thought," Joe ventured, when he thought Patricia had recovered her composure. "We wanted a godmother and a middle name for Little Joe, and Jess wanted to ask your permission, first.

She – that is, we – want to call him Joseph James, and have you and Andy as godparents."

"Why, Joe, that would be lovely!" Patricia beamed, wholly enthusiastic. "Yes, of course, you have my permission. You wouldn't mind if I let Paw-paw know, too? He has always been fond of Jess, and she and Jamie … It'll be a comfort to him, I'm sure – knowing that you both want to keep a bit of his memory alive. I'll tell Andy right now. Great heavens, what are those dogs carrying on about?"

"No idea, Pat – no idea at all. Baying at the moon, I expect." Joe replied, as Patricia laughed.

Dinner at the Walcotts – Continued

The cavernous living room gradually filled; voices, laughter, the clinking of ice in tall glasses filled with refreshing beverages *(soft drinks for the younger set, as Chris Mayall was positively unyielding in his refusal to serve alcohol to minors)*, soft music floating from cleverly-spaced speakers, as golden afternoon light sifted in from the pavilion. Beatriz and Blanca circulated with the trays of *hors de oeuvres*, trim in black and white maid livery, offering mushroom caps, mini-Scotch eggs and bite-sized crab cakes. The hard work of preparing the buffet selections was accomplished just as the first guests arrived. Richard found that he was frequently intercepted by friends, in his circulations between the kitchen and the buffet tables, even as Robbie Walcott and Bree Grant were similarly waylaid by their own friends – in spite of being clad in chef's jackets and white toques.

"Araceli, correct me if I am mistaken," Richard ventured, at a moment when it was just the two of them in the kitchen, finishing up deep-frying the last of the mini-Scotch eggs, "But it seems to me that Grant and Walcott are the envy of their young friends. Can this be true? They are working, while their peers are enjoying the lavish hospitality that Walcott Pere can provide..."

Araceli chuckled. "Chef, you aren't imagining it; they are. Bree and Robbie are having the time of their lives, because they are working for you, at the Café. You've made food service something exciting and glamorous to the kids, and that you chose <u>those</u> two ... well, the other kids are green with envy that they get to work for and learn from you every day. They've got stature among a group that is terribly status-aware."

"I cannot honestly conceive of how that would be," Richard shook his head, incredulous. "It's a brutal way to make a living; the hours are long; the pay is usually insultingly low, the chances of being a celebrity out of it are vanishingly small ..."

"Well, the same with acting," Araceli pointed out. "Or playing pro football ... but still, there are kids who want to do try."

"I will never understand Americans," Richard sighed, shaking his head, and Araceli dipped up another strainer full of sizzling sausage and bread-crumb coated eggs.

"It gives Bree and Robbie a chance to learn something useful – and to look good in front of their friends. That's all there is to understand," Araceli shrugged. Likely she was correct in this, Richard thought. Out in the hallway, a massive grandfather clock chimed the hour of 6, and the front door opened and closed on more guests, their voices echoing in the hallway. Araceli unplugged the deep-fryer and set the last batch of eggs on a tray. "All right then, Chef – that's the last of them. Another twenty minutes to start setting out the hot dishes. Better tell the kids to get back to work."

Now the living room, and the pavilion extension were gratifyingly crowded; knots of teenagers congregating around Belle Walcott and her coterie of girlfriends, shrieking with laughter. Belle appeared happy and animated, for practically the first time Richard had ever observed. There was Doc Wyler with Patricia Pryor and her husband, and a couple of gentlemanly men in formal suits ... and elaborate cowboy boots. It appeared that the local custom was to top off Savile Row splendor with Texas-peculiar accessories. Sook Walcott stood with her husband, elegant in designer splendor, draped in a rope of pearls the size of marbles and shod in towering high heels which lent her an additional six inches or more in height. The only woman more strikingly clad was Patricia Pryor, in a pale blue asymmetrical gown that was a miracle of flowing silk pleats and drapery. There was Lew Dubois, unexpectedly debonair in Continental-cut tuxedo, with a cluster of men who must be some of Clovis Walcott's Houston associates, as Richard did not recognize them. And there stood the other Walcott son; Jerry, the trained nurse, side by side with another young man whom Richard also didn't know, although they were all in a familial cluster with Sook and Clovis. The Vaughn men, Harry and Joe also sported tailored suits and cowboy regalia. They were sitting at one of the small tables with Jess, who – like Sook – was also wearing something flowing and designer-like but which did nothing to hide the much-increased baby bump. Min Kim, Halmeoni or Grandmother to the Walcotts, was also sitting there, chattering to the attentive Harry Vaughn – the only other person in Luna City outside of the Walcott family who spoke fluent Korean. Jess smiled and waved across the room at Richard, so of course he had to go speak to them.

"Nice party," Harry Vaughn growled appreciatively. "Ol' Clovis really knows how to put on a good party. How you been doing these days, Rich? Been up to much messing around in boats?"

"Not so much," Richard answered. "We've picked up so much business at the Café these days that I hardly have the time for anything but work." He glowered at Harry; his one venture in a boat with Harry Vaughn was not a pleasant one.

"I liked your Captain Kitten podcast," Jess confessed, in a comment obviously meant to keep the peace. "I'm watching them, every week. My mom never had a chance to teach me to cook. And very soon I will really have to …"

Joe reached across the small table and patted the bump, affectionately. "Kid-kind can't live on frozen pizza alone," he observed. "Just a little longe, Babe."

"We'll have dinner laid out in about fifteen minutes," Richard promised, and went in search of his apprentices. He found them with Anson Pryor, fussing over the serving tables in the pavilion, adjusting the decorations, ensuring the serving utensils were just so, and that the chafing dishes to keep the hot dishes hot were in good order, already filled with hot water, and the ones for the cold salmon and the salad were filled with ice. This unforced devotion to detail pleased Richard very much. His time and effort over the last two months had not been wasted, although Robbie was frowning over the last table.

"I need to get some more Safe-Heat cans, Chef – they're out in the van."

"Hop to it, Walcott – double-time," Richard said. "And make sure to wash your hands and put on a clean apron."

"On it, Chef," Robbie vanished with pleasing alacrity. Richard followed more slowly; reveling in the pleasure of being about to serve an excellent supper in a flawless manner to an appreciate and hungry audience. He caught Chris' eye, they exchanged a brief nod; yes, it was all going very well.

But he could hear dogs barking, as he crossed the hallway. Weren't they supposed to be in their kennel, with all the guests coming and going? It didn't sound to him like they were – in fact, it sounded like the dogs were running … running, barking, and baying like they were the embodiment of the spectral Baskerville hound, all around the house … and then the front door swung open with a mighty crash.

The palatial hallway of the Walcott mansion was instantly full of dog, excited dog, dog and more dog, two chasing the third, which had a mouthful of something live and fighting, blood spurting like a fountain everywhere. Richard stood paralyzed on the spot, hardly daring to believe the evidence of his eyes, as the horrid cavalcade swept down the hall and into the living room!

"Not the tables!" he shouted, just as Robbie yelled from the kitchen, "The dogs got loose! Mom! Dad! Come quick!"

Screams erupted from the palatial living room in the wake of the dogs, shrieks and shouts of horror, a panoply of crashing sounds – china and silver flung to the floor, a deeper and more resounding crash as something heavier was smashed to smithereens, a feminine cry of shock and pain, amid fierce growling from the dogs. Richard flung himself down the hall, in a dash which would have won him a ribbon in his schooldays and arrived upon a scene which would have done credit to the less imaginative but gorily explicit horror movie.

Before the main serving table, the three dogs were scrabbling for possession of … something so bloodied that he could not actually ascertain what it was. And that blood flew everywhere, staining the pristine white tablecloths with crimson, puddling on the floor, lavishly on the spindly gold and white-brocade upholstered furniture nearest to the serving tables, and on Beatriz's white apron, now also smeared with remoulade. It all looked as if Jack the Ripper had been at enthusiastic work, stabbing and splashing. One of the serving tables was completely overthrown, the chafing dishes and their watery and icy contents scattered every which way, a puddle of water and ruination spreading across the floor, and scattered blue flames turning to orange as they licked at the tablecloth … until Chris appeared – oh, savior of the dinner party – with a small fire extinguisher. A burst of white chemical and the fire died in a brief futile flare of blue flame and white vapor. Beatriz regained her feet – or her knees, anyway – and possession of the large platter which had been knocked from her grasp, scattering mini-crab cakes and remoulade broadcast across the floor. Dazed and shocked, she began retrieving the spilled crab cakes one by one, gathering them onto the tray. Richard stood frozen for what seemed an eternity.

"Ok, then?" Chris was remarkably composed, even as the dogs were still fighting over … what? Chris aimed a burst from the fire extinguisher at them, and they broke apart, yelping. Robbie, appearing magically from the kitchen, yelled some command words at them, at which two dogs slunk guiltily away, and the third gave up his prize, smeared with blood and still feebly twitching, right at the foot of where Richard had committed to serve an audience of a hundred in the next fifteen minutes.

"Ohmigod, it's crapped all over!" exclaimed Beatriz with a shriek of horror. She dropped what wasn't a crab cake, as Sook Walcott appeared in the living room, flanked by her husband, Harry Vaughn, Doc Wyler, Lew Dubois, and a handful of others. For sheer decibel power, Sook's outraged exclamations topped even Beatriz, who was scrubbing her fingers on a soiled tablecloth and ranting in emphatic Spanish. Robbie Walcott vanished with the dogs, presumably to return them to their kennel, but Bree appeared from the kitchen with Araceli on her heels.

"It's an armadillo!" Bree knelt next to the bloodied, writhing animal. "The dogs must have got lucky, it's the biggest one I've ever seen!" At her side, Chris put down the extinguisher and produced a couple of bar-towels to drape over the mangled armadillo – doing so very carefully, for the thing had long, powerful claws on at all four feet, and teeth that snapped at anything that moved within reach. The towels were instantly soaked with blood.

"Shut the doors!" Richard recovered his voice and his composure. "Get everyone into the pavilion, while we cope with this… this what the devil did you say it was?"

"An armadillo, son," Harry Vaughn replied. "What the folks down in the Valley call 'armored pig,'" as Sook screamed, "Thees supper – is ruined! What you do now, Reeeeechard!"

"Nothing is ruined that we can't fix," Richard snapped, and Bree asked with a voice which trembled, "Is it dead?"

"Not yet," Harry Vaughn said grimly. To Richard's horror and Bree's as well, he produced a heavy blued-steel automatic out from under his jacket. Sook screamed again, and Harry Vaughn shrugged. "Put the poor thing out of its misery!"

"Jesus, not inside!" Clovis had his arm around his aghast spouse. "Sook, darlin' – go out and tell our guests that supper will be a mite delayed. Richard, how soon can we get this critter out of here, and put things to rights again?"

"It can be done, Colonel – all hands, people." Richard raised his voice; another near-disaster supper at the Walcott house. *What else had he expected?* The tiny chatelaine of Chez Walcott shook off her husband's arm, and marched out of the devastated living room, slamming the French doors behind her as she went.

"Don't kill it," Bree begged, tearfully. "It's just hurt. Gee-Nan would call … Doc, can't you do something? Mr. Mayall?"

Doc Wyler knelt, gingerly and with some difficulty on his ninety-six-year-old knees. "Ain't as spry as I once was," he muttered. "Let me see here, little missy – it's a wild critter, an' sometimes they don't take real well to doctoring by humans. But this one is one of the biggest 'dillos that I ever laid eyes on; I'd be right sorry to put it down straight away. I got my bag out in the truck, Mayall – you want to assist?"

"Sure thing, Doc." Chris was bringing more towels. "Colonel, is there a place that we can take this critter to – some place with plenty of light and out of the way?"

Bree was big-eyed with dawning hope. "You can patch it up as right as rain, I just know you can. Gee-Nan says you haven't ever lost one of her fur-babies, ever."

"Your grandmother has an exaggerated notion of my capabilities," Doc Wyler answered. "I can't make any promises, li'l missy. But I'll do what I can for the critter, even if there's nothing to be done but put it to sleep painlessly."

"Grant," Richard commanded. "Let Doc and Chris do what they can. Meanwhile, we were about to start service for Mrs. Walcott's guests. We can still do that ... in fact, I expect us to do that. Araceli – can you assist Beatriz? Do we have a spare apron for her... look, people, we can still do this dinner in the style which we are accustomed to offer. Fresh tablecloth. Set up the chafing dishes again. Lucky thing that we hadn't actually put out the food ..."

By sheer force of will, it seemed to Richard that order was recovered from blood, puddled water, tangled tablecloths, and a stack of broken china plates. Chris, Doc, and Clovis Walcott vanished with the towel-swathed armadillo into some further reaches of the house, while Blanca and Robbie appeared, armed respectively with a fresh stack of clean plates, and mop and bucket from which the scent of powerful detergent rose like a fog. To Richard's amazement, Lew Dubois, still elegantly Gallic in his black and white evening clothes, remained in the theater of disaster.

"You will permit me, *cher*?" he asked, helping Araceli right the table. "As a comrade in the business of providing hospitality. I confess, so comprehensive a disaster as this – my sympathies are excited. Ah – and also my appetite for supper is unimpaired. My dear wife has always claimed that the way to my heart is indeed through my stomach..."

"We'll get it done, Mr. Dubois," Anson Pryor rolled in the service cart, laden with buckets of fresh ice and a fresh case of Safe-Heat cans. From somewhere in the van, Anson had also located clean tablecloths, and from the Walcott's kitchen pantry, unbroken vases to house the rescued flowers from arrangements destroyed when the table was toppled over. Richard had not considered the younger Pryor as a potential apprentice before, but the lad did have possibilities, beyond the familial BBQ food truck. Likely, the family obligations, though …

"Yes – we'll do it," Richard insisted doggedly and with new-dawning hope, as the remnants of disaster were speedily banished through the furious efforts of Araceli, the apprentices, and Lew Dubois. Nothing inspired like emergency; why now, and not at the Carême disaster? A matter worthy of consideration, Richard thought – but later. Now was too important to be distracted by overmuch thinking. Yes, the flowers did look a bit bedraggled and the replacement apron for Beatriz was an ordinary cooks' apron and not the flounced version constructed by Patricia Gonzalez by way of stills from *Downton Abbey* … the replacement tablecloth was slightly too short, and one of the chafing-dish pans was lamentably dented. But the dent could be turned to the back, and the cans of Safe-Heat lighted underneath.

In a remarkably short time, order was restored to the serving line in the living room, evidence of disaster removed, replaced, or concealed, the chafing dishes charged with the salmon, the salad, the roast tenderloin, the pilaf; Richard and Lew regarded it with immense satisfaction, although Richard thought there were still some splashes of drying armadillo blood in the doorway.

"*Alons, mes infants*," Lew said, with the air of a successful commanding general. "You have done it. And I trust that supper will be served shortly. I will tell Madame Walcott and her guests so, unless there is reason that I should not do otherwise. A triumph, Chef – a triumph most remarkable." Lew rendered a casual, military-style salute. "And perhaps … at some later time, I may discuss with you a matter most dear to my heart."

"I won't come to work at Mills Farm," Richard warned. "Get shed of that notion right away. Your predecessor had that notion, and I wouldn't touch it – or her – with a bargepole."

"I suggest nothing of the sort, *cher* Richard," Lew replied, sounding slightly injured. "No, this is to do with my eventual plan for Mills Farm's annex, and a proposal for your services as an independent contractor … but enough. Madame Walcott's guests are ready."

"Indeed." Richard nodded stiffly, by way of returning the courtesy. "Tell them – dinner is now served."

Much, much later, as Richard, Araceli, Anson, with the apprentices and Beatriz and Blanca ate their own late supper in the cavernous kitchen while music drifted in from the pavilion, Anson swallowed a mouthful of cold salmon, and ventured,

"So, Chef – you were pretty cool with disaster. Anything like that ever happened before?"

"Only once," Richard sighed. "Of that magnitude and involving an animal. It happened in Spain – early on, when I was doing a show in one of those towns that has a bull-running thing in the streets. Not Pamplona – another town. One of the bulls got lost, crashed through a barrier – and into the venue."

"Wow," said Anson, from his expression quite thoroughly impressed. "A live bull … "

"Wrecked the venue, crippled one of the grips and smashed a very expensive camera." Richard helped himself to more of the beef tenderloin, given an appetite by the memory. "I'd say that this evening we were extremely fortunate in comparison."

Talk of the Town – Late September

What's new in Luna City, Karnesville, Hobson, Mayo, Helena, and Falls City
By Talk of the Town News Hounds:
You Read it on the Internet, So You Know It Must Be True

There is a new arrival in the famous petting zoo on the premises of the Mills Farm Resort and Spa, just south of Luna City on Texas Rt. 123; a 20-pound 9-banded armadillo named Lucky, who arrived early this month thanks to a near-fatal encounter with some local dogs. Poor Lucky was mauled but rescued in time to save his life. He was treated by local vet Dr. Stephen Wyler of the Lazy W Exotic Game Ranch, who felt that Lucky would not do well if set free into the wild, due to the nature of his injuries. Added to the menagerie of farm animals at Mills Farm, Lucky the Armadillo will have his own comfortable enclosure on the far side of the Old Red Barn, next to Fred and Wilma, the donkeys.

Work begins late this month on a new facility at Mills Farm; the first step in plans for expanding recreational opportunities. An old-fashioned Victorian-style boat house will be relocated to a site on the river just north of existing facilities. According to Marketing Director Lucian "Lew" Dubois, kayaking and canoeing expeditions will be offered beginning in summer of 2018.

Isabelle "Belle" Walcott, Luna City Unified Hight School Class of '17 and First Trumpet in the Mighty Fighting Moths Marching Band was accepted to the Julliard School earlier this year, and departs for New York next week to begin her studies at the famed conservatory, which is regarded as one of the best, world-wide, when it comes to training in the musical arts. Belle, a stand-out in the marching band for the last three seasons, will be sorely missed – but everyone here at Talk of the Town extends their best wishes for a bright new star in the musical firmament!

Chief of the Luna City PD, Joseph P. Vaughn and Jessica Abernathy-Vaughn of Luna City announced to their friends last week that their baby, due early in November is a boy and to be named Joseph James Vaughn. No doubt, the Mighty Fighting Months varsity football team will have a great quarterback for the 2033-34 season, if little Joseph James takes after proud papa Joe… In other Luna City baby news, it seems that star male model Roman "Romeo" Gonzales and his wife, former high-flying corporate maven Susanna Wyatt-Gonzales are also expecting … twins, via *in vitro* fertilization and a surrogate mother who prefers to remain anonymous. Happy news for everyone involved!

Showdown at the Café

"You seem awfully calm about *A La Carte* coming to town tomorrow," Kate remarked, on the evening before Allen Lee Mayne and his crew, with the despicable Pip Noel-Barrett were supposed to roll into Luna City. Kate, Richard, and Ozzie were enjoying their usual Monday suppertime celebratory relaxation, after a weekend of sixteen-hour days, and getting the *Weekly Beacon* off to the printer in fine style.

"I am indeed, my Kate," Richard drawled. "I have achieved a most unaccustomed state of not caring. And not just because I have been imbibing this evening."

The evening was fine and clear, the breeze was cool, and just sufficient to keep off the mosquitos – either that, or Sefton's surreptitious fogging of the campground at mid-summer had a longer-lasting effect than usual. They were sitting outside, enjoying the last rays of afternoon sun, retreating behind splendidly arrayed purple and lavender-colored clouds, trimmed in fiery gold. Richard had one last glass of Sefton's magnificent red at hand, while Kate – knowing that she would be driving home in a short while – was teasing Ozzie with a cat-toy, a wand with a long string and a puffy ball on the end of the string. Ozzie leaped, pounced, and chased the elusive puffy ball with carefree abandon. Kate let Ozzie have the little puffy ball for a joyous tussle, in which he rolled onto his back and batted it with all four paws.

"How is that?" she asked, after a moment. "You were all wound up, that time at Araceli's this summer, when we talked about it."

"Mature reconsideration," Richard replied. "Also, I talked to Doc Wyler, who offered the most sanguinary advice, as well as his personal assistance. So … aside from not wanting to be caught on camera by Pip Noel-Barrett's camera operators, I am actually looking forward to a reunion with my old and dear pal."

"How did that come about? I mean, if you want to share," Kate added hastily.

"Because," Richard explained in perfect tranquility. "The good doctor convinced me that I should have it out with the egregious Pip once and for all, the good old-fashioned way."

"Oh dear," Kate took the fuzzy ball away from Ozzie. "I hope he didn't mean <u>that</u> old-fashioned way; pistols for two, breakfast for one."

"More like boxing gloves for two, bloody nose for one."

Richard, faced on the morrow with the showdown, was mildly amazed at how tranquilly he contemplated the prospect. It would all be done, and there would be no more running and hiding. Doc Wyler was a man of his word – and over the last several sessions with Coach Barrett in the Moths fieldhouse, bashing away at the hanging bag, Richard had developed an almost Zen sense of detachment. Tomorrow he would bash away at Pip, under the stern judicial eye of Doc Wyler, he would bloody that aristocratic nose and live content in Luna City, whether celebrity found him again or not. He had moved beyond caring, although explaining this to Kate was a little complicated.

"Once the deed is done ... Doc Wyler – he has a grudge against Noel-Barrett over that whole movie debacle anyway. He says that it will all be sorted, once I stand up against the smarmy little git."

"He looked awfully fit, the last time I saw him on television," Kate sounded dubious, even a little worried. "Are you sure you'll be able to lay a glove on him?"

"My dear Kate of Kate Hall, being a lazy bugger, he depends on stunt-doubles and favorable camera work to look that good, whereas I have been bicycling miles every day and working out religiously. There's nothing to worry about. Doc expects business at the Café to be good and even better – sufficiently to expand service and add a few more staff. Alas, now that summer is nearly spent, I must bid adieu to my two apprentices." Richard sighed, heavily. "Well-trained, they are now. Set out in the right direction, even if they do not choose to pursue a career in a restaurant kitchen. And now to begin training anew."

"I think summer working in the Café has been good for Bree and Robbie," Kate dribbled the puffy ball across the patio by her chair, but Ozzie merely blinked at her, indicating that yes, he was done with this game. "They learned something and got to be treated like responsible adults. I'll bet you'll miss them – but I think you'll do just as well with training new staff. Maybe you can even get to the point where you can take a day off, now and again."

"We'll see," Richard felt a slight quiver in his innards, somewhere in the vicinity of where he imagined his heart to be located. "Are you off for the night, my Kate?"

"I have to be, Rich, I need to cover the arrival of Allen Lee tomorrow, cadge an interview with him, and drive to Karnesville to file the story with my editor." She stood with a sigh. "Good night, sweet Ozzie – don't let the coyotes bite. Good night, Richard – see you in the morning, 'kay? Give Noel-Barrett a extra-good shot in the chops for me. He slipped his hand underneath my skirt and grabbed my butt the last time he was in town for that movie, and I still owe him payback." She dropped a brief, but lingering kiss on Richard's lips.

"I didn't know that…" Richard's latent anger surged; *how dare that smarmy little git lay his filthy hands on Kate!*

"No reason to," Kate neatly ducked the returned embrace. "My knee somehow hit him in his junk, and I apologized for my awful clumsiness, smiling sweetly all the time."

"Christ, Kate – he didn't put you off men … especially Englishmen for life, did he?"

"He did not," Kate consoled him with a second kiss, as brief as a butterfly alighting. "Don't worry. See you in the morning."

And she was away, the little VW Bug that was her transportation bouncing down the narrow driveway, sending up a brief trail of dust, which settled unseen in the twilight. Richard looked down at Ozzie, and sighed again. "She loves us and leaves us, Ozymandias-King-of-Kings. Do we want her to remain … or are we merely relieved at being left to ourselves? Any thoughts on the matter that you wish to share?"

"Mrrrooow!" commented Ozzie, in his usual oblique feline manner, and went to sit on the bottom step to the caravan. The sun was nearly down, and soon the coyotes would be out. Ozzie possessed a well-developed sense of self-preservation.

***

Nemesis arrived in Luna City at mid-morning the next day. In the rush to serve breakfast and prepare for lunch, Richard had managed to put that knowledge aside, existing for the moment in that state of Zen detachment which had overtaken him from the first time that he aimed a gloved punch at the hanging bag in the Moth field-house and imagined it landing smack in the center of Phillip Noel-Barrett's chiseled countenance. It was all … without meaning, impersonal, distant from the necessity to start another batch of sweet-roll dough. Which Grant and

Walcott were attending to with touching gravity and exceptional professionalism, so he left them to it, and drifted out into the dining room.

"They're here," Joe Vaughn, sitting at the small table which he usually shared with Jess, turned down the audio on the small shoulder-radio, and announced to the slightly larger than usual mid-morning crowd at the Café. "Milo says that the purple RV has just come across the temporary bridge. He sent Santos and Greg to escort them into town. All ready for lights, camera and all that other stuff?"

"Spare me," Richard said, from the doorway to the kitchen. Doc Wyler sent him a beetle-browed and quelling look from where he rose from the *stammtisch*.

"We know your feelings on the matter, Richard," Martin Abernathy said, with an air of quiet authority. "You do not wish for any notice taken of yourself – especially by the camera crew. As much as can be possible, your preferences will be honored…"

"But recall our agreement," Doc Wyler muttered, as the rest of the Café's mid-morning customers surged out through the front door and onto the sidewalk to greet the star, supporting cast and crew of *A La Carte with Quartermayne*.

It had to be one of those beautiful, early autumn days, Richard thought; the sky a perfect, cerulean blue, the leaves on certain of the massive oaks in Town Square just lightly touched with color. The sidewalks and mown grass underneath their massive branches were thick-seeded with drifts of fallen acorns; the resident squirrels were having a field day, gathering and feasting upon them. It was cool in the shade, warm in the watery sunshine. The façade of the old Cattleman Hotel loomed bright in the sunshine, looking not a day less than at least fifty years old. Flowers in the hanging baskets in front of the Stein's place of business bloomed bright and fresh; a picture of a perfect late Victorian small-town square. Richard only wished that a photographer from one of the Sunday supplements could have taken a good couple of snaps for a calendar or tourist postcards. But there was Kate, in her billowing tan trench-coat and innumerable cameras. Ah, Kate – always to be relied upon. And wheeling around the corner, Nemesis, in the form of an enormous lumbering purple, black and gold RV, elaborately labeled in swirling letters: *A La Carte With Quartermayne – The Ultimate Foodie Experience!* One of the Luna City's PD's newer and best-maintained SUV's proceeded, ablaze with lights. A large van adorned with similar swirly letters followed the RV, and as soon as Richard noted the presence of a cameraman leaning from the passenger-side window documenting the arrival of Allen Lee Mayne and his entourage, he ducked back into the recessed doorway of the Café. The three vehicles rolled to a stop under the oaks opposite the Café and Stein's Wild West Round-up. A tall, heavy-set black man climbed down from the driver's side of the RV, grinning ear to ear as he saw an audience waiting; obviously Allen Lee Mayne, since his vastly magnified and beaming countenance was also plastered across the side of the RV.

"Hey, my foodie pals in Luna City – are we ready to get down with barbeque?"

"You bet, Allen Lee!" everyone chorused, as Martin Abernathy began performing introductions; Richard, seeing that the cameraman was busy with a tight focus on Allen Lee, came out of the Café and lingered – unobtrusively, he hoped – on the edge of the impromptu gathering. Allen Lee Mayne obviously had done his homework, Richard noticed at once; he didn't need an introduction to Andy Pryor and Joe Vaughn, rather hailing them as old friends after a long time away. He looked to be in his fifties, gone slightly grizzled but not much run to fat, a little darker than Chris Mayall, whose hand he was now pumping and exclaiming, "Hey, bro! How did you find yourself here, all the way from Dee-troit!"

Surely no one would notice him…

He wanted to find Pip Noel-Barrett and issue his challenge at first opportunity, but the blighter proved elusive. *Ah-hah!* There he was, hunched in an anonymous hoodie and baseball cap, like one of the grips, lurking by the van and hiding his chiseled profile behind dark glasses and a somewhat hunted expression.

Richard altered his path, intending to challenge Noel-Barrett without attracting overmuch attention, but just as he edged past the excited cluster of Lunaites around Allen Lee, Mayor Abernathy turned around, saying, "Hey, Allen Lee, you should meet Richard. He runs the Café, over here, and makes the best coffee and cinnamon rolls in this part of Texas. But ditch the camera, please. He's a private person. There ya are, Richard! I can't believe you never ran into Allen Lee Mayne before, you got so much in common." Before he could escape, Richard's hand was enveloped in Allen Lee's enormous grasp, and *Oh-god, the horror!* There was the camera's huge Cyclopean eye, swinging around to focus on him … and Joe Vaughn stepped quietly in between, holding up his own hand in front of the lens.

"As Mr. Mayor said, Richard doesn't want to be on camera," Joe said quietly, but with powerful authority. "Not now, and not for the remainder of your visit here, Mr. Mayne."

"But …" the cameraman and Allen Lee protested on almost the same note of disappointment. Joe stared the other men down. "No buts, guys. He asked not to be, and he won't. Your word on it, gentleman." That was not a gentle request from Joe, but an unadorned statement of fact. The cameraman looked unhappy, and Martin Abernathy frowned, but Allen Lee nodded, in gracious acquiescence.

"Understood, Chief Vaughn, Mr. Mayor. No worries. Cut it for now, Alvin – go get some good B-roll of town, while I get acquainted with these nice folks. And where the hell is Phillip? He's never around when there's work to be done." There was an edge of absolute authority in that quiet voice, and now the big man was sizing up Richard with unexpectedly shrewd eyes. Whatever his past experiences on the football grounds, he had obviously not taken too many intelligence-impairing blows to his head. "So, you're that old pal of Phil's! Yeah, he told me about you. I'm impressed, man. A real chef. I'll bet we could have a good ol' time swapping recipes! Lew, man – great to see ya! It's been an age since we taped that show at Castle Mountain! Say, have you got Richard to making real N'awlins beignets for ya?" Allen Lee whacked Lew Dubois on the shoulder and went on working the small crowd with every evidence of keen enjoyment, leaving Richard to his original intent of settling the score with Phillip Noel-Barrett.

Who proved elusive after being first being spotted, for some unfathomable reason. Richard finally ran him to ground – or more precisely to van, mostly because Doc Wyler had made it easier, by already cornering Noel-Barrett against the back doors; slightly-built and ninety-six, as feisty as a bantam-rooster, the old veterinarian had already gained the despicable Pip's complete and unswerving attention. Mainly because Doc Wyler's right arm was akimbo on his waist, revealing the holstered 1911 Model Colt pistol in the holster hung from his belt, at which instrument Phillip Noel-Barrett was staring, as transfixed as a helpless bird cornered by a snake. Obviously, Noel-Barrett had absorbed and believed every BBC-transmitted story regarding the gun-toting denizens of Texas, whole and without pause for reflection.

"Don't ever piss off an old man, son," Doc was saying, as Richard approached within earshot. "We don't care, we've seen it all, and we got nothing to lose, save a year or two off a life which has been long enough anyway. I gotta bone to pick with you, Barrett, over that thrice-be-damned movie deal but Richard here has a fresher grudge. I yield to his claim on your worthless ass. Richard, you gonna step up here?"

"I am," Richard answered. "Good morning, Pip. I've been informed that you intend to expose me and my current whereabouts, condition and by extension my friends here. I see that as a malicious threat; a situation up with which I will not put. Tomorrow morning, eight of the clock, around in back of the Café; meet me there. Withdraw your threat to expose me; that is my demand to be settled. Should I be the looser in this affray – do what you will. If I win, you will withdraw your threats of personal exposure. An affair of honor, sir; you should know the process, I think, if not the general concept. The appropriate weapons will be provided to you. Will you meet me tomorrow, then? Or be seen forever in the public eye as a gutless coward? I have friends here, who will ensure that you are branded thus forever in the public eye."

"I … yes," Phillip Noel-Barrett gabbled, frantic to acquiesce, a thing which Richard took vicious pleasure out of observing.

"All right then, Doctor Wyler, Pip; we shall meet tomorrow on the field of honor. Good day to you," Richard said, and stalked off. The latest dough for tomorrow's batch of cinnamon rolls should be ready to begin proofing. As the manager of the Café, he had his priorities.

* * *

With an eye on the clock, Richard opened the Café's kitchen as per usual, although slightly earlier than normal; turning on the great coffee urn, warming the ovens for the first pans of sweet rolls and fresh-baked bread. Araceli appeared ten minutes later at her usual time, neat in her pastel waitress uniform and white apron, her thick-soled trainers tied with shoelaces which matched her dress. She came in the back door, accompanied by the sound of an auto engine, and the crunch of tires on the crumbling pavement outside; Robbie Walcott, who had taken to making a detour to the Age of Aquarius in the early morning to collect Bree, and then driving her home in the afternoon after work. Richard often saw them with other swim-suit-clad teenagers, frolicking in the cool greenish waters of the swimming hole on those hot afternoons, and rather approved, although he suspected that the Grant and Walcott parents would take an extremely dim view of what the Victorians had called "an attachment". Bree and Robbie were, after all, only sixteen.

The two apprentices appeared, a few minutes later, fresh-faced and laughing, as they tied on clean aprons. It gratified Richard that they set to

309

their assigned tasks without any further ado, or unnecessary conversation, working smoothly and unhurried; Robbie heating the grill, and Bree to prepping garnishes to adorn the breakfast plates, artfully trimming oranges, lemons, carrots and cucumbers in various shapes and slices – just as Richard had taught them. The minutes ticked by, measured by the hands on the schoolroom clock which commanded the kitchen in remorseless fashion.

At six-thirty, Richard unlocked the street door, switched on the overhead lights in the dining area, the television which burbled inanely to itself on one of the news channels, and the little neon sign which hung in the biggest window and announced "open." The street outside was dark, darker still the tree-shrouded Square beyond, a darkness only broken by the dozen antique cast-iron streetlamps, raising their opalescent globes of light at regular intervals along the margin of the Square. Before Richard even returned to the kitchen, Roman Gonzalez and three of his workmen sauntered in, the little bell over the door tinkling sweetly.

"Morning, Ricardo," Roman yawned. "Got us a hot date with a cement truck pouring a foundation over near Helena. Coffee ready?"

"Certainly," Richard answered. "The usual for you?"

"Yeah. Ya know, that full English breakfast of yours is the bomb."

"Ten minutes," Richard answered over his shoulder. No need to send Araceli to take the orders. As he came through the door into the kitchen, he was already commanding, "Full English for four, extra toast."

"On it, Chef!" Araceli ran up a full carafe of coffee, and Robbie slapped two-dozen strips of bacon and six sausages on the griddle… Richard observed all this with an overwhelming sense of satisfaction. His introduction of a proper English morning fry-up into the breakfast lexicon of the Café had proved a resounding success with those regulars who had physically demanding jobs, although many of them insisted on a dash of salsa on the poached eggs and looked askance at the prospect of plain traditional baked beans, until he offered a more local variant – what they called 'borracho' beans. Robbie worked the griddle like a maestro, Richard was pleased to note: this summer had not been wasted. The old-fashioned bell on the Café door jingled sweetly again, and Araceli shot out of the kitchen like a well-focused arrow.

"Another full English, for table two," she sang out, upon her return – and the breakfast rush began, heralded by the silver chime of the bell, and the door opening and closing, each time announced by a puff of fresh autumn air. "And Chris is here, for the cinnamon rolls."

"On it, Chef!" Bree took a tray of fresh, crisp garnishes into the cooler, and on her return, began packaging up two-dozen sweet rolls for resale in the Tip-Top Ice House, Gas and Grocery. Araceli refreshed her coffee carafe, collected a fresh-baked hot pecan-orange sweet-roll, a glass of fresh orange juice, and a side of diced mixed fruit for Chris and vanished into the dining room. Chris was another one of those regulars, whose breakfast preferences were so well-established that Araceli usually put in his order as soon as she saw him walking toward the front door.

Doc Wyler appeared, settling with a slight grunt at his accustomed place at the *stammtisch*, followed a moment later by the Steins, and then by Joe Vaughn, large, looming, and garbed for a hard day of keeping the law in Luna City and on the adjacent stretch of Rt. 123. Joe was alone, which was unaccustomed; most usually Jess Abernathy accompanied him for breakfast.

"Plain cheese omelet," Joe said to Araceli. "Toast on the side, and a cinnamon roll to go."

"Where's Jess?" Araceli asked, a swift expression of concern.

Joe held out his coffee mug for the ever-flowing bounty from Araceli's carafe. "She had a rough night last night. Little Joe was squirming like a wiggle-worm and didn't give us any rest until about 3AM. I left a note and left her to sleep."

"God knows, she'll not get any rest for months, anyway." Araceli prophesized darkly, and Joe laughed; a hollow-sounding laugh. The front door opened, again and again, the jingle of the bell a sweet soundtrack accompaniment to the morning routine as the Café filled tables. On the television set in the corner, the news reader burbled about a hurricane forming, away out in the Caribbean. Richard spared it a glance – a pastel and multi-colored chart had the proposed track heading toward the southern coast. Back in the kitchen, he glanced at the clock, remorselessly measuring off the minutes until his assignation with Phillip Noel-Barrett. Fifty-five minutes… forty minutes… then half an hour. The hand of the clock swept in its' inexorable fashion, and the breakfast rush continued.

"I'll be out in back, when you are ready," Richard murmured to Doc Wyler, who set down his own coffee mug with a grim and yet expectant expression, and replied, "You ain't see him yet?"

"No," Richard answered. "But he has half an hour. I'll be ready for him. You brought the gloves?"

"Out in the truck," Doc answered, just as the door opened to admit Allen Lee Mayne – alone but seeming to fill the doorway with his exuberant presence.

"Morning, everybody," he exclaimed, "Thought I'd try out the best breakfast chow in town, if'n y'all don't mind."

"Not at all," Richard said, echoed enthusiastically by all present. "Make yourself at home … er…" he looked around; there were no empty tables, but one or two places at the stammtisch, and at the table where Roman and his guys were enthusiastically scoffing poached eggs with salsa, beans, toast, sausage, and bacon.

"Hey, Allen Lee!" Roman gestured with a forkful of sausage. "Over here – an' you gotta try Ricardo's English breakfast special!"

"Sure thing, guys!" Allen Lee took the last chair, and as Araceli hurried over with a menu, he waved it away and added, "I'll just have what they're having!"

At five minutes of eight by the kitchen clock. Richard took off his own kitchen apron, chef's jacket, and toque, saying over his shoulder, "I'll be outside, meeting an old friend – back in a tick."

"Yes, Chef!" Bree and Robbie chorused, and Richard let the door swing shut behind him. Golden morning sunshine slanted along the alley at the back of those establishments on the northern side of the Square and fell full on the upper stories of the old First Bank of Luna City, and the white-painted and cross-crowned spire of the Methodist church beyond. Late blooming yellow Chinese jasmine in the Stein's garden next door perfumed the air, overwhelming the pong of the Café's wheelie bins drawn up in formation by the back door.

But the space where the Airstream had been parked now and again was open, sufficiently large enough for a round of fisticuffs between two grown men. The afternoon before, Richard had gone out with a broom and swept away any stones, crumbs of decayed macadam and acorns dropped or blown in from the towering oak across the alley. He regarded the space with calm satisfaction. The back door to the Café opened again, and swung shut; Doc Wyler, toting his veterinarian's handy medical bag and a lumpy dark green cloth sack which might once have carried laundry, but now contained two pair of boxing gloves.

"Eight o'clock on the dot," Doc announced, setting down both bags at the door. "Any sign of Pretty-boy Barrett?"

"Not a sausage," Richard replied, utterly tranquil. "I'd give him ten minutes and no more – let him be fashionably late. I'll water the garden while I wait."

"Good idea," observed Doc. "Waste no time – and good display of cool. Better to be shooting pool, or something, though."

There was a spigot and a coiled-up garden hose on the far side of the wheelie bins – never a space or time wasted. Richard uncoiled the hose and began spraying a light mist of water on the herbs in the raised beds; a project begun in all earnest in the summer of the year he had come to Luna

City, which had succeeded beyond all expectations. Aside from the brutal summer heat, which made daily and sometimes twice-daily watering, the temperatures were generally mind and conducive to year-round gardening … although the French tarragon plants were looking most feeble from said brutal heat, and likely the three or four varieties of basil would not withstand an almost inevitable winter below-freezing cold snap. Chives, rosemary, oregano, parsley; all throve, rampantly green. Richard had made good use of their bounty, and privately credited the success of certain dishes served in the Café to judicious use of them.

"Son, I don't think Pretty-boy is gonna show," Doc finally observed, after a study of his cellphone. "It's been fifteen minutes, now. But you done your part, in showing up with a challenge that he wasn't up to meeting himself. I'll keep my end of the bargain, and make a few phone calls on your behalf, like I said I would."

"I still want to bloody his nose," Richard complained, vaguely disappointed. He had been so ready, willing, eager to … well, perhaps a bit too eager to beat Pip Noel-Barrett to a bloody pulp. "I could do it, Doc – still might do it, if I see his ornamental phiz anywhere around Luna City. He laid unwelcome hands on Kate, and that is an insult I will not allow to pass, even if she got his goolies with her knee. This is Kate; I won't put up with a man who molests my … insults Kate."

"You got another thing to fight for, then," Doc grinned without mirth, a feral expression which would not have sat unfamiliarly on the countenance of his grandfather. Captain (CSA) Herbert Kling Wyler was commonly held to be one of the most purely ruthless men in Southern Texas during the last quarter of the 19th century; a man who cherished and nurtured his grudges as if they were prize-winning blood stock. "Good – a real man has his hostages to fortune – something or someone that he'd fight to the death for. He may get beaten down, but he has the grit to stand for something worthwhile. Anyone who would have hit on Miz Alice back in the day; I'd have done him down like a dog in the street. Get back to your kitchen, son; the breakfast rush is in full swing, but those kids of yours are holding strong. The Café did real well this past quarter. Jess's advice is to continue expanding staff – you want three new employees after the kids go back to school, you just give me their names. Jess will handle all the rest, as soon as she gets back in the saddle again."

"Thank you," Richard was dazed with a combination of disappointment, relief, and anticipation. He coiled up the hose and turned off the water, his thoughts running ahead of the morning, like horses let out from a trailer into an endless green field. *Three more staff; expand the menu certainly – and perhaps dinner service?* Absorbed in these considerations, he walked back into the kitchen, to find Allen Lee Mayne leaning against the table with the coffee urn, mug in his enormous hand and shooting the breeze with Bree and Robbie – the latter two while they worked at the last breakfast orders.

Allen Lee glanced around as the back door opened, and exclaimed, "Hi there, Chef! There you be! The kids said you were out back. Gotta say that breakfast was amazing; every bit as good as Phillip always said. Great little place you're running here. Guess there's nothing like it anywhere short of the big city."

"No, I think not," Richard answered, slightly annoyed at how the man seemed to be making himself at home, let alone disturbing the regular measures of his day.

"Reminds me of my folks' restaurant," Allen Lee confided with a nostalgic sigh. "It was in an old place like this. Nothing about it had changed in fifty years, not the menu or the tile on the floors. A place like this is home to me. Long as we're in town, I'll be over every morning for one of those breakfasts – some real down-home cooking."

"I suppose that my old pal Phillip will be joining you for breakfast as well?" Richard could not keep a slightly snide tone from his voice; it just came naturally whenever he contemplated Phillip Noel-Barrett, his person or his presence.

"As a matter of fact, no," Allen Lee's amiable countenance became suddenly less amiable, menacing, even. "Your old pal bailed on this episode, Chef; right out of the clear blue. Seems like he suddenly got a feeling he was a mite unwelcome in this li'l ol' town – that he done dirt on some folk who had a real clear memory. So he skedaddled last night, with barely a word to me. Oh, he made some cock-n-bull story about death in the fambly – but he knows damn well he is bailing on *A La Carte* for next season. Now, me; I'm a man who expects to play hurt, until the referee calls 'time' and I don't forget who has let me down when push comes to shove."

"My sympathies," Richard confessed. "I must tell you that I am one of those people with cause to think ill of your co-host, so his absence is as much my fault as anyone elses'. We intended to have it out, once and for all, but ..."

"He bailed on you too, Chef?" Allen Lee grinned; all good humor restored. "Doan worry – I was getting tired of all the time being let down by that lazy-ass clown. We good ... now and when this show gets aired. Nothing about no bad boy chef – that's for sure. My word on it."

The Great Barbeque Showdown

From the Karnesville Weekly Bulletin - Neighborhood Section
By Katherine Heisel – Staff Writer

The Luna City VFW Post was the setting last Thursday for a BBQ showdown between two mighty local rivals in the provision of good food. The event was organized by GoodEats Productions, a company owned by former Denver Broncos quarterback and Food Network celebrity Allan Lee Mayne, host of the travel and cooking smash hit *A La Carte With Quartermayne.* The segment of the show filmed on Thursday will not be aired until Spring, 2018, when the ultimate winner of the Luna City showdown will be announced.

But no one among the more than two hundred and fifty attending the event were in any doubt regarding the excellence of the various barbeque dishes offered by Pryor's Meats & BBQ, and rival Mills Farm Country Restaurant. Pryor's – owned and operated by Andy and Patricia Pryor with the assistance of their family – opens for Fridays and weekends, with a food truck available for special events across Karnes County, while Mills Farm Country Restaurant is open seven days a week, on the grounds of the well-known Mills Farm Resort and Spa, just south of Luna City. One is a small family enterprise, the other owned and managed by an international hospitality corporation – but they put up a similar and scrumptiously tasty showing to the hungry throng last Thursday.

The weather for that day was magnificent; clear and lightly breezy, although rather hot late in the afternoon. But the grounds for the contest were shaded by a grove of oak and pecan trees, as well as breezes cooled by the presence of the San Antonio River. Both Pryors' and the Country Restaurant ventured a pit-roasted whole pig, which enterprise began on the night before, with twin pits excavated by a digger operated by Roman Gonzales, of Gonzales Bros. Construction, LLC. Each restaurant buried a whole dressed and seasoned pig in a brick-lined pit piled with coals, to cook throughout the night and the following day. Pryors and the Country Restaurant both used their own secret seasonings, prep, and sauces to follow, and prepared their own versions of smoked brisket, sausages, chicken quarters, turkey legs and smoked ribs. For a small contribution, each diner received samples of both dishes, and a ballot to vote upon which BBQ selection was the best. Live music for dancing after sundown was provided by the popular Karnesville-based conjunto band *Los Maldonados.*

Although the co-host of A La Carte, Phillip Noel-Barrett *(familiar to many Lunaites since last summer's movie production)* was called away on a personal emergency, Allen Lee Mayne more than made up for that absence. Jovial, fun-loving, and a friend to all, Allen Lee seemed to be everywhere, throughout the afternoon. If he was not filming an interview with the cooks and staff of the competing restaurants, he was talking to Lunaites and guests … and at one point in the late afternoon, he and Chief Vaughn of the Luna City PD started up a rousing scratch flag football game between present and past members of Mighty Fighting Moth teams – a game enjoyed by players and audience alike. *(see pictures, following page.)*

All Roads Lead to Luna City

Richard's cellphone buzzed frantically, cruelly early on the Monday morning – that very Monday following the grand BBQ showdown on the grounds of the VFW. He shot out of bed, not quite fully conscious, dislodging Ozzie from that latter's comfortable nest at his feet. Ozzie objected with a querulous and emphatic "Mrrroooow!" as Richard fumbled for the cellphone, immured in the pocket of his trousers – hanging on a hook in the wardrobe a brief step across the narrow bedroom.

He snarled a brief crudity into it, but no – it was a pre-recorded alert, sent out to all members of the Luna City Volunteer Fire Department. There would be an all-hands meeting at the firehouse at 10 AM. Four hours from now – he blearily consulted the time after he hung up on the call. Something to do with activating the disaster preparedness center, and a drill. Or not being a drill; he was still half-asleep. Fall back to sleep again … no, not any good in that. Almost time to get up anyway. What was that all about? The hurricane wouldn't come anywhere near Luna City. Too far inland for a hurricane to truly bite, too far south for tornadoes. Not on an active seismic fault … really, what was all this about? He put on water to boil for tea, strong and hearty – as his Gran had often insisted when it come to a proper tea, 'strong enough to trot a mouse over'. So, a slightly earlier morning rising than he was accustomed to. Richard was, because of his profession – a morning person. A very early-morning person often neck and neck with the assorted roosters in the chicken run just up the hill at the Grant's Straw Castle Aquarius.

"It's because of the hurricane," Joe Vaughn explained patiently and for the second time. He was alone for breakfast this morning. "It looks to be huge, and it's barreling straight for the coast at full speed. It's predicted to make landfall anywhere between Brownsville and Port Arthur sometime in the next forty-eight hours. The authorities are already calling on voluntary evacuations from low-lying coastal areas."

"We aren't anywhere near the coast," Richard protested. "Miles from it, in fact. Is it going to be like that spring rainstorm that flooded out all along the river? I'm serving notice here and now that I am not going out in a boat on it, not with your Uncle Harry or anyone else." Joe was already shaking his head.

"More than a hundred miles, actually. We won't be evacuating, and likely the storm won't drop any more rain on us than usual – although that's no sure thing. Never is, in Texas. But we are just off a secondary evacuation route from Rockport, Aransas Pass, and Corpus Christi. I can absolutely guarantee that we'll see a lot of traffic from the coast, starting in about six hours. There will be a bottleneck at the bridge, and lots of people won't want to drive much farther than here, after a day of stop and go traffic. Especially in the rain, and at night. You might want to keep the Café open late and the coffee flowing," Joe added as he collected up his hat and his thermos. "Martin has already notified the high school to ready the gymnasium as an emergency shelter. Good thing they had that exercise last week. If Jess comes in later and I'm not there, tell her I'll break away at about noon for a bite of lunch with her."

The 10:00 meeting at the VFD proved to be just as enlightening, but at a considerably greater length. It was likely that the storm would diminish considerably upon landfall, and inconvenience Luna City no more than any other rainstorm, so there was no real cause for Richard to have to relocate the Airstream to town again. It all seemed to him to be a tempest in a tea cup … until he bicycled home that afternoon, and noted that there did seem to be more traffic on the main road than usual, and most of it going north, in the direction of Seguin and San Antonio. The only vehicles southbound were a couple of pantechnicon vans and – unsettlingly – a convoy of sand-colored military vehicles. When he arrived home at the Age of Aquarius, it was to find a campground half-full of strange RVs, vans, pick-up trucks and trailers. The only familiar vehicle was Allen Lee Mayne's lavish purple and black RV, parked next to the old Airstream.

"I thought you'd be on your way as soon as the showdown was finished," Richard said, as he propped up his bicycle against the patio support post. Allen Lee had made himself quite at home, a beer at his elbow and Ozzie romping at his feet.

"I got a cousin in Port Aransas," Allen Lee explained. "I was gonna head on down that way for a visit, once we finished that last episode, but he called and tol' me to stay here. He and his folks maybe have to evacuate, but that they'd meet me someplace. May as well hang around, I thought. Told them I'd wait for them to come this way. You got a nice place here, Chef," Allen Lee added.

"It grows on people," Richard said. "Rather like a species of moss."

Allen Lee chuckled. "I see how it might, at that." He glanced up at the sky, freckled with small puffs of cloud. "Pretty … just don't seem like there could be anything like the worst storm in fifteen years heading our way."

"Supposed to make landfall tomorrow morning," Richard nodded agreement; like Allen Lee, he just couldn't see it, either.

Morning dawned reluctantly, with a sky shrouded in dark clouds, the air thick with humidity and threatening rain. Now the Age's lumpy pasture of a campground was filled entirely. There were lights on in the conblock bathhouse, and in some of the parked RVs and trailers. People were awake at this hour; lights flickered in windows, and the faint sounds of television and radios broke a morning silence usually fractured by the Grant's roosters and peafowl. Richard passed Sefton Grant, an enormous battery torch in one hand, tugging open the rickety gate which opened onto what was normally a pasture for goats but sometimes served as an overflow campground. A large RV waited, engine idling in the road as Sefton wrestled the gate open.

"Morning, Ricardo," Sefton drawled, in the silence after the RV passed.

"More guests, I see," Richard commented, and Sefton chuckled. "They been coming in all night. Be careful on the road now. They tell me it's moving at a crawl, all the way from Beeville, an' you don't wanna get run over by some a-hole trying to cut along the shoulder."

"Thanks, Sefton. I'll keep an eye out." Richard answered. "Has the storm made landfall yet?"

"Yup." Sefton spat into the weeds at his feet. "'Bout an hour ago – at Rockport and Port Aransas. They got hundred-mile an hour winds, right now, and the usual a-hole morning guys going out and standing in it to file a live report. I hope I live long enough to see one of them cold-cocked by wind-blown debris on live TV. Anyway, it's a good way from us, yet, but I reckon the leading edge will hit here by late afternoon. You stay safe today, Ricardo."

"Do my best," Richard pedaled, now doubly uneasy. Ozzie hadn't wanted to leave the Airstream. The cat had curled up in the bottom of the wardrobe, possibly remembering a previous misadventure in horrific wet weather. Richard didn't blame him in the least, for wanting to stay safe and dry in the cozy, self-contained caravan, with a fresh pan of litter, a bowl of food and another of water at hand. The unease deepened when a pair of headlights stabbed out of the dark; a truck towing a small trailer bumped slowly down the road toward him. The driver rolled down his window, as Richard flattened himself and his bicycle into the weeds at the side of the graveled road.

"Is this the right way into the campground?" he asked anxiously, and Richard answered that yes, it was, and knew without a doubt that the legendary pretty pass had arrived on the wings of a storm. Practically no one in the traveling fraternity patronized the Age, unless broke, desperate, or knew damn well what to expect – a lumpy meadow with minimal conveniences and nothing much to recommend it by way of attractions. Anyone with funds patronized Mills Farm; those with sensibilities favored more attractive caravan parks and resorts within a few minutes' drive north, south, east and west.

The main road presented an even more unsettling prospect; a slow-moving procession of vehicles; red and white lights gleaming in the dark, casting eerie shadows in the hedges and along the verge. The only vehicles moving at anything like a normal speed were the police cruisers and SUVs, moving along the verge, and in the southbound lanes like sheepdogs patrolling a long column of slow-moving sheep. Even Richard, on his bicycle and being careful, was still moving along at a better clip. He came around a curve in the road, and nearly ran into a man with a jerrycan in either hand, standing by a big sedan with a roof-rack, piled high with suitcases and bundles, all bungee-corded together, angled off the edge of the road as if it had coasted there.

"Howdy, pal," the man said. "I've run out of gas – can you tell me where the nearest place is to fill up?"

"A petrol station?" Richard replied. "In Luna City. About half a mile ahead, right off on the verge. The Tip-Top, but it may not be open until another hour."

"No problem," the man sounded fairly chipper at that. "Thanks, pal. I left Rockport with a full tank, but it's been stop and go all night."

"Good luck," Richard said, feeling quite awkward at how he had been so insouciant about the storm, not twenty hours before. "You know, they've set up a shelter at the high school, if you need a place to stay for a while."

"I'll be all right," the man replied. "I figure I can get as far as Seguin; got friends there."

"All right," Richard pedaled on. No, this was something different then that sudden storm which appeared out of nowhere last spring, blitzed the upper reaches of the river with twenty-something inches of rain and then vanished just as quickly. Watching that great white swirling blob on the telly, as it edged closer and closer to landfall, blotting out the green landscape and blue water below was even more nerve-wracking.

To his surprise, Robbie Walcott was waiting for him at the back of the Café, the engine of the aging Volvo sedan ticking metallically, as it cooked down.

"Hi, Chef," Robbie was his usual exuberant self. "There's no school for the rest of the week, so I thought I'd come and help out. I came around by the back road. I guess you saw the jam on the main road! They're having to let vehicles over the bridge two and three at a time. On the news it says that people are just stopping by the side of the road. Dad says that …"

"I am certain that what your father says is sensible and to the point," Richard unlocked the back door. "And I'm grateful for the help."

"We're gonna do a lot of business today," Robbie burbled, quite undismayed. "Aren't we, Chef! Bree will be sorry she's missing all the fun. I guess Fort Worth 'ull be too far north ..." Richard let the remainder of Robbie's morning monologue flow over and around him. It was going to be a very busy and a long day. So – double the usual number of cinnamon rolls to be baked, and keep the coffee coming... Araceli appeared, and set to work, laying out silverware, setting out jugs of hot milk and half and half by the coffee urn, and turning on the television in the corner of the Café.

"Abuelita and the parish ladies have opened the church kitchen," she reported. "To make soup and pies. There are people sleeping in their cars, parked all over. Pat says it's gridlock on 123, going north. I expect they have already done counter-flow on the 35. You know – that's when they open up all the lanes, both sides. Rockport's getting it bad, I just saw on the news. A hundred and thirty miles an hour winds. And it's pouring down rain in Houston. But Houston always floods. Did you know that you can drown in a parking garage elevator in Houston, easily."

"How very reassuring," Richard said. "Here in the country we have to make do with low-water crossings."

There was a crowd outside the door already, when Richard unlatched it; at least half being strangers – weary-eyed and exhausted strangers. The Café filled, and filled and filled again; by eight o'clock, Richard thought they had served as many customers as they ordinarily did in three days. Miss Letty appeared, austere and professional in her vintage Red Cross uniform suit.

"The Methodist ladies have begun preparing sandwiches and cookies," she reported. "And the Youth Group is delivering them to those stranded along the way in their cars. I must say that I have renewed hope for the young people of today."

Richard didn't mind hearing that he had competition; competition handing out free food. Let the Methodist and the Catholic ladies take care of those who could not or wouldn't appear at the Café – he had sufficient to do, providing edible hospitality to those who did. When he returned to the Café kitchen it was to find another person in it; Allen Lee Mayne, seeming to be even bigger and more jovial than ever, already wearing a Café apron, working the sauté station, and plating an omelet with garnish and a side of hash-browns if he were an old pro.

"Hey, Chef," he said, with that blinding grin. "Don't mind me – I grew up in the restaurant that my folks owned, back in the day. I was watching the local news this morning and thought I might come along and give you a hand. Sefton at the trailer park gave me a lift – man, that ol' boy knows all the short-cuts, don't he?"

"Appreciated," Richard answered, rather torn between gratitude and apprehension. "I can't afford to pay more than $10 an hour, though. Which I understand is a bit beneath your dignity and experience ..."

"Don't worry about it, Chef," Allen Lee's generous amusement about filled the room. "I like this little place of yours, and I know how much community matters, where the rubber meets the road. I'd admire to work with a real trained French chef, and don't you worry, none. I won't spill to anyone 'bout what you used to be. Phillip Noel-Barrett is a spoiled little piss-ant, and it didn't take a call ... well, it didn't take a call from no one in particular. He's in violation of his contract, and his ass is let go for the next season."

Richard found himself extraordinarily and unworthily pleased at that intelligence. His Gran would have given him a lecture over that.

"English breakfast, two!" Araceli sang out, as she came into the kitchen. Robbie and Allen Lee chorused, "On it!" and set to work. Richard silently blessed his good fortune. Because – it was all on, now.

Hurricane

It is an established fact that violent tropical storms arising in the Caribbean and wandering into the Gulf of Mexico have been walloping that part of mainland North America now known as Texas for as long as … since human beings established their homes and hunting grounds there. But as there were no accurate records kept until the arrival of the Spanish in the early 1500s. Throughout that century and the one following such records which survive usually involve damage and loss caused by hurricanes to Spanish treasure ships bringing gold and silver from the New World to the Old – a circumstance which has brought meaning to the lives of underwater treasure hunters ever since. Until the Spanish began establishing settlements and missions in Texas itself – which was unthinkably remote from the center of Spanish power in Mexico and South America – such violent storms only affected the native Indian tribes. One may presume that there is evidence in their folklore for violent winds, rain, and storm surge along the coast.

But until the Texas Gulf Coast began to be settled in the early 19th century, hurricanes came and went without any particular notice being taken. The settlement of Galveston – built on a low-lying coastal island at the mouth of Buffalo Bayou, and the sheltered waters of Galveston and Trinity Bay – was struck by a severe storm in September 1818. That storm destroyed or damaged every ship in harbor, and wrecked every existing building but for half-a-dozen. The month of September would be a dangerous time of year for coastal settlements in Texas down to the present day. Eleven years later, a hurricane made landfall near the mouth of the Rio Grande, causing severe flooding. In the mid-1830s several storms beached ships and boats and capsized a ship in Matagorda Bay. Galveston was flooded in several storm seasons, but on the whole got off rather lightly, considering that it was and would continue to be one of the largest towns along the coast. For seventy years, Galveston weathered many a tropical storm. It came to be accepted as conventional wisdom that Galveston was in a uniquely sheltered location, and relatively impervious to storms, in spite of the low-lying nature of the barrier island that it was built upon.

The toll in human lives caused by hurricanes along the Texas coast did not really begin to bite heavily until the 1840s, with increased settlement along the coast as well as inland. More than seventy people were killed when a hurricane made landfall on Brazos Island – a barrier island off the coast of present-day Brownsville and Matamoros. Storms which hit the coast over the subsequent three decades did more damage to property on land and the occasional unfortunate ship in harbor. Until September 1875, when a hurricane slammed into the deep-water port of Indianola, and the storm surge carried away much of the town and perhaps up to 800 people.

Established in the 1840s at the southern end of Matagorda Bay, it was to serve initially as a landing place for immigrants from Germany brought over by the Mainzer Adelsverein. Thirty years later, it was a major deep-water port, the Queen City of the Texas Gulf Coast, with an establish steamship service to New Orleans and the East Coast. Indianola merchants shipped rice to Europe and experimented with shipping refrigerated beef and canned oysters. The 1875 hurricane destroyed all that. There was still enough left; a fine deep-water port and a good strategic location were not something to be casually abandoned. The city stalwarts rebuilt, only to be slammed eleven years later by another hurricane. The rebuilt town was obliterated, and the city fathers sadly accepted the inevitable. *(There is a scattering of vacation homes, many on very tall pilings where Indianola used to be, and a small memorial marking the place.)*

After the destruction of Indianola, Galveston reclaimed its place as the premier port in Texas. At the turn of the 19th century and into the first year of the 20th, it was the largest and wealthiest city in Texas; a center of commerce, transportation hub and port of entry, connected to the mainland across a normally placid lagoon by three railway trestles. And then came the great hurricane of 1900, which hit Galveston like a pile-driver, on Saturday, September 8. Weather experts later estimated the winds to have blown at 150 miles per hour with gusts reaching 200. There was no way to be certain, as the Weather Bureau's anemometer and rain gage were blown away and destroyed at the height of the storm. Survivors reported that the sky turned so dark that it seemed as if dusk had already fallen. The wind whipped slate tiles as if they were shrapnel. Late in the afternoon, the water came up and up, higher and higher, driving people into the second floor of whatever they had taken refuge in – assuming that they had a second floor.

That storm still stands as the single deadliest natural disaster ever to strike the United States, with a death toll equal of all later storms combined; at least 6,000 in Galveston alone (a quarter of the population at the time) and along the Texas coast. The storm surge went for miles inland, and may have carried away another 2,000, whose bodies were never found and never reported missing, as there was no one left to do so. Galveston did rebuild, and with the extra precaution of a sea-wall barrier. Sand was dredged from the bay and used to raise the level of the island nearly twenty feet. With a great deal of trouble and effort, 2,100 of the surviving buildings were elevated. All of this proved worthwhile when another hurricane of roughly the same intensity struck dead on in 1915, with comparatively minor casualties. However, dredging of the Houston Ship Channel to accommodate ocean-going ships spelled doom for Galveston as an important player in commerce and shipping. But unlike Indianola – Galveston is still there as a city. And this is why Texas takes hurricanes very, very seriously.

The Stormy Petrel

In the midst of the morning breakfast frenzy, he came out into the dining room – an automatic impulse, hearing the jingle of the silver bell over the door. The *stammtisch* was full – even over-full. The Steins sat at one corner, and there was Doc Wyler and Miss Letty; local aristocrats with privilege which overcame any petty inconveniences, graciously sharing the table with a family of hurricane evacuees from Corpus Christi, Richard gathered from overheard tags of conversation.

"… fine, when you return," Richard overheard Miss Letty. "Covered all the windows with plywood sheets; 5/8 thickness, although even quarter-inch will do, if securely fastened. And you moved all the valuable furniture to the second floor? Oh, good – sensible indeed. You should have nothing to worry about, on your return…"

(Save discovering the whole damned building demolished in the disaster, Richard thought to himself, but was sufficiently tactful to refrain from saying so out loud.)

"Waited out many a hurricane," Doc Wyler scowled, as he set a fork into his usual breakfast omelet. "Including Carla in '61. Had to rent a motor-boat to get back and forth to town. Found salt-water fish in the stock tanks, afterwards. But the wildflowers the next spring – amazing. Never seen more spectacular. Left to me, I'd order up a Cat-5 every year about this time …"

The spring-mounted shop door-bell jingled again; admitting another customer. Richard looked automatically; Jess. There was nothing the least bit out of the ordinary about her today … save that she was carrying a small suitcase in one hand, and appeared rather extraordinary pale in the face.

"Your usual?" Richard inquired, and she shook her head.

"I was supposed to meet Joe for lunch later," Jess replied, and a most curious expression crossed her countenance, almost a grimace of pain. "But something has come up," she finished, on a half-gasp. Miss Letty looked up from her own breakfast with the alert look of a hunting hound scenting game.

"Jessica, my dear – how far apart are your contractions?" Miss Letty asked, her tones as casual as if she were asking for news of the weather.

"Eight or nine minutes … since last night," Jess set down the little case. "I … oh!" she exclaimed, as if something had suddenly caused another pain. "It can't be – the baby isn't due for another three weeks!"

Miss Letty rose from her chair, setting aside her fork and napkin with a magisterial air. "Stephen, I think it's time that we should take Jessica to the hospital," She announced. Jess protested, "But Joe …"

"Is at work, in this emergency," Miss Letty replied, sternly. "There is no time to waste, waiting for him to drive from wherever he may be, and the ambulance has already been called out on another errand of mercy. Come along, dear – Stephen's truck is four-wheel-drive, and is equal to any emergency. Mr. Hall, if you could be so kind as to make up a doggie bag for me – I will have this later."

"But …" Jess protested, but to no avail. Doc Wyler confiscated the small suitcase, and took her arm, while Miss Letty took the other. They walked her out the door between them, and the silver bell jingled. Through the glass window, Richard saw Jess boosted into the back seat and Miss Letty climbing with some difficulty in after the younger woman. In a moment, Doc Wyler's lavish black pick-up with the silver logo of the Lazy W Exotic Game Ranch emblazoned on the doors went past the Café and around the corner toward the road to Karnesville and the regional hospital there. Richard took up Miss Letty's barely-touched breakfast plate and carried it into the kitchen.

"Miss McAllister and Doctor Wyler have taken Jess off to the hospital," "I think she's having the baby," he explained, and added with heavy sarcasm. "Excellent timing – today of all days, I must say."

"Not to Joe, you shouldn't," Araceli relieved him of the plate. "Not on a day when he's up to his ass in alligators and storm evacuees. And – we're nearly out of cinnamon rolls."

"Already? All right, bake up what we have in the cooler and set the ones in the freezer out to thaw." Richard sighed, very deeply. "I hate having my routine disrupted… I suppose that we should start a big batch of sweet-roll dough."

"And bread," Araceli stowed Miss Letty's abandoned breakfast into a Styrofoam clam-shell dish, and put it in the cooler on a top shelf. "I think we should start baking bread. For sandwiches. There's gonna be a lot of hungry people tonight."

Richard looked across the kitchen, to where Allen Lee and Robbie Walcott were each nodding agreement. Araceli enlarged on the subject.

"The Tip-Top likely will be sold out of what they have on hand by noon. The nearest grocery store after that is Karnesville, but I don't think anyone will be driving there, or making deliveries here. And have you seen the traffic? Pat came back this morning, shaking his head."

Both Richard and Robbie nodded, and Araceli continued. "It's gonna get worse tonight. All those people on the road now are gonna be tired and hungry. When we start getting the rain here this afternoon, they're gonna look to spending the night here, rather than out on the road. Depend on it; that's what happened when Rita hit in '05. We had Town Square packed with parked cars, people sleeping in them. They were too tired to drive any farther. Everyone who had a room to spare had friends and family staying with them, everyone who had a driveway had some stranger's car or RV parked in it."

"Right," Richard agreed, contemplating the emergency with new eyes and making the snap decision that was only his to make. "We have plenty in the way of supplies and nothing but time, so let's get to it as soon as the breakfast rush is over. No lunch service today – just sandwiches, cold fruit and coffee from now on out."

"On it, Chef," Allen Lee replied, chorused by Robbie and Araceli. Richard rolled up the sleeves of his chef's coat.

"All right, then. Set price for simple lunch on premises, from now on. I'll have to let Jess and Doctor Wyler know, of course." He snickered, "They have likely too much going on right now to say no, of course."

Allen Lee laughed, a short bark of amusement and Araceli scowled. "Honestly, Chef, sometimes you are just too much!"

The breakfast rush dribbled away in the next hour. Richard hung a sign in the window, pricing the simple sandwich plate, and turned his energies to bread and sweet-roll dough. Out in the dining room, the silver bell over the door jingled. Araceli dusted flour off her hands and went to see who it was, returning in seconds followed by Joe Vaughn.

"Where is everyone?" He demanded. "Where is Jess – she isn't at home, she called my phone a dozen times but didn't leave a message. We were supposed to meet for lunch."

Richard felt his heart sink. Joe, tall, muscular, well-armed and sporting one of those dire military tattoos on his substantial bicep promising death from above and other unexpected directions, was not a man whose temper anyone with a sense of self-preservation wanted to provoke in any way.

"She's gone to the hospital," Richard make a placating gesture. "I'm certain there is nothing wrong – just a precaution. Doc Wyler and Miss Letty left from here with her an hour ago…"

"Oh, god," Joe paled under his tan. "I've been …"

"Up to your ass in alligators, I know," Richard agreed. "Yes, I know. Never heard that expression before, by the way. Strangely apt, considering."

"We didn't expect … the OB said she wasn't due." Joe was already thumbing through the contacts list on his personal cellphone. "Babe? Thank God! Are you OK… What's h…" Joe, a tide of pure relief washing over his face, held the phone away from his ear. Even Robbie, at the other end of the kitchen, could hear the indignant squawking sounds emanating from Jess's end, as she answered Joe's questions at length and in considerable graphic detail. Finally, Joe nodded curtly to Richard, just as his official radio added its own particular squawking to Jess' obbligato. "Babe, they're calling me … you wouldn't believe … oh, yeah, you would… listen, Babe – I'm gonna stay on the line with you. 'Kay? Listen to me … deep breath in – now out; one-two-three-four. Deep cleansing breath. That's it. 10-4 Milo, on my way," he added into his official radio, the concentration in his face adamantine. He held out his coffee thermos, and Araceli silently took and filled it, adding a dollop of hot milk before capping it hand handing it back to Joe. As he departed the Café, they could hear him carrying on two conversations. Through the front window, they saw him nearly collide with Patricia Pryor, who came in, saying over the sweet chime of the bell,

"What's with Joe? He had an expression on him like a thundercloud and hadn't two words to say to me…"

"Jess is in labor," Araceli enlightened her. "Doc and Miss Letty took her to the hospital more than an hour ago."

"Oh, dear," Patricia looked stricken. "But it's weeks too early. Is she all right? Is Little Joe all right?"

"We don't know," Araceli replied, and Richard added, "But when he finally called and got through, she sounded feisty and fit enough."

"Hey, Mrs. P.!" Allen Lee exclaimed from the kitchen, over a tub of elastic and fragrant bread dough that he was working with unexpectedly expert hands. "Long time, no see!"

"You are making yourself at home, Allen Lee," Patricia responded, looking even more like the late Princess Diana than ever.

"We're doing bread for sandwiches," Araceli explained. "For all the storm evacuees."

"That's what we did for the Rita evacuation," Patricia nodded, in complete understanding. "And that's why I came over here for. I talked to Andy on the phone, and he gave the go-ahead. We have a cooler simply packed full of leftover cooked brisket and pulled pork from last weekend. It will go to waste otherwise, so we decided that we would offer it to you, and to the church ladies to feed the multitude with."

"Better than loaves and fishes," Allen Lee rumbled with amusement, and Richard felt the enormous satisfaction of one who sees a plan coming together. Not as good as that triumphant feeling after a successful and satisfying romp in bed, but infinitely better than that after a nasty and humiliating romp in the same location.

"Luna City rules OK," he said, rubbing his hands together. "Yes, Patricia – we'll take all that you want to give us. I presume that you can write it all off as a charitable donation? Look – I sometimes manage to pay attention to the business side of things," he added, in response to Araceli's indignant expression. "Jess has managed to beat that much into

335

my head, all right? We'll do the same with the bread, of course. Yesterday's baking is ready for slicing, the first of todays is cooling even as we speak."

"I'll come and help," Patricia promised. "And I'll bring the boys. They've all got their food-handling certificates, I'll have you know. Even Little Andy. There's no school today; put them to good work instead!"

"Mrs. P., I like your thinking," Allen Lee chuckled. "The cut of your jib is what they say in some circles – wish I knew what a jib is, though. I might like to buy one."

"It's a type of sail, on a sailing ship." Richard explained, glumly, certain that Allen Lee certainly could afford a sail-yacht of a small to moderate size. "A small, triangular sail, running between the foretop mast to the bowsprit. It's something one distinguishes at once … hence, the saying, I believe."

"Thanks, Chef!" Allen Lee turned the blob of dough expertly, and ran it through a couple of turns. "Hanging out here with y'all has certainly turned out to be an education. So, we bake bread and make sandwiches until the crisis is done, or we drop. 'Zat the plan?"

"It certainly is!" Patricia beamed approval, as did Araceli. "I'll be back in half an hour with the boys! Richard, that is the most wonderful idea!" She bounced up on her tiptoes, and gave him a brief, yet wonderfully-scented kiss – a chaste and wholly un-sexy kiss – on his cheek, which he was slightly embarrassed to realize was slightly bristly, such had been the rigors and the upsets to routine of this long day. And it was promised to become even longer.

By mid-afternoon, they had set up something like an assembly line in the kitchen, putting together sandwiches from the Café's bread, and the cold cooked meats provided by Patricia – along with the half of a gargantuan container of mayonnaise.

"Manufactured mayo is an abomination!" Richard insisted. "I refuse to have my good Café bread contaminated …"

"It's a good brand," Patricia argued. "We use it for our own …" and Allen Lee backed her up. "Look, Chef, mayo is what they expect on their sammitches. Trust me; knowing what works in your average little diner, drive-in and dive is my bread. And butter. Or mayo."

"I yield to your experience," Richard conceded sourly. "Which remind me," he added, with a cold disparaging glare. "I will have to teach the construction of a real and genuine mayonnaise on the next segment of Captain Kitten's Kitchen. I have hope for the next generation, if not for this one."

"Blow it out your ass, Chef," Araceli snapped. Richard was startled into silence; this was the absolute rudest bit of verbal aggression ever to pass her lips, although she was apologizing a moment later. "Sorry …"

"We're all just a little tense," Patricia spoke in soothing tones. With her manicured hands covered in blue sanitary gloves, she was wrapping sandwiches in thin plastic wrap and piling them up in the disposable tin pans normally used for catering events. "You OK, 'Celi? It's all right, Chef. We're just worried about Jess. We've all been friends for a long time – since school days, or even before." She favored Richard with one of those heart-melting smiles. "And now this hurricane! We've all been through these things before, but now, with Jess going into labor early, and poor Joe! He must be going out of his head with worry. Do you know, I saw him when I was bringing all of the meats over from our place! At the bridge, directing traffic with one hand, and talking into his phone at the same time. It sounded as if he was coaching Jess while he was working."

"A man's gotta do what a man's gotta do," Allen Lee offered this cliché with a commendably straight face. Also blue-gloved, he was slicing cold brisket with the largest knife in Richard's collection, a knife which in Allen Lee's hand, looked about the size of a letter-opener. Araceli and the Pryor boys assembled sandwiches with practiced dispatch, while Robbie and Richard monitored the baking loaves, and sliced those which were sufficiently cooled to run through the slicer. "When is it gonna start raining here, Mrs. P.?"

"Likely hit tonight, just about sundown," Patricia replied, adding another sandwich to the pile. "Well, that's enough for the first lot. You ready, boys? Remember – these are free for storm evacuees, but if they want to give a donation, that's fine."

"Yes, Mom," Anson took the first tray, Robbie the second. "Where are we supposed to start?"

"At the bridge and work your way down," Patricia counseled. Rather than try and drive in the unaccustomedly jammed streets and byways, Robbie and Anson were going to venture their mission on bicycles, which Richard thought eminently sensible. He had an errand himself – to carry the daily order of fresh cinnamon rolls to Chris at the Tip-Tip.

"I'll be back in twenty minutes," he promised Araceli, who nodded silently and kept on assembling sandwiches. "And I'll take my cellie."

"We got you covered, Chef," Allen Lee nodded, still cutting brisket with deft precision. Feeling oddly reassured by that, Richard loaded a box of ready-wrapped cinnamon rolls onto the back of his own bicycle and ventured beyond the back of the Café for about the first time in nearly ten hours.

The sky was now clouded over, with leaden gray clouds which pressed closer and closer. An intermittent wind ruffled the leaves of the sycamore tree in the Stein's back garden, and the air felt humid, nearly too thick to breath.

Town Square was not yet as crowded with parked vehicles as Patricia and Araceli had claimed it had been the last time that storm evacuees poured into Luna City, but it still presented an unaccustomed bustle of purposeful activity. There was daylight still, but there was a twilight aspect to it, as if the streetlights around the Square would soon be turning on. A Gonzalez-owned pick-up truck with a long-bed trailer of the kind which usually carried lawn mowers and small tractors from job to job was parked around behind the Methodist Church, a trailer packed high this day with folding cots. Men were unloading the trailer, carrying the cots into the Methodist parish hall, which now bore a large hand-lettered sign over the double doors: Luna City Evacuee Shelter #3. The old Cattleman Hotel bore another such sign, designating it as Shelter #4. The single large utility truck belonging to Luna City's municipal government was parked in front of the hotel, also decanting folding cots. Richard eased carefully between the parked truck and a line of slow-moving automobiles and discovered a Luna City police SUV with Sergeant Milo Grigoryev directing the stream of automobiles.

"Around the Square, then straight on until you reach a t-intersection. Turn left, and the main reception center… Yes, ma'am, there's plenty of parking. Around the Square, and straight on … Hi, Ricardo. Ya on a mission of mercy?"

"I assume so," Richard knew every one of Luna City's small police force by sight now. Heck, he even recognized them by voice. Milo was a cheerful, rotund Slavic Texan, tending toward middle age and Joe Vaughns' right-hand man, although where and how a man who looked so much like the late Joseph Stalin had ever finished up in Luna City … well, a lot of odd people had finished up in Luna City, himself being among them.

"I'll be around for some coffee, when I get relieved, here," Milo said. "You hear about Joe – his wife is in labor, and we're so swamped here that he can't get away to be with her at the hospital."

"I know," Richard answered, "I've heard. He's coaching her over the phone."

"Sooner him than me," Milo Grigoryev confessed. "He's a lucky man. Me, I was with my wife for our youngest, and I passed out cold on the delivery-room floor. The OB was mighty pissed at me … straight on around the Square, ma'am, then past the church until you come to a t-intersection. Left and then to the high school gymnasium. Just follow that green van…"

"Come around to the back door when you get your break," Richard advised him, and pedaled away, weaving very carefully between the unaccustomed traffic; toward where the outskirts of Luna City raveled out into pastures and the untended thickets which fringed the roadside of Texas Route #123, between the ramshackle business premises of Gonzales Auto Body and Engine Repair and those utilitarian and much better-maintained buildings which housed the Luna City Police Department, and the Volunteer Fire Department. The garage doors to the latter were open; he could see that the single LCVFD ambulance was in. Well, that was a good omen, at least.

He turned south and coasted along that last road which marked the outer boundary of Luna City on the east, a narrow road which ran parallel to Route 123, and debouched on the marked exit road. There was the original river crossing, marked by the historic old McAllister mansion which predated everything in Luna City save possibly an excavated ruin by the gates to the Wyler Ranch. That ruin might have been two or three times as old, but since it had been constructed of unfired adobe brick, the whole thing had melted down into the clay from which it had been made a hundred years before the McAllister house had been built of more durable limestone. The existence of a historical marker in front of the McAllister house had always baffled Richard. Where he came from, a mid-19th century native stone residence in provincial Victorian style practically qualified as modern.

He came out on the arm of road that linked Luna City proper with the main north-south road – and was gob-smacked to see the bumper-to-bumper traffic on it, although he had been more or less prepared for the sight, after listening to conversation on the topic during all this long day at work in the Café … and what he had observed on his morning commute from the Age of Aquarius, ten hours before.

Richard regarded the spectacle, contemplating for perhaps the first time, what it might mean for millions of residents of coastal towns, to have to pack up those few most-treasured possessions and drive. Drive north, out of harm's way … to where? And overcoming what obstacles in the cause of reaching shelter from the storm?

Here at Luna City, at the bridge crossing over the San Antonio River the constant stream of vehicles ground to a stand-still, waiting on for permission to cross in file, two and three at a time. The shriek of a police whistle signaling 'go' or 'wait' could barely be heard through the cacophony of engines. As Richard understood it, the temporary bridge erected to carry traffic over the river bottom while the permanent bridge was repaired could only safely accommodate so many vehicles at once. As Clovis Walcott conceded with a mordant and jovial laugh, likely the temporary bridge could bear considerably more weight than four ordinary vehicles or a single heavily-loaded tanker truck, but no one really wanted to be there on the bridge and at the wheel proving definitively that it could not. On the near side, of that bridge, the stretch of crumbling macadam which served as a parking lot for the Tip-Top, and the VFW post was also packed solid, a few with drivers standing patiently by the brief row of pumps while a large petrol tanker replenished supplies. The odor of gasoline fumed like smoke – it looked like they were nearly done.

Richard leaned his bicycle against the weather-worn coin-op newspaper racks dispensing copies of the *San Antonio Express News*, the *Karnesville Weekly Beacon*, and the *Beeville Bee-Picayune*, and took up the box of fresh sweet rolls. The Tip-Top was just as crowded inside as out; a considerable feat considering that many shelves were entirely bare of goods; Richard had never seen that before. The Tip-Top was a ramshackle place with an uneven concrete floor, and fitted out with mismatching shelf units and a couple of cooler cases which were years past their best-if-by date. Soft drinks and beer, packaged snacks and candy bars, ice and a few grocery items like bread, eggs and milk – that was the

Tip-Top at best. It looked as if a delivery van had gotten through from Karnesville, for Chris and one of his assistants were horsing cases of bottled water onto the shelves.

"Give me a moment, will ya?" Chris said over his shoulder. "Oh, hi, Ricardo – just leave them by the register. Anyone paying for anything other than gas?" A chorus of assent rose from those standing impatiently in line, and Chris dusted his hands on his grubby jeans. "Thanks – I could have sold these three times over, this morning. How's everything going at the Café?" He began ringing up sales without even waiting on Richard's reply. "Your receipt, sir – have a safe journey … that'll be fifteen dollars, thirty-six cents … Thank you, ma'am. Safe journey…"'

"Busy," Richard answered. "Nearly as busy as here. We've all turned to making sandwiches. The boys are out now, feeding the multitude with them."

"Good idea," Chris replied, his mind already on other things, but he grinned at Richard. "Luna City – we take care of our own."

"And today, everyone else," Richard said, as he took his departure. Outside, it had begun to rain, fat drops splotching the pavement, a gray veil of rain already beginning to hide the traffic jam on the far side of the bridge. The peculiar odor of summer-dried macadam newly dampened by water rose like a brief perfume. Two sedans and a high-piled pick-up crossed the span, and a whistle sounded for a pause to let the last vehicle clear the bridge. Richard squinted – yes, that was Joe; must be, with the cellphone clamped to his ear. Yes indeed, Luna City looked after its own, but today, in this emergency, Luna City pulled together to look after everyone else.

Lost and Found

"I have to say that I'm glad to have everything back to normal," Araceli confessed, on the fifth day after the hurricane made landfall. It was Monday and late mid-morning in the Café, after the breakfast rush had slowed to a trickle. "My nerves were being wrecked with worry over everything. Over Jess and the baby, and if Pat would even still have a job."

It had rained over Luna City and environs for a day and a night, then trailed off as the weakened storm moved east in stately procession. The procession of storm evacuees moved off in a slower and less stately procession. After the storm passed, traffic reversed, although not in such quantities – mostly large trucks hauling supplies and construction materials, trailed by people returning to whatever was left of homes and businesses.

"So am I," Richard agreed, wholly heartfelt. "I am a creature of habit, I'm afraid. Selfish of me, when so many others crave excitement and unpredictability."

"All that makes the world go 'round, guys," Allen Lee Mayne shook his head in mock reproof. To Richard's mild surprise, Allen Lee had stayed on at the Age for days after he could have left. He had to admit that the blinged-out purple and gold RV did make the Age of Aquarius look more upscale, just by its' presence.

And Allen Lee himself proved to be congenial company – and welcome talent in the kitchen during the hurricane crisis. He had even been perfectly agreeable when Richard turned down Allen Lee's handsome offer of a co-star turn on the next season of A La Carte With Quartermayne. "You're a natural at this – and you done it all before, or something like it." Allen Lee argued. "We'd work great together; home-boy and Brit, ebony and ivory ..."

"I couldn't," Richard had demurred, with some mild regret. "That kind of life is just no good for me, Allen Lee. I'm content here, with everything the way it is."

"Think it over," Allen Lee pleaded. "The whole concept is – I need a good foil, someone who knows the business. Anyway, think about it. I got a whole three months before starting the next season."

"Maybe Lew Dubois can think of someone," Richard had said. "Hell, even Araceli's husband would be better than me. He does damn-fine BBQ, and if the shale oil business around here doesn't do any better in the next year, he might be looking for a new job."

"I'll give it some thought," Allen Lee had mused, and then never mentioned it again.

Now the bell over the Café door chimed. "Hey, anyone home?" Joe Vaughn called from the dining room. "'Celi, Ricardo?" We wanted to stop by on our way home so y'all could meet Little Joe!"

"The baby!" Araceli beat Richard and Allen Lee to the dining room by a considerable lead. Jess and Joe stood by their regular table, Joe carrying one of those heavy baby-carrier/car seat combinations. The inhabitant of it could only be seen as a small pink face topped with a tuft of dark hair, eyes tight closed in sleep. Araceli enveloped Jess in a warm hug. "Oh, he's just precious – he looks so much like Joe!" The baby did have a scowl remarkably like Joe in a bad mood, but Richard nobly refrained from pointing this out.

"Cute little cooter," Allen Lee grinned and admired openly. "He gonna play football, of course."

"Only if he wants to!" Jess replied, even as Joe said, "Of course he is! Katie says that he'll be the key to the Moths winning division champs in 2033!"

"I regret that we have nothing to properly wet Little Joe's head with," Richard confessed. "I know, champagne is customary …"

"Never mind that," Jess sank with relief into her usual chair. "But I won't say no to a lunch. I'm starving, and hospital food just doesn't cut it."

"The usual?" Araceli didn't even bother with her order pad. Just then, Joe's cellphone rang. "Speak to me," Joe set the baby-carrier down next to Jess's chair. "Oh, hi, Lew … yes, I'm listening … found something you have to show me, right away? Yeah, I'm at the Café. Jess and the baby were released today, and we stopped on our way home. Sure, bring it to the Café. Yeah, I'm sure. Long as it isn't bleeding or recently dead, no problem. See ya in a few. Bye. Yeah, I'll have one of your hot grilled sandwiches, and a side salad with house dressing on it." Joe grinned at Richard. "Hey, I understand you had a real fun time here while we were away."

"We did what had to be done," Richard answered, pleased to be modest about the three days that he spent with his helpers, making sandwiches. "I can say without fear of contradiction that no one left Luna City hungry – not if we could get to them."

He returned to the kitchen, obscurely pleased that things were really getting back to normal. Jess out of the hospital, looking like she had every intention of resuming her work, Joe mellow with the triumph of having gotten to the hospital in time to see his son being born in the wee hours after rain began to fall on Luna City. Richard had resisted the temptation offered by Allen Lee of a return to mild celebrity, and now to pick up those plans for expanding hours and the menu … in the meantime, there was a batch of sweet-roll dough ready to be punched down for a second rising.

He was barely aware of the bell chiming again, and voices out in the dining room, voices exclaiming in dismay tempered with horror. That was Allen Lee, looming in the doorway.

"Oh, man – you better come take a look at what they found at the building site. It'll blow your mind."

"Why?" Richard could not have been less interested, but he dusted flour from his hands and followed Allen Lee. Out in the dining room Lew, Joe and Araceli were staring into a cardboard box which Lew Dubois had set on the *stammtisch* table. The dining room was empty for the moment, which was good, considering what was in the box.

"We started work, clearing brush where the boathouse foundations are to be," Lew held up a long metal knife, adorned with much rust, and a few shreds of rotted wood clinging to the rivets which had once formed the handle. "There is … how do you say – a small draw, a little gully. And this turned up in the spoil heap. Our guys didn't see it, at first."

"Let me see that," Richard's interest was piqued, for the object was strangely familiar. He rubbed dirt from the blade, just below the hilt, and held it to the light so that he could better read the letters stamped there.

"Thought so – Alex.Coppel, Solingen. German bayonet, from the First War. We had one like it in the garden shed at home, courtesy of my great-grandfather collecting war souvenirs. Singular, finding one around here … although perhaps not. You American chaps collected souvenirs; I suppose – even if late to the game as usual."

"Most curious," Lew angled the cardboard box, so that whatever was in it rolled to one side, accompanied by the sound of something small and metallic rolling with it. "And when we started with the small excavator, this turned up. This is why I called you, Chief Vaughn. I believe that we have found evidence of … murder, perhaps?"

A skull, a human skull, weathered to the color of dark ivory looked up at the horrified audience from eyeless sockets, a skull with a creased appearance across the right orbit and forehead.

"And the murder weapon." Lew reached into the box, and only then did Richard see that Lew was wearing blue latex gloves, the same sort of gloves that … well, people wore who did not want to contaminate foodstuffs or evidence. Obviously, friendship with Harry Vaughn had technical advantages when it came to an accidental blunder onto the scene of crime, no matter how many decades old.

In Lew's blue-gloved hand was a small deformed lump of metal.

"It's a bullet," Joe Vaughn identified it without any hesitation.

(To be continued … of course!)

One Half-Dozen of Luna City

Seven Buttons and a German Bayonet

Richard stared into the box; like the others present, with a mixture of horror and curiosity. No one quite wanted to touch the skull; jawless, with the open eye-holes still partly-clogged with the damp earth from which it had been dug. The bayonet with the German maker's initials lay to one side, and Joe Vaughn was quietly bagging up the deformed metal bullet in a small zip-lock bag which Jess had produced from the suit-cased sized diaper bag. There were about half a dozen small corroded metal items knocking around in the bottom of the box, objects about the size of a 10p coin. Allen Lee Mayne reached over Richard's shoulder and picked up one of them.

"A button," Richard observed. Allen Lee nodded, gently buffing away the grime and corrosion with a paper napkin. "Looky here – it's got some kinda raised design on it. Can you make it out?"

"Looks like military," Joe ventured. "An eagle and an anchor, under an arch of stars. Navy, mebbe. You got another baggie, Jess?"

"Either our mystery man shopped at the Army Navy store, or he was a soldier," Richard ventured.

Allen Lee shook his head. "Man, that's an old Marine Corps button. Really old. Their buttons have had a globe on them now, along with the eagle and anchor. My old man was Marine in Vietnam, that's how I know this shit."

"Let me look, cher," That was Lew Dubois, his expression yet more serious. "Ah, yes – what I thought; an old Marine overcoat button. My dear Grand-père Lucien for whom I am named served in the Marines. He fought in the great battle in the Belleau Wood, and he still had his old overcoat, one with buttons just like this! He used to wear it on cold mornings, when he took me duck-hunting on the bayou. He was very old, and I was just a boy, and his namesake – a special treat for me, to go hunting with my grandfather. That is why I recollect so clearly."

"I don't think that this is your grandfather," Richard belatedly wished that he hadn't spoken, for Joe, Lew, and Allen Lee all looked at him with severely condemning expressions. "Sorry; a bit of misplaced levity, chaps, for which I apologize. But the fact remains; this is a dead chap, of some vintage. Not, perchance, one of yours? That is – local to Luna City. You wouldn't have misplaced one of your own, all these years ago?"

Both Araceli and Jess shook their heads, and Jess answered, "I'd have to double-check with Miss Letty, of course, but I am pretty certain that just about all the Luna City volunteers for WWI were for the Army."

"Looks like whoever he was, he got his Purple Heart the hard way, and no mistake," Joe looked down at the deformed and scarred skull, with an expression which Richard found hard to decipher. "Not from here, then. Drifted in, flotsam and jetsam; wasn't there some local yarn about a scar-faced drifter? I'm sure Kate wrote about it, sometime back. Weird-looking guy, used to haunt the place, back during the Depression?"

"The Scar-faced Tramp," Araceli replied, and the light of blooming comprehension shone on every face. "Katie interviewed Abuelita for that story! The Tramp frightened her into running home screaming. She was only five or six at the time," Araceli added hastily, for no one could imagine Abuelita Adeliza, the elderly absolute ruler of the sprawling Gonzales-Gonzalez clan, running screaming in terror from anything less than a fire-breathing tyrannosaurus rex. "Her mother scolded her when she got home. The scar-faced man was only a poor vagrant, living in a camp in the woods, who got by on doing odd jobs for people in town. I'll call Katie – she'll be thrilled to know about this!"

"Must you?" Joe finished bagging the buttons, all seven of them. "Look, I don't want to make a big media thing about this until we have some positive answers. Give me enough time to let me set up an investigation with the county sheriff's office and whoever they have available for an emergency dig before unleashing the media hounds on us."

"Katie isn't a media hound!" Araceli was indignant. "She has better sense than that, and she is one of us: OK, second cousin by marriage – but she is one of us!"

"Indeed," Richard agreed, with a small clearing of his throat. "Miss Heisel has been … well, remarkably restrained and discrete, with regard to my own rather fraught position with the national press. I would be inclined to trust her, as being sensitive to local concerns. She's a good egg," Richard finished, with a sense that he was being particularly lame. He strenuously ignored Araceli's muttered footnote. "Yeah, she'd love to jump your bones, Chef – given any sort of encouragement," as well as Allen Lee's distinctly lewd chuckle of agreement.

"All right then," Joe nodded, as he placed the two plastic bags in the cardboard box with the skull. "Lew … I'm sorry, this will put a crimp in your construction schedule. The work gotta be on hold until forensics can go over the area. Nothing I can do about a delay, but I promise, I'll do what I can to instill a sense of urgency."

"It is not a problem, *cher*," Lew sounded extraordinarily mellow for a corporate executive whose' multi-million-dollar project was now on the tipping-point of failure – or at least, an expensive delay – through being delayed by the inconvenient circumstance of a dead body found at the construction site. Even if the dead body was – by Richard's estimate and his vague recall of Kate talking to him about her months-ago feature story – at least six or seven decades old. Now, Lew added, in philosophical tones, "There is no urgency for this poor fellow. It has been a long time. Still, we should endeavor to find out something, I t'ink. Of who he was, and of his passing. If he was a comrade of my dear Grand-père Lucien? For the honor of that service a hundred years ago, I owe him that generous consideration. My time and interest are at your disposal with regard to this puzzle, Chief Vaughn."

"Appreciated," Joe nodded, bundling up the box under one arm, and collecting up the baby carrier with his other. "Hey – 'Celi, make our order a take-out, can you? Jess is bushed, and I wanna get my family home and settled. 'Kay, Babe? Gotta cold case to work," he added to Jess, who actually did appear pretty pale, frazzled and exhausted. *(Perhaps only Richard noted the special emphasis with which Joe said those two words; 'my family.')*

"My time and interest, too." That was Allen Lee, most unexpectedly. "My Daddy served at Khe Sanh. Bravo Company, 1st Battalion, 9th Marines. Daddy would want this. Count me in. I gotta go back to California for the show production and spend the holidays with my wife and little girls – but I'll be back about February."

"Right, then," Joe said. "I'll put out the word."

Winter Newsletter

Winter 2017 Newsletter

Luna City Chamber of Commerce

5 North Town Square, Suite 4

Check out our Facebook Page

Mills Farm Country Store opens their Christmas Market on Saturday, December 2, at 10:00 AM in Guest Cottage #2, which will be completely redecorated as the home of Santa and Mrs. Santa, for every weekend until Sunday, December 24th. Come visit with the Clauses, admire the fully-ornamented Christmas tree set up in the Parlor, and explore the many fine gift ideas available. Hand-made items, gourmet chocolate and other foods, as well as original art and hand-made craft items are available in the Mills Farm Country Store.

Christmas on Town Square

The traditional lighting of Town Square is scheduled for December 2nd, at 8 PM. Mayor Abernathy will ceremoniously turn on the switch which will illuminate the Bandstand and the Trees in Town Square. Owners of storefronts lining the square will compete in decorating their own buildings and their shop-window displays. Lunaites may vote on the best display by casting a vote at Chamber offices through December 23th, when the winner and runners-up will be announced at the Annual Christmas Parade. Join us on Saturday, the 23rd for hospitality around the Square, when shops will remain open until 9 PM. The Moths Band and High School Chorus will serenade us from the bandstand in Town square all evening. The Christmas parade will begin at 7:30, with Santa Claus and his helpers arriving on the LCVFD's vintage restored 1923 fire engine. Come join us in celebrating the holiday season!

Upcoming Events

November 22

Sts Margaret and Anthony Parish Volunteer Thanksgiving luncheon and awards ceremony at the Parish Hall, beginning at 11:30 AM.

December 7

A flag ceremony in remembrance of Pearl Harbor Day will be held by Boy Scout Post 12, and members of the Karnes Company Rangers at 7:00 at the War Memorial on Town Square.

December 8

The Luna City Players present *A Christmas Carol* at the Koenig Opera House. Performances are Saturday, December 8th and 17th at 7:30.

Extreme Cold Weather Expected this Winter

Don't be caught short – prepare to shelter yourself, your pets and stock, and drive carefully on icy roads.

Luna City ISD News

Moths Band Christmas Concert Rehearsal

Band practice for the yearly Christmas Concert will be on Wednesday afternoons in the Hernando Gonzalez Memorial Gym from 3:00-4:00 on the 7th, 14th and 21st of December. Band members should be familiar with the music prior to the first rehearsal. Music may be collected.

Elementary School Christmas Program

The Luna City Elementary School Christmas program is scheduled for December 21st in the school auditorium at 1:00. Punch and cookies will be served, and students will be released for the Christmas holiday following the program.

Vote for Homecoming Queen & Court

Don't forget to vote your choice for Homecoming Queen and duchesses of her court! The slate of nominees for LCHS Homecoming Royalty is on display in the high school foyer. LCHS Alum (Class of '39) Dr. Stephen Wyler has offered to make his antique surrey (with the fringe on top) available as transportation for the Court at this year's Homecoming game!

Holiday Food Drive

Contributions for the community food pantry Holiday Dinner baskets may be dropped off during regular school hours in the decorated container marked for contributions to the food pantry, located in the Luna City High School main foyer. Holiday Dinner baskets will be distributed to local families in need on Monday, November 20th, and on Friday, December 22nd. Contributions of canned and shelf-stable foods are requested. Local churches will provide turkeys for the dinner baskets.

Community Marketplace

Smoked Turkey - Thanksgiving

Order your whole smoked turkey for Thanksgiving dinner from Pryor's Meats & BBQ no later than November 17th for delivery to your home or business on November 20-21st. Hickory, Mesquite, or Pecan wood – your choice. Order today!

From Chief Vaughn, Luna City PD

Repairs to the Rte. 123 bridge over the San Antonio River is nearly complete. Chief Vaughn estimates that all lanes will be open by the end of November. Meanwhile, extensive construction of a new boathouse facility, which will be part of the expanded Mills Farm Resort and Spa will begin at mid-month. A temporary dirt road will be cut from Rte. 123 along the southern property line of the Age of Aquarius Campground. Travelers in the area are advised to watch out for heavy equipment and construction vehicles in that area.

Luna Café and Coffee Expanding Service!

Richard at the Café expects to begin offering supper at the Café Thursday-Sunday evenings, beginning in the new year. He is looking to hire an additional cook and fill at least two full-time wait-staff positions to help out. If interested, contact Jess Abernathy-Vaughn, or let Richard know of your interest.

In the Offices of the Karnesville Weekly Beacon

"Kate!" Acey McClain, the editor and publisher of the Karnesville Weekly Beacon shouted in his usual abrupt manner. "Kate! Get in here and brief me about the body they found last week! First unidentified dead body they've found in the county in fifty years! God, you gotta love small towns. Anyplace else where they find a stiff that nobody recognizes right away, it's just a regular Saturday night/Sunday morning!"

"You bellowed, Chief?" Kate Heisel, neat and prim in her working attire of skirt-suit and flat-heeled shoes, appeared in the doorway, pencil and reporters' notebook at the ready. As a child, Kate was enthralled by the comic strip adventures of Brenda Starr. She resolved to be a reporter at the tender age of seven, just to prove that not having red hair and a glamorous appearance was no handicap for someone whose first coherent word was not 'Mama' but 'why?'

"Don't be such a damned smart-alec," Acey returned. "Of course, I bellowed – you never answer the intercom."

"Because I'm never at my desk, and the office intercom hasn't worked since the first Bush administration," Kate took a seat in the straight chair in front of the chief editor's desk – an article of furniture nearly as ornate as the White House office *Resolute* desk, but in much worse repair. Besides Brenda Starr, Kate's other reportorial role-model was Rosalind Russell in *His Girl Friday*. Curiously, this ensured that she got on rather well with Acey, who was rather a throw-back himself, and had no patience with what he called the 'sob-sister set.' "Strictly speaking," Kate elaborated as she opened her notebook. "It wasn't a body. More like 'skeletal remains.' I got the low-down from a drinking-buddy of Cousin Horatio's who works in the coroner's office. He wouldn't show me the report, but he answered my questions over a burger luncheon. I turned in the receipt to Lola, since it's a business expense."

"You're lucky that you didn't take him to a high-class joint like Panera," Acey grunted. "Whattaburger is more our speed. So – what's the bottom line on our skeletal remains?"

"A Caucasian male, in his late thirties or early forties, significant healed trauma to his skull, ribs, upper left shoulder bones, said old injuries having been inflicted at least fifteen years prior to death. It looked as if he carried a bullet, or fragments thereof in his brain for the remainder of his life. The pathologist reckoned that given the medical options of the time that surgeons left them in place, rather than do worse damage trying to get them out. Poor guy! This," Kate looked over her notebook with a professorial air, "is consistent with having been a veteran of the First World War. The skeleton was more or less intact when found, although some of the smaller hand-bones were scattered. Probably by animals, long after death, and before earth washed down from above to cover what appeared to be some kind of camp-site."

"Cause of death?" Acey had a laser-like focus on causes of death when it came to recently-discovered corpses. Like a well-masticated wad of bubble-gum, bare clinical details could be expanded into a significant bubble in the final story, not to mention the headline. "Say – was he killed by another hobo, or even by Old Charley Mills?"

"Nothing sensational like that," Kate sighed. "No, from what the pathologist report said – there were no indications of violence. The skeleton lay on its side, as if sleeping peacefully. He said that it looked like death from exposure. The guy just went to sleep and never woke up." Kate turned a page in her notebook. "I went back and looked at my notes when I did that story about the Scar-faced Tramp. He was around Luna City, doing odd jobs for about four months toward the end of 1935 and into early 1936. That period may be significant, Chief – it was the time of an intense cold wave hitting Canada and the States. As near as I can make out, the local temperatures around here were below freezing at night for nearly two weeks, and close to it during the day. It would have been even colder next to the water, and for someone sleeping rough, maybe with a drinking problem … everyone assumed that he had just moved on. There weren't any neighbors, just a thicket of trees at the top of a tall bank by the river. The old Sheffield place was the nearest house, and it was a ruin by then."

"Did they find anything that might hint at who this guy really was, and what he was doing?"

"Just a wandering hobo," Kate closed her notebook with another deep sigh. "The crew found some bits and bobs that indicated a campsite of sorts; remains of a tin kettle and a canteen, a metal grate that could have been laid over a fire in a small pit. Some metal shoe-lace tips, half a dozen buttons from a US Marine Corps cloth overcoat, and the remains of a German Imperial Army bayonet. Anything of cloth or leather was long-since rotted away. The damp, you see. And don't ask about ID tags, or anything of the sort – long gone, or never there to begin with. Just a poor anonymous soul, long gone to rest, buried deep and forgotten. But for some reason, people in Luna City are taking an interest in figuring that out. The whole thing hits home, you know. Likely a veteran – who he was, and where he came from, dying in the woods all alone like a starving animal … seriously, before most of us were born anyway? I don't know why this has grabbed people in Luna City, but it has – and that will be a story for you, Chief. It'll take a while to work out, but Lew Dubois and Allen Lee Mayne are interested in pursuing the identity angle."

Acey McClain let out a coarse chuckle. "Well, of course Lew Dubois wants this all settled, so that he can push on with his Mills Farm expansion project. Full steam ahead, the wheels of corporate enterprise!"

"It's more than that," Kate replied, in a voice of reproach. "The worksite has been cleared for construction to continue. It's not like its' some irreplaceable archeological site needing years, and years and years of sweeping away every crumb of dirt with a fine paintbrush. But Lew – Mr. Dubois had a grandfather who was a Marine, way back when. Allen Lee's father was one – in Vietnam, as well. There's a kind of fellow-feeling about it all, a sense that they all want to know … what it is to know. It doesn't make sense on this level, but they want to get to the bottom of who this man really was, and why he finished up in Luna City. I won't have the full story for a couple of weeks, Chief – but it will be front-page fantastic when I do."

"Oh – and how is that?"

"From what I have heard, Lew and Allan Lee are going to hire an outside expert to do a facial reconstruction from the skull," Kate stood up from the chair. She did know how to make an exit. "Sparing no expense. Harry Vaughn – you know, the old retired Federal marshal, who spearheaded that rescue of that family last spring" He's advising them. Gonna put him in touch with some expert professionals. As soon as they can get a bunch of specialty photographs of the skull itself, they can do all sorts of computer-generating magic to reconstruct the guy's face. And when that is done, do all kinds of searches of newspaper archives. My guess is that the guy was told to move on from all kinds of places. Police blotters, arrest records … Say, Chief, where would the *Beacon* morgue files for 1935 be?"

"In the basement," Acey McClain waved her away, his red felt-tipped editorial pen in hand. "South-west corner, to the back. Middle shelves. Take a pair of gloves to handle them and put on a mask. The last archivist to venture there caught some kind of lung-crud from breathing in mold spores."

"Thanks, Chief – anything more?"

"No," Acey scowled at his computer. He had never gotten the hang of figuring out how to attach a picture file to an email, and he was too embarrassed about this to ask Kate for an explanation … again.

From the Karnesville Weekly Beacon

January 15
Katherine Heisel, Staff Writer

Work by a well-respected expert in forensic anthropology, Dr. Martin Sommers, of the University of Michigan at Lansing, has put a face to skeletal remains found near Luna City late last fall. Dr. Sommers is an expert in 3-D computer reconstruction. As well as lecturing at the graduate level, he consults on international projects of this nature. In this particular case, the unidentified skeleton was uncovered during preparations for a new facility at Mills Farm, the upscale Texas resort and destination resort owned by Venue Properties International.

There was nothing found to give a clue to the identity of those remains, initially thought to have been those of a vagrant, known to have been living at a rough campsite in a thicket on the western bank of the San Antonio River, approximately two miles south of Luna City. There are indications that the man, who was notorious locally as the 'Scar-faced Tramp' may have been a Marine veteran of World War I. VPI's Director of Marketing, Lucien Dubois, who is heading up VPI's expansion projects, took a personal interest in this mystery. His grandfather, for whom Mr. Dubois is named, was a Marine, and a survivor of the Battle of Belleau Wood. Mr. Dubois and former Bronco quarterback and current Food Network host Allen Lee Quartermayne (whose late father was also a Marine) were put in touch with Dr. Sommers through the recommendation of Harry Vaughn, a retired federal marshal now resident of Luna City.

"Doc Sommers is a genius," Mr. Vaughn says. "I couldn't think of anyone better. Odds are, when he finishes a reconstruction, it really looks like the person in real life, which you often can't say with any confidence."

Three long-time residents of Luna City, who as children remember seeing the so-called 'Scar-faced Tramp' confirm that the facial reconstruction bears a close resemblance.

"You must remember that Mr. Wyler and I were only twelve or thirteen years old at the time, Adi Gonzales was five years younger, and that poor man was only around for several months," says Miss Leticia McAllister. "But the horrible scar on his face was most prominent and memorable. One did not like to stare; Mother told me that it would be terribly rude. He could not speak very clearly, and he shuffled when he walked. I thought it was because was terribly old, or so he seemed to me. Looking back on his appearance now, I would suspect neurological damage."

"I thought he was just the usual old soak, myself," Dr. Stephen Wyler confirmed. "I saw him working about town – stacking wood, running errands, in a slow way. Thought nothing much about it. There were so many men hitting the roads, looking for work. My father used to feed them a good meal in exchange for a little work. Most folk around here were only a little better off."

The picture of the reconstructed face of the unnamed tramp will be circulated to local newspapers in the next few weeks. Anyone recognizing him is asked to please contact Chief Joe Vaughn of the Luna City Police Department, or the editorial offices of this newspaper.

The New Hire

"Now that Jess is back to work, we can consider moving ahead with your new hires for the Café," Doc Wyler remarked, one Tuesday morning, as a gust of cold wind stirred errant dead oak leaves across the sidewalk, from where they had escaped from the trees in Town Square. Across the table, Jess nodded with her mouth full of a bite of warm cinnamon roll. At her feet, Little Joe – fast asleep in his carrier with a faint scowl on his infant features – appeared to have no objections worth making.

"I didn't think you'd be back at work so soon," Richard said to her – it was in his mind that Jess would have wanted to take slightly longer of a break, tending to the first new sprout on the Abernathy-Vaughn family tree. "What with a new baby and all…"

"After I got over the exhaustion, I was bored to tears with staying home all day, every day," Jess replied. "There's plenty of work that I can do without going very far, and Little Joe is a good baby … aren't you, sugar?" she added with a fatuous expression as she glanced down at her sleeping offspring.

"I should think he would be better off, sleeping at home in his crib," Doc Wyler grumbled. "Can't be doing him very much good, you gadding about in this weather."

Jess sighed. Her eyes met Richards' in a mutual understanding; Doc was of that generation where good mothers stayed at home with a new baby, usually until the little sprout toddled off to college seventeen or eighteen years later.

"I could take him home this instant, if I believed that," Jess answered, "And sneak him into bed but he would be awake and howling in five minutes. Honestly, he sleeps best in the car, or in a noisy office."

"Singular," Richard murmured.

Doc Wyler riffled through the stack of receipts in the folder which Jess had put before them. Finally, he looked at Richard over his reading glasses and said, "Three new staff for the Café; that was what we agreed on?"

"Full-time, yes," Richard replied. "And a part-time cook, on Saturday and Sunday, for breakfast and lunch service."

"That would be Robbie Walcott?" Jess put in.

Richard nodded. "He came along very well, over the summer. I was quite pleased with both my summer apprentices, by the way. And he wants to go on working on weekends. Why his parents approve of this I cannot imagine. Don't they know anything about the kind of people who work in food service?" Richard added, plaintively, and Jess giggled.

"Well, between you, 'Celi, and Allen Lee, I think Robbie is off to a good start when it comes to jobs. At least, Sook and Clovis are OK with him having a job in the first place."

"Builds character," Doc Wyler grunted. "My first job for pay when I was his age was working at Bodie's, stacking sacks in the feed mill. Anyway, what are your ideas about new employees? Do you have someone in mind, or do we need put an ad in the *Beeville Picayune*, or the *Karnesville Beacon*?"

"Beatriz Gonzales," Richard answered. "For the front of the house, full-time. She's worked off and on at the Café, and finished school in the spring. Araceli gave her full marks, and she has my approval. Now if we are to open for regular supper service on Fridays and weekends, I'd like to hire another cook, besides another waitress. Sefton Grant knows of a chap working at a place in Karnesville desirous of improving his situation. Sefton says he's a fair cook, worked food service at a couple of oilfield cafeterias. Currently working the grill at Sefton's favorite Arby's, which is hardly top-drawer, in my opinion," Richard shrugged. "But Sefton says that this chap's command of the off-menu specialties is without peer and above reproach. I asked to interview him here tomorrow, about 2:00, see if he is someone I can work with."

"Someone *we* can work with," Doc Wyler nodded. "Don't you forget, the investors in this enterprise expect to make a profit at the end of every year. That's how business rolls. I'll want Miss Letty to have a look-see at Sefton's friend. Best right-off-the-bat judge of character that I know. Tomorrow at two it is, then. Pass on to Sefton that his pal ought to wear his best interview suit – or the best that he has on hand."

"I will do that," Richard promised, and he did, that very afternoon, when he pedaled slowly up the hill toward the Amazing Straw Castle Aquarius, serene in its grove of bare-leaved oak trees.

"Got your chickens their daily ration of raw gourmet leavings," Richard said, as he handed the bucket of peelings and vegetable ends to Sefton. Because of the winter chill, Sefton had forsworn his usual hippy near-nudity, and for once was sensibly clad in jeans, boots, and a battered barn coat worn to the point where it was hard to see what color it had been originally. "And tell your job-seeking chum – what's his name, by the way?"

"Lucas. Lucas Massie," Sefton tilted his battered straw cowboy hat to a more rakish angle. "Wants everyone to call him Luc, with a c. Makes him sound kinda foreign. Nice kid, has the right instincts, but his social manner could use some work. What should I tell him?"

"Tomorrow, at the Café, 2:00 PM, in his best bib and tucker… er, his best interview attire. He'll be meeting with the owners, and their financial advisor, as well as myself, so a word to the wise."

"I'll … mmm … pass on the word," Sefton answered, and Richard – oblivious as he was to most unspoken social cues – did not notice that Sefton appeared rather shaken, until he ventured. "Ricardo, I ain't certain that Lucas even *has* a best bib and whatever."

Richard sighed, rather deeply. This was to be expected. A dismaying number of kitchen geniuses that he had met over his time in the field were – if not actually barking mad, located somewhere along the functioning levels of the autism spectrum. "Then you should tell him that whatever he wears should be clean. And cover up all of the elemental naughty bits."

"All right, then," Sefton's expression cleared. He took out his cellphone from the pocket of his jeans and was dialing in a number as Richard wheeled away. "OK … hey, it's on, Luc. I'll come and get you about half-past one. Your meet and audition is tomorrow at two. I'll run you out to the Age afterwards and you can tell us how it went. But ix-nay on the Arb-ay stuff, ya know? Judikins is that dedicated a vegan … See ya tomorrow, pal. 'Bye."

By means of the bush telegraph, it seemed that several other people had an interest in the potential new line cook at the Café. Allen Lee Mayne, back in Luna City again, shared an outside table with Joe Vaughn, enjoying a late afternoon sandwich lunch with Jess and Little Joe, in advance of the specified hour. It was a month after the barbeque throw-down and the hurricane emergency that followed on its heels. For the life of him, Richard couldn't figure out why Allen Lee was hanging around, still. The mystery of the skeleton, of course; a reason for him to be tight with Lew Dubois – but that was only part of it, Richard was certain.

Inside, Miss Letty sat with Doc Wyler; she had been delivered thence by Harry Vaughn, the old retired marshal, at the wheel of his classic red convertible. Harry remained, a malicious and genial smile barely showing under his drooping mustache as Doc Wyler scowled. Miss Letty seemed to have the two gentlemen well in hand, Richard thought. At least, they were not withdrawing to the rear of the Café and strapping on boxing gloves. Which, on the whole, was a good thing. Richard personally brought out coffee for all, and a plate of assorted bite-sized tarts to go with it. This was one of his trademark dessert selections, tiny fruit, nut, and custard pies, usually presented on a three or four-level tiered dish. Today, though – a simple platter. Doc Wyler nodded – still in a vile mood, which Richard devoutly hoped would not cause difficulties with the interview. Just as the long minute hand crawled from eleven to twelve, Jess came in from the outside, leaving the baby with Joe and Allen Lee. Araceli came out from the kitchen with another carafe of coffee refills, and Richard took his own place at the stammtisch.

"Did Sefton tell you much about this fella?" Doc Wyler didn't sound as if his mood had improved much. Richard cudgeled his memory.

"Young man, been working at a purveyor of fast foods in Karnesville, before that in the oilfields. Probably a competent griddle and sauté cook. From what Sefton let fall, the likelihood of him owning a suit is vanishingly small."

"Damn few of you young fellas do, these days," Doc Wyler grunted, and helped himself to a tiny nut tart. "Ah, there's Sefton – at least he's on time. That's one good mark in his favor."

In silence, they watched Sefton's disreputable, many-colored vehicle pull into a parking space between Harry Vaughn's classic red convertible, and Doc Wyler's late-model black pickup truck with the logo of the Lazy-W Exotic Game Ranch emblazoned on the doors. Sefton and Judy Grants' eccentric method of motor-transport had been cobbled together years ago from the front section of a VW bus with a pickup truck bed welded onto the chassis from a point just behind the driver and passenger doors. The whole rickety and rust-bedewed ensemble had then been spray-painted in pastel flowers, moons, and astrological signs, while mottos along the pickup side panels urged the application of human energies toward coitus rather than armed conflict.

Of all those observing this scene, only Allen Lee Mayne looked the least startled; everyone else was quite accustomed to the sight of the Grant's beater of a vehicle. Richard did notice that the cargo bed was piled high; a couple of boxes, a bright red Vespa motor scooter secured with several bungee cords, and a full drum kit, similarly secured; he assumed that Sefton must have been inveigled unto helping someone move. The driver-side door swung open, and Sefton appeared. The passenger-side door likewise opened.

"Good god almighty!" exclaimed Doc Wyler and began coughing as the nut tart went down toward the wrong way.

"Jesus jumping Key-rist on a pogo stick!" Harry Vaughn breathed, shaking his head in mystification.

Miss Letty cleared her throat, warningly, and hissed, "Young people these days often feel obliged to make a point of rebelling against convention."

"There's rebelling, and then there is nuking convention from orbit, just to make certain," Jess took out a neat file from enormous handbag-cum-briefcase and set on the table before Richard. "This will be a short interview, I'm afraid. Sefton must have lost his mind!"

"I would take no notice at all," Only Miss Letty maintained her customary serenity as the bell over the Café door jingled sweetly.

"Hey, fellas, this is Luc, that I told you about." Sefton twisted his battered straw cowboy hat in his hands, nudging his companion with an elbow. "Luc, say howdy. Doc Wyler, Miss Letty, Miz Vaughn, an' Ricardo. He's a cook, too. Doc an' Miss Letty own the place."

"Hi," said Luc tonelessly, and looked at the floor. He was in his twenties, and painfully thin, a pipe-cleaner gangle of a boy, with colorful tattoos on his arms, barely covered by the sleeves of a black tee-shirt. At least, the shirt looked clean, although with the black color it was hard to tell.

"Have a seat, Luc. What did you say was your last name?" Jess recovered her voice first. Richard tried his best not to stare; not to stare at the small silver bolt piercing through Luc's left eyebrow, the red-dyed mohawk crest over the top of his otherwise shaved skull, or the black metal-edged round holes through his earlobes, holes through which he could have put his own thumb.

"Luc Massie," Luc mumbled, as he took the chair opposite those gathered to sit in judgment.

Sefton murmured, "I'll wait outside for ya. Let me know when you're ready."

"I'll wait with ya," Harry Vaughn excused himself as well. "This is your business, and none of mine." The doorbell jingled again, and a painful silence descended in the Café. Richard gathered his own wits and posed what he saw as the first question.

"So … Mr. Massie. Tell me where you trained. What are your qualifications, and where have you worked in food service?"

"At the Culinary Institute in S.A." Luc still didn't look up. Richard presumed that this meant some kind of cooking school in San Antonio, although for all of him, it could have been South Africa. "Then … I worked for Emerald Point Catering, here and there in the Eagle Ford division. Lots of places." He finally looked up. "I got some references from them. I worked for the Arbys in Karnesville just now. See – I'm in a band. The Ozona Mud Puppies, and their schedule didn't work with those Emerald Point places. I quit."

"A musician," Richard thought that he had better shut up. The old joke about musicians popped into his mind, unbidden. *What do you call a musician who has broken up with his girlfriend? Broke and homeless!*

"Mr. Grant is a good friend, and a client of mine," Jess leaped in, adroitly, having recovered her composure. "He told us that you would be interested in working at the Café here. I would trouble you for your picture identification and your social security card. Out of courtesy, I will warn you that we will do a brief background check, prior to taking you on, if we so decided to do so. Do understand; this is a small town, nothing goes unnoticed, and neither myself or my clients are idiots."

"No problem," Luc shifted in his chair, just sufficiently to dig out his billfold out of the back pocket. Jess took them, made notes of the particulars, and returned them to Luc. He still didn't look directly at them, which Richard feared was not going to set well with Doc. In addition to his other irascible traits, the old rancher and veterinarian was accustomed to a firm handshake and a direct gaze signifying a degree of trustworthiness. But Miss Letty seemed to look upon the lad with a kindly eye, or at least an understanding one, when she took up the baton in this relay-race of a job interview.

"We require a demonstration of your cooking skills," she announced. "Really –" she added, with a side eye toward the others at her side of the table, "It is a custom of the Café, when considering an additional cook and one whom our senior chef has not personally trained. You will have half-an-hour to produce a signature dish or dishes of your choice, out of whatever we have on hand in what I am assured is a fully-stocked kitchen. No, Richard – remain here, after you have shown him to the kitchen, so that he alone will prove his mettle. Araceli can answer any questions which Mr. Massie may have. We will wait here, to continue the interview. After all," Miss Letty swept the table with one of those piercing glances which regularly cowed classrooms of every age, from kindergarten to know-it-all-teenagers. "That is the most important qualification, is it not?"

"Indeed," Richard allowed, with an interior sigh, drawn from vast and lamentable experience. He led the prospective assistant cook into his sanctuary, which now he would have to share, but which was necessary, if the Café were to expand service. Luc was *so* not the answer to every struggling restaurants' dream, but Miss Letty was right. If he could cook like a dream, and his personal peculiarities were not totally crippling – give the kid a try. It wasn't as if Richard himself hadn't been several times as obnoxious or arrogant in his first couple of essays at employment. "Luc – Mr. Massie, let me give you a brief tour of the kitchen. Don't touch my knives, though. They should be sharpened sufficiently. We have a complete stock of what we usually require, day to day. The delivery van came on Monday, and I did my customary additional jaunt into Karnesville yesterday. This is Araceli, Luc. She is occasional sous-chef and full-time head waitress, my right-hand … human being. The soul of the Café."

"Hi," said Araceli, slicing a roll of the latest batch of sweet-rolls flavored with orange-sugar-and-pecan filling, and efficiently laying them out on a greased baking sheet. "Be with you in a min, Luc. What do you want to do for your demo? Make it good, make it the dish that you know best. Don't fall flat over being over-ambitious."

"'Kay," answered Luc. For once, he had his head up and was looking around; the very first spark of professional interest which Richard had observed in the prospective new employee. "How many? Many people?" he added.

Richard answered, in a flash of inspiration, "As many as are diners sitting at the tables in the Café right now."

"Right," Luc nodded briefly. "Eight. On it, Chef!"

Which was the first reassuring indicator he had seen from Luc Massie. Richard, per his instructions from Miss Letty, left his kitchen with marked reluctance, and returned to the dining room. It was awkward beyond all endurance to sit at the stammtisch, wondering what the hell was going on in the kitchen, between this obviously anti-social millennial, and Araceli – notorious for not suffering fools of any breed, shape, or gender. He could hear Araceli's voice in the kitchen, but not what she said, or Luc's mumbled replies to her.

"I may as well tell the others to come inside," he said, finally. "Whatever he is going to cook, he's going to do it for everyone."

"Hey, just when I was getting hungry again," Joe said, cheerfully.

Harry observed, "I'll not say no to an offer of free food,"

"Neither will I," Allen Lee chuckled.

"Anything from the Café is all good," Sefton rubbed his hands together in anticipation. "Jess, how's the kid doing, so far?"

"So far, so good," Jess replied, with a cautious look at Doc Wyler and Miss Letty. "He actually hasn't begun baying at the moon and gabbling on about chemtrails and the Kennedy assassination. If he can cook to Richard's satisfaction …"

"And we can work in the same kitchen without killing each other," Richard interjected.

Sefton looked worried. "He's a good cook," he assured them all, with an expression of intense earnest.

"Arbys'," Richard observed sotto voice. Jess kicked his foot under the table, while Sefton continued. "Don't knock it, Ricardo – he got fired because he's just too good. OK – so, he looks kinda…"

"Weird," Joe Vaughn interjected; neither condemning or applauding, merely observing.

"But he's OK," Sefton continued. "Kids these days gotta signal to their peers. I'll be the first to say that his social manner is all over the damn map, but he's had a tough life. His parents moved to Portland and left him to look after himself when he turned eighteen. He got a job, couch-surfed with friends, but made it through cooking school and a couple of rounds of working for Big Corporation. And," Sefton added, as if this was a laudable item on Luc's CV. "He's in a band."

Richard was reminded again of how often the lost, halt and starving of the animal world gravitated into Sefton and Judy's household. Apparently, it was the same with the human tribe, too.

"Oh?" Joe raised an eyebrow and handed the mildly fussing Little Joe to his other domestic half. "Babe, I think he's hungry. Any group I might have heard about?"

"Well, this month, they're calling themselves the Ozona Mud Puppies," Sefton allowed.

Jess excused herself and her offspring, saying, as she departed in the direction of the Ladies' Toilet in the Café, "Sorry, I'm just not OK with breastfeeding out in public, even with friends."

"That's fine, dear," Miss Letty nodded graciously. "It's one of those intensely personal things. What a curious name for performing musicians! Are they any good?"

"They're still settling on a final name," Sefton confessed. "Grunge band, mostly, but they do some nice covers. They're OK, but not any Bonzo-Dog Doo-Dah Band. Have to say, the kid will make a name sooner as a cook than as a drummer, if y'all just give him a chance."

"So, you don't think that he'll be the next Glenn Miller," Doc Wyler summed up the matter very fairly. "Lucky that we are here to judge his facility as a cook – not as a musician."

"Well, yeah," Sefton replied.

Allen Lee spoke up, as if he was desirous of making peace in a fraught sphere, "I know it's not my place, folks – but I have done a lotta shows in a lotta places, and I gotta say that a fair number of the cooks an' staff and all, in those places where we did shows; they weren't the best at making a good appearance. But they did good food, and that's what drew the customers. If this kid can draw the customers, I'd give him a chance. Just my advice as an outsider expert."

"Appreciated, Allen Lee," Richard said. "But I still must work with the guy…" and Richard had the *nous* to acknowledge that Miss Letty and

Doc Wyler possessed the final deciding vote, "If the decision is made to take him on as junior chef in my kitchen, I will do my utmost to work with him. Piercings, tattoos, drum kit and all."

Everyone stared at the almost-empty platter of tartlets, sunk in varying degrees of morose apprehension save Miss Letty. It was a relief when Jess returned from the Ladies' with Young Joe propped upright against her shoulder, his infant cheek pressed against a small towel, while Jess patted his back.

"I wish he would learn to burp against the cloth," Jess lamented as Little Joe finally let loose an infant-sized hearty belch. "He misses half the time. By the time he's old enough to feed himself, I won't have a single shirt without a spit-up stain on it." She mopped Little Joe's face with a corner of the towel, and set him down in his carrier again, where he remained an interested spectator until he fell asleep. "How much longer, then?" Jess added.

"Five minutes," Richard made a quick check of his cellphone, just as the door from the kitchen swung open, and Araceli emerged, carrying the largest serving tray in the Café's inventory. "Well?"

"A tasting menu," Araceli announced with pride, setting down the serving tray on the nearest table to the stammtisch. "A tasting menu; hot sandwiches, burgers, and fries."

"Glory be," Allen Lee breathed reverently, as Araceli unloaded platter after platter, and distributed small plates in front of each. A bounty of hot sandwiches was piled on those platters, many if not all still sizzling from the grill. A delectable odor permeated the air; of expertly cooked and superlative meats, *(Richard only purchased the best, from Pryors, if possible)* good breads delicately browned, a small ramekin of hot beef consume sending up a delicate thread of vapor. "I'm in fast-food heaven!"

"Wait until I bring out the fries," Araceli returned smartly. "He's just finishing them up."

"As I live and breathe, still!" Doc Wyler looked over his glasses. Each selection was cut into quarters, a frilled toothpick impaling every quarter, each a little larger than bite-sized. "Hot pastrami … and Reubens. Burgers and old-fashioned patty-melts … hot French dip! What's with a wad of rabbit food on top of frankfurters?"

"Some kind of Vietnamese-style hot-dog thingy that's all the rage with foodies," Araceli said, over her shoulder, as she vanished again into the kitchen.

"Didn't I tell you that Luc does the best grilled stuff around?" Sefton neatly scooped up several sandwich quarters, which vanished with the speed of a magician making an object vanish with the pass of a hand or handkerchief. Officially vegetarian in the eyes of his adoring wife, Sefton nonetheless was an enthusiastic back-slider when it came to hamburgers and BBQ. "If there is a fast-food maestro around here, he is it. Ya can't go wrong, taking him on, I guarantee. Speaking as a member of the food-consuming public, of course."

"Oh, yeah!" Allen Lee agreed in rapture. He helped himself to one of the Vietnamese-style hot-dogs – a length of Pryor's all-beef frank, served on a short length of Richard's French-style baguette, and topped with a salad mixture of thinly-slivered cucumber, radish, and fresh cilantro. Richard eyed it glumly. It looked as if Luc had made free with the Café's consignment of fresh herbs. Araceli returned with the tray – this time laden with platters containing an assortment of French-fried potatoes – or, as Richard preferred to call them – *pomme frites*. Thick-cut, thin-cut, shoe-string cut, cut in curls, crispy, extra-crispy, slivered as thin as tissue paper and fried as delicious, crunchy rounds, or thick wedges with the skin still on, variously dusted with spices or just with plain salt. Joe Vaughn moaned a little, deep in his throat.

"Oh, man – I used to beg the guys working midnight chow to do me a special order of extra-extra-crispy. Babe, I know I don't have a vote, but

I'd say hire this guy, unless it turns out that his last couple of roomies have turned up dismembered in the morgue, or something."

"Noted," Jess answered, her tone as dry as dust – or nearly as dry as the hand-cut crispy fries on Joe's plate. Miss Letty, with all the gravity of a judge at some high-class cooking competition, helped herself to one of the Vietnamese-style hot-dogs, and a quarter of a Reuben sandwich – one of those with little fringes of sauerkraut leaking from the edges. She nibbled delicately at the sandwich, made on a thin slice of rye pumpernickel which Richard was certain had been consigned to the deepest depths of the walk-in freezer – *how had that mad tattooed berk found it?*

Richard reached for two of the hamburger sandwich offerings, not having any particular preference, and a selection of the *pomme frites*. He bit into the one made on toasted bread, fringed with slivers of caramelized onion, and dolloped with melted Emmental cheese; it was heavenly; the bread just lightly toasted to a state of crunchiness, the onions sweet, and the ground burger perfectly grilled and still delicately pink in the center. The other – a hamburger garnished American-style with lettuce, cheddar, and sliced tomatoes, was equally savory. And the *pomme frites* … heavenly, hot, fluffy on the inside, crunchy on the outside, dusted with black pepper, salt, and a suggestion of smoked paprika. Meanwhile, Doc Wyler drew to himself the platter with the French dip sandwiches and that little ramekin of au jus and selected a couple of sandwich quarters and a few *pomme frites*.

"Singular," Miss Letty murmured, as she nibbled on the Reuben sandwich margins. "Just like Schilo's always made. You remember, Stephen? Where I introduced you to Miss Alice on VJ Day!"

"You don't say!" Doc Wyler exclaimed, and snagged the last of the Reuben quarters, beating Joe and Harry Vaughn to it by a short head. "S'help me god, so it is. Give it a side of good German whole-grain mustard, and I'm sold." He added a couple of the fried potatoes, nibbled at them all judicially, and looked directly at Miss Letty. "My vote is for this kid, assuming he is not as screwball as he looks on first glance. What say you, now?"

Miss Letty swallowed the last of her selection and looked around at the table. Richard's heart sank all the way into his trainers. *Yes – the hot sandwich, burger, and fries tasting-menu was superlative! No – the cook was a mad tattooed musician-type! Yes – but he could cook! No – unbalanced and socially awkward! Yes – but on half-an-hour notice, he had ransacked the Café kitchen like a Vandal of yore and produced THIS!*

"I vote yes," Miss Letty announced. With a placatory look around the table to the others with hiring input, she enlarged on her decision. "Based on this selection, he is a more than competent cook. But we must make it clear to him; he must understand that Richard is the senior chef. I fear that Lucas is one of those children entirely bereft of social skills, and therefore somewhat difficult to work with. Richard is the ultimate authority as far as the Café, the management, menus, and all is concerned. There must be no confusion about the lines of authority. We should make this clear, and know that he understands this, absolutely, before tendering the offer of employment."

Luc in Residence

"Understood," Richard sighed and accepted his doom. "I approve hiring him – but I'm afraid that we will – er – come to clash in the kitchen now and again. I don't look forward to it, but there it is."

"Let me go and talk to him," Allen Lee offered, and such was his fatherly authority that both Miss Letty and Doc Wyler nodded acquiescence. Richard followed Allen Lee into the kitchen, where Luc glanced up from scraping down the grill station.

"That was a magnificent meal!" Allen Lee exclaimed in hearty delight. "And they tell me that you're hired on account of it. But seriously, there's some things you gotta know – and stick to, if you wanna stay in this place long enough for me to come back around and feature y'all on a repeat of my people for a new foodie throw-down."

"Sure," Luc was still looking down at the surface of the grill. "So, they like it, huh?"

"They sure did, kid," Allen Lee reassured him, hearty and enthusiastic, with an ear-to-ear smile. "You got the job – it's yours, if you want it. But understand that Ricardo is the ultimate boss in the kitchen. And you gotta remember that he's been around the track a good few times, understand that he's got the final say, cooking-wise. See – he trained at this fancy high-class cooking school in Paris …"

As Richard listened, Allen Lee expounded on Richard's training, career, experience in the field at a fulsome and almost embarrassing length, not omitting the humiliating-fail bits, although putting the best construction possible on them – a consideration for which Richard was grateful. It appeared that Luc had never heard of him and his career as a celebrity chef, although he gave every evidence of being impressed by the tale which Allen Lee spun. He did wish that Allen Lee had left out the details about the Carême meltdown and aftermath, though.

Finally, Allen Lee wound up the final threads of his narrative and tucked in the extraneous ends, concluding, "Ya see, Luc – you're solid in the kitchen, and you have the basic skills. Ricardo is OK with taking you on. But you gotta be mature about this, realize that he has a world of stuff that he can teach you, things that you don't know about, until he starts teaching you and he's done that! He's doing it even now, with teaching kids to cook with his internet series. Learn from him about the fancy French cooking stuff you didn't know! You got the skills, kid – but don't let that go to your head." Here Allen Lee paused, perhaps to lend extra drama to his final peroration. "Take the job. Don't think that you know it all, Luc. You don't, but Richard here can teach you. Mebbe you still won't know it all, but I guaran-damn-tee, you'll know a lot more. Be a good sport and learn what he can teach you."

"Sure," Luc wiped his hands on the towel at his waist. For about the first time he looked squarely at whom he was speaking to. "Thanks. For the chance, guys. I won't ever let you down, Chef. Or you either, Allen Lee."

"I'll take that as a promise," Richard accepted with the minimum required grace, as Allan Lee beamed approval. "So will I, kid. I'll tell you know, I expect great things from you – like, I come back in a season or two, and see you on my show!"

Both Richard and Luc winced slightly, at the thought of that, but Luc straightened his narrow shoulders and replied. "Sure thing." He sounded a bit dubious. No, Luc wasn't made for dealing with the public the easy, comfortable way that Allen Lee did, and which Richard had faked for so long.

Now Richard said, "Come on and tell Miss Letty and Doc Wyler that you're on. I'm sure that Jess has some paperwork to finish, now that you're accepted."

"Sure, Chef," Luc followed them out to the front, and when Richard nudged him toward the empty chair at the stammtisch, he sat down in it, with some definite signs of unease.

Miss Letty broke the ice, by saying with as much fulsome enthusiasm that a starchy, prim lady of certain years was able to bring to bear, "You will be relieved to hear, Lucas, that we were all very pleased with your audition menu, and that the decision to offer you employment was unanimous. I do believe that the selection of regular diners at the Café were enthusiastically in agreement in this. You will have fans, even before you begin your first workday in the Café."

"I'm done," Doc Wyler announced, scraping his chair back. "Places to go, things to do, cows to brand. Welcome to the Café, son – hope that you choose to remain long. Those grilled sandwiches were prime, by the way. Now I won't have to drive all the way to the city for their like. Give your particulars to Mrs. Vaughn – your current address and all, and she can process the background check."

"Already done," Joe Vaughn observed, looking up from his cellphone. "No wants or warrants; only a citation for disorderly conduct at some dive in San Antonio."

"That was … it was nothing," Luc shrugged, as if it *were* nothing. But he added, in flat tones. "I don't have a current address."

"You don't?" Doc Wyler looked as baffled as someone might, who lived on the largest ranch acreage in Karnes County since birth nearly a century ago, in a house that his grandfather had built.

"He don't," Sefton spoke, apologetically, his mouth full of *pomme frites*. "All his stuff is in the back of my van. His roommate in Karnesville kicked him out this morning. We were gonna let him stay at the Age, but that Judikins has a major problem with …"

"The m – the non-veganity?" Richard ventured.

Sefton shook his head. "No, the drum-practice. It upsets the chickens and ya know," Sefton regarded them all in a manner which begged sympathy. "If the chickens and all are upset, My Lady is upset."

"Can't have that," Doc Wyler looked with what might be interpreted as a pleading look toward the table.

Joe Vaughn murmured, "Your Lady is your Goddess; I know. If Mama ain't happy, then no one is happy."

"What about the old apartment upstairs in the Mercantile?" Miss Letty looked to have had the only sensible reaction. "If that would suit, I can make it available. I own the building, you know. No one has lived in the apartment for years. My grandfather had his business office there, and my brother used it for a while, as well."

"At the Mercantile?" Richard was boggled. "It would be handy to work, but I never knew there was any such thing in the Mercantile."

This was the narrow red-brick building next to the Café on the opposite side from Stein's Wild West Round-up, towering two stories and a commanding cornice high over the single story and a half of the Café, with the name "Mercantile Building" outlined in the façade in contrasting and permanent white-glazed brick. The ground floor was an ice-cream parlor in the early years of Luna City, noted for having been the establishment from which Don Antonio Gonzales emerged on a certain summer day in 1919. Upon encountering his mortal enemy, one Eusebio Garcia Maldonado on the sidewalk before the Café, increasingly heated words and then gunshots were exchanged in the last recorded public duel in Luna City. *(The only casualties were the radiator of Don Antonio's Model-T sedan, a city street-light and a mule hitched to a wagon parked farther down the Square, all struck by wild shots from the participants' weapons.)* The ground floor of the Mercantile Building currently housed a small and rather shabby little shop featuring the work of local crafters and artisans. It was open erratic hours, mostly on weekends. Richard had never given it much thought, save when curious weekend excursionists wandered into the Café, asking when the place would be open.

Miss Letty was explaining to Luc, and to a rather relieved Sefton, "It's a terribly spartan little place, I'm afraid. Lucas – that means that there are no comforts in it. After the Spartans of ancient Greece, who preferred to live simply. No one has lived in it for years, as I cannot afford to renovate, and probably couldn't get back sufficient in rent to cover the costs, anyway. But the view of the Square from the front windows is quite pleasant, and there is a relatively new window air conditioning unit. Sarah and some of her friends were holding needle-work classes in the front room, where the light is good. I suppose you would want to see it, first." She fished in her generous handbag, found a ring of keys, and detached on from it. "Come along, young man, and see if it will suit. I'm afraid it will be rather dusty, and of course the furniture is … minimal. But you would have it to yourself, and of course, be convenient to the Café."

"I don't mind," Luc replied. He had not much of an emotion about this, so Richard presumed that he truly didn't mind. "No roomies or neighbors to get riled up about the drums? Let me see the place."

"She's 'Miss Letty' to you," Jess hissed, in an undertone, and then added in a more normal voice. "I'll finish the paperwork once you've had a chance to look over your new quarters," She tucked away the folder, and picked up Little Joe, who in the interval of his mother having a bite to eat, had become quite restless over her attention paid to anything but him. "I'll wait, Miss Letty. Richard, do you want to go with them?" Richard really didn't want to do this, thinking it was none of his business, but as Miss Letty, Sefton and Luc went toward the door, Jess hissed in the same undertone, "Go with her! Those stairs are murder. And he will be your employee, anyway. A good commander always looks after the troops and their living conditions."

"Right," Richard obeyed with a sigh, as Miss Letty with her key led the three of them out the front door of the Café, and to a narrow and undistinguished door sandwiched between the Mercantile Building, and the storefront on the far side of it. *The door to the space in the Mercantile, over that hapless little craft shop?* Guess that it must be, Richard thought. Miss Letty fumbled with the key, in the lock of that door, which opened into a small space, into which a staircase mounted up like an arrow upwards into the dimness beyond. There was a clumsy, old-fashioned light switch just inside the doorway. Miss Letty flipped it, and two lights came on; bare bulbs hanging on lengths of flex, one at the bottom and one at the top.

"I think that you will have sufficient space for your motor scooter to park in shelter at the bottom of the stairs," Miss Letty observed. "Such a darling little machine! I've seen them used in Italy, in the old movies! I have always wanted to ride on one, but never had the opportunity. I am afraid that the stairs are so steep! It was the way of it, in Grandfather Arthur's day, you know. So many families chose to live over their shops, or at least keep offices there." She began to climb up the steep, darkened staircase, in painful, one-by-one steps. Mindful of his instructions from Jess, Richard had no compunction about following her next, even in elbowing ahead of Sefton. If the old darling missed a step, and somehow contrived to fall backward … Miss Letty was the oldest resident of Luna City, the living repository of history and legend. Her life should be preserved at whatever risk.

On the landing at the top of the stairs, Miss Letty took out her keys again, and unlocked the substantial panel door, admitting them all into a generous but empty room, high-ceilinged, and well-lit by two tall windows overlooking Town Square. Although the room was paneled with fine, if dingy carved paneling, the floor was covered with the utilitarian greenish speckled linoleum favored for public buildings anticipating rather a lot of wear and tear, and the windows filled with equally utilitarian Venetian blinds expecting the same hard-use, hanging at half-mast. A couple of folding tables and a stack of metal folding chairs leaned against the farther wall.

It was altogether a cheerless and desolate prospect as far as a living space went, but Luc regarded it with approval. "Rehearsal space! What else is there?"

"Not very much, I'm afraid," Miss Letty replied, "Through here is the bathroom, kitchenette, and bedroom."

She led them to a door in the wall opposite the windows; a short hallway lay beyond with three more doors; the first led to a miniscule bathroom, into which a depressingly modern sink, toilet and shower stall had been wedged, likely with the aid of a crowbar. The door beyond that opened into a slightly larger room, with a single window in it, overlooking the lumpy graveled area which lay behind the Café. It had been fitted with some cheap kitchen cabinets under a Formica countertop and cabinets which had never had any better days of which to boast. A couple of dead flies lay in the sink, the porcelain lightly stained by lime from an intermittently dripping tap. There was a space where a stove had possibly once been, and another filled with a refrigerator, of a mid-century design with rounded corners and a dashing chrome handle shaped like a car door handle of the same vintage.

"The icebox works," Miss Letty said, opening the refrigerator door to show that yes, there was a light on inside, and an opened box of baking soda. "I can't recall what happened with the stove, although it may be that there never was one. My brother used this as an office, when he was writing his book about the history of Luna City. He was the last person to use this place, regularly."

The final door stood half-open, to a room with another window; this one contained a single bedstead with a dusty mattress on it and nothing much else.

"What do you think, Luc?" Sefton sounded hearty, enthusiastic. "A crash pad of your own, and a job right next door, too! Might be your lucky day, after all, buddy!"

"Yeah." For all that, Luc didn't sound all that enthused, and Richard didn't blame him in the least. "I don't mind about the stove. I got a microwave of my own, so no biggie. How much is the rent?"

"I'll work out something with Jess," Miss Letty replied, sounding as magisterial as ever. "Something fair to us all, considering that this place is relatively useless to me, and offers no home comforts worth mentioning to you. A mere token of fifteen a week deducted from the salary that the Café will pay, I think. Just consider that quarters are part of your salary."

"Aw, hey, Miss Letty, it's fine. A place of my own, even if it's a dump. I didn't mean that," Luc added hastily, on intercepting a warning look from both Sefton and Richard – and *mirabile dictu* – taking it to heart after a moment of thought, in which Richard thought that he could hear the mental gears creaking and grinding. "I'll take it. It's fine. 'Specially to practice the drums. Call it my address for now, Chef."

"Good," Richard said. "You know that I'll know where to find you, when you oversleep!"

Sefton grinned. "Luc, man – don't worry about no other stuff in the place, 'kay? When our old place burned, people were real generous to us. We gotta whole trailer full of stuff that they gave us, to replace the household things that burned, stuff that we really don't need. We'll bring up your things from the van, and then I'll make a run out to the Age and bring you anything else you might need from our stores. Hey, no problem,

Luc. You know how nice it will be, not to have to drive all the way to Karnesville for a decent burger. But like I said – ix-nay on the urger-bay when you talk to My Lady. Got it?"

"Sure."

Richard was fairly certain that Luc did not quite comprehend – something about the expression in his face. The lights were on, but the person at home was hiding in a back room, hoping that the one ringing the doorbell would soon give up and go away. For himself, Richard left Sefton and Luc to make a closer survey of the apartment and accompanied Miss Letty on that perilous journey down the narrow staircase. *Trip and fall on that, you'd be well into the grass before you stopped bouncing.*

"Lucas approves of the old apartment," Miss Letty announced to Jess upon their return to the Café. Joe had already gone back to work, and Allen Lee was swapping yarns with Harry Vaughn about old times in Banff at the Castle Mountain Hotel, at the sidewalk table, enjoying the late afternoon sunshine slanting across the Square in bars of blessed golden light. Every scrap of Luc's tasting menu was gone, save a dusting of crumbs and seasonings. "That will be his home address for the time being. Poor boy; I'm afraid he has had a very difficult life. There are these odd children, you know; quite intelligent, but no grasp of the social graces, and what it takes to get on with their peers." Miss Letty turned her regard toward Richard. "I'm afraid it will fall to you, Richard, to make allowances for this, as you work together."

Richard sighed. "My dear Miss Letty, I have worked with such numpties in the kitchen that you would not believe – and both they and I survived. Well, just barely…"

Miss Letty frowned, very slightly. Too late, Richard recalled that Miss Letty had an excellent command of English slang, based on her youthful service in the European theater. "Lucas is not an idiot, Richard – just odd and very skilled at what he does. I trust that you will take his personal idiosyncrasies into account. I must say that we – Stephen and I were pleased beyond belief with his cooking audition. The boy has definite talent. If his peculiarities can be managed skillfully, I dare to venture that he will be a credit and a benefit to the Café."

"I'm certain that he will, Miss Letty," Jess came to his rescue, as she settled her son into his carrier. "So – when should we announce regular supper service?"

"I suggest in time for Valentine's Day," Richard thumbed through his mental calendar. "We can do a couple of weekends, unannounced, just to work out the kinks…" He ignored Jess's snort of smothered laughter, too late remembering that crude slang went both ways.

"Very good," Miss Letty gathered up her own notes. "Good night, then, Richard."

"Do you need a lift home, Miss Letty?" Jess ventured. "I wasn't going that way, but …"

"No; a lady always departs with the gentleman who brought her," Miss Letty replied with a wintery smile. So that was why Harry Vaughn still waited outside the Café. "It's a treat on a mild day, to travel in an open car, with the wind in your hair."

"All right, then," Richard supposed that his day was now done, some hours after he was accustomed to ending them. But this had been a special day, although he was still unsure about why this should be so. Another chapter in the doings of the Café, and of his involvement in the doings of Luna City, a place which had now set bonds – Richard refused to think of them as tentacles – so tightly now around him, that he feared that he would never be able to shrug them off and leave, even if he really wanted to do so. Kate Heisel, Ozymandias-King-of-Kings, the nurturing of the clients at the Café, for the schoolchildren which he had taken on the mission of teaching about proper food, the friendship of Joe and Jess, of Berto and Araceli and Pat, and all the others, to include the uncouth Grants … *and now the care of a fellow with no perceptible social skills?* He wandered into the kitchen, where Araceli had already efficiently cleaned up after the unexpected late afternoon spasm of cooking.

"Hey, Chef – I think we're done for the day. I guess the new guy is hired. Can we all close up and go home?"

"Yes, yes, and yes," Richard replied, whereupon Araceli favored him with a brilliant smile.

"He'll be a good addition," she assured Richard, with a relatively straight face. "Yeah – he's weird, but, hey – he knew what he was doing, and wasn't half as obnoxious as some of the other guys that Miss Letty and Doc hired. Believe me; I've seen them all and outlasted them all. Does that make me an expert?"

"It does," Richard acknowledged with weary acquiescence. "So tomorrow morning, after the breakfast rush, we all sit down and have a talk about where we are going. I've got approval to take on Beatriz for the front of the house, and another waitress of your recommendation. In a couple of weeks, as soon as we work it all out – we'll be doing regular dinner service. Neither one of us can work seven days a week, and eighteen hours a day – so, we need to work out what we can do and the proper lines of authority."

"On it, Chef," Araceli replied, smartly.

Richard had no doubt that she was on it. *What a waste of good managerial authority, in a dinky, small-town café,* he thought, as he locked up for the day. In any first-rate place, Araceli would have been commanding a princely salary. But then, so would he.

He got out his bicycle from where it had been leaning against the wall at the back of the Café, whistled for Ozzie, who appeared from the Stein's garden, hopping easily up onto the basket on the back of it, nobly taking no notice of the bucket of kitchen scraps dedicated to the Grant's chickens.

When he came around the end of the block, it was to see Luc's Vespa go by, at a decorous pace, around the margins of Town Square, with Miss Letty, sitting demurely side-saddle on the back, with one arm around

Luc's waist, the other holding onto her hat, as they stopped in front of the Café. Harry Vaughn leaned against the fender of his red convertible, obviously waiting for her – now that she had experienced a ride on that dear little Italian scooter.

Yes, that was Luna City; a world apart and all of itself. Richard waved to Miss Letty and pedaled out on the road that led home. Home, in Luna City. It had a nice sound to it.

Radio Silence

Adeliza Gonzalez-Gonzales – who was never called anything but 'Adi' back then – was just thirteen when her older brother Manuel – Manolo to the family, Manny to his Anglo friends – came to Papi and Mama and said to them, "Papi, I want to see more of the world than Karnes County, an' at the Navy recruiting office, they say that I'll get a paycheck nice and regular, and I can work on ship engines that are bigger than this house. Besides, everyone says if America gets into a war, then they'll be drafting men my age, an' I don't wanna be a soldier, marching around in the mud and all that. The Navy lives good, and they say that the food is great. Can I have your permission, Papi?"

Mama got all pinch-faced and weepy, because Manolo was her favorite and oldest child. Papi sighed and looked solemn and grave, saying, "Manolo – *mi hijo* – if this is what you truly want, I will sign the papers." To Mama, he added, "Do not cry, Estella, can you see your boy as a soldier, following orders?"

"But he still must follow orders – the Navy is as military as the army," Adeliza piped up, and Manolo jeered and replied, "Nothing like the same at all, Adi!"

Manolo packed a few things in a cheap cardboard suitcase, and climbed aboard the bus to the city, and in time over the next three years the postman delivered hastily-scrawled letters and postcards; letters with odd postmarks and postcards of splendidly colored landscapes and exotic places. Manolo came home on leave once, in the summer, splendid in his white uniform and round white cap, carrying a heavy duffel-bag over his shoulder with apparent ease, seeming to have expanded from a boy into a man. Manolo was greatly excited. His ship was being transferred from the West Coast to the Hawaiian Islands. He brought presents for the family, a breath of fresh air and tales of travels in exotic far lands. Later, he sent his little sister a scarf of silk gauze, printed with a map of the Hawaiian Islands and pineapples and exotic flowers. Adi put it in the chip-carved box where she kept her handkerchiefs and her most precious small possessions. From that time on, a tinted picture-portrait of Manolo in his uniform sat in pride of place on the cabinet radio and Mama kept a candle burning before it always, a candle dedicated to Saint Peter, who had the particular care of sailors.

A winter Sunday morning, when the breeze from the north promised chilly nights, and the frost in the shade had not yet melted in the sunshine; Papa came to fetch Mama and Adi and the other children after morning Mass. Adi sensed that there was something wrong, even before Papi spoke. There was a peculiarly grim expression on Papi's face, a hush among the congregation scattering to their houses after Mass, silence broken only by the tinny sound of the radio in Papi's car.

"The Japanese have dropped bombs on the harbor, and our bases in Hawaii," Papi said. "The war has begun, whether we wish it or no."

"What of Manolo?" Mama demanded, her hands to her mouth in shock and horror. "Where is he? Is he safe?"

"I have no idea," Papi replied, his eyes shadowed with fear. Adi said nothing. She was sixteen now, almost grown. She met Papi's gaze with a silent nod of understanding.

Two days later a card came in the mail, from Manolo, a card on which Mama fell on with tears of joy. "You see!" she exclaimed. "He is safe! This letter is from him! All will be well, you will see!"

"Mama, the letter is postmarked the week before last," Adi said, to Mama's unheeding ears. A week later, a parcel bound in brown paper arrived, addressed in Manolo's handwriting.

"Christmas presents!" Mama exclaimed, "From Manolo, of course. You see, he is safe! It is only rumors that he is missing, that telegram was mistaken."

"Yes, Mama," Adi agreed with a heavy heart and a show of cheer, for the telegraph office messenger boy had brought that small envelope at mid-December. The telegram from the war office was followed in short order by Father Bertram, then the priest at St. Margaret and St. Anthony, who had seen the messenger boy's bicycle pass the priest's residence while Father Bertram was pruning the pyracantha hedge around the tiny garden. Everyone knew that telegrams meant bad news, now that the war had well and truly come to them, but Father Bertram's intended consolation and comfort were misplaced, for Mama was not distressed in the least.

"In the government telegram, it says only that he is missing," Mama insisted, over and over again. "Missing – not dead. In my heart, I know that Manolo is safe."

In the end, Father Bertram was the most sorely grieved of them all. He departed shaking his head and saying to Adi, "Your poor dear mother – I can only think that the enormity of your loss has affected the balance of her mind."

Father Bertram's Spanish was very bad, afflicted as he was with a very strong accent, reflecting many years as a missionary in the Argentine, so Adi was not entirely certain of what Father Bertram meant. She only smiled uncertainly. No, Mama had merely decided that Manolo was safe, and doing what he needed to be doing for the war effort and would not hear any word to the contrary. Never mind that Manolo's ship – the great battleship *Arizona*, whose engines Manolo had tended lovingly – had blown up with a roar that could have been heard halfway across the Pacific. There were pictures of the battleship, half-capsized in billowing clouds of black smoke in the weekly English newsmagazine. *Poof! Like that, a candle blown out in a single breath and a thousand and a half lives snuffed out with it.* It made Adi's heart ache to think of this, and she wept, but not where Mama could see.

That Christmas and many Christmases afterwards were not happy occasions for Adi's family. They were not happy again until Adi married and had children of her own, to bury the memory of that first wartime Christmas.

She did not even cry when Cousin Nando, and Cousin Jesus Gonzales and a half-dozen of the other teenage boy cousins came to Adi after Mass on Christmas Day, 1941, announcing that they had all sworn a blood-oath to avenge Manolo. Cousin Jesus had already had his orders to report to the Army, but the other boys were intent on volunteering for the Army, the Navy, the Marines even.

"So … we meant to ask you as Manny's sister – if you would give us all a token," Jesus Gonzales affirmed solemnly. "We pledge to avenge him by killing a dozen Japs each. Our solemnest promise, Adi!"

"Don't be ridiculous!" Adi snorted. Yes, of course she was angry at the Japanese for killing her gentle brother Manolo, who only lived to get grease all over his hands and work on his engines until they were tuned and vibrated like the beating of a human heart. And they had attacked without warning, without a declaration of war, which to Adi's understanding, was sneaky and unfair. But Jesus Gonzales, who was dark-eyed, lean, and handsome like a movie star, looked at her soulfully and begged again, until she relented. "Give me a moment."

She went into her parent's house – the house in the oldest part of town, into her room, and took out the chip-carved box with her most precious small things in it, considering a sacrifice of the scarf printed with that map of the Hawaiian Islands, the pictures of a tower and exotic flowers, and blue waves crashing on a white-sand shore; the scarf which had been a gift from Manolo. *No, not that.* She took instead another of her handkerchiefs, a pretty white cotton gauze handkerchief, printed with little blue flowers and green leaves, and the sewing shears from Mama's sewing basket.

Out on the front porch, she met the cousins – dark-eyed romantic Jesus, hot-tempered Nando, and the others. "My token, that which you have asked for," Adi said, as she crunched the scissor blades through the crisp-starched handkerchief; producing a dozen smaller squares, and struggled for something to say as she put them into the hands of that boy or this, thinking that this was absurdly like something from the old legends, or the movies on a flickering silver screen. She struggled for the right words. "Not in hate … Manolo didn't hate, for he didn't want to be remembered that way. But for the right, for justice and freedom, and for our people. For Manolo …" she lost the thread of her thoughts entirely, for Jesus and Nando reverently kissed the scraps of handkerchief as they were handed to them, and so did the other boys.

"Write to me?" Asked Jesus, at the last. "Promise, Adi!"

They all went off, in the following weeks, all with their small cheap suitcases packed, taking the weekly bus that was the only public transport then from Luna City to the wider world, and to the duty and colors which called them. Cousin Nando became a pilot, Jesus a cook with the Army, the others to service mundane or heroic as chance and temperament led them. Adi Gonzales was certain that every one of them took that little square of cotton handkerchief, printed with blue flowers.

Jesus Gonzales certainly did, for it was one of those small things which she found at the end in sorting out his things, after half a century of faithful marriage; a cotton scrap, discolored with age, so fragile that it practically fell apart in her hand as she took it out from his wallet.

But Mama … No, Mama never accepted that Manolo was gone from the world of the living. Against all evidence to the contrary; the telegram from the government, that Manolo never came home again, she insisted that he was alive and well, doing his patriotic duty for the war, still working in the engine-room of the battleship *Arizona*. Mama was first to the telephone – the telephone that was almost the first in Luna City in the household of a Gonzales or Gonzalez, certain every time that it was Manolo calling, long-distance. The war dragged on.

Even when it ended and the next began, Mama smilingly assured Adi and the family, their friends that Manolo was fine and happy in his work. For she had seen him frequently – or his likeness, in pictures of sailors on one ship or another, on shore leave, or in the newsreels in the movie theater in Karnesville. Mama did not allow the star on the flag which hung in the front window of their house to change from white to gold, and there was a wrapped gift on Three King's Day for Manolo for many years to come. Now and again, Mama claimed that that she had talked to someone who had seen Manolo. In her later years, Mama even insisted that she had spoken with Manolo, on the telephone. In her final illness, she had opened her eyes one afternoon, and said to Adi – perfectly clear, "There is nothing to worry about, *mi hija*. Manolo has left insurance, to take care of us all."

Some years after both Mama and Papi passed away, Adi's nephew Roman and his wife celebrated their twentieth wedding anniversary with a trip to Hawaii. Roman and Conchita went to the *Arizona* Memorial, and surreptitiously left a bouquet of fragrant white plumeria flowers floating on the water; water still streaked with oil leaking from Manolo's ship, iridescent streaks which the locals said were the tears of the ship, crying for her lost crew.

Roman and Conchita also went to the Punchbowl Cemetery. They brought back pictures. Adi is certain that Manolo is buried there, among the unknowns from the *Arizona*. After all this time, it hardly matters, really. But she likes to think of him, the strong young sailor in his white uniform, with his hands and fingernails from which the oil and grime that came from working engines would never quite be cleaned. She likes to think of him walking among the palm trees, plumeria and frangipani scenting the tropic air, the blue water and white foam, crashing on a sugar-white strand.

Now and again, Adeliza Gonzales-Gonzalez, who has not been called 'Adi' in years thinks she has seen Manolo, in a magazine picture accompanying some story to do with the Navy, or a sailor half-glimpsed in a television newscast. She is very careful not to say anything about this, of course.

Christmas Morning in Luna City

Christmas had passed, and the New Year well-established by the time the matter of the bones of the Scar-faced Tramp emerged, metaphorically, from where they had been consigned. Richard had only the mildest of interest in the matter, mostly because Kate was fascinated, and kept bending his ear with progress reports. The matters pertaining to the Café absorbed most of his energies, especially when it came to the holidays. For Thanksgiving dinner, Richard accepted an invitation to Pat and Araceli's, on condition that if Pat persisted in his plans to deep-fry a whole turkey, would Pat would kindly refrain from setting fire to their home with it. Christmas morning, which dawned cold and frosty, fell on a Monday so that it was a holiday for him.

On Christmas morning, Richard brewed a pot of tea and regarded the pile of neatly-wrapped gift parcels with a feeling of mild anticipation. Kate had brought him a small potted holiday tree, decorated with glitter-covered Styrofoam balls, to serve as a Christmas tree on his brief patio. It was too cold to sit outside. The ground was covered in white, crunchy frost, which would evaporate as soon as the sun rose higher in the pale blue sky, laying rosy beams of light across the campground meadow. Ozzie, tucking his paws beneath him as he sat on the tiny table at the banquette end of the Airstream, kept him company along with a cup of steaming hot tea. Richard had not felt this lively sense of anticipation since he was a very small boy on Christmas morning, contemplating the Christmas tree and a mountain of gift-wrapped boxes piled up underneath expensively-decorated branches.

He drew the closest to him; a gift bag from Kate. It contained a thick book; a cook's compendium of local recipes of the kind not covered in Larousse, published by a tiny specialty publisher in San Antonio. Ozzie had a present from Kate in the same bag; a cat-sized pleather motorcycle jacket, with a set of small goggles. On to the next parcel: from the Grants, who gifted Richard with an assortment of Judy's hand-made organic goat-milk soaps in various herbal scents, and a jug of Sefton's well-aged vintage mustang grape wine. The small box with the logo of the Wyler Exotic Game Ranch custom-printed on the top contained a personal check for an eye-wateringly substantial amount and a personal note signed with Doc's scrawled initials. *"Have fun with this – and don't spend it all in one place!"*

Jess and Joe provided a Christmas fruitcake in a tin; a cake which proved to be amazingly good, when Richard cut a slice from it and took an experimental nibble. Miss Letty – Richard was pretty certain that it was meant as a tactful reminder regarding thank-you notes – sent him a box of stationary and a vintage fountain pen. From Patricia Pryor and her family; a box of specialty smoked sausages and a small ham, cured Parma-style. Araceli and Pat's gift was a brand-new chef's jacket, embroidered with the coffee-cup logo of the Café, and his name above the pocket. *"Now you can replace that old one from Carême"* read the note in Araceli's handwriting. Two large boxes remained, and Richard went for the heaviest first. That box contained a heavy roll of what Richard thought was canvas, but unrolled, revealed a small hand-hooked rug, with the image of a smiling, many-rayed yellow sun on it, and the command "¡*Levántate y brilla!*" worked into the light blue background. Another note in Araceli's handwriting fell out of the rug. *"Abuelita worked this for you – it means in English – Rise and Shine!"*

Richard thought about it for a moment – the best place *(indeed, practically the only place)* would be next to the bed. Hell, it would be nice to put bare feet on something soft, first thing on a frosty-cold morning. He spread out the rug in the narrow space between the bed and the dresser, but Ozzie immediately sprawled as much as he could of himself on the rug and looked at Richard with his single unblinking eye as if he were daring the human to take it back.

"All right, you crafty little bugger," Richard said, poured himself another cup of tea, and went to open the final box, from Chris at the Tip-Top, who also volunteered as a medic for the Luna City VFD, and Sylvester; one of the myriad Gonzales/Gonzalez tribe, and like Chris, also a veteran, although his specialty was all things technical and internet. *"Merry Christmas; we think you have the right to wear a pair of these now!"* was written on the gift card taped to the top of the box. *(P.S. They should fit, and don't ask us how we knew what size to get. If we told ya, we'd have to kill ya. Sprinkle talcum powder on the inside, the first time ya put them on)*

Richard opened the box; within lay a pair of tall bronze-leather boots, ornately stitched Western-style, with a pattern of plumes and vaguely-floral shaped motifs in cream-colored thread on the tall shaft of the boot. His initial reaction was one of mild horror. *Really, could he wear these at work in the kitchen?* But then, all the mystique of all the Western movies he had ever watched as a child in Bickley came rushing back, as well as his inchoate longings to be one of them. Yes, these were the boots of the sort which John Wayne and Randolph Scott wore, boots to slide into the stirrups of a bronc-busting, cattle-punching saddle, the boots which won the West … Doc Wyler wore boots like these, as did Joe Vaughn and his

Uncle Harry. Pat Gonzalez, too – even if Pat drove a tanker petroleum truck. They were all born to wear boots like this. They were practically Clovis Walcott's sartorial signature. Georg Stein, at least as much a foreigner, although a mad Western fanatic, also wore famously ornate tall boots as he tended to his business in the Wild West Round-up.

The presentation of these boots, Richard sensed, was a signal rite of acceptance into the tribe, even more than being a volunteer for the fire-fighting company! Sylvester was one of the tribe from birth, Chris an adoptee; all that had to count for something, as a signal of his ultimate acceptance. Luna City <u>was</u> a tribe, eccentric, unfathomable, curious. Somehow, he had hit on all the right notes, in his blundering way. No, he would never be able to map the way of it, even to himself.

But here he was … in possession of a pair of boots. A present from the other members of the tribe. Richard was enormously touched. The boots were new, smelling faintly of leather and saddle-soap, their soles unscratched, unworn. He found a pair of thin socks in his wardrobe, drawer, the tin of talcum powder and with some effort, pulled the boots on over them, one after the other. They felt … ok, although they cramped his toes a bit.

"What do you think, Ozzie-King-of-Kings?" he asked of the cat, luxuriously squirming on the little hand-hooked rug, as though the fluffy wool nap scratched an itch which couldn't be relieved through any other means.

"Mrrrooow!" Ozzie replied, in his usual judicious manner. Which meant either that he approved of the boots, or of the rug. It was a pity that Kate would not be able to admire them in person for some days yet. She was spending Christmas in Karnesville with her family – and Richard was just as happy to spend a solitary holiday in the Airstream, neither having to make pleasant conversation or put himself out for anyone, or anything – except for Ozzie.

The Face from the Past

"Hey, Chef," Robbie Walcott said, "I nearly forgot. I saw Chief Joe on my way over here. He says that he's calling a meeting with you and some of the other guys at the VFW, this afternoon at four-thirty. Be there, he said – or be square."

"I have no notion of what he means by that," Richard answered. It was early Thursday afternoon; the day when he and Robbie consulted with Luc and Araceli about the Friday night and weekend menus at the Café. Robbie's enthusiasm for working at the Café was unwilted, even after a brutal summer spent in Richard's ad-hoc apprenticeship program.

"Neither do I, Chef." Robbie answered. "But that's what Chief Joe said. Hey, the new guy is pretty cool. Weird, but cool. He runs the grill station like a boss!"

"He does, that," Araceli put on her coat, her workday complete with the conclusion of the strategy session. Luc had also departed – coatless, apparently being impervious to extremes of temperature. His band – whose name had changed almost overnight from the Ozona Mud Puppies to Other People's Money – was performing tonight at a battle of the bands in Southtown, San Antonio. Richard publicly wished him well, privately hoped that the event didn't get all too raucous, and that Luc did not look overlong at the wine when it was red. There was the Café to run, and an unreliable assistant cook was an obstacle to that end. "Did Joe say what it was about, Robbie?"

"He got something about the set of bones an' stuff," Robbie answered. "By overnight FedEx from Allen Lee in California. Hey, I hope he comes back to Luna City soon! Now Allen Lee is a <u>boss</u>!"

"Indeed," Richard answered in dry tones. He couldn't help but like Allen Lee, in spite of the celebrity which the big ex-football champion seemed to enjoy. A little niggling envy of that celebrity sent up the occasional tentative shoot in the smoothly-raked tenor of Richard's present life. "And a damn good assistant cook himself, all things considered. He will be back; there's some kind of gourmet food line that he's working with Lew Dubois on, for Mills Farm. He'll be back, before he has to hit the road for the next season of *A La Carte*."

"Fascinating," Araceli collected her handbag from under the cash stand. "And you know about that, because …"

"They asked me, when they were putting it together," Richard answered. "And I said I'd only do it as an anonymous consultant. Lew had a notion to put my name on the line when it came to advertising, and I said no, when he suggested it …"

Richard had turned it down with much stronger language than that. *'No, Lew; look, you're a brick – heart of oak, and all that – but I can't go back to perpetuating that ghastly fraud. Just doing Captain Kitten's Kitchen is as far into a public face as I want to go.'* And Lew had looked startled, then smiled and replied, *'Not to worry, cher. Allen Lee has volunteered; a good move, n'est-ce pas? But your advice and judgment in our test kitchen – your skills would not go unrewarded. But we should talk about this another time.'*

'*Perhaps,*' Richard replied, considering the available funds in his local bank account with a critical eye.

Yes, he earned sufficient for his needs at the Café, and through the occasional special catering job, and he was content with that, for the nonce. But he had the responsibility of Ozzie to consider, and possibly a future with Kate. At some future point in time, all the parties whom he had left in the lurch when he walked away from Carême and his old life, might come demanding substantial recompense for their trouble and loss; yet another good reason to remain anonymous and unheralded. But it would be nice to be able to make those outraged creditors – when and if they appeared, waving demands – to go away and never bother him again, ever. When he first lighted in Luna City, potential angry creditors had not loomed so large in his personal reckoning. But he had a position now, a position of responsibility, a pair of proper Western boots, some apprentices and a couple of employees. Somehow, he should contrive to do better by them, in the event that his past came calling with more determination than that demonstrated by the detestable Pip.

"I'll be there," he said to Robbie. "OK, we're set for the weekend menu? Good. See you all tomorrow morning."

"At the crack of dawn, Chef!" Robbie answered cheerily and went on his way. Richard locked up the Café, turned out all the lights, and wended his own way to the VFW – long established as the primary *(although not exclusively)* male refuge in Luna City. The building itself was a sand-pink repurposed temporary classroom, moved from the high school when an expansion of the facilities made the temporary building redundant. Now it sat in an open space on the riverbank, behind the Tip-Top Icehouse, Gas & Grocery. The riverside terrace behind the old classroom, shaded by a couple of tall sycamore trees, was the venue for barbeques and pot-luck picnics in more temperate weather; the inside was comfortably yet eccentrically fitted out with a bar, an assortment of military memorabilia, and sufficient tables and chairs to serve the purpose. Even so, the 'V' still retained the air of the classroom that it had once been. When Richard walked his bicycle around the corner of the Tip-Top, he could see a scattering of familiar cars parked there.

Inside the VFW, three tables were pushed together to make one; Joe and Jess, with Little Joe, Chris from the Tip-Top, and Sylvester were already gathered, casually, with their chosen refreshments – mostly soft drinks, since it was not quite five PM and time to open the bar properly. Fortunately, there was a coin-op soda dispenser.

"Hey, Ricardo!" That was Roman Gonzalez, the construction contractor, a key pillar of the Gonzalez-Gonzalez clan, as well as one of Luna City's main employers. "I didn't know you were a part of this ruckus!"

"I didn't know, either," Richard sighed. "But I am curious, just as a matter of course. Kate is caught up in it, so I suppose I'm involved, by extension."

"Kate just called," Joe said, from the bar. "She's on the way. I thought she might want to be in on this. Uncle Harry's on his way in with Lew, so we'll give them all five or ten minutes."

"I still don't know what this is all about," Richard dug out change from his pockets and got himself a plain ginger ale. "Robbie said you'd gotten something sent express from Allen Lee in California."

"I have," Joe nodded. "The pictorial results from the reconstruction of our mystery skull." Joe looked tired. He sat at the head of the impromptu conference table, with an opened FedEx envelope at his hand. "I'd like to wait for the others, if you don't mind – show you all at once." At that moment, one of the doors opened, admitting Kate, borne on a gust of winter breeze that sent her oversized trench coat swirling like the cloak of a medieval hero.

"Hi, Joe!" she gasped, "I got here as fast as I could! Rich!" Those beryl-green eyes of hers lit up in a blaze of happiness, and Richard felt his own heart – still exercised from the bicycle ride from the Café – beat a little faster. "I didn't know you'd be here!"

"All the better," Richard couldn't think of anything else to say. He grubbed in his pocket for more change. "What's your pleasure, my Kate of Kate Hall?"

"Coke, please," Kate answered, and Richard – feeling that this was a kind of irrevocable step – nerved himself up to drop a brief kiss on Kate's forehead as he handed her the cold aluminum can.

"Thanks, sweetie," she answered, planting a return kiss on his cheek in return. "I am so out of breath! Best not tell anyone how I busted the speed limit in getting here, Joe."

"What the eyes don't see," Joe said, and he and Jess exchanged a wry smile. Richard was almost afraid to meet the knowing glances of everyone else in the room; the first time that he and Kate had demonstrated exclusive affection before an audience. But at that moment, Harry Vaughn and Lew Dubois came in from the other door. Through the bank of windows at the back of the VFW, Richard caught a glimpse of Harry's little tin cockleshell of a motorboat, drawn up on the shallow sloping bank. Ah, yes, he knew that little boat painfully well. Harry and Lew must have been out on the river in it, surveying the progress of Mills Farm's new expansion from the viewpoint of a boat on the water.

"You've got the final facial reconstruction from Doc Sommers?" Harry demanded, almost before the door closed behind him. "Let's take a look!"

"Get a drink of your choice and take a seat," Joe replied, tersely, and such was his authority and their own curiosity that everyone obeyed, even Jess, who had Little Joe cuddled against her shoulder. The baby, mercifully, was in his slumbering mode, eyes tightly closed, and a scowl on his infant countenance which was comically the very expression that Joe had on his. "All right then; this briefing is open, now that everyone is present. I'll be letting Allen Lee know, regarding what has transpired here.

It's his right, since he footed the bill for this; a not inconsiderable sum, considering that he paid for the time and expertise of a master of the craft."

"Worth every cent," Harry Vaughn murmured with a nod. Meanwhile Joe took out a thick folder from the envelope and dealt out a single sheet of heavy paper to all present; a sheet of thick paper, enough to carry a high-resolution photograph, and to a selected few of them – Kate, Sylvester, Harry and Lew – a small thumb-drive.

"This is our guy," Joe said. "Katie, I have all of the professor's pics on a thumb-drive for the *Beacon,* and for those of you who are internet savvy and have a lot of contacts. Honestly, I don't think more than a dozen people in Karnes County will recognize him from this, being that our guy was in the area more than seventy years ago, but it's a start. I'm thinking of spreading the word far and wide. Sometimes we get lucky. What do you think, people?"

Richard looked down at the photograph laying on the tabletop before him, trying to gather his thoughts; yes, a splendidly human, lifelike representation, indeed. A heavy-browed face, furrowed with the lines of hard living and harder luck, gouged along the right cheek and forehead with a massive scar, which subtly twisted the angle of the nose and the lie of those narrow lips, as well as denting in the mans' forehead. The reconstruction artist was sufficiently a master of the craft to limn the eyes with a haunted expression and visualize the subject with an indifferent shave and thinning gray hair, as lank as frost-killed weeds.

"I'll show this to Abuelita," Kate was the first to speak. "And to Miss Letty, too. Poor fellow…"

"He looks like every wino I've seen with a cardboard sign, begging on a big-city street-corner and claiming to be a veteran," Joe said. He drew out another folder and passed out another photograph to each. "Now, look at this. The professor did another version; what the Scar-faced Tramp probably looked like sixteen or seventeen years before, without the scar."

"Nice!" Kate breathed, and Jess nodded silently. For some reason, Richard wondered if Jess was about to weep. This picture – based on the very same skull – presented as a very young man, little more than a boy, although with the same rather heavy brow and narrow, sensitive lips. His face was smooth, unscarred, clean-shaven, short dark hair parted in the center and combed neatly. The reconstruction expert had added a telling detail; a high-collared military tunic with the military insignia of the American Marine Corps.

"One of our boys," Harry Vaughn said at last, and Lew Dubois nodded silently. Joe cleared his throat, as Sylvester murmured, "A fellow Marine. We don't leave our own behind, ever." Sylvester, like Joe and his uncle – were veterans as well.

"We didn't opt for doing an analysis of his tooth enamel to determine geographic origins. That's expensive and takes a little bit longer. Might come to that, eventually, though. But Allen Lee and the professor both think that these a good enough to get us started."

"So, what is the plan now, Chief?" That was Chris – almost the first words he had spoken.

"It's this," Joe replied. "Allen Lee already has his part and knows what to do with it. Roman; show this to Abuelita Adeliza, and all the others you can think of who might be old enough to have seen the Scar-faced Tramp. Long-shot, I know. Kate; take this all to Acey at the *Beacon*, write him up a story to go with these pictures that plays *"Abide With Me"* on the heartstrings. Hell, send it out to the regionals; *Express News* in San Antonio, the *Houston Chronicle*, the Dallas-Fort Worth papers. Maybe the national press will pick it up. You never know. Now – I'm going to distribute this to some of the local police departments. Yeah, I'm sure they'll drop everything to go back into their booking records from fifty years ago and search for a match. But you never know. If I have time, I'll drive over to Beeville, and burn an afternoon or two, seeing what I can find in their old arrest records. Now, you guys," Joe turned his regard to

Chris and Sylvester. "You put this out to your mil-vet social media networks, everyone that you are in, or know of. *Dysfunctional Veterans, Uncle Sam's Misguided Children* – the lot. Ask your friends, their friends, friends-of-friends and people they have barely heard of. I know this guy's service was so long ago that most people think of World War I as a legend happening about the time of the dinosaurs ..."

"Hey, Joe – this is part of our Knowledge!" Sylvester protested.

"Cast a net wide enough, you'll draw up something, for sure," Harry Vaughn noted, with satisfaction. "What about us, Joe?"

"Work your network of old retired law enforcement officers," Joe replied, promptly. "Look, I know some of your old pals must be getting bored as hell playing golf and yarning about the old days. Rope them in and get them to work on it: our guy, where he came from, who he was, how he finished up doing odd jobs and living in a tent in winter. What you said about casting a net. Now, Lew ..." Joe turned his regard on Lew Dubois. "We need you to do the same, with your corporate contacts and interests. You got friends in France ... all over the world. You never know what might turn up. It's a gamble – a game on the roulette table, where you spread a lot of little bets across the table, knowing that the number will come up, somewhere. This is a list of mine and everyone elses' email addresses, or number for a text message. Keep us all informed, of whatever you find, as soon as you find it." Joe dealt out a final round – half sheets of paper with a list of contacts on it, even Richard's.

"Understood," Lew gathered up his share of photographs, list, and thumb-drive. "*Mon vieux*, I have friends in far places, and some of them devoted to obscure areas of knowledge. I will send them this ... and see what we have, once we have cast our bread upon the waters."

"Good," Joe gathered up the two folders, and Richard – out of sense of pique, since he was the only one present not tasked with a mission – asked, "What shall I do then?"

"Keep the coffee and the cinnamon rolls coming," Joe replied, with a grin that quite took the sting out of it. "The Café is now the command post for this. Hope you don't mind, Ricardo. From now on, anyone who comes up with anything, send a message out to the group and meet at the Café at 9 AM sharp to brief the others."

"Thanks, I think," Richard couldn't help feeling a little sour over this.

Lew Dubois chuckled and said, "The great Napoleon, he said that an army marches on its' stomach. For this, my dear Richard, our enterprise marches on your coffee and a bounteous supply of your delightful cinnamon rolls."

"Mine marches on a good English breakfast fry-up and tea strong enough to trot a mouse over," Richard answered, to a general chuckle, and everyone gathered up their copies of stuff. As they went out one of the two doors, Richard managed to say to Kate, his bonny, fearless Kate, whose' first spoken words in her life had been, *'Why?'* "Come over to my place for supper, as long as you're in town?"

"Sure!" His beautiful, beryl-eyed Kate replied, although with something of an absent expression, and Richard said, with a small sigh,

"The internet reception is fine, out at the campground this week. You can work, as I cook for you, Kate of Kate Hall."

"Fantastic," Kate replied, absently, her eyes were already far away; Richard could only suppose that she was already writing the heart-string tugging story in her head, but then Kate seemed to shake herself and look at him with her regular attention. "Really – it would be fantastic. What are you going to fix for supper?"

"Something simple," Richard answered. "An omelet, with salad?"

"Perfect!" Kate beamed with such a heartfelt expression that all of Richard's resentment over being relegated to food and drink support vanished utterly.

On the River in Spring

"Ramona," said Lew Dubois on the afternoon of a day which had begun cool and foggy, but which had the promise by afternoon of being fair, cool and bright, "Take messages from everyone who calls, save from my wife and the children. I wish to spend another afternoon on the river, examining the work done – and I must be able to consider matters without distraction."

"Yes, Lew," his senior assistant and executive secretary replied, veiling her mild annoyance that Lew would be out of pocket during regular business hours yet again. Ramona had come to VPI's corporate office some fifteen years previously, with the highest possible recommendations from an agency which specialized in providing experienced and bonded C-level staff to a select corporate clientele. She had never quite become accustomed to Lew Dubois' penchant for informality, to the extent of routinely spending one morning a week *(when matters allowed)* in the Country Kitchen restaurant, bussing tables, or taking orders, out with the golf-course or garden maintenance crews, mowing the grass or digging holes for new plantings … or other, even more lowly work.

Her previous executives had been nothing like that. Ramona would never forget the occasion when another director from the Houston main office called for Lew and would not accept her adamant assurances that Mr. Dubois was unavailable, and could she take a message? Eventually, she had to admit that Mr. Dubois helping to run a mechanical snake though a blocked sewage outfall from one of the guest cottages.

"What shall I tell anyone who persists in asking where you are?" Ramona entertained the faint home that Lew would be doing something … something not embarrassing.

"On the river, dear friend Ramona – examining the work done so far on the boathouse and the stables. And then, I think I will go into town with Harry, and observe progress on the hotel renovation."

"You know, Lew," Ramona ventured; she had become confident in being equally informal with Lew, "You have people whose job is to make reports to you. You don't need to waste time seeing for yourself; you're a manager!"

"Ah, but the time is never wasted, *chère* Ramona. Besides seeing matters for myself, I find that they are more willing to speak honestly when I am there, with my feet in the mud, and my hands dirty – just so as they are. It is how I have always managed – how I have built two of VPI's grandest properties – and you will help me to build a third, *n'est-ce pas?* By managing my office so that I may manage by walking around. Be at ease. I shall return no later than half-past four, and I will keep my telephone turned on."

"Yes, Lew," Ramona acquiesced gracefully. She had worked for Lew in the Houston office for several uneventful years, to their mutual satisfaction. Starchy, middle-aged, given to dress for the office in very correct skirt suits and sensible shoes, Ramona was nonetheless a secret reader of the most lady-like romance novels, and privately made weak in the knees by a man speaking with a deliciously French accent, besides being a supremely capable star in the VPI firmament. Lew stepped into his private office, made a single terse phone call, and donned his barn coat, slipping his more than usually elaborate tablet phone into the biggest pocket, and departed, whistling.

It was all going very well, even with the delay of a month, caused by discovering the bones of that poor unfortunate. A sad thing, but Lew was a man with many fish to fry and pots to tend, as Grand-père Lucien was wont to say, and quite capable of keeping a very good eye on all of them. Now Lew walked quickly down through Mills Farm, noting both routine preparations in hand for spring, and those in hand for the planned expansion; a new roadway and additional gardens, to lavishly adorn the grounds and perpetuate the illusion that such had always been 'just so' at Mills Farm, a row of young and soon-to-appear mature native trees, some artfully-arranged thickets of shrubs and flower-meadows, all to beautify the short road leading toward the new recreational facilities – a road designed with equal art to suggest that the distance was actually somewhat greater than it was.

Past the Country Store, and the restaurant, past the rebuilt Riverbank Cottage, and along to where there was a new and expanded dock – built as part of the expanded riverine excursion program, to be offered in the coming summer. Harry Vaughn waited patiently there in his little aluminum motorboat, the boat rocking gently on the clear green water.

"How's it going these days?" Harry asked

"Very well, *mon vieux*," Lew replied, stepping carefully from dock to boat, settling himself on the center seat. "And if not – it soon will be. I have only to say the word – and sometimes only to appear sorrowful, that I have been let down by those in whom I have placed such trust."

"No one writes a ticket for a guilt trip quite like you do, you sneaky old bastard," Harry said, pulling the cord to prime the motor, which caught with a roar and a sudden gust of gray smoke, then idled under Harry's expert hands to a relatively quiet hum. "All right then – let's go take a closer look at your new facilities. They looked damn good, when I came down-river."

"Excellent," Lew beamed. "Even with the delay in beginning … I have been told that construction of the stables is ahead of schedule, and the boathouse is nearly on time."

"Promising a generous completion bonus for every day ahead of the contracted schedule does have results," Harry snorted. "Again – you are one sneaky old bastard."

"A bonus, like a sentence of being shot at dawn the following morning, concentrates the mind of man most wonderfully," Lew observed. Harry chuckled. "They've finished the dock, so we can put in, and walk around a bit. You've got a lot riding on this, haven't you?"

"Not as much as I had on the Castle Mountain project," Lew replied. "At least with this, my old, there is an established resort of much beauty and appeal. It is if I am overseeing the quiet nip and tuck, and the work of a brilliant new stylist for an aging beauty of the silver screen. The aging beauty has appeal; I merely oversee renewing it."

The little boat chugged around a bend in the river, past a sweep of water-burnished gravel, where a couple of feather-leaved cypress trees dipped knobby knees into the shallows, where tiny fish hatchlings and tadpoles squirmed and darted in the sun-warmed and stone-bottomed pool, in water that reflected the golden of the sandstone where currents never vexed or chilled. Lew could see them plain, from the boat at idle in the deeper water; such a marvelous sight – and how marvelous to share, like the twilight spectacle of fireflies later in the spring, darting among the deep grass and the taller shrubs like animated sparks of lightening.

Now, Harry steered his little cockleshell around the farther bend, to within sight of the muddy slope where the fresh new wood of a dock ran out into the water, and the bones of a new structure sprang from the steep slope above.

"A note," Lew spoke into his cellphone. "Ensure that the wood of the dock and boathouse are suitably aged, before and after final painting. Consider duck-egg green as the final color for the boat house." He observed Harry shaking his head in mock-despair. "Details – the Devil resides among them. Now, shall we alight and consider this aspect on my new project? We hope to open formally at the time of Spring Break – to appeal to the younger set, of course."

"The younger set want to go carouse and screw at the beach," Harry grunted, cynically. "Can't blame them much for that – it's all that I wanted when I was eighteen and dumb and full of …"

"Perhaps," Lew shook his head. "But I remain convinced there are those of our children who are not so enchanted by such. A romantic age … they yearn for the ideal, for perfect romantic love, and yet the world conspires to make them feel ashamed for admitting such. The 19th century has certain charms, *mon vieux*. Even the bare suggestion of the old verities – proprieties, politesse, of the old way of conduct between men and woman – these may yet suffice to influence. We … you and I – we have lived long and seen much. This place – this blessed parcel called Luna City – has seen even more. We should remember, my old friend, and bend every effort into recalling those memories and more to the young. They have nothing, aside from silly, trivial, and passing matters – the modern scourge of social media, whatever silly prank they are encouraged to by their equally silly friends, a trivial romantic fling, forgotten by the next morning. We should take the time to show them what endures; otherwise, what are we?"

"A shadow, a rag, fretting himself from day to day…" Harry angled in the boat toward the new-built and solid dock. He tied up the boat with the absentminded skill of a lifetime of expertise, and he and his passenger stepped ashore. Lew looked around with the visionary gaze of one seeing the final product in this scrambled miscellany of half-reassembled structure, of muddy and churned-up earth, and of the construction vehicles parked haphazardly close by. Harry only spat into the nearest clump of straggling, frost-killed brown grass and observed, "Not much to show so far, Lew."

"Ah – but the possibilities!" the other man exclaimed, as he looked around in delight. "Imagine this, my friend – a pleasant greensward, suitable for picnics … a game of croquet, perhaps …" he spoke briefly into his cellphone, adding another note-to-self, which Ramona would later transcribe fully and faithfully. "A breath of the past, and a nod to the present and future …'Allo, Roman! How goes the work today, my friend?"

"Swimmingly," Roman – the construction boss, and responsible for just about all the building projects, large and small, in the vicinity of Luna City *(and even as far as Beeville)* – tucked a small spiral notebook under his arm and surveyed the worksite with guarded satisfaction. "The roofers have started on the stable building. If we are finished here by Saturday, they can move on to this building without wasting a day. All the better for your schedule, Lew?"

"Indeed," Lew replied, open and cheerful of countenance. "Your fellows are doing splendidly, Roman. They say that Texas is of the South, but I say – not so. Texas hustles, whereas the South, for all its many charms, is languid, leisurely. Not to criticize; seeing life and all its charms without hurry, but it is refreshing; to see that work is accomplished on time and on schedule."

"Well, yeah," Roman answered. "We have a reputation to keep up. It's not like we're the only construction firm in the county, ya know? What do ya think so far?"

"I reserve opinion until I have seen the stables," Lew replied, with a touch of austerity. "But the boathouse will be the centerpiece of our publicity when we open the expansion ... to the stables, then."

"Good – got your hard hats?" Roman answered. "Good – better put them on. Ya wouldn't want to get beaned by a guy dropping something. Ruin your whole day, that would."

There was already a finished driveway, curving up around the back of the boathouse, past an area marked off by flags on short stakes driven into the ground, and two workmen industriously tamping level a stretch of sand. A half-dozen pallets of bricks were stacked at the edge; this would be the permanent parking area.

The stable building stood on the top of the low rise in the bend of the river, where once the old Sheffield mansion had been; a series of paddocks and corrals now ran nearly to the border fence with the Age of Aquarius. A few curious goats lingered on the Age side, eyeing the lush and new-green grass longingly, as Roman, Lew and Harry strolled along the muddy track which the passage of many vehicles had gouged in the clay-like mud during the months of construction. A new utility road ran out to Route 123, which would service the stables and the boathouse discretely through an employee-only gate. At the moment, that gate enabled Roman's crew to come and go without disturbing the regular guests at Mills Farm. The new metal panels on the stable roof gleamed like silver in the watery spring sunshine, and the regular pneumatic-bang sound of a nail-gun floated distantly down the hill.

"Looking good," Harry remarked admiringly. "Going with the classic red with white trim, I see."

"It's what the guests expect," Lew explained, eyeing the painters at their efficient work, as the three men approached the new stables. "And it looks as much like the barn at the main enclosure."

The barn at the main enclosure served as shelter for the various petting zoo animals on the ground level, while the hayloft level housed

Mills Farm's supremely efficient security department. This new place was intended for horses and ponies, their feed, their comforts, their tack and saddles. Right now, it smelled of fresh paint, and new-cut lumber.

"Ten horses, half as many ponies," Lew waved a careless hand at the stalls, beautifully archaic, fitted out with wood and wrought-iron mangers. The only thing missing was a scatter of straw and wood-shavings on the floor, and the horses themselves. "To start with, of course. Room for expansion, when demand increases. We'll move man-camp trailers up here, to house the horse-excursion staff. With the animals, best to have a few employees close at hand." He paused to admire the hand-wrought hinges on the nearest door. "This looks very good, Roman – a local source, I trust?"

"Got an enthusiast non-profit in Goliad to do those," Roman answered. "Bunch of old guys, love blacksmithing, and beating iron into anything useful. They did those, and a lot of the other fittings. Look good enough to be in a museum, don't they?" Something fell with a heavy thump and a metallic clatter on the roof above, attended by a heartfelt outburst in emphatic Spanish. Roman muttered under his breath and shouted a question in that same language. The answer floated back down; Roman looked relieved. "Just dropped his nail-gun," he explained. "Sounded worse from down here, though. Glad I reminded you about helmets?"

"Yeah," Harry answered. "But it's all good, as long as there's no blood."

Meanwhile, Lew murmured a few notes into his cellphone. Now he said, "All good, *mon vieux* Roman. Unless we are sidelined by abject misfortune, I anticipate that we shall be able to stage the grand opening in time for Spring Break."

"Good," Roman nodded, with a somewhat abstract expression, his mind already on other things. Lew and Harry took their courteous departure, and picked their way down the hill, toward the boat house, and the dock with Harry's little motorboat bobbing gently in the current.

"Nice little place," Harry commented with a nod toward the boat house; a two-story confection built out over the waters' edge, with three garage-like bays at water level, and a generous exterior staircase along one side and angling up the back to an open-sided pavilion on the second level. A shallow hipped roof crowned with an onion-domed tower and a weather-vane completed the vision. "New-build, or relocated?"

"New-build," replied Lew. "Copied exactly from an original on an estate on the shores of Lake Mackinac. Dates from 1912. We're going to call it the 1912 Boathouse. Not terribly creative, I know – but my wife has designed a most enchanting logo for it. Ah, my old – you cannot imagine the satisfaction from having achieved the ultimate victory in a project such as this!"

"I can imagine," Harry mused, in Sahara-dry tones, as he stepped into his little boat, and busied himself with unwrapping the mooring rope from the completely authentic forged-iron ring which secured it. "Must be rather like the feeling I had, arresting a waste-of-flesh perp for bashing some innocent grandmother over the head and shoulders for the cash and credit cards in her handbag, leaving the poor old girl in a wheelchair for the rest of her life, afraid to venture out of her own home – and watching the scumbag get locked up for thirty years as a serial menace. There's a mighty load of personal satisfaction to be had in taking out the trash; a job well done is what I used to tell myself."

"Indeed," Lew agreed with a sigh. "We both deal with housekeeping, my old friend."

"That we do," Harry fired up the motor, with a couple of expert pulls, and steered the boat out into the center of the river, and around the next bend. This bend afforded the deepest and most popular location for swimming; a traditional locale for the youth of Luna City over the previous half-century and more. It was too early in the year and still too cold for anyone to indulge in that pastime. Come summer, and temperatures at a high in the eighties at the very least – there would be bathers splashing around in that pool.

Slowly the cockle-shell tin boat worked its' way upstream, past the cream-colored tower of Straw Castle Aquarius, rising triumphant on another gentle rise, attended by an attentive grove of oak trees, the clattering windmill, and the colorful banners, fluttering in the slight breeze.

"A charming place," Lew observed. "And an interesting enterprise. By all logic, it should not exist, but still…"

"Damn hippies," Harry grunted. "Stink up the place, wherever they go."

"The Grants are an exception," Lew protested, mildly. "They are neighbors of the most charming and accommodating spirit. Yes, eccentric in their way; such is the spice of an ordinary life. They are the touch of garlic, or truffle, which enlivens the whole dish."

"Truffle and garlic both stink," Harry insisted, and Lew shrugged, a particularly Gallic gesture which might have signified either agreement or otherwise. The distant crowing of one of the Grants' roosters, and the scream of a pea-fowl serenaded them, over the gentle rumble of Harry's outboard motor, until they rounded another bend.

Presently, the spires of the First Methodist Church, the square bell-tower of Saints Margaret and Anthony, and the dome of the Cattleman Hotel rose before them, standing proud and tall from a huddle of lower rooftops and trees freshly-green with new spring leaves. Harry steered the boat to a place where the bank fell steeply from the area in back of the Tip-Top Icehouse, Gas and Grocery, a bank reinforced with concrete slabs. There was sufficient space to tie up the boat, and step ashore, although some slabs were smeared with the clay-like local mud, which made footing perilous.

"I left the truck here," Harry said. "Save us a hike."

"You're living in town now, aren't you?" Lew ventured, and Harry nodded.

"Renting the Abernathy place on Oak Street, now that Jess and Joe are settled into the Vaughn's old house. Suits me fine, not having to shovel snow in Moose Pass and keep the lights burning, all of a winter long. Splendid place, but the long winters finally got to me. And I wanted to be close to family, after all this time."

"So do we all, *mon vieux*," Lew climbed up into the passenger seat of Harry's pickup, now adorned with Texas license plates, although there was still a peeling *Alaska – The Last Frontier* bumper sticker on the tailgate, next to a newer one that said, *Here, Fishy, Fishy!* "My old, shall I buy you a drink at the V, on the way back?"

"You read my mind," Harry grinned.

The side of the Square in front of the Cattleman was fenced off, reserved for workmen's trucks, and deliveries of building materials; bricks, lumber both plain and fancy, industrial-sized buckets of paint, sacks of plaster, grout and cement, sheetrock by the pallet, and other contents too obscure of purpose to be identified by the casual observer. A gridwork of scaffolding masked at least half the façade, while the part not obscured stood revealed in the afternoon sunshine as clean and polished; bandbox new, as of from the hands of the original builder. Donning their safety gear, Harry and Lew strolled in through the door-less opening, Lew explaining as they did so, strolling through the lobby, now shrouded with hanging sheets of thick plastic,

"We sent the oak doors to a specialist, to be refinished, and have the stained-glass panels re-leaded. Alas, my old – the work required will not be accomplished any sooner than autumn, at least. The condition of the electrics!" Lew made another one of those Gallic gestures, this one of amused despair. "It is miraculous that the place was not set on fire by an electrical malfunction. Mr. Gonzales' electrician has become most devout in his religious observances, since he came to work on this project! The condition of the plumbing; inadequate beyond the imagination to handle new in-suite bathrooms on every floor. Of course. I did not expect otherwise. I can guarantee that the public rooms will be finished by the Founders' Day observances, but the third and fourth floors must be stripped down to the studs in order to accommodate the new installations. Fortunate for us that they were originally plain and unadorned … but the ballroom will be the work of months alone!"

"What about the bar? That's the part of the Cattleman that all the old-timers cared about most, you know."

"Ahh," Another Gallic shrug from Lew. "The ground floor is the priority, my old. The walnut paneling, the fittings – most magnificent. The bar shall be the show-place, so I insisted that an effort be made. Shall we see what has been done? They put up a temporary door, to keep the dust out, now that the paneling has been reinstalled." He led the way through a utilitarian door in a wall roughed out of plain plywood, and they stood in the pillared entrance to the bar – which contrary to Harry Vaughn's unvoiced and low expectations – looked perfectly splendid.

The work here was nearly done; only one worker doing touch-ups to the paint on those walls which were unadorned plaster, and another, atop a tall ladder, assembling light fixtures of a suitable archaic design, and creamy-gold matte glass lampshades. Which, when finished and lit – would cast an atmospheric light on the ornate bar, the mirrored back-bar, all set about with swooping curves and ornaments of carved Circassian walnut – mottled and tiger-striped in shades of rich brown and gold, lacquered and polished to a high sheen. The back-bar, eventually to be piled high with serried ranks of cut-glass tumblers, and bottles of expensive liquor, was a thing of High Victorian glory, even empty.

"I gotta hand it to you, Lew," Harry spoke at last. "I had no notion of how good this old place might look. No wonder your predecessor wanted to buy it all for a song, knock it down and move the whole show to Mills Farm."

"A man of good taste, but little tact and judgment," Lew replied, austere in condemning his predecessor in management by several degrees. "He knew well what a gem this place might be, but wrenched from its proper setting, and trampling over the wishes of your good people? It is a failing in managers of a certain persuasion, my old; to see the objective, but not that one must necessarily work with people, patiently as a skilled artist does with paints. Now, visualize how this room will perform, by this time a year from now! We will have restaurant service – for the dining room, and for those tables in here nearest the windows. Our guests will dine on the finest, regard your beautiful Square and retire to their rooms upstairs, in perfect contentment, as they look forward to a day spent on the water, along the trail. Mills Farm will be the destination extraordinaire, as Castle Mountain has been, as the Chateau always was."

"One thing," Harry mused, "Have you mentioned to Richard at the Café … about your plans for a world-class kitchen here? Or even – Stevie-boy Wyler?"

"No, I have not," Lew replied, settling his safety helmet more firmly on his head. "But I will – when the time is ripe."

Spring Newsletter

Spring 2018 Newsletter

Luna City Chamber of Commerce

5 North Town Square, Suite 4
Check out our Facebook Page

Mills Farm holds their traditional annual Easter Egg hunt on the lawn and gardens below the Mills Farm Dance Hall on Saturday, March 31, at 10:00 AM. This year marks the 45th anniversary of this event, which began on the Saturday before Easter in 1973. To mark the anniversary, Mills Farm will offer a bonus of ten golden eggs, hidden somewhere on the Easter Egg Hunt grounds, each egg containing tokens allowing the finder to claim a large, solid-chocolate egg and a variety of valuable prizes, including an all-expenses three-day paid stay at any Venue Properties resort in the continental United States, Mexico or Canada.

Spring Season of Luna City Players

The Luna City Players launch a new year of local drama with a special presentation of Oscar Wilde's classic comedy *The Importance of Being Ernest*, March 10, at 7:30 in the ballroom of the newly-refurbished Cattleman Hotel. President and long-time director of the Luna City Players, Patricia Pryor makes a rare on-stage appearance as the imperious Lady Bracknell. *The Importance of Being Earnest* was the first full-length play put on by the officially-organized Luna City Players, in November 1898. Until then, the Players had been known as the Lunatics, who performed in a variety of short skits, musical numbers, and farces. The ladies of the town desiring more elevated theatrical fair, they put their heads and considerable talents together under the leadership of Minnie Crane Bodie, the newly-wed wife of Gregson Bodie, who in her native Chicago was a mainstay of a local theatrical group – and the rest, as they say – is history.

Luna City, Texas – Home of the Mighty Fighting Moths

Upcoming Events

February 14

The Luna City Café & Coffee initiates regular dinner service Tuesday-Sunday evenings with a Sweethearts Dinner special!

February 21

A brief ceremony to observe President's Day will be held at the flagpole in front of the LCVFD & Police Department at 7:30 AM

March 10

Venue Properties Intl., opens their latest attraction, the 1912 Boathouse and Stables. Admission is free for those in appropriate early 20th century vintage costume.

Eagle Scout Project

Scout and member LCHS Class of '19, Robert Scott Walcott is raising funds to cover burial expenses for LCpl. Michael D. Walters, USMC, a veteran of the First World War, who died an indigent near Luna City, 1936.

Page 1 of 2

Luna City ISD News

Junior Firefighters

High school members of the Luna City Volunteer Fire Department have an opportunity to dress up in old-timey VFD uniforms and demonstrate use of the reconstructed steam-powered water pump, as part of festivities on March 10. This will take place on Town Square, as part of the grand re-opening of the public rooms at the historic Cattleman Hotel. Contact Captain Bodie if you are interested in participating, or becoming a junior member of the LCVFD .

Senior Spring Break Road Trip

The Luna City HS Class of '18 Senior Break Road trip is scheduled for March 26-29th. Our seniors will head off to Dallas-Fort Worth, by way of Austin and Waco. Visits are scheduled for the State Capitol in Austin, the Texas Ranger Museum in Waco, and the historic Fort Worth Stockyards. Permission slips must be signed and turned into the office by March 9.

Spring Job Fair

Local employers will have tables at the third annual summer job fair, in the gym on Friday, April 5 during lunchtime from 12:00-1:00. Information and applications for summer, part-time and full-time jobs with Mills Farm, the Wyler Ranch and the Karnesville Parks & Recreation, and other enterprises will be available to interested students.

Eagle Scout Public Service Project

Robert S. Walcott, a member of LCHS Class of '19 will be selling home-baked goods Monday through Friday outside the cafeteria at lunchtime. Robert is raising funds through this daily bake sale to pay for a memorial stone and proper burial for a WWI veteran found during recent excavations on Mills Farm's new extension. He will take special orders, to be delivered the following day.

Community Marketplace

Ground Floor Renovations Complete!

Renovations to the ground floor public rooms of historic Cattleman Hotel have been largely completed. The main lobby, saloon and the ballroom will be open on March 10 to the general public. Work continues on the guest rooms. The Cattleman will reopen as a hotel in January, 2019, under the management of Mills Farm/Venue Properties, International.

From Chief Vaughn, Luna City PD

Residents of Luna City and the near neighborhood are reminded that with the opening of the Mills Farm extension – especially with the open house on March 10, that traffic is expected to be heavy on Route 123 for the entire weekend. It is also spring break time. With the extreme popularity of Rockport, Corpus Christi and Padre Island for the 'Spring Break' crowd, Chief Vaughn warns everyone to expect more demonstrations of drunken juvenile idiocy on the roads than usual.

Valentine Dinner With Your Beloved

Richard at the Café opens regular dinner service with a special Valentine's Day menu on Wednesday, February 14th. Treat the one you love to one of Richards' special prix fixee four-course suppers

Five Men and a Baby

"The whole thing came up at the last minute," Joe Vaughn groaned. He sat at one of the picnic tables in back of the VFW, while a mild spring breeze stirred the leaves of the monumental sycamore tree overhead. Sitting in a monumental car-seat/baby carrier/rocker set on the table top, the infant Little Joe sucked on his tiny pink fist and regarded those gathered for guest night with eyes which had already gone as dark as blackberries. "I've been subpoenaed to testify in a court case – Monday in San Antonio. Not in Karnesville, which would be a walk in the park. God knows how long the trial will drag on; I guarantee I'll be sitting on my ass in the Bexar County Courthouse for a week, at least."

"I don't see what the problem is," replied Richard, sitting across from Joe, and nursing a very respectable ale produced by a local small brewer. *Really*, he reflected privately; *there were subtle advantages to this place, which no one coming from the outside would ever have considered.* It was guest night at the VFW. He was enjoying the ale, and the company of Joe, Chris, young Berto Gonzales (who had inadvertently delivered him to Luna City nearly two years previously) his cousin Sylvester, and Jerry Walcott, oldest scion of the new-money Walcotts, brother of Richard's occasional assistant cook, Robbie Walcott.

Joe sighed, heavily for dramatic effect. "Baby-sitting, Ricardo. Jess is away at the Methodist women's retreat as of yesterday – until next Sunday."

"So?" Richard sank another satisfying draft of ale and ventured a friendly wink at Little Joe, who merely chomped again on his baby fist and scowled in reply.

"Everyone – that is, every one of our female kin is also on that same retreat," Joe answered glumly. "Every single one of them. Even Miss Letty – she would advise me as to who would be a good fill-in. Pat and Araceli chose this weekend for a get-away to the coast for some relaxation, or I would ask them. Look, guys – this is Jess and mine own first-born child. Handing him off to strangers, or giggly teenagers every day all day for a week is just not an option."

"Tell me about it," Richard acknowledged in a morose tone of voice. Beatriz and Blanca were filling in adequately, as far as front-of-the-house service went, between giggling, with Luc and Robbie in the kitchen, but dammit, this was a disruption to his routine! Richard did not welcome disruptions or handle them gracefully when they occurred.

"What about your parents?" Berto asked, in a tone of voice which suggested an attempt at being helpful. Naïve, hapless – that was Berto, being helpful.

"Off on a Caribbean cruise," Joe replied, dolefully. "They flew out yesterday – not back until two weeks." He fetched up a deep sigh, from the very core of his being. "Screwed, blued and tattooed, guys. I need a babysitter for Little Joe, or else I take him into the Bexar County Courthouse every day and giving him to the bailiff to hold when I am called to the witness stand."

"What's the problem with that?" Berto asked, in genuine curiosity.

Joe sighed again. "Look, the bailiffs aren't there to do that job. Anyway, have you seen the stuff you have to take along with a baby? They search everything, just getting into the place. It will take me half the day just to get through security at the courthouse alone. God; think of the bugs that he would be exposed to! Just from being in that old building, with all those people! He's too young to be exposed to all those viral cruds; kindergarten is soon enough."

"They're so small," mused Sylvester, dapper in his usual retro-nerd wardrobe – today a pair of classic chinos and a fetching short-sleeved aloha shirt printed with images of palm trees, surfers, and pineapples. "Babies, I mean – but all their stuff! That takes up so much space!"

"Tell me about it," Joe grunted. Under the table was a diaper and sundries bag the size of a small steamer trunk.

"We could take care of him for you, Joe," Jerry Walcott was home in Luna City for the weekend; a gentle and competent late-twenty-something, who worked as a nurse at the Karnesville Medical Center. "Really," Jerry added, in serene response to the skeptical looks on the faces of the other men at the table. "I did my last rotation in pediatrics. It'll be a gas to look after a healthy kid. Serious, you guys."

"I can help," Berto offered, and in response to several questioning looks from those assembled, added "It's Spring Break. I gotta help Papi at the garage during the day, though."

"I'm done at the Tip-Top 'bout half-past five every evening," Chris ventured, thoughtfully. "Ricardo, you're free in the afternoons, aren't you?"

"Well…" Richard temporized. "I'm busy at the Café from about five in the morning until after lunch."

"We can do it in shifts," Sylvester pulled out a small spiral notebook. "When are you done at the hospital, Jerry?"

"Six AM," Jerry replied.

Richard protested, "Look, chaps, I don't know anything about caring for infants. I've barely worked up to having a cat."

"Nothing to it," Jerry answered. "Bottle at one end, clean diapers at the other, and keep them from being too hot or too cold."

"A piece of cake, as long as I don't confuse one end with the other," Richard meant to sound derisive, but both Berto and Jerry were impervious to sarcasm.

In any case, Sylvester was already mapping out a schedule. "Ok, five of us – we can cover the baby-sitting duties round the clock. Four hours and forty-five minutes each – no sweat."

In the space of five minutes and another round of drinks, Sylvester had worked out a rotation, while Jerry gave a swift demonstration of applying a bottle to the appropriate end of Little Joe and a diaper *(accompanied by hygienic wipes and sticky white diaper-rash ointment)* to the other. Berto and Sylvester volunteered to spend their nights at Joe and Jess's house for their shifts – "Hey, the kid can sleep nights in his own bed, 'kay?"

At around 6:30, when Jerry got home from the hospital, he would take Little Joe for nearly five hours. Then it would be Richard's turn, for the afternoon, until Chris finished at the Tip-Top. The plan had Chris delivering Little Joe home to Sylvester and Berto after supper, to begin the whole cycle again. Still, Joe's expression as he looked around the table and regarded his offspring, was torn between gratitude and worry.

"I owe you guys," he confessed at last. "But I dunno about handing him around like a hot potato. I mean, Jess will have a conniption fit..."

"Babies thrive on the stimulation," Jerry said. "And doesn't Jess take him with her, when does her client consultations?"

"Yes, but ..."

"I don't see the difference," Jerry said. "If he's used to it, he probably likes it."

Richard had a feeling that Joe didn't precisely agree, but in the face of a workable solution, he had no other choice.

"We'll start on Monday," Sylvester folded away his notebook, after writing down a copy of the schedule for everyone else. "Any questions?"

Richard briefly considered asking for release from the schedule, but then he considered Little Joe, and his own long-term plans to inculcate an appreciation for good food into a younger generation. *Really, how much younger could you get than a six-month old?*

This merited careful consideration, but when he asked it of the table, both Jerry and Joe laughed. "At this age? Rice cereal, and not much of it," Jerry replied, and Joe snorted.

"Mother's milk. No – really. The fridge is full. Jess began stocking up weeks ago."

"Moth – oh, I see," Richard considered that he had already looked enough of an idiot in front of the others; best now enjoy the weekend, before flinging himself into the baby-minding rotation.

He had nearly forgotten about it all; or at least, shoved the trepidations to the farthest and most neglected corner of his mental attic, when the Café's door opened and shut to a musical jingle, and Jerry appeared, with the baby – a tiny pink-faced morsel dwarfed by a monumental stroller. Richard could verily swear that he had seen smaller motorcycle sidecars. The enormous necessity bag was stowed at the back of the stroller. With some difficulty, Jerry maneuvered it through the dining room and into the kitchen. Richard was there alone; Robbie and the girls having capably dealt with the with the most immediate pressing post-lunch-rush chores and departed to their own infant-unencumbered lives.

"Here we are!" Jerry announced. "Little Joe is all ready to spend quality time with Chef Richard." He almost succeeded in concealing a yawn. "He's already had his midday bottle. You'll want to give him another just before five. It's in the side pocket of his diaper-bag with an ice-pack to keep cold. Just warm it up before you give it to him. Blood-warm is about the right temperature. Remember, how I showed you how to hold him for feeding? Yeah, that. Remember to burp him, when he's done and check his diaper, too. He'll probably poop again, just to make room for the fresh intake."

"What do I do with the little … little tyke until then?" Richard demanded. He had almost made himself forget his promised child-minding obligation.

"No idea," Jerry yawned again. "Talk to him. Play simple games, pay attention to him, stimulate his imagination. That is, when he isn't sleeping, eating, or pooping. Use your own … sorry … imagination. See you tomorrow, the same time. Chris will take over from you at five-thirty." Upon delivering this dispiriting intelligence, Jerry took himself out the door, the bell chiming musically at his departure. Little Joe and Richard looked at each other.

"Goosh," commented Little Joe, blowing a spit-bubble. It sounded philosophical; neither hostile or overly-affectionate.

"The same to you, my little man," Richard replied. That took care of the social niceties. "Look, young chappie-my-lad, you're a little young to become a kitchen apprentice. And I'm told that … well, you aren't quite old enough to start cultivating a sophisticated palate. How about just keeping me company while I prep for tomorrow?"

"Goob-gurgle," replied Little Joe with perfect amiability.

"Right then," Richard said, and fetched one of the three high-chairs from the front of the house, setting it up next to the big all-purpose table which served as prep-space. Summoning up all of his nerve and silently sending up a prayer to the heavens that he not inadvertently damage the little sprout in any way, shape or form – since Joe and Jess between them had the capacity and will to inflict horrific damage on anyone who harmed a single one of the barely-visible hairs on the head of their tiny offspring

– he lifted Little Joe from the stroller and settled him into the high chair. Regarding his handiwork, Richard thought the infant was sagging a little too far to one side in the chair, which would accommodate a much larger child. A pair of small cushions wedged in on either side of Little Joe did the trick. The two of them regarded each other solemnly across the worktable, and Richard continued his prepping for the following day's business.

"Cinnamon rolls," Richard ventured. "It's cinnamon rolls for tomorrow."

"Goo-goosh!" commented Little Joe, and Richard was heartened. *Didn't Jerry advise talking to the little sprout? Stimulate his development, or some such child-rearing mumbo-jumbo?*

"They're a mainstay at the Café, don't you know? Well, you should; I think your mum had one every morning. So, here's the dough for them. Been rising in the warmer for a couple of hours. Now, this is the mixture that goes onto the dough, once I have patted it out just so. Light on the flour, by the way…" he continued in this vein, as if he were explaining and training a new apprentice, as he worked the dough with the expertise of long practice, and the yeasty odor of newly-risen dough filled the workspace. Little Joe was even drooling a bit. "Pity you're just not old enough for a taste," Richard commiserated. "Never mind, Young Chum; soon enough, soon enough."

He had run out of prep-work to demonstrate to Little Joe well before five o'clock; for the last hour and a half of his stint, he pulled in a chair from the dining room, opened his trusty edition of Larousse, and read aloud from it to the child. It was impressive, the drama potential which could be invested in the chapter regarding the preparation of various kinds of court-bouillon. Little Joe did begin to fuss a bit, when Richard began on the varieties of crab and their preparation for various tasty dishes; *Oh, bottle-time.* Recalling how the bottle must be served up warm, Richard half-filled one of the smallest saucepans in the place with water and set it on the burner, just as a ripe odor began permeating the air. Richard swiftly ran the source to earth; it was strongest in the vicinity of Little Joe, now eyeing Richard with a reproachful expression.

"Sorry, Small Chum," Richard gasped, lifting the baby out of the chair – and there was a distinct, squishy feel around the child's bottom. Richard's left hand felt something soft, malleable ... and the stench intensified. "You might have waited!" Richard exclaimed. *Oh, god, he would have to deal with the unspeakable; changing a diaper!* And a more than usually disgusting one, from the feel and the smell. Holding Little Joe out before him, both hands firmly grasping the little wiggler around the chest, Richard made a run for the commodiously-equipped Ladies' lavatory in the Café – that facility four times larger and three times better-lit then the male equivalent. One of the additional benefits of the Ladies' *(in addition to a fully-lit makeup mirror and a full-sized chaise-lounge)* was a fold-out changing table, installed to address the very problem he faced at this moment.

Holding Little Joe one-handed, he put down the table, laid the child upon the surface, and begin striping off those abominably-saturated lower layers. Off came the lower-reaches of the onsie-stretchy-terry thing which was the infant's garment, which fastened up the front and down the legs in a series of snaps ... oh, god, they were hideously-soaked, about the lower margins, with a vile-smelling materiel which rather looked like yellow-tinted large curds of cottage cheese leaking out from the diaper. Richard stripped garment and diaper from the small, pink, wiggly infant and swabbed Little Joe's nether regions with dampened paper towels. *Oh, god, he had neglected to bring in the diaper bag, that fount of fresh, clean coverings!* And no, he could not leave the little wiggler unattended on the fold-out changing shelf in the Ladies' – by god, he could not! Little Joe might roll over, roll over and off the shelf, falling onto the floor ... and Joe and Jess would kill him for injuring their precious first sprout on the family tree. His reputation in Luna City would be utterly destroyed.

Richard took up the naked infant, holding him in one arm, praying desperately to all the powers that might or might not be, that there would be no more demonstrations of Little Joe's digestive system being in perfect yet smelly working order. He went out from the Ladies, grabbed the Brobagnignian-sized diaper bag with the other, and dragged it back to the Ladies'. Fresh diaper, fresh clean onsie – Richard set about reassembling the baby in his garments, realizing that he would have to take out the soiled diaper and paper towels to the outside dumpster, otherwise the disgusting reek rising from the trash receptacle would permeate the whole place. He prayed that the food safety inspector would not pick this particular moment to pay a visit.

Replacing Little Joe in the safe confines of the stroller, Richard rushed back to take out the Ladies' room bin, holding his breath as much as possible, then to wash his hands as per iron-clad kitchen-management practice. But a stink still lingered in the kitchen – a throat-catching stink of … burnt milk, and scorching plastic! He caught up a towel, cursing under his breath, and pulled the saucepan off the burner, cursing even more.

The saucepan with Little Joe's bottle in it had boiled dry, melting the bottom of the bottle, and covering the saucepan with a volcanic mixture of seething milk and bubbling plastic. Richard swore again. This was insupportable! Adding to the fraught atmosphere, Little Joe began whimpering.

"A minute, Small Chum!" Richard exclaimed, knowing to his own ears that he sounded desperate. Was there another bottle secreted in the depths of the bounteously bottomless diaper bag? Thank god, there was. But this one was only half-thawed! Resolving to pay better attention this time, Richard filled another saucepan, settled the second bottle into it, and decided that there was no other way to comfort the little wriggler, other than to pick him up from the stroller, and hold him while the new bottle warmed.

"There, there, Small Chum – not so bad, is it?" Richard settled into the chair from the dining room, hoping that this would suffice to comfort the baby. Which it did, for a few minutes, anyway. Blast! Little Joe scowled, looking more and more like his father in a very bad mood. "Look, Small Chum – maybe some more about *crab a la bretonne*? All right, then." Tucking the infant into the crook of his left arm, Richard opened up Larousse with his right, and began to read, giving proper RADA dramatic intonation to the words.

Alas, Larousse was not quite the soothing influence it had been all afternoon. Little Joe's unhappiness became ever more marked. Richard got up several times to check on progress of the bottle-warming. Turn up the flame higher – and speed the warming process! No; the disgusting remains of the previous attempt still sat in the bottom of the main sink. *God, that saucepan might very well be ruined!* Richard went from sink, to stove, to chair, pleading under his breath for peace and understanding to the infant balanced in his other arm, and read some more Larousse to Little Joe.

At least that seemed to be working. And in the fresh saucepan, the water burbled gently. Richard plucked forth the bottle, shook it, and turned the business end of it toward the inside of his wrist – that wrist attached to the arm cradling Little Joe, who eyed with bottle with gluttonous interest as it came within his near-sighted baby vision. Victory – the milk within was blood-warm, as he squeezed the bottle and splashed a small spurt against his wrist. Richard settled into the dining room chair, remembering to hold the bottle at the proper angle, while Little Joe sucked with energy. How readily those lips resembled a carps', closed around the bottle nipple, suctioning out the nourishment within!

Maybe this baby-sitting job couldn't be so hard as all that. Warm, fed, change out where they had crapped … sort of like a cat, save that Ozzie was rather more self-cleaning. Richard, sitting in the Café kitchen, with the comfortable, warm, and pliable weight in his arm, experienced a fleeting sense of … what was that – contentment? A kind of fulfillment enveloped him. Really, wasn't this a kind of human core experience? Caring for the helpless young of the species, nurturing, caring, training them up in the proper paths …

And then Chris came in through the back door of the Café, exclaiming, "Jesus, Rich – what is that godawful smell?"

"I can't think what the hell you mean!" Richard answered.

Chris chuckled, in an insultingly knowing manner. "Yeah, you do – ya let the bottle fry, and had to change a diaper. God, what a stench. Like a *hadji* latrine. Is Vaughn-Junior ready to ride? OK, I'll take him as-is. Never mind about the burping. We're gonna go for my nightly run. He'll get all the good burping he needs – k'ay, Little Trooper? Knew you would! See ya tomorrow, Ricardo – same time, same baby-sitting station!"

"Gush-goob!" Richard heard faintly from the stroller, as it vanished with Chris out the front door. Chris must have walked from the Tip-Top, a distance of only two blocks or so, since he did not hear the sound of a car engine. The Café seemed suddenly empty, as empty as Town Square, drowsing in the late afternoon sunlight.

Richard closed up the Larousse, suddenly feeling about a decade older than he had a mere half a day ago. He put the mutilated saucepan to soak, spent a few moments tidying up, and opened a few of the transoms over the tall windows, in order that the place might air out a bit, overnight. Being spring, it was not yet so warm as to require the air conditioning to work around the clock, although that time was coming, and coming soon, if the lushly-blooming wildflowers along the verge of Route 123 were anything to go by. Faintly, from the apartment windows in the Mercantile Building, the sound of Luc at his drums floated out into the mild spring air. He locked the back door, whistled for Ozzie, who appeared as if by magic from underneath the hedge that separated the back of the Café from the Stein's tiny garden. Ozzie hopped nimbly up into the plastic crate bungee-corded to the back of Richard's trail bike, and Rickard swung a leg over the saddle. His day was done. Now for the commute home to the Age of Aquarius.

This, Richard thought, as he pedaled the brief few blocks toward the outskirts of Luna City, was almost his favorite time of the year. All was lush and green, the meadows and verges strewn with wildflowers; pink primroses, purple wild verbena, and dark blue and white bluebonnets. The scattering of fruit-trees in the backyards of sprawling residences – some of them mere double- or triple-wide trailers – were also in clouds of bloom; white ornamental pear, pink-and-white apple blossom, dark-pink plum. The sky arched above, a pure blue, shading toward pink and golden in the west, where the sun was sliding down toward the horizon. A few clouds floated in that sky, clouds trimmed around their edges with a narrow rim of gold, where the setting sun inflamed them.

Richard pedaled around the edge of Town Square; his heart lifted once again at the sheer aesthetic beauty of the place. Pure late Victorian Beaux-Arts, a harmonious symphony in brick, tile, glass, with carved stone embellishments, and all the civic grace notes that a proud little town could provide, back in the day. He was reminded again of the saying that in America, a hundred years was a long time, and in England, a long distance. There were so many plummy-voiced intellectuals who – in his experience of watching various television programs – had poured elaborate scorn upon late Victorian civic sensibilities. Yet, Luna City Town Square remained a wonderfully harmonic, attractive, and most importantly – livable example of the best which that era had to offer. Human-scaled, pleasingly ornate, and leavened with the green space provided by the oak trees and lawn of the Square itself, by the hanging baskets of ferns and flowers offered by such public-minded mercantilists as the Steins, the Abernathys, and now the new leasees of the Cattleman hotel. Yes, this was his place, and he would defend it to … well, possibly not to the death, since Richard had a well-developed sense of self-preservation. But to the exhaustion of his capabilities as a relatively small cog in the wheel of commerce in Luna City…

To the edge of Luna City, in the golden late afternoon dazzle, Richard pedaled in a rising sense of satisfaction and hope for his next four days. Only four more to go. He followed his usual route, out past the VFW, the Tip-Top – and across Route 123, the McAllister house, standing severe and proud as Miss Letty, supervising the traffic over the bridge *(now that repairs were complete, all lanes were open, both north and south)* with a kindly, distant eye. The road boasted a generous macadam shoulder, sufficiently wide to accommodate a couple of bicyclists, and an equally generous green verge, starred with wildflowers wherever whoever had been charged earlier in the year with mowing them had missed a few stands. It heartened Richard do see that the mowing crews had gone around those stands where the wildflowers were thickest. Thus did Luna City, or those subcontractors working for the state road system, uphold their responsibilities toward nature.

A little south of the bridge, and halfway home, he overtook a solitary runner on the verge; a runner unmistakable at a distance for the blade prothesis on his left leg. Richard caught up level with him.

"Faster, faster – we're catching you up!"

Over his shoulder, Chris replied, genially but unprintably. Richard kept level with him – coasting on his bicycle.

"You talk like that in front of Little Joe? *Rockabye baby, or Daddy will spank, Mummy's at Aldershot, driving a tank … when the war is over, Mummy will return, and Oh, what a lot of new words you will learn!*" Little Joe, apparently lulled to sleep by the regular motion of Chris and his daily workout runs, did not reply, but Chris did.

"Hey, he likes this circuit. It burps him, and I have the benefit of running with additional weight. See you tomorrow, Ricardo. Hey, try not to fry any more bottles, will ya? Jess only has about eighty or a hundred of them in the freezer."

Richard favored him with a splendid one-hand gesture. "See you tomorrow, Young Chum," he called over his shoulder, as he put some energy into it, and pulled ahead. Never had the sight of the Straw Castle Aquarius, serene and glowing like a Chinese paper lantern on the oak-shaded hill, been more welcome, that and the tidy, non-smelly interior of the Airstream. It was like retreating to a cozy monks' cell. His spirits rose even further, for it was Monday, and Kate's little VW bug was already parked next to the Airstream.

Kate herself sat on the folding lounge chair, her sensible shoes kicked off. Ozzie leaped out of his traveling crate and ran up to her, launching from ground to her lap in one smooth, cat-leap.

"Ooof!" Kate remarked, as he landed on her stomach. "Ozzie, my sweet, you land like a ton of bricks! Hi, Rich; what have you been feeding our star kitten? You're late and you smell like scorched cottage cheese; was this some godawful kitchen disaster?"

"Only the usual, my sweet Kate," Richard leaned down, for a brief and comradely kiss. "God, what a day. It's five o'clock on the east coast. What's your pleasure – the red or the white?"

"White," Kate's eyes narrowed, as she looked at Richard. "You look exhausted. Did something really horrible happen in the Café?"

"You could say that," Richard admitted. "Not that it would be a suitable event for the *Beacon*, though. Let me pour out the evening libations, Kate of Kate Hall. You look somewhat disheveled yourself – anything you wish to share with the class?"

"We shall swap accounts of the horrors of our day," Kate replied. "And commiserate accordingly over the wine. Shall you go first, or shall I?"

"Ladies, as always, first." Richard thought he might as well bring out the whole bottle, as well as a pair of mis-matched, yet chilled glasses. When he came out with the wine and their glasses, Kate already looked less frazzled, and Ozzie lay purring under her regular caresses.

"Thank you! Bliss indeed. I already feel better about having wasted my day in the archives. Ugh!" she shuddered, involuntarily, and Ozzie laid a paw on her hand. "Spiders, silverfish and dust. I don't think anyone has been in the archives in decades, or not in the oldest part. They're in the cellar, you know. It's like a cave down there. I had to take a battery lantern just to be able to read the dates on the spines, then lug them one by one upstairs."

"What were you looking for?" Richard poured out his own and took his own chair. Over the far side of the campground, the sun had begun a gradual slide behind the upper branches of those trees lining the riverbank, painting long bars of shadow and gold across the campground.

"Any information about the Scar-faced Tramp," Kate leaned her head back against the lounge. "I thought sure that we'd get more leads, once the facial reconstruction was publicized, but the whole matter is so old, it's not even a cold case anymore to anyone outside of Luna City. I thought I'd start in the *Beacon* archives first."

"Because they're handy, and it's the nearest big town to Luna City," Richard completed the sentence. After six months of … whatever it was that he and Kate were doing, he had a pretty good idea of her thought processes.

"Yes," Kate nodded. "The *Beacon* was a daily back then, so I had to go through every issue. I thought I would never get the smell of old paper mildewing away out of my nostrils, and it took most of the afternoon to go through 1934 and 1935. I don't know if there is anything to be gained through going farther back. I suppose I'll move on next week and try Beeville. At least the San Antonio papers are likely to be in microfiche. So how was your ghastly day, then?"

"Not quite as dire," Richard reported. "As it only involved some four hours of baby-sitting the Vaughn offspring."

"Oh, really!" Kate began to giggle. "How on earth did that happen. I know Jess and Sarah and all the other ladies in the congregation are off on a retreat. What happened to Joe? Daddies should be just as good at child-care as mommies; this is the 21st century, you know."

"That fact has not escaped me, my Kate of Kate Hall. At the last possible minute, Joe had to testify at a trial in San Antonio," Richard explained. "So Berto and Chris and Jerry Walcott all volunteered to take it in shifts. I did not volunteer, my sweet Kate; I was drafted. They made me an offer that I could not well refuse, not without looking like an utter cad."

"My poor put-upon knight of the Chivalrous Gard," Kate still looked amused. "You have worked up from looking after a plant, to a cat, and now to practicing on an infant. So, how did it go?"

"Not too badly, I confess," Richard looked with morose attention at his glass. *How had it become so empty so suddenly?* He remedied that lack before continuing. "The Vaughn-spawn … is that clever, or what, my Kate? – is too old to be fed occasionally and then to slumber peacefully for the greater part of the time, so as to be safely ignored but for basic maintenance, and yet not quite old enough to be taught anything useful or contribute to an amusing conversation. I don't know how parents endure the wait until they can carry on a meaningful conversation or have a useful interaction with children. I really only want to have dealings with those whom I can teach something useful."

"Never mind," Kate reached across the gap between their chairs, and patted Richard's hand – the hand which did not hold a wine-glass. "They grow old enough, soon enough. It seems that one minute, Berto was making an appalling mess in diapers …"

"Don't mention that situation, Kate!" Richard begged, and Kate continued as if he had not spoken.

"And then he was driving for Uncle Tony and dating a movie star. Honestly, sometimes I wonder where the time goes."

"Into the drink, Kate – into the drink. Shall I pour you another? No…"

"Little Joe will be old enough to learn from Captain Kitten before you know it." Kate assured him. "Speaking of which; what have you planned for supper?"

"You only love me for my food," Richard accused.

Kate grinned and answered, "Not just that, my paladin. Your sparkling wit, your undemanding companionship; I adore you for all of that."

"Temptress," Richard poured another glass for them both. "How about paella. It's fast, and in one pan. I have some lovely imported saffron, and a bag of assorted frozen seafoods. Not completely authentic, but since I cannot shop regularly at a decent fish-market…"

"Tempt me, indeed." Kate twinkled at him, and Ozzie only stretched and yawned.

Sufficient was the day were the evils and the baby-sitting responsibilities thereof, Richard told himself, as he set to heating olive oil in the shallow pan which would have to serve in the stead of a proper paella pan. This evening was his and Kates'.

The following day was much like the one before, only with the addition of Luc to the ménage in the Café to enliven Richard's afternoon, when Jerry arrived as before, trundling the enormous baby carriage through the front of the Café.

"Slight change of schedule today," Jerry said, as soon as Little Joe was decanted from his personal set of wheels and into the high chair which Richard had dedicated for his use for the duration of the emergency. "Sylvester and Chris have swapped shifts. Chris's evening manager didn't show up. He has the flu or something, so Sylvester's going to take over from you this afternoon."

"Not a problem," Richard replied, feeling rather more cheerful than the day before. Having accomplished a bottle feed, a diaper change *(the latter just barely)* and the hand-off to Chris without significant disaster *(other than melting a bottle and near to destroying a perfectly good saucepan)* he could afford to be insouciant.

"Hey, a baby!" Luc looked up from shaping seeded rye-bread dough for the following day's bread requirements. "Where did it come from?"

Richard was attempting to fill in the gaps in Luc's culinary experience and practice. Using anything but commercially-provided breadstuffs was a new experience for Richard's latest kitchen apprentice. So far, he was adjusting well, if slowly, but on several occasions, Richard had to step out of the kitchen and address his heartfelt remarks to the sky overhead. In his own way, Luc required as much special handling as Little Joe.

"That is correct," Richard answered. "High marks for observation on your part. As to where they come from, there is no truth to the rumor that they are often found underneath cabbage leaves. This is Jess and Joe Vaughn's child. As Chief Vaughn must testify all this week at a trial in San Antonio, and was unable to find a suitable and acceptable nanny on short notice, a number of their friends – to include myself – are stepping in."

"Cool," Luc replied, giving a wad of dough several turns and turning it into one of the pans standing by. Sarcasm was lost on him. "Under a cabbage leaf, uh? I'd never heard that one. So, what are you gonna do with the baby, all afternoon."

"Alas, he is too young to be put to work, making bread for tomorrow." Richard got down the trusty volume of Larousse, a copy of which he now kept in the Café in order to better torment his apprentices and staff. "So, until it is time for his nap, I propose to add to his education, and to yours, by reading aloud. Are we ready, then? Good."

It did not escape his attention that both Luc and Little Joe appeared to find Larousse soothing; monotonous, but soothing. Richard had gotten through most of the chapter about broths and soups, and Luc had put the last of the bread aside, by the time Little Joe began making faces like a small carp sucking in water, by which Richard deduced that the child was ready for his afternoon bottle. This time, he prayed, that warming it would go without a problem.

"Chef, is there anything more for me?" Luc already had divested himself of his kitchen apron, and donned his jacket, which to Richard was a hint that Luc assumed that he was done for the day and merely wanted Richard to formalize the matter. "OPM is gonna play at the Roadside in Beeville tonight."

"No, nothing more. Break a leg, then."

"I ... hadn't planned on it," Luc was baffled.

Richard sighed. "It's a traditional means of wishing a performer good luck."

"It doesn't sound very lucky ..."

Richard briefly considered explaining that it was bad luck in the theater world to wish good luck on a performer. No, Luc would not be able to grasp that, not without a short instructional video and a long talk accompanied by a presentation on flipcharts. "Just let it go then. See you tomorrow. We'll work on pastries and pies, so refresh your memory in that regard."

"G'night, Chef."

The front door jingled as Luc let himself out, and Richard looked at Little Joe, still making carp-faces. "Goog-gush," Little Joe commented, a line of drool making his chin unpleasantly shiny.

Since the sprout seemed to have grasped the concept of agreeable conversation, although nothing like the vocabulary necessary to make it meaningful, Richard replied, "Indeed. Well said, young chap. Ready for your afternoonses, then? Right. I haven't managed to destroy another bottle, so chalk me up another pip on being a good child-minder, eh?"

"Goog-gush," Little Joe answered, agreeably, adding a bubble of spit for emphasis. Richard sprinkled a little milk on the inside of his wrist, as Jerry had instructed – just exactly blood-warm. He swiped his wrist with a clean towel, settled down with Little Joe propped against his arm, and applied the nippled end of bottle to Little Joe's mouth.

"Just wait until you can be a help around the kitchen," Richard informed him. "What shall we teach you do make first? A good mayonnaise, I think. By hand, with a whisk, none of this blender nonsense. Crack an egg, a dab of mustard, some lemon juice – freshly squeezed, of course, and whisk vigorously to blend. Add pure extra-virgin olive oil in a steady stream until it emulsifies. Calls for a bit of coordination, but at least sharp knives and hot hobs aren't involved. Your mum definitely won't let you mess about with any of those things for a while. Although, it might be a salutary experience – learning to manage dangerous things at an earlier age ..." he ruminated in this vein, while a steady stream of tiny bubbles bisected the diminishing level of milk in the bottle. The hands of the kitchen clock slowly ticked toward half-past, the moment when Sylvester Gonzalez appeared in the kitchen.

Richard eyed him with sudden suspicion; normally, Sylvester affected a kind of retro male chic; button-down short-sleeved shirts, chino trousers, and a pair of Buddy Holly glasses with heavy black frames. Now Sylvester sported a floppy bow tie, and a sports jacket of an archaic cut, in addition to his usual vintage fashion eyewear. Richard eyed him with suspicion.

"Why the sudden sartorial splendor?" he asked, as he sorted out the last of Little Joe's milk afternoon meal, rinsing out bottle, nipple and all, and stowing them in the humongous bag of infant necessities. "You look like you're going someplace. I thought you had baby-sitting duty."

"I am, and I do," Sylvester replied, looking at his archaic and totally vintage wristwatch. "Hey, I've got to hit the road, so can we do the *Readers' Digest* version. Is Little Joe all refreshed and ready to rumble?"

"Fed, burped and cleansed," Richard answered. Chastened by the experience of the day before, he didn't think he had done too badly; the young Vaughn-spawn was already settled and half-asleep in his Harley-sized pram, drowsy with a tum full of mother's milk, warm and content – and possibly with infant dreams of kitchen supremacy dancing in his head.

"Oh, good," Sylvester replied. "I'd be P-Oed, if he spit up on this. Vintage Brooks Brothers; got it at Thrifttown in San Antonio. Great stuff to be found there, Ricardo; a five hundred-dollar item on the rack in menswear for thirty-five bucks and change. Worth a road trip if you ever want to upgrade your wardrobe."

"Thanks, I'll leave that to you," Richard answered. He truly didn't care about clothing, as he suspected most men didn't either – just that garments be comfortable, in the neighborhood of fitting, and be fairly decent as far as the naughty bits being well-covered against exposure of several different varieties. But Sylvester was one of those rare straight guys who were inexplicably entranced by clothing. Richard supposed that it had something to do with how Sylvester was painstakingly detail-oriented in all matters. "Whither are you bound with our mutual infant responsibility? I ask, only that I will have a good and convincing story to tell Jess and Joe upon their return."

"Sure," Sylvester took over the stroller, and guided it from the kitchen. "Mensa meet-up in San Antonio. Regular thing; I'm already committed."

"Mensa …" Richard was slightly boggled. "I see; one of those clubs where you sit around and admire each other's bulging brains? S'help me god, I never thought there'd be a reason to use the words 'Marine' and 'Mensa' in the same sentence."

"Yeah, that," Sylvester replied, as he maneuvered the stroller out the front door. "My once-a month social occasion and opportunity to meet intelligent women who aren't cousins. Don't worry, I'll drive carefully, and probably won't bring any of 'em home with me."

There was no possible answer to that which didn't sound … well, whatever; sour, envious, or totally bitchy. Richard locked the front door of the Café, seeing Sylvester's Accord sedan head off around the margin of Town Square toward the road northwards – driving most cautiously, he was pleased to observe. Another day of baby-sitting under his belt, with no harm done to either party – although he did fear that the one saucepan with plastic melted all over the bottom was ruined for good and all. He retrieved his bicycle, whistled for Ozzie and pedaled home slowly in the thin spring sunshine, contemplating a quiet evening and a solitary meal, consumed while watching the sun go down, attended by the gentle clamor of the Grant's goat herd, the distant screams of a pea-fowl, and the clattering of the old-fashioned daisy-wheel windmill that pumped water from the Grant's well.

Wednesday brought a blessedly sudden end to the baby-sitting responsibilities, when Joe Vaughn appeared in the Café, toweringly official in his best uniform coat, buttoned up against the weather, which had – with the swiftness of stunt driver in a high-speed movie chase – pivoted from mild to gusty and chill. Jerry Walcott, not even attempting to hide his yawns, had delivered Little Joe, just as the lunch rush was dying down. Richard had not even had a chance to decant the infant from pram to high chair when Joe strode into the kitchen.

"Hi, Rich – your troubles are over; the judge declared a mistrial, and I'm sprung! How's my Little Buddy doing?" Joe scooped up his offspring and lifted him high overhead. "I've already been to the house to let Chris and Sylvester know they're off the hook. Bet you've been a rotten little pain in the butt to Ricardo, haven't you, Little Buddy?"

"He has not, as such," Richard felt lightened with relief but also a trifle disappointed. Aside from the matter of disgusting messes inadequately contained in a diaper, Little Joe was a perfectly companionable small chum. He did not display quite the same indifferent attitude as Luc did, or ask as many questions as Robbie Walcott was prone to do. "We … actually had a rather pleasant time. I discussed the matter of the first recipe what I will teach him … How do you feel about small children handling knives, by the way?"

"As long as they're not cutting open the sofa cushions to see what's inside," Joe replied. "Which I did, with the first penknife my grandfather gave me. Yeah, when Grandma finished wearing out my backside with a switch, she gave Grandpa a good ass-chewing as well. Knives are fine. After that, it'll be shooting BBs at tin cans from the back porch. Hey, I want to thank you and the fellows for helping out." Joe tucked his son, like a small football in the crook of his arm and looked seriously at Richard. "It was a load of my mind, having y'all step up, like this. I won't forget."

"It was … my pleasure," Richard answered, feeling rather that it had been. "I can't speak for the other chaps, of course,"

Joe grinned. "Sylvester says that he took Little Buddy to the Mensa meeting last night. Talk about perfect date bait! Better than having a cute little dog on a leash, I guess. Sylvester says he was beating women off with a stick."

"It does take a village," Richard replied, serene in the knowledge that for now, at least, his bit was done. Still – he wondered how it would have worked out if Kate had been around …

"Thanks, anyway. Hey, drinks are on me for you guys at the V, on Friday. No argument – I buy, you drink."

"No argument from me," Richard said. Yes – it did take a village. Or a Luna City.

The Deathly Wood

1918 was not the year that the 19th century died; died in all of its boundless optimisms and earnest faith in advancement of the human condition. For Europe – cynical, cultured, hyper-superior old Europe – that could be said to happened two years earlier, along the Somme, at Verdun, in the tangled hell of barbed-wire, poisoned gas and toxic, clay-like mud, the burnt ruins of the centuries-old Louvain university and that priceless library, destroyed by German 'frightfulness' tactics in the heat of their first offensive. Perhaps the 19th century died as early as 1915. It depended on which front, of course, and the combatants involved, still standing on their feet, but wavering like punch-drunken, exhausted pugilists. One may readily theorize that only blood-drenched enmity kept them propped up, swinging futilely at each other, while the lists of casualties from this or that offensive filled page after page of newsprint; all in miniscule typeface, each single name – so small in print, yet a horrific, tragic loss for a family and community hundreds of miles from the Front.

All this was different for Americans, of course; sitting on the sidelines, gravely concerned, yet publicly dedicated to neutrality, and firmly at first of the conviction that Europe's affairs were not much of Americas' business. But softly, slowly, slowly, softly, American sympathies swung toward the Allies, even though there were enough first- and second-generation Americans among German and Irish immigrants to have swung American public opinion among non-Anglo or Francophile elements toward maintaining a continued neutrality. After all, it was a war far, far, away, and nothing much to do with Americans ... at first. But events conspired; the brutality of the Huns in Belgium (documented by American newspapers), unrestricted submarine warfare which extended to American shipping (and, inevitably, American casualties), and finally, the publication of the Zimmerman Telegram – and in the spring of 1917,

President Wilson formally requested of Congress that a declaration of war on Imperial Germany be considered and voted upon. Said declaration was passed by an overwhelming margin, and by summer of that year, American troops were arriving in France – first in a trickle, then a flood.

The Belleau Wood was a forested tract thirty or so miles northeast of Paris; a hunting preserve in a stand of old-growth European forest, the refuge of wildlife, and for those whose favored recreation was hunting them. At the northern edge of the forest was two-story octagonal hunting lodge; built of stone, it was a place to shelter hunters for a night, during momentary bad weather, or a hearty meal, mid-hunt. Until the spring of 1918, it had been relatively untouched by a war which had turned acres and acres of French and Belgian farmland into muddy, barbed-wire entangled wastelands, many of which are still poisoned and unsafe, a hundred years after the end of that war. That forest tranquility ended when the expected German spring offensive slammed into the Allied lines – lines which now included the Americans – and punched through to the Marne River. The Germans had hoped to break through before the sufficient of the American Expeditionary Force arrived to make a difference in the wars' outcome.

Late in May, German forces reached the Paris-Metz main road – and if they managed to break across the Marne and reach Paris, that one last throw of the dice would pay off for Germany; perhaps in victory, or perhaps in a negotiated and face-saving settlement with the equally exhausted and embittered French and British.

An experienced career soldier, General John J. "Black Jack" Pershing commanded the US. Expeditionary Force. He had rejected British and French demands that the Americans be parceled out piecemeal among Allied units, and essentially fight under the command of French and British officers. This would not do; likely Black Jack was polite yet forceful about it. *(His nickname came from him having commanded a troop of black cavalry early in his career as a young officer.)* The AEF's

3rd Division went into the line to counter the German advance at Chateau-Thierry – the 3rd Division, which included a brigade of Marines, had initially been held in reserve – was brought forward in a hurry. The Marines were pretty much seen as a second-class by the Army brass, according to some accounts: good enough to do rear-guard and support duty, and only thrown into what was expected to be a quiet sector because every able-bodied American serviceman was needed, in the face of the German spring offensive. Checked by stiff resistance at Chateau-Thierry, the German advance poured into the woods, where the 3rd Division had just arrived. Retreating French troops, exhausted from the fight to keep from being overrun, urged the Americans to do likewise, whereupon one of their officers is supposed to have riposted, "Retreat, Hell – we just got here!"

Of course, the newly-arrived American troops were keen as mustard; champing at the bit, as it were – especially the Marines, few of whom were of the career old breed. Many were recent volunteers. Up until that moment, the Marines had been a rather small, and somewhat specialized service; more inclined to security on board naval ships and at US embassies abroad, perhaps a small punitive expedition where American interests were concerned in South America and the Caribbean; a military constabulary, rather than hard-charging infantry. Still, it was a service that took pride in having been founded by an act of the Continental Congress in 1775, recruiting at the Tun Tavern in Philadelphia, beating the official establishment of the US Army by more than a decade. *(Yes, there was a Continental Army during the Revolution, but it was more like state militias seconded for service in the colonies' united cause. The US Army wasn't quote-unquote officially established until the 1780s. Upon this kind of minutia are friendly service rivalries built.)*

Throughout the month of June 1918, the Marines fought with bitter tenacity through the deathly woods; sharpshooting at first, with deadly effect, and eventually to point-blank, then with bayonet, knives, and hand-to-hand. They kept the Germans from moving out of the wood, and then fought them back, yard by yard, trench by trench. The trees in the forest, the boulders at their feet were shattered by artillery and machine-gun fire. The stench from the bodies of the dead – too many to bury, under the existing conditions in the early summer heat – revolted the living to an unimaginable degree. And still – they went on, clawing back the wood to Allied control. More Marines were killed in that single month than had been killed in action since their founding in 1775. The Corps would not face another butcher's bill to equal it until the taking of Tarawa, a quarter of a century later, and half the world away. It was a special kind of hell, this fight in a 200-acre French woodland, fought by relatively untried young troops, motivated by pride in service, by devotion to comrades, and by the leadership – which in many instances devolved onto NCOs, and even individual Marines, like Sergeant Dan Daly, a scrappy Irish-American career Marine *(who had been awarded the Congressional Medal of Honor – twice, for actions in the Boxer Rebellion, and then again in Haiti)*. In legend he is said to have rallied the troops with a shout of "For Chrissake, men, come on; do you want to live forever?!" *(Or similar phrasing. The war correspondent Floyd Gibbons later wrote that he had heard a similar expression shouted by a senior NCO, and the legend attached itself to Dan Daly.)*

In the end, the Germans were driven from the woods, at a horrific cost; 10,000 casualties among the Marines, including nearly 2,000 dead. There is no definitive record of German dead, although there were around 1,600 Germans taken prisoner. But the Marines had clawed back the deathly woods, blunted the last-ditch German offensive … and in November of that year, Germany threw in the towel. By agreement, it all came to a temporary end on the eleventh hour, the eleventh day, the eleventh month. Such were the enmities and resulting bitterness that the armistice held only for the time that it took for a baby boy born in that year to grow up and serve in his turn.

The shattered forest was christened anew after the battle; it has been called since then the Wood of the Marine Brigade and an adjunct to a American war cemetery. The American 4th Brigade was recognized by the French government by the award of a military honor, the Croix de Guerre. To this day, active-duty Marines serving in the 5th and 6th Marine Regiments are authorized to wear the French fourragere – an elaborate garnishment of looped and braided cords – on their left shoulder as part of their dress uniform, in honor of that unit's service in the Deathly Wood, a hundred years ago. To this day, successfully completing Marine Corps basic training means completing the "Crucible" – a 54-hour marathon march on short rations and little sleep, featuring grueling marches, obstacle course and team-driven combat-problem-solving exercise – some of which was drawn on the experience of the fighting in the deathly woods.

The Email

From: Joe V <lctopcop@gmail.com>

To: <tweetynemesis@gmail.com>

CC: All in Group

Subject: Found Our Man

Have a match, found in the booking records of the Beeville jail for 1935. Scan of the page attached – top row, second from left. Note the facial scar and cut of military overcoat. I'm positive this is our guy. Name: Michael Delaney Walters, age 37, origin Columbus, Ohio, no fixed address noted. Arrested for vagrancy and public drunkenness on November 19, 1935, released a week later on his own recognizance, on account of being a veteran, with the understanding that he leave town on the day. Given five dollars from some public charitable fund, on condition that he beat feet immediately, and never set foot in Beeville again. Statement in the records says that he claimed to have been a Marine.

Meet tomorrow at nine for discussion.

Joe

A Name to the Face

"All righty then," Joe said, by way of opening a brief meeting at the Café the next morning, a meeting to consider the identity of the Scar-faced Tramp. Richard was the last to slip into a chair at the *stammtisch*, when the morning rush of those Lunaites who urgently needed to get to their places of business diminished to a trickle. Only Kate was absent, being tied up in a city council meeting in Karnesville, but Araceli would brief her, with expanded commentary at the earliest opportunity, and Joe's email had gone out to everyone. "You all had a chance to compare what I sent yesterday? Yeah, I know the page I sent you was pretty small, but I had Sylvester work some of his computer magic last night, which I think will confirm the Beeville identity. Show 'em, Sylvester."

"On it, Joe," Sylvester unzipped the black case which contained his laptop computer, and taking it out, turned it so that the computer screen faced most of the others gathered around the table. "See – I manipulated the transparency of the mug-shot scan that Joe located Beeville … and here we have the reconstruction. Now, let me expand the mug-shot image…"

As he talked, he moved his computer mouse. The reconstructed image of the scar-faced vagrant gazed out at them. The black and white mug-shot image bloomed on the screen, and then went strangely transparent, as insubstantial as a veil, as Sylvester scooted it to overlay the reconstructed countenance. The darting arrow-shape moved to the corners, adjusting the image in position over the reconstruction. "See – exactly the same size. Now, see how they match, when I play with the transparent overlay?"

Some more fiddling with the mouse, and the image on the overlay intensified and darkened, then thinned again. Joe sat back with a sigh, as Araceli topped up the coffee all around. "So, what say you all?"

"Looks like a good match to me," Chris replied, voicing the assent from around the table. "The eyes and chin match, not to mention the scar. I'd say that this Michael D. Walters is the man."

"I do, too," Joe said. "And I base my opinion not just on the match but the fact that Kate and I between us haven't found any other local records that come anywhere close; only this one. Did Miss Letty and Mrs. Gonzales confirm when you showed them the reconstruction, Roman?"

"Abuelita couldn't be certain," Roman answered. "It was a long time ago, and she was just a little girl, but Miss Letty was as certain as she could be. The scar … it's pretty damn memorable. I showed it to Tio Jaimie, just on a whim. He was around back then, and he remembers the scarred tramp, too. Says that the man worked for about a week, helping Tio Jaimie's dad Don Antonio dig fenceposts. It was a damn long time ago, but Tio Jaimie was really impressed by that scar."

"Yeah, there might have been a dozen identically-scarred veteran tramps hanging around other places in South Texas in late 1935," observed Joe. "Thanks, Araceli. The odds are in our favor. Law enforcement <u>always</u> plays the odds; hear hoofbeats and whinnying in the street, the intelligent bet is on horses out there, not on zebras. We'll operate on the assumption that Walters is the name to attach to those bones sitting in a box in the Karnesville morgue. What can we dig up, and where to we look, now that we have a name to go with the face?"

"National Archives," Sylvester replied, and his face assumed a frustrated expression. "The depository in St. Louis is where all the records for enlisted Marines who separated after 1905 are stored. Earlier records are in DC. There's an alphabetical card file listing, by surname, all the way back to the late 1700s, but it's not on-line. That would give us his enlistment record, years in service, decorations, units assigned, disciplinary and hospitalization records and when discharged from service – if someone can actually eyeball the physical records."

"So, somebody must actually go to the archives, search the card file, and then hit the muster rolls for each year in service." Joe nodded.

A short and depressed silence fell on the *stammtisch*, eventually broken by Lew Dubois gently clearing his throat. "I will have business taking me to St. Louis, which will allow me time, or I will make time – to visit this archive, but alas, not until later in spring."

"We wouldn't want to put you to the trouble," Joe said, after an exchange of glances with his uncle. "Maybe Allen Lee can do it, on his swing through Missouri, this season. Uncle Harry, if Allen Lee can't do it, will you and Sylvester sound out your contacts and see if anyone is in a position to spend time at the Archives or do heavy historical research? Being a Marine; small pool of players, you know?"

"Even in the Second MEF, as it was then?" Sylvester nodded. "Yeah, not more than a couple of regiments. Eight hundred to four thousand men each – going by todays' arithmetic, which likely doesn't apply to a hundred years ago. I'll have to put out the word to the guys," he added, with a significant glance at Chris. "The odds that anyone still alive knew this guy personally diminish every year, ya know. It's been a hundred years since the end of World War One. But there might still be younger family, cousins, neighbors…" Sylvester finished on a discouraged note.

"Ya know," he added, irreverently, "They say that there are degrees to death. When no one remembers your name, even – that's the final degree."

"Don't sweat it, pal," Chris assumed his best authoritative and comforting 'EMT to accident victim' manner. "We'll get the word out – he'll be remembered. By us, if no one else."

"If he fought at Belleau Wood as did my Grand-père Lucien," Lew Dubois mused. "He may have distinguished himself there; I am certain that is the case, for it was a most historic battle, and there were many dead and even more wounded. I had an interest, since Grand-père never said much of what he had experienced there. I was most curious on that account, and so I have collected books and memoirs, about it, looking for what Grand-père Lucien would never tell. But all those books are at our home in Houston. My dear wife can send them to me, and I can search them for mention of this name."

"Good," Joe said, as Sylvester silently closed his computer and returned it to his carry-all. "Any questions?"

"I have one," Richard ventured. "Why does this all matter so much to you?"

"Because we never leave one of our own behind," Sylvester and Chris replied almost as one. Chris added, "And this poor bastard got left behind, when the victory parades were all over, that's for certain."

"He needed help," Joe shrugged. "And never got it. Maybe he was even too proud to ask for it in the first place. But he finished up here in Luna City. We just sort of feel responsible for sorting out what has been left over, even if it is about seventy years too late to make a personal difference to him."

"Just thought I'd ask," Richard replied, feeling slightly stung by the reproof.

"Keep us informed by email," Joe scraped back his chair, and took up his notebook and car keys. "Anything of significance, I'll call a meeting here."

Celia Hayes & Jeanne Hayden

The Grand Opening

Howdy, Neighbors! Come visit us all day Saturday, March 10, beginning at 9:00

Help us celebrate the Grand Opening of the 1912 Boathouse & stables!

Tour the elegant new boathouse, and stables, sample fine food at the Country Kitchen, and join us at the Campfire Circle for a sing-along!

Admission $10, $5 for Children

Free admission to those wearing period garb

Tickets available on-line, and at the Main Gate

This is Phase One of our expansion during 2018-2019

Consult our website for information on the grand re-opening of the

luxurious Cattleman Hotel, scheduled for early 2019

Grand Plans

"We have a special event coming up," Richard announced to his staff, on a chilly afternoon in mid-February, once the luncheon rush had ended. This was the time and day that he liked to have what Sylvester called, 'all hands-on-deck' briefing; new items on the menu, any deviations from routine, suggestions relayed from customers to front-of-the-house staff for anything from menu items to the color of the tablecloths for dinner service. "The new extension at Mills Farm is being launched on March 10, and I – that is – we – have been asked to participate."

"I thought they already had a restaurant out there," Luc mumbled. Richard nodded. "Of course – they do. But they are expecting an avalanche of guests on that occasion – and we have been offered the prize position." He waited, anticipating a heightened degree of interest from those present; Araceli, Beatriz and Blanca, Luc, and Robbie. Robbie, young and ingenious, was the only one to rise to the bait.

"Where will that be, Chef?"

"At the Boathouse itself," Richard replied, still hoping for a greater manifestation of interest and enthusiasm than he was getting. "A picnic buffet, served in the riverside pavilion atop the boathouse; diners may set themselves at tables in the pavilion, or take their meal at leisure on the lawn by the riverside."

"Cool!" Robbie exclaimed. "And Belle will be home for Spring Break, so she can par-tay!"

"That will be nice," Araceli allowed, with more restrained enthusiasm. "So who else is going to be serving up at the grand opening, besides us and the Country Store restaurant?"

"The Pryors are going to do BBQ from the back of an authentic chuckwagon at the Campfire Circle location," Richard answered. "The Country Store restaurant will do their usual fare, only for a greater than expected crowd. And a nose-bleedingly high-end restaurant from San Antonio will do a lavish twelve-course meal for a selected few, in the dining room of the Homestead House. Some directors' wife decided it would make an enormous splash among the high-rollers, and for reasons known only to himself, Lew Dubois has approved."

"Why didn't they ask us?" Beatriz pouted. "You've done grand suppers, Chef!"

"Lew did offer it to me," Richard answered. "And I turned it down – not much of a challenge, you see. I'd rather that we do the picnic buffet at the Boathouse. That's where most of the crowd will be, and it's the opportunity for us to shine. Mr. Dubois has decided on a theme for the grand opening, you see."

"What kind of theme?" At least Blanca was impressed.

"A theme befitting the Edwardian era," Richard told them. "It is the 1912 Boathouse, after all, so everything we will serve will be appropriate for a picnic luncheon of the time. This obliviates the need to cook anything on-scene, save perhaps for hot tea and coffee. Everything, and I do mean everything, will be prepared beforehand, refrigerated, and served chilled.

In spite of that restriction, the menu will be lavish. Mr. Dubois advises me to expect no less than five hundred." He was not deterred by the gasps of astonishment from his crew.

He was certain they were up to it, especially after the venture with Patricia Pryor's wedding party event. *Of course, then, he had the assistance of the good ladies of Saints Margaret and Anthony ... perhaps they had a word with their Higher Authority? Best not to think on that, too much.* "Cold salmon with mayonnaise sauce, cold sliced lamb with fresh mint sauce, chicken salad, game pie, cold ham with mustard sauce, mixed green salads with an assortment of dressings, cucumber sandwiches – do not forget the cucumber sandwiches – hardboiled eggs – bread with fresh butter, and a cheese platter ..."

"Cold fried chicken," Luc suggested. Richard nodded. "Sliced bread, and rolls. Three or four kinds, I think; to suit every taste. Pastries and little cakes, as we did for the last buffet supper at the Walcotts'. Fresh fruits, jellies and ices – that is, sorbets and ice creams. And one more thing ..."

"Yes?" Araceli raised a practiced eyebrow.

"We will have to dress appropriately. The ladies in long dresses, Robbie and Luc and I in ... well, striped shirts, and butler's aprons and boaters. Because of the theme, and all."

Araceli shrugged. "Not a problem. I'll see what Patricia can do for me. The girls already have their maid's outfits from ... remember that time when the Maldonados were supposed to play, and they got into a fight instead?"

"I spent months trying to forget that particular contretemps," Richard shuddered. Every catered supper he had done at the Walcott manse had been marred by some spectacular and unforeseen disaster. If it weren't for Clovis Walcott (Colonel, USAR, Ret.) being so damned generous, he would have run screaming from every proposal put forward by the good colonel and his lady. Sook Walcott was also the most demanding tiger-mother in Luna City, a domestic terror without peer and seemingly above reproach. She was also Robbie's mother, although the kid seemed to be charmingly undamaged; perhaps inoculated by constant exposure to the contagion that was Sook Walcott.

"Never mind, Chef," Araceli consoled him. She had been there for that first and then the most recent disaster at Chez Walcott. "This is for Mills Farm. There's no way that the hex could carry over."

"It's at Mills Farm!" Robbie pointed out, sunny and optimistic. "Not at home ... gee, it really was odd, how things kept happening. But Dad says ..."

"He does, doesn't he?" Richard brutally cut off another panegyric to the wit and wisdom of Walcott, Senior. "Your father's thoughts are usually to the point, no need in repeating them to us all. All right, troops. The event is on March 10. I propose that we commence preparing for it all during the week previous. Practically everything can be done in advance and held in the freezer, or in cool storage ... yes, Walcott – what is it?"

"Chef," Robbie was fidgeting in his chair, as if he was considering raising his hand like a good student. "Did you know that Bree Grant is coming back to Luna City until fall? She can help out, too."

"I did not," Richard was oddly pleased by this bit of information; Bree and Robbie were his apprentices during the last summer holidays and trained to his exacting and exhausting specifications. "That is possibly the best bit of good news I have heard so far. Very good news – would she be willing to return, at least part-time to the Café? I was under the impression she had another year of school to complete."

"She does," Robbie explained. "But she's being home-schooled now. Bree Grant," Robbie explained to Luc, "She's Judy and Sefton's granddaughter; you know, who provide us the eggs and local seasonal produce? She apprenticed at the Café last summer. She's wicked smart," Robbie added, without a trace of envy. "Honors and advanced placement, and she finished high school early. She's taking college courses on-line right now. She says she will start her first year at UT as a sophomore and graduate before she is twenty."

"Cool," Luc still didn't appear impressed. If Miss Letty was correct, he was one of those odd, socially-inept children, singularly unimproved by the passing years. No matter: Robbie and Bree possessed sufficient self-assurance to equip at least three other people.

"I will consult with Mrs. Vaughn and Doctor Wyler, to see if the Café can afford hiring Miss Grant on at least a part-time basis," Richard concluded the meeting. Yes, having Bree on board for the Boathouse event would resolve much of the pre-prep challenge. "All right then – Luc and Robbie; familiarize yourselves with prep for the new items on this weekend's supper menu. We'll prepare them for sampling on Friday for staff luncheon so that you," he nodded towards Araceli, "And Beatriz and Blanca will be able to describe them to diners. And do your homework; come up with suggestions for the Boathouse menu along the lines that I have proposed; the sauces, the game pie, the jellies, ice creams and cakes."

"On it, Chef!" the company chorused with an enthusiasm which quite warmed Richard's heart, or that space where he presumed that organ rested.

Miss Letty Contemplates Her Garden in Spring

Miss Letty McAllister, the oldest person in Luna City at the age of 97 and three months, sat on the front porch of the McAllister house on a mild afternoon late in February and thought about her garden. Mid-March was the last time in the spring that a hard freeze was likely, so of custom and accumulated experience, Miss Letty did not begin any serious projects in her garden until then … although this did not prevent her from regarding the stretch of lawn – now winter-browned and straw-like – the leafless stands of brown sticks which were the perennial borders of hydrangea, or the rhododendrons, to which some dark green leaves still adhered, and the bare tumbled earth in which colorful annuals would soon make glad the heart of Miss Letty. The sight would also gladden the hearts of those passing by on Route 123, who would glance at the tall stone house, with the faded green metal roof, the bay window, and the deep porch all trimmed with Victorian fretwork bric-a-brac, and think in mild envy – *'Oh, what a beautiful old house! I wonder what the inside looks like, and who lives there?'*

In the meantime, and for another three weeks until the danger of frost passed, Miss Letty made plans, sitting in her comfortable wicker chaise, looking at the garden, and watching the occasional vehicle flash past. *Good heavens; there went that enormous purple RV with the logo of that television cooking show plastered along the side! So Allen Lee was back in town for another visit!* Miss Letty was not particularly a fan of football played by professionals (only by high school or perhaps college students), or the Food Channel, but she approved in a rather distant fashion of Allen Lee, who (somewhat against her private expectations) had turned out to be an upstanding citizen, a responsible father, and a credit to his upbringing. Miss Letty hoped that he would remain a little longer, next time. He was a gentleman and had been such a help during last autumn's hurricane evacuation emergency.

She left off thinking about Allen Lee and surveyed her garden once more. The grounds of the old McAllister place were not without a promise of verdant beauty, even as a Texas winter yielded to another spring. Soon, the daffodils would soon be poking little green shoots out of the earth in the circular bed around the birdbath, and wisteria rambling over the lath-house at the back of the property would burst forth into hanging festoons of pale lavender flowers, although that splendor would linger only for about a week, before reverting into a featureless tangle of light green leaves on rampant vines. In the little greenhouse set against the south-facing wall, Miss Letty already had tomato sprouts, cucumbers, lettuces, and pole bean seedlings sending up tiny, tender leaves. Soon would be the time to put them outdoors in a sheltered spot to harden ... and then, when all danger of frost was past, to plant them in the kitchen garden plot. Miss Letty's mind turned briefly to thoughts of crisp fresh green beans, cucumbers, and tomatoes – warm from sunlight, fresh-plucked from the vines. *Nothing like the taste of fresh home-grown tomatoes, and garden greens newly harvested.*

A familiar automobile on the southbound lane slowed and pulled across the center line, into the parking area at the Tip-Top Ice House, Gas and Grocery; the Walcott's black SUV, lavishly trimmed with chrome. Blinged-out, as the younger people would say. Miss Letty observed with mild interest. *Oh, yes, Sook Walcott, and was that young Belle?* Her school must be on their Spring Break, Miss Letty concluded. It must be nice for Sook to have the girl at home, with Clovis away in Dubai for six months. There was Chris, who lived in the apartment over the old stables in back of the McAllister house, pinning something to the public noticeboard outside the Tip-Top. He saw Miss Letty and waved. Miss Letty returned the gesture.

In a moment, Sook Walcott emerged from the Tip-Top with a gallon of milk in one hand, followed by Belle, eating what appeared like one of the Café's cinnamon rolls. *Good for her*, thought Miss Letty – the child was still too thin. Sook sounded as if she were rebuking her daughter, though. Miss Letty considered what she might say, with all tact, to Sook when next they encountered one another. Well, she would say something, for all the good it might do; only her duty as a stalwart Methodist and gardener.

Miss Letty contemplated her garden again, as the Walcott's SUV backed out of the parking place and returned to the road; this time mentally surveying what she considered her larger garden. That would be the garden of Luna City and those living in it. Miss Letty had never seriously considered marriage; in her opinion that would have been like devoting lavish care and attention to a single plant to the exclusion of all others. She considered herself to be a gardener of human character; tending unobtrusively to all; especially those who were of a stormy nature and therefore most in need of careful nurturing.

Miss Letty thought that those she felt to be in her care in the larger garden fell into two general types. There were those who were mercurial, turbulent in character; often very bright, gifted and burdened equally with enormous talent. And then there were the ones who were of a more equable temper, stolid and philosophical; often every bit as talented, but more evenly balanced. It had been Miss Letty's experience that a marriage between two of the latter sort was almost always a happy, successful one. Young Araceli and Patrick were one of those stable arrangements, a success which Miss Letty had predicted with confidence even before their wedding. Marriage between the two opposites in temperament was not automatically doomed, as Miss Letty also had good reason to know; look at her own long-time friends, Stephen Wyler and dear sweet-natured Alice. Stephen's own hot temper had been tamed by the decades, of course, but also by his wife's tranquil influence. Miss Letty felt strongly that this was also true of Clovis and Sook Walcott, who otherwise wouldn't have been more different than chalk and cheese; a perennially angry virago, whose fury bounced almost unnoticed off her spouse, like rain off a polished granite block. On the whole, Miss Letty thought it was a good thing that Jerry, Belle and Robbie all reflected the even-tempered nature of their father in their personalities, although in time, Belle – with her musical talents and training – might yet develop diva-ish inclinations more like her mother.

A car emerged from Luna City, waiting in obedience to the stop sign at Oak Street and 123, in spite of being no traffic. An aged Volvo, with a careful young driver: Robbie Walcott. It must be the end of the working day for him at the Café. Miss Letty observed with approval that the Grant's young granddaughter was in the passenger seat, the teenaged girl who had spent all last summer at the Age of Aquarius. Brianna – that was her name; Young Sefton Junior was her father. Miss Letty had taught Young Sefton to read above grade level when he was barely six years old. A very clever little boy; hard to think that all those years had passed so rapidly, and Young Sefton was now nearly middle-aged. Brianna; such a pretty name and she had good manners for a child of this era, too – had worked at the Café all last summer. *Didn't Jessica say something about Brianna working at the Café again?* Robbie must be taking her home; another courtesy of which Miss Letty heartily approved. Good manners were most important, and consideration for others was a social good which had become sadly in abeyance.

Brianna and Robbie would be a good couple, Miss Letty considered and concluded in her magisterial way. Although Sook Walcott would probably be most unhappy about such a relationship. She was one of those mothers who lived overmuch through their children; almost always a blueprint for disaster and disappointment, in Miss Letty's view.

Ah – the day at the Café must be over; there came Richard on his bicycle, coming along to the same intersection, with that darling little cat riding along in the basket strapped on the back. Miss Letty raised her hand and waved at him. Such was the custom of Luna City, to exchange such a brief greeting. She was mildly surprised when Richard not only returned the greeting but pedaled across the road.

Leaning the bicycle against the fence around the McAllister place, he called, "I've brought you some baked goods for your approval, Miss McAllister; a baguette, some cinnamon rolls, a couple of muffins and some of those little cakes that were the result of me training Luc in the pastry arts. A little too rough in appearance to serve to customers, but good enough as far as taste goes. Are you receiving visitors?"

"Of course, I am," Miss Letty rose from the chaise with some difficulty and the assistance of her handy cane, as Richard came to the bottom of the steps, holding out a pastry box for her to see. "Oh, my! They look delicious. Would you like to sit down and have a cup of tea with me? It is about that time, you know. And I can put out a treat for your little friend. Salmon – the secret weapon that no cat can resist."

"Thank you, I will," Richard answered. "Do y'know, Miss McAllister, you are the only person I know in Luna City who can make a decent cuppa, besides myself."

"Then let me take this inside, and put on the kettle," Miss Letty took the box, ignoring Ozzie, who was twining himself around her ankles in his usual bid for female affection. "Sit down and enjoy what view of the garden that there is, on this afternoon, and listen to me talk about my plans for this year. I am considering trying to grow this particular hot-weather variant of summer squash. A friend of mine sent me the seeds…"

She carried the box, and the baguette inside, courteously declining Richard's offer of assistance, but asking him to make certain that Ozzie was not where she might tread on the cat – by way of ensuring that she did not trip and fall over him. It gratified her to see that Richard did so, almost immediately. *Richard had graduated from a potted plant to a pet cat.* Miss Letty found this development extremely gratifying. She had hopes for Richard, in that distant, master-gardener sort of way. The Heisel girl was an excellent prospective match, in accordance with Miss Letty's theory regarding compatibility. Katherine Heisel was one of those even-tempered, philosophical personalities; an excellent counterpart for one inclined toward extremes in temperament.

Miss Letty understood that these days, medication was often preferred, in dealing with such children, a method which she deplored with every fiber of her being, and the experience of nearly half a century in a classroom filled with small unsocialized children. Natural remedies were much to be preferred to the chemical, especially the balm provided by the wisdom of elders. In her day of teaching kindergarten and first grade, nothing quite put the starch out of wriggly little boys than being sent to run three or four times as fast as they could, around the monumental building which housed the Luna City Elementary School. Such remedies had gone out of fashion; a lamentable development, in Miss Letty's considered opinion. Organic methods were so much more …

satisfying. By the time she had finished with a class of children, they were quite well-socialized, thank you very much, and well on the way to being good small citizens, politely-mannered, and accustomed to the ways of the adult world.

The kettle purred, with the boiling of water in it. Miss Letty poured bubbling-hot water upon the tea leaves in her brown-glazed pottery teapot. Yes – the proper proportions, the proper proportion of leaves to boiling water. The English were so particular about their tea. *There was a particularly dear friend who had* … Miss Letty firmly wrenched her memories from that direction and set them onto the present. She carried out a small tray with two cups, saucers, a little pitcher of cream, a sugar bowl, a little cracked bowl, a can-opener and an unopened can of salmon.

"I'll bring out the plates when the tea has finished steeping," she said, setting gown the tray on the small table between her chaise and the chair which Richard had claimed. Miss Letty deftly opened, and scooped out flakes of salmon, while Ozzie demonstrated that for the moment, a person wielding a can-opener was his very favorite human in the whole world. He fell to scarfing salmon, emitting tiny mews of pleasure, as well as slurping noises. "I've never known a cat to turn down a taste of salmon, until they had run through every one of their lives to the last moment," she observed, and then turned an assessing eye on Ozzie's personal slave. "We have been very pleased with young Mr. Massie working in the kitchen. I hope that you have found working with him to be satisfactory."

"Oh, yes," Richard answered, with a sigh. "He's still an odd fish – but quite willing to learn from me. Which is really all that I ask. Sometimes I think he comes back late in the evening and works in the kitchen all night long, especially when an enthusiasm for perfecting a recipe takes him. I had to give him a key to the back door, since he will be my relief cook."

"Single-minded in pursuit," Miss Letty replied, inwardly rather relieved. Richard agreed. "I've worked with those who were madder, certainly."

"You are happy in your own situation here?" Miss Letty ventured. "It occurs to me that someone of your background and world experience might find Luna City to be a little … limiting, professionally. Wouldn't you be tempted to move on, eventually?"

Richard was already shaking his head. "No, not limiting at all. It's restful. Exceedingly restful. I can focus on that which matters to me. Cooking. Teaching people to appreciate good food. A regular routine. I find that a routine is satisfying. I used to laugh at all those old codgers on the telly who wanted everything just so, but now it unsettles me to have an interruption in how I am accustomed to conduct matters."

Ah, thought Miss Letty. *He is one of those odd children, after all. He and Luc have more in common than he will admit. His social skills are just more highly-developed. Douglas used to say that the English had a higher toleration for eccentrics. Richard attended a private school as a child – perhaps there is something to Douglas' theory.* Aloud, she said, "The most curious thing – about fifteen minutes ago, I saw Mr. Mayne's RV pass by. Is he in town again, or was he just passing through on his way to another one of those televised cooking competitions?"

"No, he's here for a bit," Richard answered, and leaned down to give Ozzie a brief head-scritch. Ozzie had finished all the salmon on the dish, regarding his servant-humans with disappointment when no more was forthcoming. "He messaged me, on his way into town. He'll be staying at Mills Farm, actually. He and Lew have a project on. And he …"

"What?" Miss Letty prodded gently, when no further comment seemed to come.

"Reminded me of a previous offer of professional employment. Which I had declined on first being offered … Tempting, though."

Miss Letty regarded Richard's countenance and divined the offer and the process of declination. *Really*, she thought – *there are matters which I think are so plain to be seen, but so obscure to others. No wonder old women were burned as witches in the old days. They could see the obvious through their long experience; an insight which no one else could fathom.* Aloud, she said, "I assume that you did not accept his offer to be his co-host for the following season of that show of his. Very sensible, I think. Your first venture into that exercise did you no good at all."

"It paid damned – sorry, Miss Letty. It paid excessively well, which ensured a constant supply of fame, sycophants, and free totty – and that was about all the good it did for me. I finished up in a hell, a hell that I built for myself, which was even worse." Richard shuddered, and Miss Letty kept wisely silent. He had the look just now of someone who had looked into an inferno and recoiled at the very brink. "I finished up in a black-out drunk and sobered up just enough to realize what had been going on, up mid-way across the Atlantic. The trouble is that the temptation to get back into that hell is harder to resist than I thought it would."

"For what shall it profit a man, if he shall gain the whole world, and lose his own soul?" Miss Letty quoted.

Richard confessed. "I like it here. Oddly enough. I shouldn't – but I do. I can feel like a human being, living with other human beings. People who do nice things for each other, people living ordinary lives … well, as ordinary as it can be around here, what with insane treasure hunters, zombie movie producers, elderly mad hippies, and all that. I'm pretty certain that giving that up … would not be good for me. But the temptation is pretty strong, now and again, right up until I remember what it felt like, in the middle of that flight from London to New York. Never going to risk experiencing another pitch-black night of the soul like that, ever again."

"Good," Miss Letty smiled, a mild smile of satisfaction. "As Socrates is supposed to have said – although many other wise Greek philosophers may also have said it, 'know thyself.' Such knowledge, my brother used to say, is the beginning of true wisdom." She reached for her cane, adding, "Are you ready for tea, now? And you can tell me all about what you have planned for the buffet at the grand opening. I do believe there has even been a story about it in the San Antonio newspaper. I must say, I am very impressed with what Mr. Dubois has done with the old Cattleman, too. What a pity he is going away on vacation. I suppose that once his projects here are completely finished, he will return to Houston for good."

"And you can tell me about your garden plans," Richard replied – Miss Letty noting that he looked more immediately cheerful.

"I will do just that," Miss Letty answered, allowing a very slight smile. "And I will bring out another cup for Mr. Mayall, who should nearly be done with business today at the Tip-Top. He is in the habit of having tea at about this time, when his duties allow. On the whole, my garden is coming along very well this spring, which is enormously reassuring."

Both gardens, Miss Letty thought, as she went into the house to get the tea pot, and another cup for Chris.

Mr. Dubois' Grand Hotel

"I think you'll be pleased with what we have worked out," Richard reported to Lew Dubois, the following week. At the latter's request, they met in the lobby of the Cattleman, now that the refurbishment of the old grand hotel had progressed to the point where the ground floor public rooms were finished, or nearly so. Richard had walked over from the Café, with his thick notebook in hand, stuffed with lists, recipes, and illustrations of the finished menu selections.

"Excellent!" Lew beamed good cheer. "Let us sit down in the old ballroom – the kitchen, alas, is not nearly as far along. Had you ever seen … no, you would not, I think. The old offices and back of the house were in a parlous state."

"It looks … very nice now," Richard had no need to call upon his slender reservoir of tact, as they walked through a wide, neo-classical archway from the lobby and into the ballroom – a noble space with a second-floor gallery around three sides, and a raised stage and ornate proscenium on the fourth side. It all looked perfectly glorious. The gleaming parquet floor had been restored to gleaming gold. Overhead in the ceiling, elaborate plaster-work garlands and ornamentation were repaired, repainted and re-gilded. Only the stage and window curtains had not been re-hung, nor had the light fixtures been returned to their position. Several inexpensive folding tables and a scattering of chairs sat at one end, obviously intended for the use of the workmen.

Lew made a deprecating gesture. "Wait until the central chandelier and the sconces have been restored and replaced. Then this room, and the dining room will be of a magnificence I could not have imagined, in the beginning. Did you know that the light fixtures are all original and authentic Lalique glass? Excuse me for the moment, *chère...*" He took out his cellphone, begging a further pardon of Richard for doing so, and recorded a note regarding insurance and security, when restoration of the Cattleman had been completed. Once done, he stowed the cellphone in the pocket of his lamentable working-man's jacket and fixed Richard with the intense interest of a man with no time to waste, and no intent of wasting anyone elses'. "Now, show me what you propose for the Boathouse opening; this will be the most popular among the crowd, I foresee."

"But the Country Kitchen ..." Richard began, and Lew waved his words aside with a brief gesture.

"Everyone who has ever visited Mills Farm has eaten there. Nothing to astound, and surprise, even for a special event of this nature. They do what they do, well, and consistently; but astonish with creativity, originality? Not what we require in the normal day of doing business, but in this instance, that is your task."

"To serve up a splendid and authentic 1912-appropriate picnic luncheon spread," Richard opened his notebook, to the menu page. "I took the trouble of printing you a copy of this, and of how they will appear as part of the buffet. I have worked with my staff and your finance office to create a selection of items which will appeal to every taste and be within your fixed costs, assuming you approve. Let me know of any selections which do not work for you and your corporate vision, of course."

"I will," Lew answered, and such was his managerial expertise that Richard was certain that Lew had taken it all in, considered and rendered a solid verdict, of which he would be informed of in due time. "I will sign and sent the contract to you, with the initial payment, and any changes that I see as necessary, as soon as I have had a chance to review this project in detail. I am certain that everything is satisfactory – such is your reputation and my experience at the Cafe. Would you like a tour of the project? I value your opinion as to the kitchen, since we must of necessity begin from scratch in the modernization of it."

"I would be honored," Richard admitted, somewhat in reluctance; he had only expected to spend twenty minutes with Lew and spend it strictly on the matter of the picnic menu. He did have to admit to considerable curiosity regarding the transformation of the dingy and verging-on-decrepit old hotel into a shining star of the VPI firmament.

"Excellent!" Lew beamed. "You have seen this room, of course. We will use it for special events, perhaps as an overflow dining room, when the occasion demands. You have also seen the lobby. This room and the lobby were kept in good repair, by the Historical Association, and the city, as they were in regular use. But the electrical system was in a most unfortunate condition. Roman tells me that some of the wiring installed … bare wire and ceramic posts, within the wall space. Now on my first project – there had been no electric system installed at all, and only the most rudimentary gas-lights."

"That place in France," Richard dredged some fragments of VPI's publicity materials from his memory.

"The Chateau, yes," Lew nodded, and led the way out into the lobby – a noble space, like the ballroom, on two levels. A grand staircase swept down from the floor above, and light streamed in from the tall windows over the main entrance. A few pieces of overstuffed furniture – a circular ottoman and a number of armchairs upholstered in crimson and gold-patterned brocade which matched the colors in the carpet – had been moved into the lobby, along with a pair of palm trees in bathtub-sized bronze urns standing sentry on either side of the door.

The reception counter with the bank of little message boxes for each room stood against the paneled wall below the staircase. A bronze nymph on tiptoe on the bottom baluster held aloft an elaborate torch above her head, a torch with flames of brilliant, diamond-like glass.

"We had to have a copy of the original carpet woven to order," Lew remarked, as they crossed the lobby. "The existing was too worn to be repaired. Now, this is the main bar. There will be a smaller establishment on the second floor, adjoining the gallery above the ballroom. In the original plans, it was the gentleman's smoking salon."

"My god, how perfectly splendid!" Richard gaped, in astonishment. He had been once or twice in the Cattleman's bar, on the brief occasions when it had been open for nostalgic business as part of Founders' Day celebrations; the ornate plaster ceiling dark with years of cigarette smoke and accumulated dust, the woodwork obscured by the same. Now all was fresh, polished, ranks of glassware reflected in the mirror behind the bar, everywhere panels of tiger striped Circassian oak seeming to ripple like silk through a courtesans' fingers. The only thing missing on this day were the serried ranks of jewel-colored glass bottles of liquors … and of course, customers.

"The bones of this place are superb," Lew replied. "The original owner and his builder spared no expense. All the fittings – the wood, stone, the glass and metal – were of first quality, and for the most part, maintained well, until the hotel closed for good. Since then – benign neglect, which is often the best which can be hoped for. So now, the dining room. The furniture is about half original, but restored, the rest replicated from the designs in modern materials."

"This could be ..." Richard began, as they walked out through the lobby and into the second arched doorway. "It could be every bit as ... never mind." It was on the tip of his tongue to compare it to Carême, the glorious restaurant, every stick and stone of it his own making, until the fateful opening night. There were no cloths on the tables, no place settings of china, cut-glass and silver plate – merely the chairs and bare tables, in serried ranks. He was aware of Lew's sideways glance, and hesitation before speaking. Ah, this would be the VPI marketing manager speaking, possibly with an offer to make to a once-famous chef, now refugee from his own celebrity.

"It could be splendid, or it could be yours, you mean?" Lew asked, his voice gentle, neutral. "It could be, you know. You have only to say yes – and a generous contract as house chef of the renewed Grand Cattleman Hotel would be yours."

"You know how to tempt a man," Richard sighed, heavily, recalling the words of Miss Letty, reiterating the lessons which he had doubtless listened to as a bored boy, forced to attend church services. *"For what shall it profit a man, if he shall gain the whole world, and lose his own soul*? I would be in the spotlight once again, as the executive chef of your palace hotel – probably as soon as the doors opened, and the paparazzi flooded in. I can't do it, Lew. I even said no to your predecessor, when I first got here, and she twigged who I was. Narrow escape, that. I said it before – no."

"And you said no to Allen Lee, when he asked you to co-host with him?" Lew smiled, slight and knowing. "Ah, yes – do not look so astonished, *chère* Richard. Allen Lee told me, as a friend. You fear to lose your soul, then, to fame."

"Fame is a bitchy, demanding mistress," Richard complained bitterly. "Other chaps would cheerily wrap up their soul in brown paper and hand it to the Devil in a shopping bag in exchange; I would have, ten, fifteen years ago. That was then, this is now, and I know better. Trust me – I'd be back where I started again, within weeks; black-out drunk, wrecked and dumped in a foreign city, yet again. It's a handsome offer, Lew. Thank you for considering me, but I will not venture down that road again. Leave me to the Café, and my catering ventures. I'll gladly do the occasional event; just another local working stiff in the catering trade, but not an exclusive contract with VPI's organization. No hard feelings, then? Look, if you want me to advise you on the kitchen layout – be glad to. As a friendly neighborhood expert. Lay on, McDuff. I do confess to being eaten up with curiosity."

"This will be the last room on the ground floor to be finished," Lew explained, as he led the way through to the kitchen. "I had hoped to see it completed before the Boathouse opening, and my wife and I take our vacation – but alas, events conspired, as they often do. I am leaving one of my associates to oversee progress over the summer. Georgina Mason; she is not only the wife of one of my colleagues, but she has some knowledge and experience in interior decoration. Our CEO thinks highly of her skills, as she has done some work in our headquarters offices … and she is … personable." Lew gave one of those inexpressible Gallic shrugs.

"Ah, but is she able?" Richard asked, with understandable cynicism.

"I have no objection to her," Lew answered. "And the major reconstruction on the upper floors has been completed, in any case. All that remains is the decorating, and it is not as if she can do much harm, in any case."

Famous last words, as Richard would later discover. But that would be much, much later.

The Young Volunteer

The message from Joe was terse. *To All in Group. Subject: New Information available on our guy – Meet tomorrow at nine in the Café.*

That was the first hint to Richard that things to do with the unearthed skeleton were about to enter a whole new phase. The second was when Allen Lee swaggered into the kitchen at half-past eight, all a-beam, and saying, "Hey, Richard! Can I have one of your awesome fry-ups? The guys are meeting at nine. I've got the Walters records, and Harry and Sylvester say they've come up with stuff as well."

"Don't you love it, when a plan comes together," Araceli remarked, as she came in to load up her coffee carafe. "Hey, Allen Lee – welcome back! We were beginning to think we'd never see your smiling face around here, ever again!"

"I can't stay away from my favorite breakfast, at my favorite little café in Texas!" Allen Lee exclaimed, and dropped a gallant kiss on that hand of Araceli's which wasn't holding the coffee carafe. "Or my very favorite waitress! Girl, you have got to run away and marry me some time! What about tonight! We can catch a flight out of San Antonio, be in Las Vegas by midnight, in one of those emergency wedding chapels! What do you say?"

"Well, besides me being happily married, and you the same," Araceli replied in the same teasing tone, "I have a PTA meeting tonight, and then I have to wash my hair. Some other time, Allen Lee?"

"Heartbreaker," Allen Lee answered with another huge grin, and absented himself to the dining room, while Richard and Luc looked on, in slightly stunned amazement.

"Hey," Araceli demanded in sudden indignation, "What's with the fish-eyed goggle? Is there some rule about flirting in the Café that I haven't been told about? Allen Lee's a man, I'm a woman. There's absolutely nothing serious about acknowledging the fact that we like each other and are not dead from the waist down. A good unserious flirt is about the most fun that mature adults can have these days. Lighten up, Chef. You too, Luc." She added, in a pedantic voice, unconsciously rather like Miss Letty explaining something to a rather slow child, "There's nothing serious in it. He asks me to run away and marry him, and I come up with elaborate reasons as to why I cannot. It's just fun. You know, adults can have fun without taking their clothes off; right?"

"A form of verbal give-and-take," Luc's expression cleared of the cloud which had hung over it. "Oh, I understand now."

"Exactly," Araceli took her full carafe off to the dining room, leaving Richard and Luc contemplating the baffling ways of confident women who knew their own minds. Sylvester drifted in, along with Chris Mayall; Araceli sent in Chris' breakfast order even before the silvery chime of the bell on the Café's door heralded their arrival. Then Harry Vaughn and Lew Dubois pulled up in Harry's candy-apple red convertible, just ahead of the Luna City PD cruiser.

"The sleuths are assembled," Richard observed to Luc, who gave him a puzzled look, as he started an omelet for Chris. "I don't get it, Chef."

"They are trying to figure out about the skeleton that they found, doing the initial land-clearing for the Boathouse project," Richard explained.

Luc brightened. "Oh, yeah – that was on the news. I saw it before my old roomie in Karnesville pawned my TV without asking. So – what did they find out about this guy?"

"A name," Richard replied. "And that he had been in the military in the First War. They must have discovered a lot more, since then." He sighed, a small private sigh. When he looked around the door, there was Kate Heisel, her oversized tan coat flapping like a sail behind her, as the door chimed again. She flashed a beaming smile at all sitting at the stammtisch table and came into the kitchen.

"Hi. 'Celi! I guess I'm not too late. Richard!" she went on tiptoe in her sensible flat-heeled pumps, planted an affectionate kiss on his cheek. "I just barely made it, even denting the speed limit. Acey's all eaten up with curiosity about my potential scoop. I've been putting off finalizing the story since forever! I got Joe's message … Oh, hi, Joe! Is all that you be telling me today be embargoed, or can I finally file the story, complete and entire? Acey's getting darned impatient."

"You can now do with it as you like," Joe replied, most dour of expression. "And Acey McClain can be grateful that I'm not gonna tell him to fold it until it's all corners and stick it where the sun don't shine. Calling me every day for a month and threatening me with an FOIA request is not the best way for your boss to win me over, Katie."

"Acey's a bit old-school, Joe," Kate replied, in an almost superhuman demonstration of apologetic tact. "But you can depend on me to be straight with y'all. You know that, Joe."

"I do." Joe helped himself from the coffee urn, splashed cream into his mug and went out into the dining room. Kate followed him.

"He's already eaten," Araceli came into the kitchen, brisk and smart. She rattled off the breakfast orders, adding, "Kate just wants one of our croissants and a bit of fruit. They want you to join them, Chef – so you'll be in the loop."

"God knows why," Richard gave a swift turn to the patties of sausage turning on the griddle, and Araceli put on an expression of thinning patience.

"Because you are the manager of the Café," she said. "It's always been the hub. Everyone comes here, they talk… And you were one of the first people to see the bones, and you figured out right away that it was a German bayonet – an old Imperial Army one."

"Right," Richard did have to admit that he was curious about what the sleuths had found; this was straight out of a vintage Hardy Boys mystery, his secret and guilty reading pleasure. "It's just that this interrupts my workday!"

"Rise to the occasion, Chef," Araceli displayed a notable lack of sympathy. She filled the coffee carafe from the urn, snapping the lid shut with a violence which spoke volumes, as Luc said,

"I got it, Chef – don't worry."

Richard took a mug of his own, filled with coffee and cream, and sat at the last empty chair at the stammtisch. Joe, Allen Lee, Sylvester and Harry Vaughn all had folders or heavy envelopes before them; Kate had her own reporter's notebook open, pencil at the ready, with a spare stuck through her usual sloppy bun.

"Right then," Joe began, without preamble. "This is a working day for folks, so we'll be short. Allen Lee, you came the farthest to this meet-up and did the heaviest digging, so the floor is yours."

Allen Lee cleared his throat and opened the folder in front of him. "I have some kin in St. Louis, so it wasn't that far out of my way. I spent a couple days searching the archives. Got copies of Walter's enlistment and service records." He fanned out a handful of copied documents; archaic forms filled out in scratchy old-fashioned penmanship, a copy for each. "Michael Delaney Walters enlisted in the US Marine Corps on June 2, 1915, in Philadelphia, Pennsylvania – local boy, from Marlton, just outside of the city. This was a few weeks after the sinking of the passenger liner *Lusitania*. Folks got pretty heated up around that time, 'cause of Germany declaring unrestricted submarine warfare. Walters did pretty good in training, an exemplary Marine, from all accounts. Good marksman, too. Nothing derogatory in his records; disciplined once for being late reporting for guard duty. He'd just graduated from high school, was supposed to be going to college. Stood apart in those days, if you had finished twelve years of school – which he had."

"A real bright spark," Harry Vaughn shook his head. "Patriotic as all get-out. Knew a lot just like him in Korea. Go on."

"By the summer of '17, Walters had been promoted to Lance Corporal, and assigned to the 6th Marine Regiment, at Quantico. Shipped to France later that year, became part of the 4th Brigade, 2nd US Expeditionary Force. Did nothing much for the rest of the year, save being trained by the French…"

"Please, no witticisms regarding dropping weapons and surrendering," Lew Dubois murmured, somber as a man at a funeral of a friend. "France had bled near to white by that point. Continue, my old."

"From all reports, Germany had achieved much the same," Joe interjected. "And in the next year, they threw everything they had at the Western Front, having been relieved of having to fight on the Eastern, since Russia was out of the war. Well, Russia was out of the war against the Axis: Not out of that against the Mensheviks and the Whites. One last gamble to win the war, before we arrived to save the day. Hey, I had to read about all this. Professional military education. Carry on, Allen Lee."

"Sometime during May 1918, the 4th Brigade were assigned to defend a length of the front just south of Chateau-Thierry and Belleau Woods, against a German force trying to punch through, over the Marne River. The fighting there got pretty hot and heavy early in June."

"My Grand-père Lucien was wounded there – the first time," Lew Dubois nodded. "By a fragment from a German grenade, which killed the man next to him,"

"It's part of our lore," Sylvester was looking down at the copied forms in front of him. "The first time the Marines went all-out in a big land battle. Trenchworks, bare fists, bayonets and all that."

"Grand-père only spoke to me of it once," Lew Dubois mused, as if looking back over the decades past. "When I was about … thirteen or fourteen. There was a man who drowned in a summer flood on the bayou … and it was our misfortune to find the body a week later, cast up in the reeds near to Grand-père's favorite place for hunting ducks. You may imagine the condition of it, of course."

Both Joe and Chris nodded, with bleak expressions.

"The smell," Sylvester said, and Lew Dubois agreed. "Grand-père was as white as a fine linen handkerchief. And he vomited over the side of the boat. I say, 'Grand-père, are you all right? Did you eat something bad?' An' Grand-père, he wipe his lips, with a hand what shook as if he had the palsy, an' he say, '*Chère*, it smelled like that, a thousand times worse in that Hell Wood, where I fought in France. The smell of death, an' we could not escape it, for the dead were all around us and we could not begin to bury them.'" Lew shrugged. "Only that time, did he talk to me about it. He never went back to that place to hunt ducks again. No matter. What of our man? Was he also wounded in Belleau Wood, like my Grand-père?

"Walters was lucky there, according to the records," Allen Lee continued. "But in July, his regiment – or what was left of it after Chateau-Thierry – were part of a counter-attack near Soissons, as part of the Aisne-Marne offensive. His unit walked into stiff resistance as they were advancing toward Parcy-et-Tigny. Lance Corporal Walters's company had a surprise argument with a German machine-gun and lost. He was one of about half a dozen survivors, all of them badly wounded. He spent the rest of the war in various military hospitals before being medically-discharged, about a year later. The bare bones of this is in the copies that I have handed out to y'all."

There was a brief moment of silence while all digested this, along with breakfast. Sylvester was the first to speak.

"We earned the nickname of Devil-Dogs there, of course. And the 4th Division got awarded the French Croix de Guerre. Named the whole woods after us, too; Woods of the Marine Brigade. I put the feelers out to some veteran-support websites. Some of the guys are into history. There's a memoir written by another WWI Marine who was in the same unit, near as I can figure. The writer mentions his pal 'Wally' Walters from New Jersey, a couple of times. Said he was a hard-charger, guts to spare, and went on about how Wally should have been put up for a decoration, for something he did in the fighting there. But that memoir was privately published in the Forties, and surviving copies are as rare as hens' teeth. I've asked my friend to scan those pages and send them to me, but he hasn't gotten around to that, yet. So, what happened to Walters, after termination from service?"

"Short medical write-up attached," Allen Lee replied. "No loss of mental function, but somewhat physically impaired, to the point of being unable to continue serving. And in any case, the war was over."

"Know the feeling," Joe Vaughn muttered, to Sylvester's silent nod of agreement.

Allen Lee continued. "He was badly scarred, and this at a time when plastic surgery was basic, at best. Nothing much they could do for him, past a certain point, back then. That's as far as the military records go. He was awarded a small stipend for an inability to do the work that he might have been able to do before being wounded. Not much, though. The government then, as now, worked exceedingly slowly."

This comment elicited a weary and cynical chuckle from Sylvester, Chris, and Joe.

"Harry worked the genealogy angle," Joe picked up the thread of the meeting with commendable alacrity. "He tracked down a couple branches of the Walters family tree of Marlton, Noo Joisey. Over to you, Harry."

"Right," Harry Vaughn opened his own folder, and cleared his throat in a professorial manner. "Now, lucky me; I didn't have to drive all the way to Philadelphia or St. Louis, even. A paid account at Ancestry.com, some database searches, and a lot of phone calls. Got a line on the next of kin almost at once. Michael Delaney Walters was the youngest of five children; five surviving children, let me correct myself. Parents were Alexander Walters who owned a grocery store in Marlton, and Mabel Delaney Walters. Seems to have been a prosperous enterprise; I checked on it, and on the Walters house on the Sanborn fire insurance maps, and they both were damned nice places for the time, with every modern convenience. Alexander was on the ball, businesswise. There were two deceased as infants or small children between him and the next-oldest sib, a sister named Iona, who married a guy named Arthur Pratt in 1915, according to the census and the parish records of their church. You young folks might not realize that once upon a time, it was the usual for parents to lose a few sprigs off the family tree, in the generations before vaccinations and antibiotics became widespread. Our Michael Walters had another sister, and three brothers, all very much older; married or out of the Walters home before that time. This we got from tracking the family trees and the US Census in previous decades. The 1920 US Census has Michael D. Walters, no occupation noted, living with the widowed Mabel Walters, along with Iona Walters Pratt and two small children, Arthur Pratt having died the year previous in the great influenza epidemic. Alexander Walters died in 1922, and Mrs. Walters inherited the residual estate, but apparently not his business sense. I think that we can make some suppositions from this data."

"He was the baby of the family," Kate Heisel replied, at once. "Doted on by Mom and next-older sister. Returned to the nest to recover and work out what to make of life with a disability."

"PTSD, too," Christ put in, "Only they called it shell-shock, then. Old problem; just the name of the diagnosis changes."

"Safe assumption," Harry Vaughn nodded. "Now then, as to what happened next: I had several long telephone conversations with Iona Pratt's granddaughter, Mavis Harrison. She's the one who tracked down all this about her family. Nice lady, sixtyish, had a thing for family history, and remembers the stories that her grandmother told about her family, including the great-uncle who was terribly wounded during the Great War."

"What stories did she have of this great-uncle?" Lew Dubois asked, his voice particularly gentle.

"That he drank, could not keep any kind of employment, and was a particular concern to the family, especially to his mother. Alas, she – the great-grandmother died at about the time of the great stock-market crash, and all was lost. The business, what remained of it – the house, everything. Iona Pratt and her children moved in with relatives of her husband in Dayton, Ohio. The great-uncle, who was our Michael Delaney Walters, went wandering. On the bum, looking for work, like hundreds of other hoboes, back then; riding the rails, hitch-hiking, walking – whatever. Mavis says that her grandmother received a letter, a post-card, now and again, over the next five years. The last was a Christmas card, from someplace in Texas in 1935. The card is long-gone, of course, but I'd bet anything you like short of my candy-apple-red convertible that it was mailed from Luna City."

"Miss Letty said that her mom mailed a Christmas card for the scarred tramp, the year that he was here," Kate Heisel, her beryl-green eyes lively with interest, scribbled a note, and shuffled through the pages of her notebook. "Ah, here it is; "*Mother and Father hired him to cut firewood from some trees felled at the back of the property, and to help Father clear away the debris from the vegetable garden and dig it up for spring planting. And on the day that he finished, and came to the back door to be paid, he took out an envelope from the pocket of that old overcoat, saying, 'I have written a Christmas card for my sister, and I'm feeling poorly, too poorly to walk into town. Can you put it in the post for me, ma'am?' Mother said that she would and that was the last we saw of him. We thought that he had moved on, because that was the way of the fraternity of the road, so Father said. It was in mid-December, as I recall. The envelope already had a stamp on it, so Mother was not put to any expense. Money was so tight, at that time – and she was just grateful that he been so considerate."*

"Anything more for us, now?" Joe said, after exchanging one of those inscrutable looks with Sylvester and Chris. "Write up what you want from this, Katie. Make it a matter of public record. Hell, most of it is already in the public records…"

"One more thing," Lew Dubois put in, gently. "I am told that one of your local Boy Scouts has taken it as his project to raise the burial expenses, to include a proper marking stone, in the town cemetery. An admirable project, in my opinion. Harry, my old – you might wish to inform your contact, Mrs. Harrison, of this enterprise. I intend to support young Walcott in this project, of course. He will be permitted to solicit donations at the opening of the Boathouse for this purpose."

"Good idea," Joe replied, absently, as his official radio shrilled for his attention. "Yeah, Milo – ok, on it. Sorry, folks," he addressed the table at large. "Crime waits for no man. Gotta go. Any new developments, email us all in group."

He absented himself hastily from the Café, not before grabbing his thermos for a fill-up. Richard got up from the table and followed him into the kitchen.

"So, it sounds as if our mystery is solved and sorted," Richard said, as Joe topped up his thermos with cream.

Joe capped it, and replied, "Pretty much, yeah. All over but for the shouting and the victory parade. Walcott's kid prolly will do all the rest. Still," Joe sighed. "A hundred years ago, and someone we didn't know, save through moldy old paperwork. It still hurts, thinking of a straight-up Marine stud, curling up and dying all alone in the woods like a stray dog hit by a car."

"It wasn't as if there was no one who cared," Richard answered. "Look; from today, plenty of people in his life did – the sister, at the very least. Miss Letty's parents. It was just … some people need to go away into the woods and get sorted – away from everyone. It's … it's a bit like having a sore place in your soul that you just don't want anyone touching – because then it hurts even more."

"Ah," Joe regarded Richard, with what seemed to Richard to be dawning respect. "You know the feeling then, I guess."

"I might," Richard answered, in a noncommittal fashion.

The Pursuit of Love

"Bree, you haven't experimented with … the sex-magick, have you? You know; with a boyfriend of your age?" Gee-Nan asked, anxiously. Bree Grant looked at her grandmother with eyes rounded in mild astonishment. *What on earth could have brought that on?* It was the first day of Bree's return to the Age of Aquarius; suppertime in the Straw Castle Aquarius, a high-ceilinged tower of a place with a domed roof. Her parent's car had vanished up the narrow road into the Age that very morning, trailing a smudge of dust and leaving Bree behind to spend spring and summer with her grandparents.

Bree, seventeen, intense and outgoing, replied in shocked surprise, "Ick, no! The male of our species," Bree continued with a magisterial air, wondering why Grampy was stifling laughter. "Is simply not at their best at this stage of development. Really, Gee-Nan, they're either all zits and obsessed with cars or football, or Goth and emo. The very thought; it is to make me throw up. It would generate an overwhelming quantity of synchrotron radiation from the upper dreckosphere of the suckularity, too much even to contemplate. Besides, the guys I know have no savoir-faire at all. I have standards, you know!" Bree directed a severe look at her grandfather who was still snickering. "I demand a degree of savoir-faire in a lover. Absolutely, at a minimum."

"Bree Pumpkin, do you even know what savoir-faire means?" Grampy asked, over his plate of quinoa and feta-cheese salad; a dish which Bree had made herself, rather than risk a serving of Gee-Nan's signature and revolting Lentil Surprise.

"Sure," Bree serenely scarfed up a forkful of salad. "It's from the French, actually. It is defined in the dictionary as *'a polished sureness in social behavior.'* I really don't think that is too much to ask for, Grampy – and what is so funny about it?"

"Nothing, Pumpkin," Sefton still grinned, which Bree found quite baffling. Not as baffling as when Judy laid down her own fork and looked earnestly at her granddaughter.

"You are of the age to consider experimenting with sex-magick, you know. It is a powerful force in this world, and not one to be lightly considered."

"I know, Gee-Nan," Bree reassured her grandmother. "Trust me; I have thought about it all very carefully. There's no real future in sleeping with every guy you meet. I mean, really. They forget you the next day, or never call … I'd rather be the one they remember forever for <u>not</u> having gone to bed with them. When I do decide," Bree helped herself to more home-made organic okra pickles and bit into one of them with a satisfying crunch. "To practice sex-magick, it will be spectacular. Perfect. On satin sheets at the top of the Eiffel Tower, or under a Tahitian waterfall with the scent of frangipani hanging in the air … That kind of perfection takes time, and he will really, really have to be worthy."

"What about that Walcott boy?" Gee-Nan ventured, having – as Bree assumed – totally missed the point. "He's quite nice-looking, for his age. The two of you are quite compatible, astrologically-speaking."

"Gee-Nan!" Bree was horrified. "Robbie's my best friend in Luna City, practically! He's just a kid. He can't possibly do the magick correctly!"

"Might surprise you," Sefton Grant murmured and looked innocent when Bree glared at him. Judy compounded the horror with a further suggestion. "Bree Pumpkin, if an older man, knowledgeable about working the sex-magick properly is what you are looking for, consider Richard, at the Café. He is also compatible, astrologically … and very handsome. And an accomplished lover, by all that we have heard…"

"Oh, double-ick!" Bree, shocked out of all impulse to be polite to her elders, slammed down her fork, followed by her fist on the table, which being of sturdy make from native cedar cut on the property by Sefton, only trembled slightly. "Gee-Nan, that's positively gross! He's old enough to be Dad, practically! Besides, he's my boss! I just may throw up at the thought. If anything, he's sweet on Kate Heisel. And I mean – ugh. I wouldn't do another girl dirty by screwing her boyfriend. That's just gross!"

"Calm down, dear! It was only a suggestion!" Judy protested, her eyes filling with tears. "I meant it in your best interests. You want your initiation into the magick as a woman to be perfect, with a considerate and skilled practitioner of the arts!"

"But not incestuous!" Bree retorted. "Jeez, Gee-Nan! At that rate, I might just as well throw myself at Chief Vaughn, or Coach Garrett! Can I just be allowed to sort out my own life?"

"We want the best for you, Pumpkin," Judy wiped away a tear on her napkin.

Sefton came to her rescue. "We know," he said. "Leave it alone, Judikins. Bree Pumpkin, your Gee-Nan means well. We'll let the subject drop as of this moment, all right? Good. Now, Richard asked me yesterday morning, since you were to be back in Luna City – are you free to work a special event, come Spring Break? Not full-time," Sefton added hurriedly. "Just to help prep for a big bash at Mills Farm early in March."

"Sure, Grampy," Bree sniffled. "Yeah, I can do it." She glared at her grandmother. "But not another word about me and my love life, 'kay? I'm almost eighteen, I'm practically through my first year of college, I can sort that shit out for myself, Oh-Kay?!"

"Agreed, Pumpkin," Sefton agreed, keeping his relief private … although Judy was still sniffling, slightly. "So, you do your studies in the morning, work a coupla-times a week at the Café in the afternoon?"

"I'm a big girl now, Grampy," Bree spared a serious glare at her grandmother. "I can handle it!"

"Good," Sefton replied. "Now, who wants another sliver of that marinated barbequed tofu?"

A week later, Bree had settled gratefully into a schedule which had the happy effect of exercising her mind and her physical self, returning to the familiar environs of the Café, and picking up the threads of friendship with Robbie, Araceli, and the cousins Blanca and Beatriz. The new cook, Luc, rather startled her at first.

"He's really weird," she remarked, to Robbie. Robbie had returned to his summertime habit of driving her home from the Café, and hanging out at the Straw Castle Aquarius, since it was too cold yet to go swimming. "Is he really a drummer with a rock and roll band?"

"Yep," Robbie signaled for a left-hand turn, into the unpaved and indifferently graveled driveway which led into the campground and to the Grant home-place. The driveway might have been mistaken for the entrance to a dumpsite, an oil-pumping donkey-jack or a long-neglected ranch pasture, and in any case, there was no traffic on either side of Route 123. But Robbie was a careful driver, a scrupulous observer of established rules, no matter who minor or who might be watching.

"You are such a Boy Scout!" Bree giggled. "Why did you even bother signaling?"

"Dad says that character is what you are when no one is watching," Robbie answered, unperturbed. "And besides, I <u>am</u> a Boy Scout. I'm working on my Eagle project; raising money to bury that dead veteran properly in the Luna City cemetery. With a nice headstone, and all. You know; Michael David Walters, the skeleton that they found when Roman Gonzalez's crew started working on the foundations for the boat house? Yeah, that one. Poor guy; there's some kin they found in Ohio, someplace, but he's just a name on a family tree chart to them. Why should they bother?"

"Why should you?" Bree asked, in all seriousness.

"Because it's the right thing to do," Robbie confessed, in touching earnest. "And because it's a good project. Everyone was thinking about who he was, where he came from; no one thinking much about what to do about what was left of him, until I suggested my project to Coach Garett – he's my scoutmaster, you know. And …" Robbie slowed the aged Volvo sedan, to circumvent some particularly deep ruts in the road. "Chief Joe and them. They found out that Michael Walters was exactly my age when he enlisted. Seventeen and a half, although it looks like he told a bit of a lie about his birthday to the recruiter. It made a difference to me, knowing that. A personal difference. He was plenty bright, they say – supposed to go to college, like me. But he enlisted instead. And when he came back, he was seriously messed up. Coach Garrett, Chief Joe; they both say we owe them something to the guys that got their lives messed up, fighting in a war for us. Even if it's nearly a hundred years later, I'm paying back a bit of that debt."

Bree was silent for a good few moments, as the aged Volvo bumped along the track, past the goat pasture, past the campground, where the clattering windmill stood guard over the concrete-block wash-house. "It's a good project," she said, at last. "And you're a great person for even thinking of it. One of the best people I know, my age. Did you ever notice that so many of our peers are idiots? Is it because of their parents, or just having to hang with other idiots, all the time?"

"I dunno," Robbie drove into the somewhat-more-thoroughly-graveled space which lay before the Straw Castle and put the Volvo into neutral gear. This was another reason that Bree liked Robbie; he could drive a vehicle with a standard shift. Somewhat of an arcane skill, but Bree appreciated such. "See you tomorrow, Bree? Chef wants to get an early start on the meat pies for the picnic spread."

"Yeah. See you tomorrow," Bree echoed. She made a gesture to open the passenger door, before looking at her friend, and venturing, "You know that Gee-Nan likes you a lot. She thinks it's okay if we have sex. Before you get all hopeful, *I'm* not keen. It's awkward. I like you *lots*, but it's awkward. Maybe someday, though. We can think about it then."

"Yeah," Robbie answered, and Bree noticed that the tips of his ears and his cheekbones were reddening. "It's awkward. The only place that we could do it is the back seat."

"Uncomfortable and just plain tacky," Bree restrained a shudder – not that the back seat of the Volvo was all that gross, or that the prospect of doing with Robbie was an unpleasing thought. "It would mess up a friendship, you know. I like things between us the way that they are. Besides, your Mom would be furious when she found out."

"She would find out," Robbie agreed, and it seemed to Bree that he was a bit relieved as well. "And the screaming would be epic. She'd scream at you, too, for good measure."

"Just as well, then. See you tomorrow, OK?"

"Sure thing," Robbie answered. *Yes, he definitely was relieved.* Bree waved at him, as he turned the Volvo around and headed back down the road.

Love, Etc.

Bree loved being back in Luna City, with Grampy and Gee-Nan, living at the sparkling-new Straw Castle Aquarius; such a wonderful change from the old yurt! To her, that place had always smelt faintly of moldy wool and indifferent drains, dark and dreary on the inside, with the only natural light coming down through the smoke-hole in the top, or the door when it was open. She had never been able to fathom why her father was so fond of the nasty old place. She couldn't see why on earth anyone would be sorry it all had burned, burned so thoroughly all left had been insubstantial ashes.

Now Grampy and Gee-Nan had a tall, thick-walled castle tower, flooded with light on the one side, open to the outdoors and a sun-lit pergola, which commanded a view of the riverbank, at some distance. She could see what she was cooking for them, of an evening, when Grampy came in from the pastures and the chicken-coops, with buckets of goat-milk and baskets of eggs, and Gee-Nan from brewing up her soaps and candles, in the old trailer which served as her workroom.

"You are an old soul, Bree," Gee-Nan remarked, when Bree had commented on how free and energized she now felt, now that she was not locked in to a tiresome day in a sprawling brick compound of that prison called a high school. "The Establishment is not for you."

Bree agreed, although she was not entirely certain that Gee-Nan meant about The Establishment. Except when it came to school. Really, how had she not seen clearly how stifling it all was, moving from cell to cell, in obedience to the hourly unfeeling bells? Most of the teachers there were lame, indescribably lame, and as for her fellow pupils! *That was to barf, just thinking of it all.* The cliques among students, the tiresome organized happy fun of school programs, being confined, like sheep – at least goats were intelligent and rebellious! How wide, how wonderful the world now open to her was; full of interesting people and fascinating subjects, now that she could gorge her natural curiosity to the widest possible extant! No longer had Bree to raise her hand and wait to be called on! She could grapple, intellectually, with topics which interested her. As for the other inmates of the educational asylum – how had she ever come to think of them as friends? Like Meryl and Cher, they were inchoate rebels against the system, lashing out, rebels without a clue.

Now Bree could see clearly that they had gone about rebelling in exactly the wrong way, a way guaranteed to end in disaster. Mom and Dad were right about that, although Bree was still too embarrassed about how she had acted over the issue to apologize to her parents. Grampy and Gee-Nan; they had been rebels in the righteous old way, staking their claim and livelihood on a bit of land. *So, OK, Gee-Nan had inherited the property* ... but she and Grampy had built an enterprise on it, and lived on their own terms for ... well, since forever.

Bree felt that she had grown up enormously in the last year and a half; living at the Age with Grampy and Gee-Nan over the summer, working at the Café, being friends with Robbie, and bossed by Chef. That was as far from being a kid as it was possible to get and still actually be a kid, and one who couldn't yet vote. But getting a driver's license was still in the cards, assuming that Mom and Dad would spot her a car … even a beater like the Walcott's battered old Volvo sedan.

Speaking of cars, that small dust trail on the drive to the Amazing Straw Castle must be Robbie, come to take her to work. Bree's spirits lifted. She liked Robbie enormously. He wasn't a total yuck-fest, like most of the boys in the classes that she had left behind in that gulag called a high school. *(Bree had only just learned what a gulag was, although freely admitting that she was perhaps exaggerating in making the comparison; high school for her was every bit as cruel and soul-killing as the Soviet Russian variety.)*

"Gee-Nan, I'm off to work!" Bree caught up her bag, into which she had put her wallet, iPad, and a paperback copy of *One Day in the Life of Ivan Denisovich,* a thick notebook in which she was accustomed to scribble notes on any topic which took her fancy, and a clean chef's jacket with the embroidered logo of the Luna Café and Coffee on the front. *OK, for the moment, she was only part-timing, but Chef said she had earned the right to wear that coat.* Bree was one for standing on rights for which she felt she was entitled.

"Hey, Bree," Robbie said, through the rolled-down drivers' side window. "You remember my sister, Belle? She's gotta go to Karnesville in the car, while we're at work. But don't worry – she'll be back in time that I can run you home when we're done." Robbie frowned slightly in bafflement, which Bree thought was simply adorable and added. "I can't remember if you two know each other."

"We do," Belle answered tonelessly and without much interest. "We met last summer. Maybe when Pop was overseeing the rebuild out here. I remember; at Dad's send-off party for me, and the Abu Dhabi project.

Where the dogs came in and about murdered that armadillo. Weren't you one of the catering people?"

She was sitting in the passenger seat of the Volvo, a tall, skinny, dark-eyed, and dark-haired girl who looked like Robbie's female clone. Bree was inclined to detest her on sight, or at least, for the tone of bored dismissiveness in which she voiced that last remark. Robbie set the brake, got out of the car, and opened the rear passenger-side door for her. Slightly irked, Bree took the seat directly behind the driver. *Yeah, she could see the back of Robbie's head from there, and also his sister in three-quarter profile.*

"You're in college, aren't you?" she ventured, determined against her first inclination to be civil, as Robbie swung the elderly Volvo through the graveled space with served as a drive and parking space at the Amazing Straw Castle.

"Yeah," Belle replied, in tones flatter than Kansas in boredom. "Julliard. You *might* have heard of it. In New York. I'm studying trumpet."

Bree racked through her repertoire of potentially-polite-yet-socially-savage responses and came up with one of Gee-Nan's favorites. "How very nice for you." Daringly, she added. "I guess that means that you blow … a nice horn."

"Yeah," Belle replied, not budging her tone of voice a single degree from bored disinterest. "Dad bought me a Monette for school. I guess you still work with Robbie in the kitchen?"

"Yeah," Bree answered. "I'm doing college – independently. On-line courses, and all. I should get my degree in another year."

"How very nice for you," Belle replied. *What a total bitch*, Bree concluded silently and also that she was finished with being social and civil. She sat in the back seat, maintaining an air of frozen politesse, until Robbie wheeled through the back alley and parked the Volvo in the space behind the Café and the other storefronts lining Town Square. There was

Luc, with the sleeves of his own chef's coat rolled up, harvesting herbs from Chef Richard's carefully tended raised beds in the space behind the Café.

"Who's that?" Belle asked, in a tone of voice suggestive of mild curiosity. "I don't know him. Does he work at the Café?"

Robbie answered, "He's the new cook. Bit of a weirdo, though – but he's a musician, too."

"Oh?" Belle asked, as Robbie – with touching gravity, held the door open for Bree, and then went around to hold the passenger-side door open for his sister.

"Yeah," Robbie answered. "He's a drummer, in a grunge band called OPM. Either it stands for Other Peoples' Money, or Ozona Mud Puppies, Objective Parallaxes in Motion, or maybe something else. They keep changing it."

"That accounts for why I've never heard of them," Belle replied, as Robbie tossed her the keys to the Volvo.

"Be back from Karnesville by four," he said, as seriously as he had exercised the door-opening-courtesy. "We're done by then. I promised that I'd drive Bree home."

"Sure," Belle answered, still flat and emotionless, but as she and Robbie went into the Café, she could swear that Belle and Luc had their eyes fixed unswervingly upon each other; Belle with the keys in her hand, Luc with the basket of cut herbs in one of his and a pair of kitchen scissors in the other. Some twenty minutes later, Chef was cursing under his breath, and about snapped Bree's head off, when she asked why.

"Thyme!" he snarled. They were laboring to debone two quarters of venison, several rabbits, and a haunch of boar; the sliced or cubed meats to marinate overnight, the bones intended for the stock pot, and the meat scraps and pig-fat to make a kind of sausage for the pie filling. It was a very complicated recipe.

Bree glanced at the kitchen clock and replied, "Half-past one, Chef."

"No, imbecile! The herbs! Luc was supposed to fetch them for the marinade."

"On it, Chef," Luc replied, as he came through the back door at that moment, the small wire basket piled high with slightly-wilting oregano, parsley, thyme and basil." He looked mildly stunned; so close to his usual expression that Bree didn't think anything much of it. The familiar sound of the Volvo's engine echoed briefly in the kitchen, diminishing in the distance, as the back door fell closed.

"Any time now, any time now!" Chef was agitated, impatient. Bree had worked long enough in the kitchen to know that. Chef wanted everything to go as clockwork, everything in place; timing was everything. He got freaked about the simplest things. Bree – from the great height of her experience as an apprentice – could sympathize. The kitchen had to go like clockwork, everything in the *mise-en-place* ready to hand, or else … disaster. Chef now cast an exasperated glance at Luc, but it sounded as if he were trying his best to control his tone. For some reason, he didn't give Luc the rough side of his tongue, as he had when she and Robbie were training last summer.

"Break up the bones, and start the stock," Chef commanded, and Bree bent her head over the task at hand. This was an interesting-looking recipe, for a sort of cold meat pie with a hot-water raised crust. *Must be a peculiarly English thing*, she decided. Anyway, they would be part of the grand picnic. She and Robbie talked about it in undertones as they worked, all though that afternoon of mincing, slicing, trimming, and Chef's intermittent lecture about the theory and practice of hot-water pastry raised crust pies, while the rich scent of bubbling stock perfumed the kitchen. Bree listened without particular resentment, as Chef was almost always interesting, and his accent was so pleasant-sounding.

"It sounds perfectly grand," Bree said quietly to Robbie, when Chef seemed to be done lecturing for a moment. "We could see them working on it, from the upstairs windows. My grandfather says the goats were just fascinated by all the activity."

"There's been stories on the San Antonio TV news, all this week," Robbie agreed. "One of the news crews even came in for coffee the other morning. They talked to me about the fundraising for my Eagle project. Mr. Dubois an' Sylvester Gonzales, they even located an antique Marie Corps uniform for me to wear. You know, Dad is heavily into reenacting? I'm kind of in two minds about wearing it, but Sylvester said it would be OK, and he promised to coach me on proper bearing. The news crew taped me talking about my project, but I don't think it made the news that night. But Dad said it was on the news in Abu Dhabi! I'll bet we'll see people coming in from everywhere for the grand opening. It will be fantastic!"

"It will be exhausting, too," Bree pointed out, with slightly less enthusiasm. Meanwhile, Chef poured brandy and port over the vat of meats, adding a couple of allspice berries, and finely minced thyme.

"Stir until it just combines," Chef commanded, and then he and Luc covered up the tub, shifted it onto one of the kitchen carts and rolled it into the walk-in cooler. "Now," he added, closing the cooler door, "All done for today – tomorrow the pastry, and the baking. Is the reduced stock cool enough to add the additional gelatin, Luc? Ok, whisk it in, and put it way in the cooler. We'll assemble the pies and bake them tomorrow."

"Are we done for the day, Chef?" Luc asked, which was a surprise – he was not normally a clock-watcher. In fact, he seemed to have little awareness of the concept of time, which was why he was often at work in the Café kitchen in the wee hours, a habit vastly preferred by those living in the other apartments on Town Square to Luc practicing on the drums in the front room of that little apartment in the Mercantile Building.

"Pretty much," Chef agreed. "Just clean up before you go."

To Bree's mild surprise, the Walcott's beater Volvo was parked in back, and Robbie's sister was perched on the hood, her feet resting on the substantial front bumper, waiting for them with every indication of patience.

"Hey," she said, as she tossed the keys to Robbie. "I'm gonna wait for Luc – he said he'd give me a ride home. It's just cool about him being in a real band. He thinks it was neat, me being in Julliard and playing with *Los Maldonados*. Don't tell Mom, 'kay? She'll have a meltdown. Just say I'm hanging out with some old friends; I'll be home before she even notices."

"Look, Belle," Robbie answered, a serious expression on his face. "If the subject comes up with Mom, I won't lie outright. I won't blurt out that it's Luc, but I won't say anything more than you're hanging out with a friend at the Café."

"'Kay," Belle replied, with a marked lightening of the sullen expression. Bree looked over her shoulder. *Yes, Luc was running out a bagful of kitchen trash, and that unedifying sight was sufficient to make Belle glow like ... like the glass wall of the Aquarius Tower, when the sun set on the far horizon, all mellow and golden.*

Settled in the accustomed passenger seat, as Robbie backed out of the Café's small parking place, Bree asked, "Hey, do you think that your sister is in love with Luc? She has the look of someone who wants to practice the sex-magick, all right."

Robbie laughed, in a way that Bree thought was so essentially male, knowledgeable, and superior. "Heck, no – Bree! He's a drop-out musician, in a busted-flat band, going nowhere. They can't even decide on a name! What does she have in common with him?"

"Only that she's a drop-in musician," Bree replied, and then they laughed together, and forgot about it all. Because this was Luna City.

Georgina Mason Rocks Inner Space!

Staff Writer Meaghan Turner
Houston Chronicle Life Style Magazine – October 2017 Issue

Visionary interior designer Georgina Mason is the hot new interior and party space designer in the upscale River Oaks neighborhood these days. A native of New York, and a graduate of the prestigious Pratt Institute with a BFA in Interior Design, Georgina worked briefly at several cutting-edge design firms in New York before devoting herself to raising a family with a rising young executive with Venue Properties, Intl., Gregory Mason. When Gregory was transferred to VPI's headquarters in Houston, Georgina put her talent and visionary skill to work in transforming their River Oaks home into a showcase. She was briefly a partner with Stubbs & Associates, before hanging out her shingle to practice independently, as "inner space by georgina" *(she is a fan of poet ee cummings)*, first among her friends and neighbors in River Oaks, and then as favorable word of mouth got around, to homes, offices, and retail spaces around Houston. Each space designed by Georgina is visionary, personal, and ultra-modern. One of her most striking interiors is the employee breakroom at VPI, which Georgina designed as a favor at cost. The breakroom is dazzlingly futuristic – and yet comfortable and well-lit – a suitable place for the employees of an international hospitality chain can recharge their mental batteries during the course of a busy day by relaxing in one of the personal 'people pods' under a thirty-foot tall 'jungle' of indoor plants– or socialize with friends and co-workers around the coffee bar.

"Everyone needs their own personal space, reflecting their tastes and experience," says Georgina, when we met at the trendy Backstreet Café for a quick brunch of bucatini and spicy crab. "And my job is to refine that experience and desires into a suitable ambiance. It's a challenge, sometimes … but I find that bringing synthesis and order out of chaos and bad taste is supremely rewarding."

Although the VPI breakroom is not open to the general public – as are most of Georgina's commissions – a few are; notably in the Houston Galleria, at the BoxLunch store, the Café Dolce Gelato, and at Nieman Marcus on the second-floor level. Check them out – and consider the dazzling visions of 'inner space by georgina' for your next party or home redesign.

Mills Farm, Inc. – Owned by VP, Intl.

The Glorious 1912 Boathouse Opening

On the morning of the opening, Richard and his crew, both kitchen and front-of-the-house – absent Robbie, who was extraneous to their buffet-serving needs and had another project to work on anyway – were transported out to the venue from the Café by a Mills Farm hired minibus; a luxury which Richard appreciated no end. The bus was followed by a pair of hired refrigerated vans boasting temporary Mills Farm Country Kitchen decals, stuffed full with their pre-prepared pans and trays of comestibles, and two obliging assistants who helped them transport the contents to the lower floor of the boathouse, where a small and efficient kitchen tucked away in back of the boat docks, had been equipped with a couple of enormous, industrial-sized refrigerators.

"Looks as though you have enough to feed an army there, Chef!" remarked one of the helpers, and Richard replied, "Such is our expectation!" He was already in an off mood, which he could not quite explain. Everything had gone like clockwork: every item on the menu had been pre-prepped according to plan. Indeed, he and Luc had been up since four in the morning, blearily assembling sandwiches for the multitude. The meat pies, the fruits, the tarts, and hardboiled eggs – everything! All had been assembled, packed into tubs and pans, stowed in the back of the refrigerated vans, checked off on a list by the ever-vigilant Araceli ... and now, it was nearly curtain time.

A curtain which would rise on a performance which would last until mid-afternoon, a long haul of six hours from now, and then conclude by a return to the Café for supper service. But long hours held no terrors or weariness for Richard now. It was just that there was something ... something lurking at the edge of awareness. And what was more aggravating, he had no idea of what it might be, since everything was going ... perfectly. They had been working full-out for the last four days. Even Belle Walcott had been roped into service by her brother to make lists of ingredients and prepared foodstuffs, after mooning around the kitchen, waiting to take the Volvo someplace, although to Richard's view, she was more interested in coy conversation with Luc, who – surprisingly – seemed to rise to the occasion.

"Start the coffee and the hot-water urns, as soon as you and the ladies are changed," he said to Araceli. "The buffet opens at 11:00, but we may offer coffee and tea at 10:00, when the event begins."

"On it, Chef!" Araceli replied, smartly. Her outfit for the day, and those for the other women were already hanging in suit-bags in the back of the bus clean, starched, and ready for 1912 service. So were the outfits for Richard and Luc. Richard sighed a small, hopeless sigh on observing that. He regarded the venue with an assessing eye. Yes, he had visited several times, to assess the general layout and the conveniences available, but during the first visit, the boathouse interior offices were just being painted, and on the second, he was impeded by several trucks unloading specialized equipment.

The venue – the magnificent boathouse – was undergoing those last throes of preparation. The groundskeepers and gardeners who kept the golf-course and the gardens of the main complex in immaculate trim were busy putting the last few colorful annuals in the flower beds, mowing the velvet-green swath of lawn, and sweeping up those dead leaves which an inconsiderate wind had deposited in the pristine surrounds overnight – probably blown in from the Grant property. Judy and Sefton were notoriously disinterested in appearances of a conventional sort, and the leaves from their grove went wherever the wandering winds took them, and dropped them where they wished, or lost interest and velocity. A pickup truck with the logo of Mills Farm on the doors was already parked in the brick-paved area adjoining the picturesque greensward sloping down to the riverbank. Another crew unfolded folding tables and chairs of a suitably archaic design, deploying them across the grass and covering them with crisp white cloths.

"I think they're going to offer the Boathouse as a wedding venue," Araceli ventured. "It makes sense, Chef, especially if the weather is nice. Hold the ceremony by the riverside, host a catered reception by the Boathouse; Mr. Dubois thought out this bit very cleverly, I think," she added in some awe. "I guess that's why he gets paid the big bucks, then."

"As long as he passes … those big bucks on to us, on the odd occasion," Richard added, although he did not think he meant to sound as sour as he did. This would be an excellent event venue, in temperate weather; a constant in Texas not to be relied upon any more than in England. Well, if all came to thunderstorms and rains, there was always the covered second-floor pavilion – which, he noted, was now equipped with gently rotating ceiling fans. The theory was, he had been told, that the fans would blow off all but the most persistent of biting insects. In case that theory proved invalid, they had come equipped with a quantity of old-fashioned screened covers for the food dishes. There would be no weather worries today, according to the forecast, which Richard checked and re-checked obsessively; clear and mild, with a light easterly breeze and highs in the low seventies. Otherwise, a perfect, mild spring day in South Texas.

The contents of the refrigerated vans went into those restaurant-sized refrigerators, stashed discretely in the that small kitchen at the back of the Boathouse. The stand-alone freezer was packed solid with bags of commercial ice. Richard regarded that facility with guarded approval. It wasn't large enough to seriously prepare a gourmet-level meal for hundreds, but sufficient to hold and stage already-prepared food items in quantity. Someone, possibly Lew Dubois himself, with his passion for detail, had foreseen the need for sufficient ice.

"Set up the buffet pans but hold off on adding the ice for another half-hour," Richard ordered. "And don't start setting out the food until a quarter of eleven." The back of minibus was piled high with buffet servers, and pans to hold ice. Richard was certain that Mills Farm would eventually lay out for specialized hot and cold food tables, if they were intending to do this regularly, but the old-fashioned manner for today just looked more in keeping with the archaic theme. One of the refrigerators contained an assortment of vases, large and small, already full of tasteful flower arrangements, with a note pinned to the largest vase. Richard let out a low whistle, when he saw that.

"The large bouquets are for the serving tables," Araceli noted with approval, upon reading the note. She and Richard were standing at the downstream end of the pavilion, observing the activity taking place on the riverbank and in the brick-paved area directly below. "All the small ones go on the guest tables. Araceli and the others had already gotten into their 1912 black and white serving-maid garb; Richard was still holding out. The only place to change was the mens' restroom, at the other end of the boathouse from the kitchen. He figured that Luc, with his tricolor mohawk, tats and body-modification would need the best part of an hour to even begin resembling early 20th century man. "There's supposed to be some staff coming to set them up. What's the plan, Chef? You and Lew confabulated all last week, but you didn't tell us much…"

"Customers will hand their pre-paid tickets at the bottom of the staircase there," Richard nodded toward the exterior staircase leading to the upper level. "Go through the buffet line, and either set themselves at one of the tables there … or go down again to a table on the lawn … or to a picnic blanket. Likely the pavilion and the tables will fill up fast. Mr. Dubois has thought of everything; he has additional staff who will circulate among the tables on the lawn, dispending additional drinks – ice water, sweet tea *(Richard shuddered at that: his Gran would condemn in strongest terms, the custom of pouring of perfectly good albeit cold tea over ice cubes)* and lemonade. He located an old-fashioned ice-cream cart, to circulate among the crowd. And his staff will take care of clearing the tables and such outside the pavilion. You only need wait on those sitting at tables in the pavilion."

"An ice-cream cart?" Araceli beamed. "How cute! Abuelita would love that! Her Uncle Hernandito used to sell ice-cream from a cart like that. He was the father of Nando, the jet-fighter ace that they named the high school gym after." She heaved a slightly regretful sigh. "I would have gotten *so* many social points back then, telling everyone that the gym was named after my Uncle Nando. Trouble was, just about every Gonzalez and Gonzales in town could say the same."

"Your family tree is a Gordian Knot," Richard agreed sourly. "Or one of those exotic ficus trees with a braided trunk; otherwise impervious to any attempts at untangling."

"You're in a bad mood today, Chef," Araceli sent him one of those shrewd sideways glances. "Any idea why? This should be one of our Café catering triumphs. And everything looks good!"

"That's just the trouble. Everything has gone to plan," Richard sighed. "It makes me nervous. I keep expecting disaster; the longer it is put off, the more horrific it will be. Rather like that ongoing curse on your school homecoming game. I have overheard Joe and Jess discuss the matter. When did all of their careful preparation ever forestall the inevitable disaster?"

"Chef, don't worry so," Araceli replied in that irritatingly calm voice she had when faced with temperament. "We've covered every possible contingency. The weather is predicted to be fine today: no storms, no high winds, no nothing but clear skies and light clouds. And if there are any dogs here, they will be on leashes and under control. *Los Maldonados* are playing up by the campfire ring, so it's not like they can get into a fight and ruin the day … well, not here. Anyway, they're nothing to do with this part of the event. What do you think might go wrong, Chef?"

"I don't know," Richard was still depressed, in spite of Araceli's heroic effort to buck up his mood. "I keep trying to skull out all means by which this event might come to disaster, and taking steps to forestall all of those which I can see, but …"

"You're a perfectionist, Chef," Araceli replied. "And a bit of a control freak. But you don't need to go borrowing trouble. Honestly, just relax and enjoy the day. Really. I will. So will the crew. Look, there's Patricia, and the rest of the cast."

"Oh. My. God." Richard breathed. "What are they doing – and what's this all in aid of?"

Araceli followed the direction of his gaze. "Oh, it's the old surrey from the Wyler place. Doc let them use it for the Homecoming Queen this fall, remember? That's Patricia and some of the cast for tonight's special performance."

From the direction of the new stables – a gleam of aluminum roof gleaming like silver beyond a distant clump of dark green oak trees – came the sound of horses' hooves clopping and clumping along the road. Around the bend came a pair of dapple-gray horses drawing a canopied surrey-cart, into which five people *(including the driver)* had managed to squeeze; three ladies in the rear seat, their lace-thatched gowns and monumental hats seeming to overflow the space entirely. A man in black and white clerical robes sat in the front seat next to the driver, an achingly handsome blond man in a in a well-cut suit and old-fashioned top hat who handled the reins with authority; Bodie Madison, a connection of the family who owned the Bodie feed mill in Luna City -- sometime rodeo rider, and briefly the object of Richard's jealousy over Kate's affections.

"What performance?" Richard inquired, still a little shaken by the initial intensity of his dislike for the handsome Bodie, although he had been put wise as to the man's sexual orientation almost immediately by Chris and Joe.

"Tonight, in the Cattleman ballroom; a special presentation of *The Importance of Being Earnest*. It's kind of an homage; the first formal play that the Luna City Players ever presented. Up till then, they only did minstrel shows and skits. Lew Dubois put it up to Patricia and the Players, months ago."

"Well, he is a man who makes long-range plans," Richard replied. The surrey drew up to the brick-paved open area, the three women waving cheerfully at them, as the handsome *(if flamingly gay)* Bodie Madison busied himself with securing the horses to the staircase railing. The churchman – Canon Chasuble, if Richard remembered his Wilde well – assisted the ladies down from the conveyance.

"Ricardo!" the oldest of the three women waved up at him. With a bit of shock, Richard finally recognized Patricia Pryor, elegant if theatrically aged, costumed in the most elaborate of Edwardian day dresses, and a hat the size of a bushel basket, skewered to a voluminous pile of gray hair. Richard assumed it must be a wig: Patricia in real life was stunningly blond; a thoroughly American, and subsequently much happier avatar of Princess Diana, if that lady had lived past the age of forty and been blessed with a bountifully happy and productive marriage. "Ricardo – is the coffee ready? I am perishing for a cup of your coffee, since we have been up since six, getting ready! We are to meet Lew and his wife here, just before the rush of the crowd…"

"The coffee is ready!" Richard called down, "And … I may have some small pastries to go with it, if you have the time and inclination. Patricia – you are … stunning." Well, that must be the right word, for Patricia twinkled happily, as she climbed the stairs. "I almost didn't recognize you, or the others in costume."

"The shoes are killing me," Patricia replied, deploying her skirts, parasol, and handbag with the expertise of a master, as she reached the top of the stairs. "Celi', you look absolutely charming, the very image of the perfect parlor maid! I don't know if you remember the other members of the cast, Ricardo; but this is Marina, who is playing Miss Prism the Governess, and Caroline, our Emily Cardew. And Orlando Biggs is our Reverend Canon Chasuble, of course."

"I remember Bodie," Richard said, as the two women curtsied to him; an elaborate flourish for no better reason than that Lunaites adored role-playing, no matter what the costume or venue. He thought he recognized the other players from the farcical presentation a year or two previous, when he damn near had to play a part himself at the last minute as an unwilling understudy. "Is he playing Worthing or Moncrieff?"

"Moncrieff," Patricia sank into the nearest chair. "Oof! I will be crippled tomorrow for sure, if I need to walk very far in these shoes. Is Lew here? We were supposed to meet him, as he does one last run-through. Did you know that his wife Annie is here for the opening? Isn't that sweet? She worked up so many lovely designs and sketches for this development, without ever laying eyes on it. He has worked so hard, no wonder that she is taking him off for a good vacation… their wedding anniversary, did you know? To France, of course. With the whole family."

"It's grand," Richard acknowledged honestly. "Lew is a good chap. He and his chapess and chums can drop in on my Aged P's any time they are in the Luberon. They live in retirement on a vineyard, not far from that hotel that Lew first set up for VPI. All he need do is say the word, and Mum and the Pater will make them welcome for as long as they like."

"Lew and Annie would adore it!" Patricia exclaimed. "Oh, coffee – 'Celi – before anything else. And I don't suppose you have any cinnamon … You do? Bliss indeed. We are famished!" Beatriz appeared, magically, with a gigantic serving salver, laded with coffee, china and silverware, and a small plate of two-bite-sized cinnamon rolls, and grinned as Patricia admired them extravagantly. Having finished securing the horses, Bodie Madison sprang nimbly up the steps and joined his fellow Players, bantering affectionately with them all, to the point where Richard simply had to remove himself. It was time to go put on his own antique attire anyway, now that Luc had returned from the men's loo, having tamed the wild mohawk. The ear enlargements were still in evidence, which quite spoiled the intended effect. Richard didn't want to know by what means the tats were hidden, although it was possible that industrial-strength concealer had a lot to do with it.

"Better luck next time," Richard murmured to himself. It was twenty to ten; and he couldn't put it off any longer. He took his own suit-bag into the men's, and when he returned, one of the Mills Farm electric carts sat at the foot of the boathouse stairs – an electric cart with a dashing canopy trimmed with fringe, very like that of the surrey-cart. Three more had joined the happy group of Patricia's cast: Lew Dubois and two ladies of moderately-indeterminable middle age. Neither were in the first fleeting bloom of youth, yet thanks to discreet work and expensive skin-care regimens, neither could be taken at a squint for being much over their fourth or fifth decade on this green earth. Richard hoped that the pleasanter-appearing lady, clad like Patricia in a flowing vintage Edwardian day dress and brandishing a dainty parasol, was Mrs. Dubois. The other, dressed in modern jeans and a gauze tunic strewn with turquoise-colored beads and sequins in vaguely Southwest-ish Indian motifs, was looking around at the topside boathouse pavilion with what

Richard judged was barely-concealed distain. This woman was dark-haired, not an artfully-maintained blond, yet she reminded him irresistibly of Susannah Wyatt, an unrequited admirer of his, and potential bunny-boiler, presently and productively wed to Romeo Gonzales, who apparently was able to keep those stalkerish impulses of hers under control … or at least, Richard assumed so, since it had been at least a year since Susannah had last blighted his life and darkened the doorway of the Airstream.

"Lew, old chap, how absolutely splendid you look!" Richard put on his best welcoming manner; Lew did, clad in a dapper seersucker suit of an old-fashioned cut, a high-collared shirt with a string-tie and a straw boater. With his rough-cut, weathered countenance, he did indeed look like a country farmer dressed in his best, at the order of his wife and master. Lew grinned.

"Cher Richard!" he exclaimed. "You look splendid yourself! I see that you are well-prepared for the deluge of the public! They tell me at the gate, that better than half of those purchasing meal tickets are opting for the Boathouse buffet."

"We are prepared," Richard managed a stiff bow. "My staff is now all in readiness. And might I say that we appreciated the ice for the tables … and the generous assistance of your staff in laying out the tables outside…"

"I pride myself on my foresight," Lew demurred. The comfortably middle-aged woman in the flowing dress giggled most deliciously, and exclaimed, "Well, ever since he accepted a job – and then found out the job was in France! I swear, he has never been caught out since then!" She extended a graceful, and authentically-gloved hand to Richard, adding, "Anne Dubois. My husband has said so many nice things about you, especially your coffee and perfect cinnamon rolls."

"I am flattered, Madame," Richard bowed over the hand and kissed it, going by his best social manner. Archaic good manners seemed to be the best way to go. Anne Dubois giggled again. She was not beautiful – but round-faced, her eyes sparkling with intelligent interest. Any woman who could indulge her husband to the extent of wearing a trailing skirt and a monumental hat on a spring day in Texas, for the purposes of playing along with his vision of old-school hospitality … well, good on her, and matrimonially a keeper. "Alas, he has said very little about you, Mrs. Dubois. His devotion to business is such that we have had very little opportunity for extraneous social conversation. It is my understanding that you came up with the overall design for this establishment, and the stables, too – as well as some of the other charming period elements…"

Here, the other woman made a brief and resentful face, as if she had bitten into something sour, which Richard noticed only in passing, as she summoned the attention of the hovering Araceli and peremptorily demanded coffee. "*With* agave syrup and almond milk," she added, with an air of authority. Araceli murmured, "I am sorry, ma'am. All we have is ordinary sugar, and half-and half."

"Black, then," the other woman replied, with an air of martyrdom and a deep sigh, which suggested that such a lack was a hardship unimaginable to civilized beings. Araceli's expression was one of practiced neutrality, but Richard knew her of old and what that brief flash of irritation in her eyes meant. He hastily intervened.

"Lew, you haven't introduced me to your other charming companion," he said, and Lew Dubois smiled, a rather guarded smile, as he answered, "I have been amiss, *chère* Richard: this is Georgina Mason. Georgina *chère*, my I present Richard Astor-Hall, of the Luna City Café, whom I have not been able to inveigle into working for VPI on an exclusive basis – only occasionally as a caterer. If I can tempt you into trying his pastries, especially the cinnamon rolls, my triumph here would be complete! To my regret, I have not gotten him into producing proper New Orleans beignets … but I have that as a goal!"

"Charmed," Richard averred, as he bowed likewise over Georgina Mason's hand. She snatched it away almost as soon as she decently could, as of the regard of a mere caterer were something unclean.

"I guess that Lew thinks you are important," she replied, with a stunning lack of grace, in a voice like a raspy corncrake.

Oh, a snob, then, Richard thought, as he mumbled something noncommittal in response. *And one to walk warily around – she looks as if she is just aching to find fault and throw an epic scene.* Lew beamed impartially upon them all, adding, "Georgina is here in Luna City to acquaint herself with the charming locality, and with those whom she must work, as she will be overseeing the work on the Cattleman rooms, while my dearest Annie and I celebrate our anniversary."

Oh, crap, Richard thought, crap on a gourmet biscuit with a side of caviar: She is exactly the wrong person for Luna City. Doesn't Lew see this? She will unravel every scrap of local goodwill that Lew has woven over the last year, I guarantee it. Oh, well – good thing I haven't committed to work for VPI much farther than this. At least I'll be out from under the fall-out when the fewmets hit the fan. Pity about the Cattleman, though. Could have been a smashing little place; elegant and popular in the old style … Aloud, he said, "Here comes Araceli with your coffee. The best of luck for today, Lew – and the best of luck to the Players. Patricia, will there be a place for me in the balcony, if I come see the performance?"

"Certainly, my good man!" Patricia boomed, in the voice of the commanding Lady Bracknell. "Here; a ticket for you and in the front row!" she winked at Richard and added in her normal voice. "We're giving out free tickets today, to the most amusing people! Enjoy the show … you know, we have all been listening to you speak! I hope that we got the accents right. Of course, some of us have a better ear for dialect than others. You should come, as well, Georgina; here's a ticket for you, too," she added in such a bland voice that only one sharply attuned to social matters could detect the veiled malice.

"Ohh, playing an older woman? Just somehow seems so natural for you," Georgina murmured. "I can hardly wait." Richard looked between them, and was boggled, all over again. What – Patricia! Malice? This Georgina woman must be an even bigger blight on the landscape than Richard assumed; Patricia Pryor, the uncrowned queen of Luna City, generous patron of the arts, hard-working member of the community and friend to all, heir of Doc Wyler and his considerable lands and fortune – Patricia did not like Georgina? And Georgina was tactless enough to be openly vicious? That was as far as Richard could go with it. He had too many other matters to think about, right this very minute. Like ... the wave of customers for the buffet, those appearing in a human wave ... or a human wave, appearing slowly on foot, and by electric surrey, from the direction of the main Mills Farm establishment. Both the Players and Lew's party drank the last of their coffee, excusing themselves with merry grace, although Georgina Mason still looked as sour as if she had found half of a slug in her cinnamon roll. A quarter to eleven, by the hands of the antique station clock set in the roof-peak at one end of the pavilion.

"All hands, to the tables," Richard murmured to his crew. "Beatriz, Blanca – handle the coffee mob, ''kay? Tell them that lunch service begins in fifteen minutes. Here comes the first of the day ..." The girls bustled off with Luc, to load up the service carts and bring them up by the long curving ramp which connected the two levels. Araceli was laying out more silverware, already bundled in napkins banded with paper, as was customary in the Café, while Richard set out the little silver-framed labels identifying the contents of each pan: Game Pie, Chicken Salad, Cold Salmon with Cucumber Sauce, Cold Fried Chicken, Cucumber Sandwiches and so on. The labels and frames had been provided by Lew; detailed to the extent of being done by hand, in elaborate calligraphy, likely by Annie Dubois.

"The man thinks of everything," Richard admitted, in grudging admiration. "I must say, it looks most splendid. I daresay that Georgina – that is Ms. Mason – will find it impossible to meet his standard ..."

"Her?" Araceli snorted, contemptuously, and added a few choice words uncomplimentary to Georgina Mason's appearance, character and professional abilities. Not that Richard was particularly surprised, for Araceli was unsparing of a certain kind of person.

"I cannot for the life of me figure out why you and Patricia have taken such an instant dislike to Ms. Mason," he said.

Araceli replied, crisply, "She's a bitch and it saves time, Chef."

The sound of merry music echoed faintly from the direction of Mills Farm's main establishment. Down on the river, a pair of kayaks splashed around the bend, paddled by two pair of giggling teenagers. In a twinkling, the quiet riverside lawn was transformed, animated by a bustling crowd.

A few were in some variant of early 20th century raiment; most were not, although Richard generously complimented the young man and woman clad in period swimsuits – which attire covered them from knees to neck, as they went through the serving line, during a pause in the general rush, because of Los Maldonados performing live at the Campfire Circle.

"They're both authentic," the woman admitted cheerily, as Richard dished up a sliver of game pie, at which selection the two of them looked with dubious expressions. "My grandmother never threw away a darned thing! Say what is this stuff?"

"Game pie, in a raised crust," Richard answered. "Made with venison, and locally-sourced wild-boar sausage mince." Richard profoundly hoped that this was the breaking wave of diners – having swelled, crested, and made considerable of a dent in their supplies. The game pie was the only thing they had plenty of, still. He was disappointed. This should have been one of their most popular items, being made with generous lashings of local meats.

The young man in the two-piece striped turn-of-the-last-century male bathing suit brightened with interest. "You don't say ... it looks interesting. You hunt it yourself, Mr... Mr. Astor-Hall?"

"He's Captain Kitten," his female companion reminded him, brightly. "You know; the guy in the cat-head, who teaches kids to cook, on-line. He has this neat website!"

"Cool," replied the young man. He lifted his slice of pie in one hand, took an experimental bite, chewed meditatively, and swallowed. "Say – that's pretty darned good. Is the recipe a secret 'r something?"

"No ... I'll ask my web-master to post it on Captain Kitten," Richard replied, and then he had to step away from the serving line for a moment, to regain his composure, whilst wondering if living in Luna City was not akin to descending the White Rabbit's burrow into a mad and hectic world, where the mundane danced a *pas-de-deux* with the eccentric on a daily basis.

The surge of diners diminished over the following half-hour of Los Maldonado's concert, music to be heard faintly over the soughing of wind in the trees, the musical jingling of the bell on the ice-cream cart, the pleasant murmur of those guests relaxing on the pleasant greensward or splashing about in the water, even though it was chilly where the deep current ran. Richard, in a quick private survey of what was left in the refrigerators in the little kitchen, congratulated himself on his accurate estimations of the quantity of food prepared. There was just enough of most menu items left to continue service until the appointed hour, although there would be leftover game pie, and hardboiled eggs. Well never mind. They could make egg salad sandwiches for tomorrow's luncheon at the Café. And if anyone asked for it at the end of the day, he would sell remainders of the game pie, in part or entire, in a take-away container ...

He returned to the open-air part of the pavilion just in time to greet Sook Walcott, attended by her younger children; Belle in her mariachi regalia when she performed with *Los Maldonados*, and Robbie, solemn in period uniform, buttoned up to a high collar and topped with a flat-brimmed campaign hat of the kind that Mounties and Boy Scouts used to wear. Apparently, the US Marines favored that campaign hats of that style as well.

"Hi, Chef!" Robbie exclaimed. "How did it all go! Sorry I couldn't help out today! But Lew said that the best place to be to hand out information about my project was at the main gate. I'm all out of flyers and cards, and Mom wanted to eat here, since what Belle and I told her about the buffet sounded so good." He looked at the diminished serving dishes; although Richard and the crew had done their best to keep them topped up, maintaining the illusion of culinary abundance, some of them did appear a little ravished. Especially the salmon. Richard would have sworn that cold salmon would not have been as big a hit as it was. And the cold fried chicken was to the point where they might as well just put the last pathetic pieces on a smaller platter and be done with it. "Is there anything left for us?" Robbie added, with a touch of pathos, suggesting that he was perishing of starvation."

"Of course, there is," Richard replied, heartily. "You turned in your meal tickets, of course … then, what would be your pleasure? There's plenty of seating now in the pavilion, of course. Half-an-hour ago, you would have to have used a pry-bar to wedge in another chair. Shall I make up plates for your mother and Belle? Your sister looks quite exhausted."

"She played two encores with Los Maldonados," Robbie answered. "It was so good! Bee got a standing ovation, and Javier kissed her, right in front of the crowd! They're all so proud of her, going to Julliard and all. And she started with a *conjunto* band, right here in Karnes County!"

He burbled away for a bit, in his usual artless fashion, while Richard thought about what was left downstairs in the boathouse refrigerators, how many minutes to go until they could close the serving line, what to do with the leftovers. He was tired – and there was still supper service at the Café to oversee, although the bulk of that would all fall on Luc. He himself would walk over to the Cattleman with his ticket and settle into a front row seat for the Luna City Players' presentation of *The Importance of Being Earnest*. Maybe, if any of his friends were going out toward the Age of Aquarius afterwards, he could cadge a ride from them. He would be exhausted beyond all measure, after today's schedule. Luc hovered over the serving table with Beatriz, dishing up slices and helpings of this or that for Robbie, Belle, and their imperious mother. Luc was really being quite assiduous in his attendance on the family Walcott, which Richard viewed with satisfaction; the younger mans' social competence was coming along nicely. Miss Letty would be so pleased.

Beatriz, ever on the hostessing ball, showed the three to a pristine table, exchanging laughing remarks with Robbie and Belle. Richard now recalled that the three "B's" had all been classmates and graduated together at what was essentially the local comprehensive, where the offspring of those who would have gone to a public school *(which in this country was a 'private' school)* mixed socially and every other which way, with those who in past times and in another country, would have attended the local grammar and gone to work as soon as they were sixteen. Somehow, it all seemed to work, although he could not quite sort out why. An American thing, or a Texas thing, or maybe a purely Luna City thing? He had no notion of how that all operated. After all, he was still a foreigner here, having spent all but the last three years of his life in another world entirely.

The cold salmon and cucumber sauce was pretty well finished as a menu item, with the last scattering of those preferring to dine after the concert. From the serving line, he could see a good-sized group of people, walking purposefully along the wandering path from the main establishment. More potential customers Might as well take the serving pan and the little framed card off the table, move the other serving pans closer to hide the gap.

"Go down to the kitchen," he told Luc, "Take these with you. I think we can top up the cold ham, and let's put out all of what we have left in the sandwich line. Those items won't be any good after today anyway. Might as well sell them to the punters while they're still fresh."

"On it, Chef," Luc replied, with becoming alacrity. Good; he was, at this late stage of development, becoming properly socialized. Miss Letty would <u>definitely</u> be pleased. Richard messed about for a bit in the serving line, filling the plates of those few stragglers for a late lunch. *There went the last of the cold fried chicken. What to do about the game pie?* He fretted about that, through the next influx of diners. They would have leftovers and game pie wouldn't be good after a day or two, even frozen. He ruminated to himself about this for a good few minutes.

"Hi, Chef," He started. That was Belle Walcott at his elbow. Still thin, still nervous-looking. "I … well, where is the … umm Ladies' room?"

"Downstairs," Richard answered, absently. "At the bottom of the stairs, the third door along."

"Yeah … thanks, Chef." Belle vanished down the exterior staircase. It looked as if Sook and Robbie were still taking their time over the meal, for which Richard didn't blame them in the least. The day was perfect, the food – in all modesty, divine – the view from the open pavilion was perfect, the river flowed limpid green in the deeps and golden in the shallows, a scattering of purpose-planted, or maybe they were wild and unfettered trees planted at random, starred the new green on the far banks with dark-pink blooms. All was … perfection. The end of a successful day, another catering triumph for Richard and the Café, another disaster avoided. Perhaps he had escaped this time; was there something about Mills Farm which negated the curse? As the hands of the clock crept up to two of the hour and he ruminated over that, and the means of disposing of what was left from today's bountiful spread, Sook Walcott approached the serving line, in her usual preemptory fashion.

"Ree-chard, I need to use the bathroom … and where is my daughter! She is still in the bathroom!"

"My dear Sook, I have no idea why she needs to take a bath," Richard answered, slightly bowing. "But I will show you to the …. To the facilities. Just follow me, Mrs. Walcott."

With a silent nod to Araceli, Richard walked down the staircase, wondering what on earth was taking Luc so damned long. The riverbank side of the boathouse was open to the river, through three garage-sized swinging doors leading to open bays. Each bay would accommodate kayaks and motor launches a little longer than Harry Vaughn's little tin cockleshell. The facilities, an equipment storage locker and the kitchen occupied the landward side of the boathouse. Even though the afternoon was warm, it still seemed cool inside, with water occasionally splashing against the dock supports as someone paddled past, out on the river itself.

"Through here, Mrs. Walcott, past the kitchen. The … erm, facilities are at the far end." Richard waved a hand in that general direction, still wondering what was keeping Luc.

He pushed open the kitchen door. And stood rooted to the spot in horrified amazement, for there stood Luc and Belle, their arms wrapped tightly around each other, locked in a passionate embrace.

Oh, shit, he thought, paralyzed.

Sook Walcott's dreaded steam-whistle shriek of outrage could doubtless be heard all the way to Mills Farm's main establishment.

"You, crummy cook! You no canoodle with my daughter!"

(To be continued … of course!)

Celia Hayes & Jeanne Hayden

www.ingramcontent.com/pod-product-compliance
Lightning Source LLC
Chambersburg PA
CBHW031957060726
47497CB00015B/114